EAST END TROUBLE

Dani Oakley and D. S. Butler

If you would like to be informed when the new Dani Oakley book is released, sign up for the newsletter:

http://www.danioakleybooks.com/newsletter/

Copyright © 2016 Dani Oakley and D. S. Butler

All rights reserved.

http://www.danioakleybooks.com

For My Family x

1

MARY DIAMOND PICKED UP THE soapy brush and started scrubbing her front step. She did it every Tuesday afternoon without fail.

In her opinion, the state of a front step said a lot about a family. Alice Pringle, who lived next door, kept hers spotless, but the family across the road were another story altogether. The front of their house was a disgrace. The windows were smeared and dirty, and the front door had a panel missing. The old man was a drunkard, and the wife wasn't much better. Mary made sure she had nothing to do with the likes of them.

The June sunshine flooded down on Mary as she scrubbed. It was too blasted hot for this kind of work. She pushed back a damp curl of grey hair and smiled with satisfaction at her lovely clean step. She dropped the brush she'd been using into the bucket of soapy water and got to her feet. She carried the bucket through the passage towards the kitchen at the back of the house. She was parched and could murder a cup of tea.

She had another half an hour before her daughter, Kathleen, would be home wanting her dinner. Even though there was no one around, Mary beamed with pride as she thought about her only child. It hadn't been easy bringing Kathleen up alone after her good-for-nothing father had run off with his fancy woman when Kathleen was barely out of nappies.

Mary filled the kettle and put it on top of the stove to boil. She wiped her wet hands on her white apron.

As the kettle came to a boil and began to whistle, Mary reached for the teapot, but before she could start making the tea, she heard a knock at the front door.

Who could that be at this time? It was an odd time for a visitor to call. Everyone would be home preparing the evening meal. It had to be Kathleen. The silly child had probably forgotten her key.

Mary opened the door, and her mouth dropped open in surprise as she stared at her visitor. It wasn't Kathleen.

It was Babs Morton.

What on earth had brought that woman to her door? They didn't exactly move in the same social circles, and Babs wasn't the type to drop in for a cup of rosie and a chat.

Babs Morton was married to the notorious gangster, Martin Morton, and Babs waltzed around as if she was Queen of the East End these days.

It was boiling outside today, and Babs was standing on Mary's freshly scrubbed front step in a bleeding mink coat! What a stupid cow. Not that Mary would ever have said that to her face. She wasn't daft.

"Babs, what a surprise. Er…why don't you come in?" Mary stammered, finally finding her voice and remembering her manners.

As she was closing the door, she caught sight of her nosy

neighbour, Alice Pringle, craning her neck over the fence to get a good look at what was going on.

Mary gave her a hard look and then shut the door firmly behind her.

"Come through," Mary said. "I was just about to have a cup of tea. Care to join me?"

Babs looked around the small kitchen and turned up her nose as if she'd stepped in something nasty. "No," she snapped. "I won't waste time, Mary. I'm here for a reason."

Mary licked her lips nervously and patted her hair, feeling very self-conscious about her bedraggled state in comparison to Babs' perfectly groomed appearance.

"And what reason might that be, Babs?"

Babs scowled, and all the lines around her mouth puckered up. "My friends call me Babs. You can call me Mrs. Morton."

Mary flushed. The uppity cow. Coming around here like she owned the place. Her little two-bedroom house might not be the height of luxury, but it was clean and well-looked after. Mary was proud of the fact she'd managed to hold onto it, meeting the rent by taking on two cleaning jobs after Kathleen's father had done a runner.

Babs Morton might like to put on airs and graces now that she was married to Martin Morton, but Mary knew she'd grown up in a house just like this one.

Mary bit back the sharp words she wanted to say. It wasn't worth risking the anger of Martin Morton. She would just have to wait for Babs to say her piece.

"What can I do for you, Mrs. Morton?" Mary asked coldly.

Babs flapped open her coat and fanned herself. "It's like a bleeding furnace in here. I don't know how you stand having a pokey little kitchen like this."

Mary didn't respond. She knew Babs was trying to rile her for some reason. She would have loved to have pointed out to the snooty cow that if she wore a mink coat in the middle of summer then of course the daft mare was going to be hot.

Mary folded her arms across her chest and waited.

"It's about that daughter of yours," Babs said.

Mary felt her stomach clench. "Kathleen? What on earth has she got to do with anything?"

"She's been sniffing around my Martin. And I'm here to tell you if you don't put an end to it, I will."

"It must be some kind of misunderstanding," Mary said. "Kathleen is just a kid."

"I hope for your daughter's sake it is a misunderstanding. Otherwise, she will have me to deal with."

Mary felt sick. Martin Morton was in his forties. There was no way her Kathleen would be interested in the likes of him.

Babs had clearly been to the hairdressers that morning and wore her makeup as if she'd plastered it on, but as she looked at Mary with an ugly scowl on her face, Babs looked every single one of her forty years.

If Martin had developed an eye for the ladies, Babs wouldn't like that one bit.

"Well, are you going to talk to her? Talk some sense into that empty little head of hers?"

Mary wanted to slap the old bitch and then hit her over the head with the frying pan for good measure, but instead she just nodded.

"I'll talk to her when she gets home from work. But I'm sure this has all been a misunderstanding. Kathleen is a good girl."

Babs gave a cold laugh. "The mothers are always the last to know, aren't they?" She tossed her dark hair and stalked away, letting herself out of the front door.

When she had gone, Mary eased herself into a wooden chair next to the window. Her legs felt wobbly after that encounter. She couldn't believe that her Kathleen would have gotten involved with a man like Martin Morton, but something must have tipped off Babs.

For the life of her, Mary couldn't think of any reason for Babs to be jealous of Kathleen, other than the fact that Kathleen was a pretty little thing and more than twenty years Babs' junior.

Mary held her head in her hands. She would have it out with Kathleen as soon as she got home. There would be a simple explanation for all this. There had to be.

Kathleen wasn't stupid. She would listen to reason. The Mortons were not a family to be messed with.

Mary felt a shiver run up her spine. God help them if what Babs said was true.

2

AS MARY DIAMOND SAT WITH her head in her hands, her daughter, Kathleen, was squeezing herself into a bright red miniskirt.

"You don't think it's too much, do you?" she asked her friend Linda as she gazed down at her exposed legs. "It didn't look this short in the shop."

"It suits you. You've got a fantastic pair of legs so you may as well show them off." Linda gazed up at her friend through a heavy brown fringe. Linda was a sweet girl, but she wasn't much of a looker.

"Your outfit is nice too," Kathleen said to her friend.

Linda was wearing a blue and white striped dress that flared out at the waist and stopped just above the knee. She was a little on the heavy side, and the dress didn't flatter her figure, but Kathleen wanted to bolster her confidence. She didn't want Linda to back out of going with her to Morton's club tonight.

"I dunno. I'm not sure about this. Think what your mum would say if she found out. She wouldn't be happy," Linda said.

"What has that got to do with anything? She's too old

6

fashioned and wouldn't understand. This is my chance, Linda, and I intend to grab it with both hands. You should follow my example and find yourself a man. There'll be loads of them there tonight." Kathleen nudged her friend and giggled.

She had sent Linda's brother over to her mother's house with a note telling her she wouldn't be home for dinner. That way she avoided having to ask her mother's permission to go out tonight. She didn't want to risk it. If her mother refused, it would mess up all her plans.

She was eighteen years old and quite old enough to look after herself, but her mum was set in her ways, and Kathleen had learned it was easier to go along with them, or, at least, pretend to.

The girls left Linda's parents' house, linking arms as they walked down the street. They'd had a little of Linda's mum's secret stash of sherry before they left the house, and Kathleen wobbled a little on her high heels. Linda helped keep her upright.

As they got closer to the club, Linda seemed to get more and more nervous. "Let's go back now, Kath. I don't want to go to Morton's. It's not a good idea. What if your mum finds out what you've been up to? She'll go spare."

Kathleen let go of her friend's arm. "Stop being such a baby. I don't know why I bother being friends with you. You've got no ambition that's your trouble."

Linda's lower lip wobbled and her eyes filled with tears. "It's not me who is the problem, Kathleen. You're going to get yourself in trouble."

Linda whirled around and ran back up the street towards her house.

Kathleen stamped her foot and fumed. Stupid Linda. Why did she have to go and ruin things by being such a baby? Well, Kathleen wouldn't let her ruin her evening. Her mother would never find out she spent the night at the club rather than Linda's, so she intended to enjoy herself.

She hadn't gotten all dressed up for nothing. She had spent a fortune on this new outfit to impress Martin Morton, and she was determined he would see her in it.

Kathleen tossed her hair and stalked towards the club.

By the time she got there, her feet were already sore. Her heels were a little too tight and had rubbed the skin on her toes painfully. She ignored the pain, adjusted her miniskirt. The warm buzz she'd gotten from the sherry was starting to wear off.

There was a man wearing a suit on the door. Kathleen had seen him before, but he wasn't one of Martin Morton's inner circle. Kathleen scowled at him as he looked her up and down. There was a small gathering of people outside, queueing to get in, but Kathleen strutted right up to the front of the line.

"Oi, you're pushing in," a voice from behind Kathleen shouted.

"Shut your mouth," Kathleen snapped and turned her attention to the bouncer. "I've come to see Martin."

"Of course you have, love," the man on the door said with a smirk on his face. "You and all the rest of them."

Kathleen put a hand on her hip and narrowed her eyes. "You'd better let me in now. Martin won't be happy when he finds out you've kept me waiting."

A flicker of doubt passed over the bouncer's face. "What's your name?"

"Kathleen, and you'd better make sure you remember it for next time."

The bouncer exchanged a few words with someone inside and then returned to the door, opening it wide so that Kathleen could pass through.

She gave him a cold smile as she entered the club. She wanted to ask the bouncer if Martin was here yet, but she didn't like the way he was looking at her. Deciding to find Martin herself, she sashayed into the club.

The music was loud, and the club was already in full swing. She looked around for Martin, but she couldn't see him. She made her way to the bar, feeling a bit self-conscious without Linda by her side. She wished she had her friend with her now. Linda could be a dopey cow, but she always made Kathleen feel more confident.

A bald man with an enormous belly bumped into her, spilling his pint, and leered. "All right, darling. Can I get you a drink?"

Kathleen sneered and was about to tell the man to piss off when she remembered she didn't have enough money to buy her own drinks all night, and she could do with one now that the effects of the sherry had worn off.

"I'll have a rum and Coke," she said, intending to drop the man as soon as she got her drink.

Unfortunately, when the man returned with her drink, he wrapped an arm around her shoulders and had no intention of letting her escape.

Kathleen pulled away and took a sip of her drink. The man smelled sweaty and dirty.

"So, what's your name, sweetheart?"

Kathleen ignored him and looked around the room,

desperate to see Martin. There was no sign of him. Perhaps he was out the back.

"Oh my goodness, look at that," Kathleen said and pointed at an imaginary object in the distance.

"What?" The bald man turned and gawked in the direction Kathleen had pointed.

Kathleen took the opportunity to slip quickly away. She made her way to the bar and caught the attention of one of the barmaids who looked vaguely familiar.

"Is Martin here tonight?"

"Not yet. He'll be in later, though."

Kathleen sulked as the barmaid turned away. Great. She was only able to get away for a couple of hours without her mother noticing anything was awry, and Martin wasn't even here. Her shoes were pinching her feet, and she had to be up early in the morning for work. Tonight had been a complete waste of time.

Five minutes later, Kathleen was draining her glass of rum and Coke and considering going home, when there was a change of atmosphere in the club. The music continued, but the voices in the club died away as a strange hush fell over the bar. Kathleen looked towards the door.

Martin Morton had arrived. He wore a sharp suit and tie, and his hair was closely trimmed at the sides in a fashionable style. Kathleen felt her heart race as he looked over at her and smiled. His gold tooth glinted as the club lights shone down on him.

Kathleen smiled shyly as he made his way towards her.

His brother and right-hand man, Tony Morton was behind him along with another man Kathleen had seen before but didn't know by name. His bulky frame loomed behind

Martin, and Kathleen knew enough to know that the man was some kind of bodyguard.

Kathleen turned her attention back to Martin.

"Hello, Princess," he said and nodded to her empty glass. "Did no one get you a drink?"

"I've just finished this one." Kathleen put the glass back on the shiny wooden surface of the bar.

"Another." Martin snarled at the bar staff.

"Yes, sir."

"I don't know what I'm paying them for. A bunch of jobsworths."

Kathleen giggled nervously.

"I don't want to see this girl with an empty glass again. Understand me?" Martin ordered.

The barmaid nodded. "Yes, sir. Sorry, sir."

Martin put his hand on the small of Kathleen's back as she took her new drink. "Let's go through to the back," Martin whispered.

Kathleen felt a thrill of excitement as she walked beside Martin. Everyone in the club was looking at her, and she basked in the attention, loving every second of it.

This was it. Kathleen Diamond had arrived.

3

MARTIN MORTON HAD A FLAT over the bar that was decked out in the top of the range furnishings.

"It's a lovely place," Kathleen said, running a hand admiringly along the sofa cushions.

It put her mum's tired old furniture to shame. Kathleen looked around the room happily. She could see herself living somewhere like this. Everything was sleek and modern and had no doubt set Martin back quite a bit.

Martin watched her with an amused grin on his face. He stood behind a small cocktail cabinet and held up a bottle of rum. "Another drink, Princess?"

Kathleen smiled back at him. "I'd love one."

She swayed her hips as she walked towards him, trying her best to look seductive.

When the huge man standing in the doorway cleared his throat, Kathleen jumped. She'd forgotten he was there.

"I thought we were going to have some privacy, Martin," Kathleen said, pouting.

Martin nodded at the big man. "That will be all for now, Tim. Go through to the back room."

Tim nodded and leaned forward so far it almost looked as

if he was bowing to Martin. He left the room and closed the door behind him.

Kathleen took her drink from Martin and settled herself down on the plush cushions of the sofa. She considered taking her shoes off. The bloody things were killing her. But she didn't want to seem forward.

She decided to keep the shoes on for now, and she crossed her legs, allowing her miniskirt to slide higher up her thighs.

Martin looked at her appreciatively. "You've got a lovely pair of legs, girl."

Kathleen took a sip of her drink. She knew she had a good body, and she wasn't afraid to use it to her advantage.

She patted the sofa. "Well, aren't you going to come and sit beside me? I'm starting to feel lonely over here."

"Well, we can't have that, can we, Princess?" Martin grinned as he took a seat beside her on the sofa and slid his arm around her shoulders.

He pulled her roughly towards him and crushed his lips down on hers. Kathleen was taken aback as he thrust his tongue into her mouth. It wasn't quite the romantic evening she had planned. Martin Morton clearly didn't believe in taking things slowly.

He clutched the nape of her neck, messing up her hair, and Kathleen briefly considered pushing him away. But she couldn't do that. You didn't push a man like Martin Morton away.

It wasn't long before Martin had stripped off her blouse and was unhooking her plain white bra.

Kathleen winced and wished she had been wearing something a little sexier. The white bra had been washed so many times it was starting to look grey, but Martin was moving so fast, he didn't seem to notice.

Martin pushed Kathleen back on the sofa, so she was wedged in the corner. He had just shifted his body over hers when there was a knock at the door. Whoever it was didn't wait for an answer. Kathleen felt a cold rush of air on her exposed body as the door opened.

She felt the weight of Martin's body lift from hers as he looked up angrily at the person who had interrupted them. "What do you want?" He snarled the question.

Kathleen clasped her arms over her breasts and gasped in horror when she turned and saw the large man from earlier standing in the doorway looking in at them.

Bloody pervert!

Kathleen reached out quickly for her blouse and used it to cover herself.

Tim averted his eyes, and the red stain of embarrassment climbed his neck to his cheeks making them look blotchy. He looked down at the floor.

Martin's bad mood seemed to dissipate as he laughed at Tim's embarrassed reaction. "Anyone would think you had never seen a pair before, Tim."

Martin stood up as Kathleen shoved her arms in her blouse and started to do up the buttons.

"Sorry for the interruption, boss, but we've got a problem," Big Tim mumbled, still looking at the floor.

Martin followed him out of the room, closing the door behind him and leaving Kathleen sitting on the sofa.

What the hell was she supposed to do now? Things had been moving very fast. She could take the opportunity to rush off home now before things went even further. But as she looked around the modern furnishings in Martin's flat and the fancy cocktail cabinet at the end of the room, she decided to stay put.

She reached into her handbag and pulled out her compact. She hardly recognised the flushed face that stared back at her. Carefully, she applied a fresh coat of pink lipstick and then grabbed her rum and Coke and gulped it down to steady her nerves.

Opportunities like this didn't come along very often. This could be Kathleen's only chance to hit it big, so she leaned back on the sofa and tried to relax.

It seemed like ages since Martin had disappeared with Big Tim, but it was really only five minutes before Martin stormed back into the room.

"You'd better go home, Princess. Something has come up. A bit of business."

Kathleen tried to look relaxed. "I don't mind. I can wait. I'm quite comfortable here." She treated him to what she thought was a sexy smile. "What's it about anyway? Anything I can help with?"

"Don't talk daft, girl. And never ask questions about my business. Now get your arse home before I lose patience."

Kathleen flushed red. She was glad nobody else was here to witness her humiliation.

She clenched her fists and got to her feet, then patted down her hair in an effort to look respectable. She reached down to get her handbag, and by the time she turned around, Martin had already gone.

She walked slowly down the stairs and back into the club, which was noisy and full of people having a good time. No one even glanced at her. She ducked through the crowds. Kathleen couldn't wait to get away from this horrible place.

She'd been stupid. At least, she now knew one thing for certain: Martin Morton certainly wasn't the man of her dreams.

4

MARTIN MORTON STEPPED INSIDE THE back room. Cigarette smoke hung thickly in the air. Gathered around the dining table were his closest associates, his most trusted men.

As Big Tim sat down, the two other men in the room stopped talking and looked up at Martin, clearly eager to know what he wanted them to do about the situation.

Big Tim was also known as Tim the Tank for obvious reasons. Henry Patterson, known as Henry the Hand, had been working for Martin the longest. He had a fearsome reputation in the East End, and despite the fact the man was knocking fifty, he still commanded respect. Henry understood the importance of reputation. He knew how to use it to his advantage, and he loved his nickname. Henry the Hand had come about because he'd lost two fingers while working in a factory when he was fifteen years old. But most people didn't know that version of the story.

Only a select few knew the truth, so how Henry had lost his fingers was a matter of speculation and gossip. The most popular theory among the East Enders was that he'd had them chopped off while being tortured by a rival gang, and he'd given up his fingers rather than sell out his men.

Red-haired Freddie sat next to Henry. In Martin's opinion, Freddie was one of the ugliest bastards he'd ever seen. He had a sharp face like a weasel and pockmarked skin, but he was a clever bastard and loyal to a fault, and Martin valued that trait over everything else.

Martin grabbed the bottle of single malt from the sideboard and poured himself a hefty measure. He downed the glass in one go, and then looked at his three most trusted men.

"Right, who wants to tell me about it then?"

The three men exchanged anxious looks. They didn't want to risk displeasing him by delivering bad news. Martin had been known to shoot the messenger in the past, literally.

In the end, it was Henry who spoke up. "I'm sorry to say we've got a traitor in our midst."

Martin's hand tightened around the glass, but other than that he didn't betray his feelings. He moved back towards the sideboard and poured himself another drink.

"Who?" he asked, keeping his voice steady.

"It's Keith Parker," Henry said. "He's been on the fiddle, messing with the books."

"It's worse than that, Martin," Tim said. "We found out tonight he's been working with the Carters."

"What? The little shit has been working with Dave Carter behind my back?"

Tim nodded, the tension on his face obvious. "He's been selling beer and fags for them. I don't know how deep it goes, or how long it's been going on, but he's definitely working with Dave Carter."

Martin felt all the muscles in his body tense, and he

yearned to be able to smash his fist into something.

He forced himself to calm down. You never got anywhere in this world if you went off hot-headed. Revenge was a dish best served cold.

"Keith Parker is a traitor," he said. "And we all know what happens to traitors."

Before Martin could say anything else, the door to the dining room opened, and his brother, Tony Morton, stood there looking angrily at the three of them.

"What is all this then?" Tony said as he looked at Martin. "You never said we were having a meeting."

Martin looked at his brother, not bothering to hide his dislike. Tony was younger than him by three years and a right pain in the arse. He never showed any respect and just expected to share in Martin's little empire, even though he hardly ever did anything to help.

"It wasn't planned," Tim said, trying to pacify the situation. "Something came up."

Tony's eyes didn't leave his older brother. "Is that true?"

"You would have known about it if you'd been here," Martin said. "Where have you been? Didn't you fancy working tonight?"

Tony looked smug. "I've been visiting our old mum. You should get around there yourself," he said. "She told me you haven't been around to see her since Easter."

Martin ran a hand through his hair. The smug bastard. Tony knew he was his mother's favourite, and that rankled Martin. It always had.

Tony had always been Mummy's little boy. He could do no wrong in her eyes. Despite the fact, it was Martin who constantly had to bail Tony out of trouble. She never seemed to appreciate the fact it was Martin who paid her rent and made sure she had money for a few little luxuries every week. Every time he'd seen her recently she had just gone on and on about how he should be nicer to poor Tony.

Poor Tony? That was a bleeding joke. Tony had it easy, and he knew it.

In the end, Martin had stopped going around there just to save himself the earache.

"We're here to talk about business, Tony. Not family," Martin said, pouring a large whisky and handing it to his brother. "We're talking about how to deal with Keith Parker. He's been working with the Carters."

Tony's eyes widened. "You need to make an example of him, bruv," he said. "You can't let this go unpunished. It will make you look weak if you do."

"When have you ever known me to look weak?" Martin said in a dangerously low voice. "Keith Parker will be dealt with appropriately. Mark my words, he won't know what's hit him."

When Kathleen got home from the club, her mother appeared at the top of the stairs wearing a winceyette nightie, her hair in rollers and her skin greasy with Pond's Vanishing Cream.

"Good grief," Mary exclaimed in horror, looking at Kathleen's clothes. "Please tell me you haven't been out in public like that. You look like a tramp, young lady."

"Oh, don't start, Mum. I've had a horrible evening, and I've got to get up early for work."

"Well, you should have thought about that before staying up all hours. And I know you weren't at Linda's. I went round and visited her mother. She said she hadn't seen you since seven."

Mary marched down the stairs and followed her daughter into the kitchen.

Kathleen sighed, poured herself a glass of water and then turned on her mother. "Oh, did I say Linda's? I meant Tracy's. I went to see Tracy, and we went for a drink, that's all."

Mary stared at her daughter with narrowed eyes. "And where did you go for this drink?"

"Oh, nowhere you would know," Kathleen said irritably and took a large swallow of water. "It's a modern place. You won't have heard of it."

"It wouldn't be Morton's by any chance, would it?"

Kathleen was so surprised that her mother knew where she'd been; she forgot to guard her expression and keep up the pretence. "How did you know that?"

"You can't go there again, Kathleen. I absolutely forbid it."

Mary put a hand on her daughter's arm, but Kathleen wrenched it away. "You can't tell me what to do. I'm not a child."

As Kathleen stormed out of the kitchen, her mother quickly followed.

"Kathleen, wait. I need to talk to you. I had a visitor tonight."

Kathleen turned back to face her mother. "A visitor? Who?"

"Babs Morton. She came round here to warn you to stay away from her husband, Martin. I told her it had to be a mistake. There is no way you would get involved with a married man, let alone a gangster like Martin Morton. That's right, isn't it?"

Kathleen flushed. "Babs Morton?" She felt sick. She hadn't realised Martin's wife had any idea about her and Martin.

"I don't know where she got that idea from. It's not true, Mum."

Mary stared hard at her daughter's face, trying to determine whether she was telling the truth. "I hope to God you're not messed up with that family, my girl. Otherwise, our troubles have only just begun."

5

THE FOLLOWING MORNING KATHLEEN FELT absolutely terrible. Her mouth felt dry and furry, and her head was banging. She winced and clutched her head as she got out of bed. Her mother clattering things around in the kitchen didn't help matters either. Kathleen was sure she was doing it on purpose. It took her longer than usual to have a quick wash and get ready for work.

Mary set a bowl of porridge in front of her daughter, but Kathleen barely touched it. She just moved the lumpy grey porridge around with her spoon. "Sorry, Mum. I've got no appetite this morning."

"I can't imagine why," Mary said pointedly, removing the bowl and scraping the wasted breakfast into the bin.

"Just you remember what I said last night. You stay away from that family. Do you hear me?"

"Yes, Mum." Kathleen said meekly and got to her feet. "I'd better go now otherwise I'll be late for work."

She met up with Linda at the front door to Bevels, which was the clothes factory where they both worked as machinists.

Linda looked at her hopefully and gave her a smile.

Kathleen had been intending to give her friend the cold shoulder that morning and teach her a lesson, but she felt so terrible, she couldn't be bothered. Linda was good at sympathy, and that was exactly what she needed right now.

"So, what happened last night?" Linda asked. "I hope you didn't get into any trouble."

Kathleen looked at her friend who was wearing a brown, shapeless cotton dress with a cream cardigan. Her thick brown hair was her only good feature, and even that was ruined because her mother made her tie it back for work.

Kathleen pinched the bridge of her nose between a thumb and forefinger. "I've got a terrible headache, but to answer your question, no, I didn't get into any trouble, and I had a fantastic night. You should have come."

Linda bit her lip. "I'm sorry for letting you down, Kath. But I was just worried. I've heard some really bad things about Martin Morton, and I didn't want to go to his club."

Kathleen gave her friend a disdainful look. "All that stuff doesn't bother me," Kathleen said. "I'm not a child anymore, Linda, and I can look after myself."

Linda nodded. "I wish I was as confident as you. You're so glamorous."

Kathleen smiled, feeling a lot warmer towards Linda now. They headed towards their respective sewing machines. The bloody noise from the infernal things wasn't going to help Kathleen's headache at all, and she wouldn't be able to talk to Linda until they'd had a break later.

Three mind-numbing hours later, Kathleen stood up from the sewing machine and stretched. She reached for her bag and rummaged inside for the sandwiches her mother had prepared that morning.

Linda leaned against her sewing bench. "Let's take our sandwiches outside today," she said. "It's lovely and sunny."

Kathleen nodded, thinking that the fresh air might do her headache some good.

As the girls left the factory floor, they passed through the reception area, and on the reception desk, there was a huge bouquet of red roses. The scent of them filled the air.

"Oh, look at those," Linda said. "They are so beautiful. I wonder who they're for."

Mrs. McClair, the secretary who sat behind the desk, gave the girls a disapproving look.

"It's terribly inappropriate," she said in a nasal voice. The secretary thought she sounded posh, but Kathleen thought she sounded like she had a constant cold. "They are for you, Kathleen. They arrived this morning, but, of course, I couldn't interrupt your working hours. I must say Mr. Bevel is very unhappy. He doesn't believe young women should receive flowers at work."

Kathleen ignored Mrs. McClair's disapproval and gasped with pleasure, turning to smile at her friend.

"Oh, look, there's a card."

She plucked the card from between the rose stems and read it.

To Kathleen, sorry about last night, Martin.

Despite the fact that last night Kathleen had sworn she never wanted to see Martin Morton ever again, she found herself softening towards him. He must be very sorry. Otherwise, he wouldn't have apologised with such beautiful flowers.

Linda's eyes widened as she read the card over Kathleen's shoulder. "Martin? They're not from Martin Morton, are they?"

Kathleen gave her friend a sharp nudge in the ribs to shut her up. She didn't want Mrs. McClair to overhear. On the other hand, if she thought Kathleen was stepping out with Martin Morton, it might make the snooty cow treat her with a little more respect.

"Ouch." Linda rubbed her ribs "What was that for?"

"I'm afraid I'll have to leave them here until I go home," Kathleen said to Mrs. McClair. "I'm sure that won't be a problem, will it?"

"Just make sure it doesn't happen again," Mrs. McClair said.

Kathleen rolled her eyes and looped her arm around Linda's, dragging her friend outside.

"Sour old cow," Kathleen muttered under her breath. "She's just jealous. I bet she's never had anyone send her flowers."

"You're probably right," Linda said agreeably. "Hang on a minute…" Linda stopped dead in the middle of the pavement, causing a woman carrying her shopping to almost bump into them.

"What is it?" Kathleen asked. She wanted to get to the park and eat her sandwiches. She was ravenous after missing breakfast.

"Isn't that…?"

Kathleen looked in the direction Linda pointed. "Oh, my God," Kathleen whispered. "Quick, let's go before she sees us."

But the girls were too late. Babs Morton was crossing the road heading directly for them.

"Kathleen Diamond, isn't it?" Babs Morton asked.

Babs' dark hair had been carefully curled around her face. She wore a deep shade of plum eyeshadow, and her lips were painted a dark pink, matching her nails. She wore a heavy gold chain around her neck and a bracelet that looked like it was dotted with sapphires and diamonds.

Kathleen was dazzled. "Yes, that's me," she said in a quiet voice.

"And I am Linda."

Babs ignored Linda completely. "I've been hearing certain rumours, Kathleen. A girl like you ought to be careful. Once a reputation is ruined, it's impossible to get it back."

Kathleen didn't know what to say. She just stood there gaping at Babs.

"Morton's club isn't any place for a lady. You would do well to remember that."

Kathleen swallowed hard and then nodded as Babs Morton walked past them, leaving them in the trail of her violet-scented perfume.

"What was all that about?" Linda asked. "Those flowers were from Martin Morton, weren't they? Oh, God, Kathleen. If you're messing about with her husband, Babs Morton is going to kill you!"

6

KEITH PARKER WAS SWEATING BUCKETS, and it had nothing to do with the hot weather. He walked along Blocksy Road and nervously looked over his shoulder. There was no one there. The whole street was deserted.

Old warehouses lined up along Blocksy Road. Occasionally a truck pulled out of one of the gates, but other than that it was pretty quiet, and that was why Dave Carter had picked one of the warehouses as his headquarters.

Keith was heading to the warehouse now.

He should have been over the moon. He was dropping off Dave's money and picking up thirty quid as a nice little kickback for selling the black-market cigarettes. He had Dave's money in his pocket, all rolled up and carefully counted.

The trouble was Dave Carter had asked to see him. Usually, Keith handed the money over to one of Carter's henchmen and arranged to pick up the cartons of cigarettes from them. He never dealt with Dave Carter in person, and now this summons out of the blue had him worried.

People saw Dave Carter as an old-fashioned gangster, polite and courteous. He wasn't known for violence like

Martin Morton. Dave Carter was a businessman, and if you treated him with respect, he treated you the same way.

All that might be true, but Keith had heard stories about people who had chanced their luck with Dave Carter and tried to take advantage of his gentlemanly nature. Those people were never heard of again. Unlike men who crossed Martin Morton, they weren't tortured or murdered in a showy, grotesque way. They just simply disappeared.

Keith pulled a handkerchief out of his pocket and mopped his brow and the back of his neck. He wasn't only worried about Dave Carter. The thought of Martin Morton finding out Keith was also working for his rival made him feel sick to the stomach.

He shouldn't have done it, but when the opportunity arose it seemed too good to pass up. All Keith had to do was go round selling the fags in different pubs around the East End. Black-market fags were incredibly popular because they were so much cheaper than getting them from the shops.

There was something in the way Big Tim had looked at him last week that made Keith think that they were on to him. He wasn't really doing anything wrong, at least, nothing that would hurt Martin Morton. But there was a deep rivalry between Carter and Morton.

Martin Morton thought he owned the whole patch, but Dave Carter had other ideas, and it was the silly sods like Keith who got caught in the middle. He was just trying to earn an honest living. Well, maybe not honest, but it wasn't as if he was hurting anyone.

When Keith approached the entrance to Dave Carter's warehouse, he pulled on the collar of his shirt. Perhaps he could tell Dave today that this was the last job he would do for him. If Dave was the gentleman everyone said he was, surely he wouldn't mind finding someone else to do the job Keith had been carrying out for the past few weeks.

But as he walked forward through the large steel gate that led to the truck loading bay, he had a horrible, sinking feeling that he wouldn't get out of it that easily.

As he approached the warehouse, Charlie Williams, a tall skinny man with a handsome face, stepped into view. He was clearly the lookout. He wore a suit that had seen better days but had on a smart waistcoat and gold pocket watch.

Charlie nodded at him and then called over his shoulder. "It's only Keith Parker." He turned back and nodded at Keith. "How are you, mate? Keeping well?"

Keith shrugged. "Not bad. Yourself?" He wasn't really in the mood for conversation. He just wanted to get this over with.

The metal rolling door clattered as someone in the warehouse pressed the button to raise it. The noise made Keith jump.

Charlie smirked. "You look like you're on tenterhooks, Keith. I hope you haven't got a guilty conscience. Have you done something silly?"

Keith blinked and looked up at Charlie. "Silly? I ain't done nothing. I'm an honest man."

"I'm just messing you about, Keith. Don't take things so seriously."

As Keith followed the man into the cavernous warehouse, he was glad of the cool and dusty air inside. It was baking outside today.

Their footsteps echoed as they walked across the empty storage hall towards a small room at the side that used to be used as the security man's office but was now Dave Carter's private headquarters. Carter didn't go in for show, unlike some of the other gangsters Keith could mention. Dave Carter was a practical man, and the minimalist space suited him down to the ground.

Dave was sitting talking to one of his men when Keith entered.

He looked up and smiled. "Nice to see you, Keith. Let us see the colour of your money."

Keith shivered as the sweat on the back of his neck cooled. He was far more comfortable dealing with one of Dave's minions. It was easy to collect the cigarettes from them and pay them their share of the money. But for some reason today, Dave Carter had insisted on seeing Keith in person. And that scared the living daylights out of him.

"Nice to see you, Mr. Carter," Keith said, trying to smile. He dumped the rolls of money on the desk. "It's all there. I've counted it more than once."

Dave nodded slowly and then brought his fingers together in a triangle beneath his chin as he sat forward and leaned on the desk. "Thank you, Keith. I appreciate your contribution." He stared at Keith hard for a few moments, and Keith felt his knees wobble.

At this rate, neither Dave Carter or Martin Morton would need to do him in. The way his pulse was pounding he thought he'd probably have a heart attack before either of them could get to him.

"I hope everything's to your satisfaction, Mr. Carter," he said, his eyes nervously flicking about the room as he realised that another two of Dave Carter's goons had appeared out of nowhere.

"Absolutely, Keith," Dave Carter said and peeled off a couple of notes from the cash rolls Keith had given him. He held the money out in front of him.

As Keith reached out a hand to take the money, he saw to his embarrassment, he was shaking.

"Thank you very much," Keith mumbled.

"We've been hearing a few rumours," Dave Carter said. "About Martin Morton."

"Martin Morton?" Keith stammered, and his mouth went dry. "What rumours would they be?"

"You seem nervous, Keith," Dave Carter said. He looked the epitome of cool. He was dressed in a full suit jacket and tie, but he didn't look the least bit hot and flustered. Keith on the other hand, had started sweating again.

"Nervous? Not me. Why would I be nervous?"

Dave Carter gave a smile that made Keith's stomach flip over.

"I'm a fair man, Keith. As long as you keep doing good work for me like this, you'll continue to be paid well. But a little dicky bird has told me you've got a foot in both camps. Are you working for Martin Morton?"

Keith didn't know how to respond. It was pretty much common knowledge that Keith had worked for Martin Morton in one way or another since he left school. He'd never exactly been a player, only taking on odds and ends whenever Martin needed someone for a low-risk job.

He'd never been involved in anything violent, and although he broke the law on occasion, it was never anything that Keith considered really bad. If he lied and said he had nothing to do with Martin Morton, Dave Carter would be sure to find out. On the other hand, this could be a test to see if Keith was going to be honest with him.

If Dave Carter really did deserve the reputation of a gentleman gangster, then perhaps Keith should tell him the truth and throw himself on his mercy.

"I've worked for Martin in the past, Mr. Carter. I've done a few jobs for him here and there."

Keith waited anxiously for Dave Carter's response.

For a minute or two, Dave Carter said nothing and just stared at Keith. Then finally, he said, "Do you understand what a conflict of interest is, Keith?"

Keith shook his head. "Not really," he stammered and tugged at his collar.

"Well, you see, Keith, it's like this, Martin Morton is my competition. I can't have people working for me and passing on certain information to him. That wouldn't do at all. Do you understand me?"

Keith nodded frantically. "I'd never tell anyone anything about your business, Mr. Carter. Of course, I wouldn't."

Dave Carter gave a single nod, but his eyes didn't leave Keith's face.

Keith looked around the room desperately. "I'd never betray any of you lot. I'm not a complicated man. I just want to earn a few bob to look after my family."

"That's good to hear, Keith. I think I can trust you, can't I?"

"Of course, you can. I'm completely trustworthy."

Keith heard one of the men laugh behind him. He turned around, but not fast enough to see who it was. His heart was thumping in his chest.

"All right then, Keith. I'll see you next week," Dave Carter said.

Keith reached out for the nearest chair to support himself. His legs were wobbling like crazy. "Is that it? I can go?"

Dave Carter smiled. "Yes, Keith, you can go."

7

AFTER HIS ENCOUNTER WITH DAVE Carter, Keith needed a drink — a strong one. His hands still hadn't stopped shaking. It wasn't as if Dave Carter had threatened him exactly, but there was something about the look in the man's eyes that terrified Keith. People might refer to him as the gentleman gangster, but Keith thought there was a monster lurking underneath the surface.

He walked up the Whitechapel Road and headed straight for the Blind Beggar. He ordered a pint and a whisky chaser and downed his whisky straightaway.

"Cor blimey, Keith," Brian Epswhistle said. He was standing beside Keith at the bar.

Brian was a regular. If he wasn't in the Blind Beggar, he could be found in the betting shop on Victoria Road. He wasn't a bad sort, but Keith didn't fancy talking to him today. He felt like he never wanted to talk to anyone again in case he let the wrong thing slip.

"Do you want another, Keith? You look like you've seen a ghost," said Molly, who was working behind the bar.

Keith nodded, and as the whisky hit his bloodstream, he felt himself start to relax. Dave Carter hadn't actually threatened him. In actual fact, he'd said he was pleased with the work Keith had done for him. There was no real reason for Keith to be so frightened.

"I've just had a tough morning, that's all," Keith said picking up the whisky glass as soon as Molly had put it down in front of him.

"It looks like it," Brian said. "I take it Martin Morton's men caught up with you then?"

Keith dropped his glass, and it smashed on the floor.

"Oh for God's sake, be careful," Molly said irritably and reached for the dustpan and brush behind the bar.

"What did you say?" Keith asked Brian in a whisper.

"Martin Morton's men," Brian said. "They've been asking after you."

"When was this?" Keith's pulse rate was galloping along. This day had just turned from bad to worse.

"Not sure. Old Bob mentioned it this morning."

Keith picked up his pint, planning to take it over to the table and get a bit of peace and quiet, so he could try and make sense of the situation.

It wasn't good. He couldn't think of any reason why Martin Morton's men would be after him other than the fact they'd found out he was working for Dave Carter.

"Maybe they've just got a job for you," Brian suggested cheerfully "I'm sure it's nothing to worry about." He slapped him on the back.

But Keith knew he was wrong. This was definitely something to worry about.

He was carrying his pint over to a table in the corner of the room when the door to the bar opened, and Keith got the fright of his life. Standing in the doorway and blocking out the sunlight stood Big Tim and Red-haired Freddie.

Keith froze where he was in the middle of the pub as Tim turned his attention to him and smiled. "There you are, Keith. We've been looking all over for you."

Keith felt his whole body tremble as Big Tim and Red-haired Freddie walked towards him with big grins on their faces.

"Be a good lad and drink up, why don't you?" Big Tim said, looking down at Keith. "We've got a lot of catching up to do. I thought we could take a drive."

"A drive?" Keith's lower lip trembled.

"Yes, out in the country somewhere." Red-haired Freddie leaned close to Keith so that he could whisper in his ear. "Somewhere nice and quiet."

"I look like a bleeding squashed sausage in this thing!" Linda said, looking at herself in the full-length mirror in her mum's bedroom.

"No, you don't. Stop making such a fuss. It's one of my best dresses. You just need a nice pair of heels to set it off," Kathleen insisted, eyeing her friend critically.

Linda was wearing a little black dress. On Kathleen, it draped over her curves and looked shapeless. Kathleen had always thought it made her look older than she was, but the dress made Linda look all boobs and backside. It clung to every curve, and Linda had lots of curves.

Linda looked close to tears as she tugged on the dress. Her cheeks were flushed. "A pair of bloody heels aren't going to make any difference. There is no way I am wearing something like this in public."

"Fine. Suit yourself. I was only trying to help," Kathleen

said irritably, scowling at her friend. Just recently Linda seemed to have developed a backbone, and Kathleen didn't like it one bit. She was used to her friend looking up to her and thinking she was the font of all knowledge, so she didn't appreciate this sudden change.

"I suppose now you'll say you're not coming to the club tonight because you've got nothing to wear."

Linda struggled to unzip the dress herself. "I said I would come, didn't I? I will just wear one of my own dresses."

"You'll look like a right square," Kathleen mumbled under her breath.

"What did you say?"

"Nothing." Kathleen picked up her eyeliner pencil and carefully drew a line close to her lashes. She sat back at Linda's mother's dressing table, pleased with her new look. She'd seen it in a magazine about film stars.

She turned to her friend. "Well, at least, let me do your makeup."

"Okay," Linda said as she pulled a yellow cotton dress over her head and then sat on the edge of the bed,

As Kathleen applied some blush to Linda's cheeks, Linda said, "Are you going to see Martin again? I don't know how you can be so brave. I would be terrified of that Babs Morton."

"She doesn't scare me," Kathleen said and picked up the eyeshadow. "Besides Martin has told me he's just biding his time before he leaves the nasty cow."

"He's going to leave his wife for you? But what about their children?"

Kathleen slammed down the eyeshadow brush. "You're so naive Linda. Their marriage isn't working anymore. He stayed with her for the sake of the children, but now it's time he had some happiness himself."

Linda kept her mouth shut as Kathleen applied some glossy lipstick. When Kathleen was finally satisfied with her handiwork, she put her hands on her friend's shoulders and turned her towards the mirror.

The makeup had worked wonders on Linda. She never normally wore any as her mother said it made her look like a trollop, but the blusher had given her clear skin a warm glow, and the eyeshadow had made her big, brown eyes look even larger.

Linda beamed happily. "Thanks for doing my makeup, Kath. It looks great."

Kathleen put the lid back on the lipstick with a click and handed her friend a pair of cream heels. "You do look nice, Linda. Maybe we'll find you a man tonight, eh?"

Linda giggled. "Shall we have a glass of Mum's sherry?"

"No," Kathleen said, standing up. "Let's get round to the club now, before it gets too busy. Martin told the bar staff to give me free drinks whenever I want. I'm sure I can get you some too. "

"Oh, lovely," Linda said as she followed Kathleen out of the bedroom like a faithful puppy.

8

KEITH PARKER KNEW HIS TIME was up. He lay across the back seat of Henry the Hand's car with his wrists and ankles tied together. His bladder was full to the point of bursting after his drinks in the pub, but needing the toilet was the least of his worries right now.

They'd been driving for a while. Henry was at the wheel. From his position on the back seat, Keith couldn't see properly. All he could see was Henry's three-fingered hand coming down to rest on the gear stick every so often. It gave him the creeps.

After helping bundle Keith into Henry the Hand's car, Red-haired Freddie had walked back into the pub laughing. Keith could still hear that horrible cackle echoing in his ears. When he'd seen that Big Tim was waiting for them in the car, he'd almost wet himself.

He didn't know what they were going to do with him. He hoped they had a gun and that way it would be over as quickly as possible, but from the stories he'd heard, Martin Morton's men didn't favour quick deaths.

"Please, Tim, I haven't done anything wrong. This has all been a misunderstanding."

Keith had already taken a smack around the earhole from Henry for talking too much, but he just couldn't stay quiet. He had to try. Even if there was the slimmest chance he could get out of this, he had to take it.

"You've made your bed, Keith. Now you have to lie in it."

His mother had always used that saying as well, and Keith had never understood it. What did making a bleeding bed have to do with anything? He was glad his mother hadn't lived to see what would become of her son. She had passed five years ago; God rest her soul.

"Please," Keith sobbed. He could feel the wetness from his tears underneath his cheek on the car seat.

"If you don't shut him up, I will," Henry the Hand growled at Tim, and he reached over, keeping one hand on the wheel, trying to smack Keith in the face with his horrible, disfigured hand.

Keith squealed in terror and tried to wriggle further back on the seat.

"Keep quiet," Tim said in a perfectly calm voice. "We are nearly there."

Nearly where? Keith wondered. They'd sped along smooth roads for a long time, but now the road they were on was bumpy, and from glimpses out of the window, he could just about see a lot of trees and green stuff. They had promised to take him to the country. Essex was his best bet. They were probably going to dump his body somewhere where it wouldn't be found for ages. They'd leave him as food for the wildlife.

The car came to a stop, and Keith's pulse was going through the roof. This was it. This was the end.

The car lifted as Big Tim got out. He opened the back door

and grabbed Keith by the scruff of the neck and the belt of his trousers, yanking him out.

Keith yelped in pain and refused to walk. He wriggled and tried to make himself as difficult as possible to carry. It made no difference. Big Tim didn't get his nickname for nothing. The man was all muscle.

Keith looked around, desperately trying to see some way of escape, but there was nothing in front of them but a deserted country lane. Tim hoisted him up and carried him under one arm towards a small group of trees.

Keith felt his bladder release, and a hot stream of urine ran down his leg, dripping onto Tim.

"Ugh, that's disgusting!" Tim dropped Keith on the floor.

Despite the fact his wrists and ankles were tied up, Keith did his best to wriggle away, but it was hopeless.

Henry grabbed one of his arms, and Tim grabbed the other. They lifted him between them, keeping their distance from Keith's urine-soaked trousers.

"You're not going to get away, so you may as well face up to it, you dirty bastard," Henry the Hand said.

"But what am I supposed to have done?" Keith pleaded.

"You know what you've done," Henry said. "You double-crossed Martin Morton, and nobody does that and gets away with it."

"I didn't. I swear I didn't. I was just selling a few fags, that's all. I would never double-cross Martin."

Keith was unceremoniously dumped on the floor.

"Well, you will never get a chance to do it again," Henry said, and from the back of his waistband, he pulled out a pistol.

As terrified as he was, Keith felt a strange sense of relief flow through him. At least, his death would be quick.

"Wait, I—"

Keith didn't have time to finish his sentence.

Henry raised the gun and shot him squarely between the eyes.

9

"THAT GIRL WILL BE THE death of me, Alice," Mary Diamond said.

She was sitting at her kitchen table with her neighbour, Alice Pringle. Alice was known as the neighbourhood gossip, and Mary wouldn't usually be talking to her about a family matter, but she was at her wits end and had no one else to turn to.

"She's had it too good for too long, Mary. You've worked your fingers to the bone for that girl. You've given her everything, and how does she repay you? She becomes some gangster's tart."

Mary Diamond bristled. She wanted to give Alice a slap for saying something like that about her daughter, but deep down she knew it was true. She had spoilt Kathleen, giving her everything she could afford to, trying to compensate for the fact Kathleen had grown up without a father.

Everybody had heard about Kathleen's relationship with Martin Morton now. Mary had overheard people talking about her in the butcher's and had to turn around and run out. She had never felt so ashamed. She felt ostracised.

"She's not a bad girl really, Alice. She's just easily led

astray." Despite everything, Mary couldn't really believe it was Kathleen's fault. That bastard was to blame. Martin Morton had turned her head, and Kathleen just didn't understand the consequences.

"If you ask me, the girl needs a damn good hiding," Alice said and plucked a cigarette from the packet on the table before offering them to Mary.

Mary took one. She didn't often smoke, but right now she needed one.

Mary picked up her stewed cup of tea and took a sip. "It's too late for hidings, Alice. She's too big for that now. I'm just going to have to hope she comes to her senses before it's too late."

Alice took a deep drag on her cigarette and then watched the smoke as she exhaled. "It might be more than just Kathleen's reputation at stake in all this, Mary."

"What do you mean?" Mary set her tea back down on the table and looked at Alice intently.

"Well, for one thing, I've heard that Babs Morton is pregnant."

Mary set her lips in a firm line. How could Kathleen runabout with the husband of a pregnant woman? Maybe she didn't know? If Mary passed on the news, then Kathleen might start steering clear of Martin Morton.

"How do you know that?"

"I know Frieda Lyons, and her daughter, Maisie, works as a receptionist at the Doctor's surgery."

Mary frowned. She didn't like the idea of nosy Alice having access to everyone's private medical records.

"And another thing," Alice continued, using her cigarette to emphasise her point. "This is probably even more important; I've heard rumours about Dave Carter." Alice lowered her voice as she said Dave Carter's name, even though no one could overhear them in Mary's kitchen.

"What has Dave Carter got to do with anything?"

Alice leaned forward over the table and moved her half-full cup of tea to one side. "I've heard whispers that Dave Carter might be making a move, trying to muscle in on Martin Morton's patch." Alice raised her eyebrows. "And you know what that means, don't you?"

Mary nodded slowly. She did know what that meant. It meant that there would be bloodshed very soon and an ugly battle for territory. Kathleen's involvement with Martin Morton meant her darling daughter would be caught right in the middle of it.

At the same moment as her mother was worrying about her future, Kathleen sat up in bed with Martin Morton, her naked body covered with a thin cotton sheet. She smiled in delight as Martin handed her a navy blue velvet jewellery case.

Kathleen's eyes widened. "What is this?"

Martin grinned showing off his gold tooth. "A present."

Kathleen snuggled up beside him. "I like presents," she said and squealed with glee as she opened the box to find a solid gold Rotary watch.

"Do you like it, Princess?"

"Oh, Martin, I love it!" She threw her arms around him and kissed him on the lips.

Kathleen had been getting a bit fed up lately. She'd wanted Martin to take her out to a fancy restaurant in the West End, or at least somewhere other than the club, but he refused to go. He told her he couldn't risk anyone seeing them together yet.

But the present had made her forget all that. It more than made up for it. Kathleen held out her arm as Martin fastened the watch around her wrist.

Martin got out of bed, stretched and then turned back to Kathleen. "You better get off home now, Princess. I've got work to do."

Kathleen tried her best not to look hurt. It was just Martin's way. She nodded, threw back the sheets and started searching the floor for her underwear.

There was a horrible niggling feeling deep down inside her. A little voice kept saying if Martin really cared for her wouldn't he give her a lift home, or, at least, make sure she got home safely? But he always left Kathleen to walk home alone, again telling her he didn't want to risk people seeing them together.

Of course, things would be different as soon as he got his divorce. Martin had told her he was going to tell his wife about them next month. He said things were complicated at the moment, but by next month, everything would be out in the open. Kathleen was already dreaming about her engagement ring. She could picture it clearly. She put the fact that they'd only been seeing each other for a couple of weeks out of her mind. Time didn't really matter when you were in love after all.

After she had gotten dressed, she walked through the bedroom and into the living area as she wanted to say goodbye to Martin. As she reached the doorway, the phone rang.

Martin snatched up the phone. "Is it done?" he asked.

There was a pause as he listened to the person on the other end of the phone, and then Martin smiled.

"Excellent," he said and then hung up. He walked across to the cocktail cabinet to fix himself a whisky.

"I'll be off then," Kathleen said.

"All right," Martin said, not even bothering to look up from his drink.

Kathleen felt deflated as she walked out of the club and into Hollins Lane. It only took five minutes to walk home, but she didn't exactly enjoy walking alone in the dark. She always imagined there was someone in the shadows waiting to pounce.

She glanced down at her watch, trying to cheer herself up. She didn't know why she was feeling so down after getting such a lovely present. Surely she should be happy. And she planned to be happy, just as soon as Martin got his divorce through and everything was settled.

She had just turned the corner into her street when somebody grabbed her from behind and thrust her up against a brick wall. The scream died on Kathleen's lips as she stared into the eyes of Babs Morton.

Babs leaned her arm against Kathleen's throat. The pressure was so intense she could barely breathe.

"You little bitch. You've just been with Martin, haven't you?"

The weight of Babs' arm on her windpipe meant Kathleen couldn't speak, so she just shook her head instead.

"What has he told you? Did he say he's going to leave me for you? He says that to all of them, you daft cow. He is only seeing you because I'm pregnant."

Kathleen felt like she'd been punched in the stomach.

Pregnant? No, that wasn't possible. Clearly Martin didn't know about this. Otherwise, he would have said something.

Oh, God. He'd never leave her now that she was pregnant.

It couldn't be true. It just couldn't.

"You're lying," Kathleen croaked out.

Babs released her grip and started to laugh. "You really are just a silly little girl, aren't you?"

She pulled her dress flush against her stomach, so despite the fact it was dark, Kathleen could see a rounded bump.

Her eyes filled with tears. "You haven't told Martin. He doesn't know…"

"Of course, he knows, you daft mare. And I'll tell you this, he'll never leave me for the likes of you. So you'd better get yourself another man. Preferably someone who isn't married."

Babs poked a bony finger at Kathleen's chest. "I fight for what's mine. Everyone is scared of my Martin, but it's me you need to be afraid of."

10

AFTER BABS MORTON HAD THREATENED her, Kathleen had stayed away from the club and Martin.

She tried to convince herself she wasn't disappointed that Martin hadn't bothered to contact her. There were no roses this time, not even a note asking if she was okay. Did he know Babs had found out about them? Or had he found out that Babs was pregnant and decided to dump Kathleen without telling her?

She didn't appreciate being ditched in such a humiliating way, but her friend Linda insisted Kathleen had had a lucky escape.

If nothing else, her mother was pleased. In fact, that was an understatement. Mary Diamond had been bloody ecstatic when she realised things between Martin Morton and her daughter were over.

Kathleen leaned back on her bed and sighed. It was the weekend, so there was no reason to get up. She didn't seem to have the enthusiasm to do anything anymore. Linda had come round last night, trying to get her to go out for the evening, but Kathleen couldn't be bothered. Linda had stayed for a while, trying to interest Kathleen in gossip about a girl who had just been sacked from Bevels. Normally Kathleen would have enjoyed the salacious details, but last night she just sat miserably listening to Linda going on and on.

There was a bang on her bedroom door. "Come on, Kathleen. You can't stay in bleeding bed all day."

Kathleen put a pillow over her head. That was exactly what she wanted to do. She didn't want to see the outside world. She knew people had been talking about her behind her back. She quite liked being gossiped about when she thought they might be impressed that she'd landed a man like Martin Morton, but it was a completely different matter now she knew they were laughing at her. She wanted to shrivel up and never leave the house again.

Her mother wasn't one to take no for an answer, and she barged into Kathleen's room, pulling back the covers and gave her a slap on the backside. "You lazy mare. If you get out of bed, you can have a treat."

Kathleen peered out from under her pillow. "A treat?"

Her mother nodded. "Yes, I've decided you need a little something to cheer you up. I thought we'd go down the Roman and get you a new dress. What do you say?"

Kathleen shuddered at the thought of going to the busy market where lots of people would see her. She'd always loved shopping in the past, particularly if it was something for her. She was about to shake her head and tell her mother to go away when she saw the concerned look in Mary's eyes. Her mother was really worried.

Kathleen knew she could be a little self-centred at times, but she did love her mum, and she didn't want her to worry. She had stuck by her through all of this, after all.

"All right, thanks," Kathleen said, trying to muster up some enthusiasm.

Mary beamed. "Good girl. I'll be downstairs."

Mary went downstairs and poured a cup of tea for Kathleen. She was really worried about the girl. Kathleen had been moping around the house and only picking at her food, which was very unlike her.

She knew it seemed like the end of the world to Kathleen right now, but gossip died down in the end, and most people didn't believe Kathleen was a bad person. They thought she'd been a silly little girl, led astray by Martin Morton.

It had been a couple of weeks since Kathleen had last been out in the evening, so Mary knew she hadn't been seeing that horrible man. Violet Craig, who worked in the greengrocers next to Bevels dress factory, liked to keep an eye on passers-by, and she'd informed Mary that she had never seen Martin Morton step within a few feet of the place. Mary was satisfied that this horrible incident was over, and they could now put it behind them.

Later that morning, Mary and Kathleen walked along the Roman Road market, trying to avoid the puddles. After an unusually hot start to the summer, the rain had returned with a vengeance, and now it looked like they would suffer a soggy August too. Mary didn't much mind; she'd been getting hot flushes recently, so the cooler weather was definitely a relief.

She shot a sideways glance at Kathleen, checking the girl was all right. She didn't look her cheerful self, but at least, she was looking about at the stalls and the brightly coloured clothes. It wouldn't be long until she was back to normal.

Mary decided when she went home she would have a

word with Linda and encourage the girl to see a bit more of Kathleen. In Mary's opinion, Linda was a very good influence.

A pink dress fluttering on a hanger caught Kathleen's eye, and she wandered across, reaching up for the material and rubbing it between her fingers. It was a heavy crêpe and Mary thought it would look good on her daughter.

"How much?" Mary asked the man on the stall.

The man gave his price and Mary balked.

"Not on your Nelly," Mary said, folding her arms under her bust and giving the man a stern look.

Kathleen smiled. Her mother loved the pantomime of the market. She loved haggling and getting a bargain.

A movement out of the corner of her eye caught Kathleen's attention.

She gasped and shrank back, trying to hide behind the stall.

It was Babs Morton, striding along the street as if she owned it and behind her were her two children, Ruby and Derek. Derek looked around five years old, and Ruby was scarcely more than a toddler.

As Babs turned around to hurry the children along, she caught sight of Kathleen and scowled. Her belly looked full to bursting now, and Kathleen guessed it wouldn't be long before another little Morton was in the world.

Kathleen let out the breath she'd been holding when Babs simply turned away and carried on walking. She felt her shoulders slump as she realised Babs didn't think she was worth worrying about anymore. Babs had been right all along. Martin hadn't cared about her at all. She'd just been one more notch on his bedpost.

She turned back to her mother, who was still haggling happily with the stall owner. She hadn't noticed Babs, and Kathleen was glad.

She was sick of being the victim. Sick of feeling sorry for herself. Sick of going to the same boring job every day, and sick to the back teeth of not being able to afford the nice things she believed she deserved. It was time to make a change. Kathleen was determined to do something with her life, and she wouldn't let the Mortons, or anyone like them, tread all over her again.

One day, Kathleen would get her revenge. She would pass Babs on the street, decked out in diamonds and furs and look down her nose at Babs Morton and her horrible family.

11

DAVE CARTER SAT IN THE little office at his warehouse surrounded by his men. Everyone was tense.

Dave Carter and Martin Morton had been rivals for a long time, but the tension had been ratcheting up over the past few weeks, and today it had shot up to the highest level yet.

Martin Morton was being a difficult bastard, and Dave Carter had decided it was time to make a stand. He had his men gathered here today to go over their plan to raid a pub that was on Morton's patch. The raid was an act of revenge. Just last week, one of Martin Morton's men had waltzed into a car workshop that was under Carter's protection and stolen a car. The whole thing had caused Dave no end of headaches. It was just one car, but the lack of respect had far-reaching consequences. It was a deliberate act that Dave knew had been intended to rile him.

Dave wasn't one to act on the spur of the moment. He liked to bide his time and weigh up his options, but when he did act, it was decisive and often deadly.

The last thing he wanted was a turf war. He was sure Martin Morton, like him, first and foremost, wanted to make a living. If they were distracted by violence, it meant they weren't concentrating on their money-making ventures and risked other gangs muscling in while they were otherwise occupied.

"I don't want any violence," Dave said. "This is just a warning, all right?" He looked around the office at his men. Charlie Williams was there, and in the last few months, he'd really proven himself an asset. Dave was sure he could rely on him.

Frank the Face wouldn't meet his eye and kept his gaze on the ground. He was called Frank the Face because the left-hand side of his face drooped downwards. It looked like he'd had a stroke, but he hadn't. The rest of his body was unaffected, and Frank's disability had never caused any problems with his job, until recently. Dave had noticed that Frank's hands had a tendency to tremble, particularly when he was stressed or angry. He knew him well enough to know he wasn't a coward, so the trembling had to be caused by something else.

"No problem, boss," Brian Moore said. He was a short man, but wide, with the biggest shoulders Dave Carter had ever seen.

Dave nodded. "We need to show our strength, pass the message on that we are no pushovers, but there won't be any protection at the pub tonight, only civilians, so don't get trigger-happy." Dave looked pointedly at Charlie, who nodded.

"Okay," Dave said, satisfied. "It will go down tomorrow night. Martin Morton won't know what's hit him."

Everyone turned and made their way to the door except Charlie Williams. He hesitated beside Dave's desk.

"What is it, Charlie?" Dave asked when the other two men

had left the room.

"I'm worried about Frank," Charlie said and looked over his shoulder to make sure that the other men had gone.

Dave nodded. If he had noticed Frank trembling, then it was no surprise that Charlie had too.

"He's not safe, Boss. He gets the shakes. I don't know what's causing it, but my old man had the same tremors. Alcoholic, he was."

Dave shook his head. He knew Frank's problem wasn't alcohol withdrawal. It went deeper than that.

"Frank has always been loyal to me, Charlie. He's a good worker."

"I'm not saying he's not a good bloke, but it's getting to the point where he is a liability. When we collected the booze last night, he only went and dropped his bleeding gun, didn't he?"

Dave frowned. This was the first he'd heard of it. "Last night?"

Charlie nodded. They'd gone to their usual pickup last night to collect the bottles of black-market spirits that Dave distributed to the pubs under his protection. It was a routine job and very unlikely to go wrong. The boys only carried guns for show. But the fact that Frank had dropped his gun was very worrying indeed. If it had happened during a different job, it could have had a very different outcome.

Charlie began, "I've talked to Gary about it-"

Dave Carter cut him off. "And why would you do that?" he asked coldly.

Charlie's eyes widened. "Um, I thought… I mean, he is your brother."

"Exactly. He's my brother. He's not in charge, is he?"

Charlie shook his head. "No, of course not," he stammered, looking uneasy.

Dave loved his brother, but he wasn't as cool and level-headed as Dave. Gary could be hot-headed, and armed with this information, could do something stupid.

"It's me you deal with, not Gary. Understand?"

"Yes, boss," Charlie said, hanging his head in shame.

Satisfied that Charlie was sufficiently sorry, he said, "Send Frank in to see me."

A moment after Charlie had left the room, Frank the Face entered.

The left side of his face hung slackly down, but the right-hand side of his mouth turned up into a smile. "You wanted to see me, boss?"

"That's right, Frank. Have a seat." He nodded to the chair on the other side of the desk, and Frank sat down.

"This sounds serious." Frank gave a little chuckle, but Dave could tell he was nervous.

Dave didn't skirt around the issue. He didn't want to prolong Frank's misery. It was better to confront things head-on. "I heard you dropped the gun last night."

Frank leaned back in the chair and looked away in disgust. "Bloody Charlie Williams, that rat."

"No, Charlie did the right thing by telling me. I'm worried about you Frank. The shaking is getting worse, isn't it?"

Frank's whole body tensed up. "No, it isn't. I'm fine. It was just a stupid mistake. It could have happened to anyone."

Dave folded his arms and leaned forward on the desk. Frank was a good man and a proud one. The last thing Dave wanted to do was take his livelihood away from him, but he just couldn't be trusted with the front-line jobs anymore.

"I've been thinking it might be time to transfer you. I thought about getting you involved with the car business. I am planning on expanding, and I need someone I can trust to keep an eye on everything. What do you say?"

Dave kept his voice level and tried to keep his tone light. He didn't want to hurt Frank's feelings, and he didn't want him to think this job offer was some kind of charity, although of course, that's what it really was.

"Give me another chance, boss. It was a stupid mistake. It won't happen again."

Dave noticed that Frank's fists were clenched in his lap. "You've always been a good and loyal worker, Frank. I appreciate that."

Dave paused and studied the man's face. The droop had even reached his eyebrow now. The left one hung down lower than the right. "Have you been to the doctors? If money is a problem, then–"

"I'm fine," Frank burst out.

"Watch yourself, Frank. Remember who you're talking to."

Frank bowed his head. "I'm sorry, boss, but don't do this to me. Don't take away my job."

"I'm not taking anything away from you, Frank, I'm just giving you a new opportunity, and I strongly suggest you take it."

"I don't have any other choice, do I?" Frank mumbled. He sounded defeated.

"Look at it this way, it's a kind of retirement plan. I'll see you and your family are all right for money. Come and work on the cars for me, Frank. I don't want to lose you."

Frank nodded. "All right," he murmured. "I'll do it."

12

FRANK THE FACE LEFT THE warehouse after talking to Dave Carter and headed for the canal. He needed the fresh air and a walk to try and cool off. Sodding Dave Carter. He wanted to scrape Frank off like shit from his shoe.

The trembling had started again in his left arm, and he clutched it, pulling it tight against his body to keep it still. It was rage, he told himself. He was only trembling because he was so angry.

He looked down at his reflection in the canal water and studied his face. The ripples on the surface made it look worse than usual.

Why did this have to happen to him?

He couldn't go back to the warehouse now. He was far too worked up. He decided to go home and talk to his wife, Maisie.

If he was honest, he wanted some sympathy. He wanted to moan about the treatment he'd received from Dave Carter without any comeback. It had to be Maisie because he couldn't trust anyone else not to go back to Dave and tell tales.

He realised his mistake as soon as he got home and hung

his coat on the peg by the front door.

"What are you doing back at this time, Frank? What's wrong? Have you been getting the shakes again?" Maisie asked after she rushed up to him.

Frank closed his eyes and sighed. Twenty bleeding questions was not what he needed right now.

Maisie reached up, trying to stroke his face, but he pushed her away.

"Stop bothering me, woman," he said. "I've had a real bastard of a day. I've lost my job, and the last thing I need is your nagging."

Maisie gasped and put her hands over her mouth. "What are we going to do, Frank? The rent is due at the end of the week."

Frank didn't tell her that Dave Carter had offered him another job and promised him he wouldn't be out of pocket. He knew it was cruel of him to let Maisie worry, but at that moment, he didn't care. He wanted her to be as upset as he was.

"Oh God, Frank, what are we going to do? The kids will be home from school soon."

Frank felt defeated. Going home had been a mistake. What he really needed was a drink.

He reached for his jacket. "I'm going out."

"But you've only just got home. I hope you're not going to the pub, Frank. We can't afford it if you've lost your job."

Frank ignored his wife and opened the front door. He stepped out onto the street. He raised his head as he felt the first gentle drops of rain begin to fall. Bloody typical. Just his luck.

"Wait, Frank!" Maisie shouted from the doorway as he

was walking down the garden path. "Promise me you'll go to the doctor."

"Get inside," Frank snarled. The last thing he wanted was the neighbours knowing his private business.

Frank hunched up his shoulders against the rain and started to walk down the street in the direction of the Queen Victoria pub.

It was no use Maisie asking him what they were going to do because Frank didn't know himself yet.

All he knew was he would make Dave Carter pay for his disrespect if it was the last thing he did.

Babs Morton walked into the parlour of her house in Poplar. She loved everything about the four-bedroom house. They'd moved there soon after getting married. Derek had been born there, followed by Ruby. It was the first place she and Martin had lived in together. When they'd moved in, Babs thought the place was like a palace. It was twice the size of her parents' place, and it even had a large backyard.

Over the years, she'd had a new kitchen installed and luxurious new carpets. It might be sentimental of her, but she'd developed a real attachment to the house.

Last night, Martin started talking about moving to the country. It wasn't the first time he'd mentioned it.

Babs wasn't daft. She knew what he really meant was that Babs and the kids would move to the country while Martin would stay in London and be able to entertain his fancy ladies without getting caught.

That wasn't going to happen if Babs had anything to do with it.

Babs lit a cigarette and leaned back on the sofa. She'd done her jobs for the morning, and now it was her time to relax.

"Mummy, can I have a biscuit?" Ruby said, tottering into the front room.

"No, you can't," Babs snapped. "You'll get fat."

Babs felt a twinge of guilt as Ruby's lower lip wobbled.

She got to her feet. "Oh, all right. Just one, though."

She walked to the kitchen, pulled the biscuit tin down from the shelf, opened it up and handed a custard cream to little Ruby.

Martin was hardly ever at home these days. He spent most of the time in that flat of his, and he hardly ever saw the children.

His visits lasted for five minutes at a time. He didn't like dealing with the everyday things. Martin liked it when they looked pretty and kept quiet.

Babs rubbed her stomach and wondered if the new baby would be a boy or a girl. She'd been lucky enough to have one of each, so perhaps she shouldn't have a preference. She thought Martin would want another boy to follow in his footsteps. She knew he already had plans for Derek. For that reason alone, Babs hoped she'd have another girl, that way she wouldn't be dragged into all the gangland nonsense.

Martin had seemed so glamorous when she'd first met him, and he'd swept her off her feet. Now, the gloss had worn thin, and she saw the danger and the cruelty of it all.

As far as Babs knew, Martin hadn't seen that silly tart, Kathleen, again. Babs had always tried to make it her business to ensure that Martin behaved himself, which was a full-time job in itself.

She knew she wouldn't be able to stop all of them. Martin had always liked the ladies, but Kathleen had Babs worried.

She'd lasted longer than Martin's normal tarts. It wasn't just that, though. When she'd looked into Kathleen's eyes, she saw something that reminded Babs of herself at that age: ambition.

On the other side of London, Kathleen sat in a doctor's surgery with Linda by her side.

"Why are we in Kennington?" Kathleen asked Linda in a whisper. "It's miles away."

"Exactly," Linda said. "That's the point. No one's going to know you over here, are they? Dr Morrison's clinic is known for its privacy, so we won't have to worry about your mum finding out."

Kathleen nodded. That did make her feel a little better. She knew nosy Alice from next door had a friend working in the local doctor's surgery, so Kathleen definitely couldn't have gone there.

When the nurse called Kathleen's name, she jumped and squeezed Linda's hand tightly. "I can't do it. It's all been a mistake."

Linda pulled her friend to her feet. "You can do it. I'll come in with you if you like."

Kathleen shook her head. "It's all right. But you'll wait for me, won't you?"

"Of course, I will."

Kathleen left Linda in the waiting area and followed the nurse through to Dr Morrison's consulting room.

The nurse closed the door on them, and Kathleen stared at the doctor. He wasn't as old as she'd expected. Kathleen guessed he couldn't have been older than thirty. It didn't feel right, seeing such a young doctor. Her usual doctor was an old, white-haired man.

"What seems to be the problem, Kathleen?" Dr Morrison asked, smiling at her pleasantly.

Kathleen's stomach was in knots. He was going to ask if she was married, and then he was going to look at her disapprovingly and send a letter to her mother, she just knew it.

Kathleen shot a glance at the door.

"It's all right, Kathleen," Dr Morrison said. "I'm a doctor. You can trust me."

Kathleen took a deep breath and clutched her hands together in her lap. In a quiet voice, she said, "I think I'm pregnant."

"Well, that's good news, isn't it?"

Kathleen felt close to tears. No, it wasn't good news. It was the worst news in the world.

After Dr Morrison had examined her and taken a urine sample, Kathleen wandered out into the waiting room in a daze.

Linda had been flicking through a magazine and looked up as her friend approached. "Well," she whispered. "What did the doctor say?"

Kathleen shook her head miserably. "I won't know until later. I have to come back for the results or telephone."

As Linda pulled her into a hug, Kathleen felt like crying. The next few hours were going to pass agonisingly slowly.

13

FRANK HAD HAD FAR TOO much to drink. But no one dared tell him that as he staggered about The Queen Victoria, spilling his pint. He noticed people were still looking at him warily. They wouldn't dare cross Frank the Face, not when he had the backing of Dave Carter, and everyone knew he worked for him.

He could kiss goodbye to that respect as soon as people found out that he wasn't working for Dave anymore, at least not in any proper capacity. As Frank felt the melancholy descend upon him, he ordered another drink. The barmaid shot a look at the landlord, but the landlord simply nodded, instructing her to give Frank what he wanted. But suddenly, Frank didn't want another drink, at least not here. It wasn't real respect these people had for him. They were only treating him well because they feared Dave Carter.

"Forget it," Frank the Face snarled and turned around, heading for the door.

He bumped into a couple of people as he went, not bothering to stop and apologise.

"Wait up, Frank. What's the matter?" It was Brian the landlord calling after him. "Come back and have another drink, eh? No hard feelings."

"Sod off," Frank said, heading for the door.

He had somewhere better to be. He knew someone who would genuinely be very glad to see him.

Frank smiled as he walked outside and staggered in the direction of the Morton club on Hollins Lane.

When he reached the outside of Martin Morton's club, Frank hesitated. He may be drunk, but he still had some logic whirring away at the back of his brain. If he did this now, there would be no going back. This decision couldn't be reversed.

Frank shoved his hands in his pockets and stared down at his shoes. He'd spent many years working for Dave Carter and had a lot of fond memories of the man. Before today, if anyone had said a bad word against him, Frank would have taken it as a personal affront, and made it his mission to smash some sense into them.

But that was before...

As the memory came back of how Dave had treated him, he felt a coldness creeping into his heart. Dave Carter had tried to get rid of him, and nobody got rid of Frank the Face, no matter how far back they went.

He looked up again at the sign over Martin Morton's club and then moved towards the door.

Inside it was noisy, much busier than a normal pub. Frank didn't really care for this sort of place. It was full of youngsters trying to dance and getting pissed. He was the oldest bloke there by at least ten years.

It was so crowded he could barely move, but he finally managed to inch his way to the bar.

"What can I get you, love?" One of the barmaids, a brassy

blonde, asked him.

Frank suddenly felt completely sober. "Is Martin around?"

The barmaid nodded in the direction of the door behind the bar. "He's upstairs," the barmaid said. "Why don't you have a word with Big Tim?"

Frank nodded and then jerked his head in Tim's direction. He didn't have to worry about trying to attract Tim's attention to have a word. Tim had spotted him the moment he walked in. That was to be expected, of course, because he was one of Dave Carter's men and a rival, or, at least, he had been until today.

Big Tim towered over Frank. "What can we do for you, Frank?" he asked. His tone was polite, but suspicion was written all over his face.

"I want a word with Martin."

Tim stared at him for a long time, but Frank refused to be the first to break eye contact.

Finally, Tim said, "Get yourself a drink. I'll let him know you're here."

Frank nodded and turned his attention back to the barmaid, who had been hovering beside them, listening to the conversation with interest.

"I'll have a Scotch. Make it a large one."

By the time the barmaid had given Frank his drink, Tim was back downstairs. "This way," he said jerking his chin in the direction of the back door.

They entered the hallway and then started to climb the set of stairs. The stairs creaked under Big Tim's weight.

Frank's mouth grew dry, and the ice cubes in the drink he carried started to rattle against the glass. He transferred the drink to his other hand.

Tim didn't ask him why he was here. He stayed silent as he led Frank upstairs and opened a door into a large open plan living area.

Sitting on the sofa, smoking a cigarette, was Martin Morton.

Martin flashed a smile, showing off his gold tooth. "Well, what a nice surprise. Have a seat, Frank," Martin said, indicating the armchair opposite him.

Frank sat down. His palms felt sweaty, so he wiped them on the legs of his trousers.

Big Tim remained standing beside the door.

"So to what do we owe this pleasure?" Martin said and took a drag on his cigarette.

"I've got a little bit of information," Frank said, sounding more confident than he felt.

Martin looked intrigued. He leaned forward. "And what would that be, Frank?"

"Dave Carter is planning a raid on one of your pubs. And I can tell you which one."

"And why exactly would you do that?" Big Tim's voice boomed from behind Frank.

Martin's head jerked up and shot Tim a scathing look.

Tim shut up immediately.

Frank shrugged. "Let's just say Dave Carter and I have parted company as of today."

Martin smiled coldly. "What a shame. Now, what are you expecting in return for this information?"

Frank hadn't got as far as thinking about that. His mind was focused purely on revenge. But then again, a little bit of money wouldn't go amiss, particularly now he was officially out of work.

Frank smiled as Martin pulled out a roll of notes from his pocket and began peeling them off. He handed Frank a wedge. "Is that enough?"

Frank smiled. "That will do very nicely, thank you, Mr. Morton."

"Where and when is this raid going to happen?"

"At the Three Grapes," Frank said. "Tomorrow night, just before closing."

Martin's face transformed into a wide grin. "Then we will be ready and waiting for them."

Martin beckoned Tim over and then whispered something in his ear.

When he turned back to Frank, his eyes were cold as he said, "I think it would be best if you stayed here until after the raid. We wouldn't want you to get caught up in it now, would we, Frank?"

14

FRIEDA LONGBOTTOM BUSTLED HER WAY into Morton's club, carrying her buckets and cleaning supplies. She'd been cleaning at Morton's club since it opened a couple of years ago. Before that, she'd been employed in a few other establishments owned by Martin Morton.

He was a picky bastard, but Frieda didn't really mind. He paid well above the going rate, and that was all Frieda cared about. She let herself in with her key and propped open the doors to let a bit of fresh air inside. The place always stank of old booze and stale cigarettes when she got there in the morning.

The bar staff had already collected all the glasses the night before, but all the tables were sticky from spilled drinks, and there were fag ends dropped on the floor.

Frieda gave a sigh and rolled up her sleeves, ready to make a start. She filled her bucket with hot water from the sink behind the bar and began to wipe the tables. She had a method: tables first, then sweep the floor, then mop it and finally she would turn her attention to the WCs.

It was hard work, but it only took her a couple of hours, which allowed her to look after her grandson in the afternoons. The cheeky little blighter was the only thing that kept her going sometimes.

After she'd finished the bar, she usually gave Martin Morton's flat the once over too. He could be a bit funny about that and had strict rules. She was forbidden from going into the small second bedroom that he used as an office, and every single item of scrap paper, even the stuff in the waste paper bin, had to be ripped up into tiny little bits so nobody could read it. Even if it was something as simple as a shopping list.

In Frieda's opinion that was more than a little odd, but of course, she didn't say anything. She just took Martin Morton's money and kept her mouth shut.

After she'd cleaned the tables, buffing the polished wood to a shine, she set to work on the floor. Bending over with the broom always made her back hurt. It was a large area to clean, and there were a great deal of tables and chairs to move around, and Frieda wasn't getting any younger.

When she'd finished mopping the floor with the lemon scented cleaner, she straightened up and stretched her back.

She had earned a cigarette. There was nobody around to mind. But just in case, she nipped into the ladies' lavatories. Martin Morton paid by the hour, and she didn't want him docking her wages if anyone caught her having a crafty fag.

Frieda lifted up her cigarette and leaned back against the sink before taking a long drag.

As she exhaled the smoke, she looked in the mirror over the sink and grimaced. Time hadn't been kind to Frieda. She hadn't lived an easy life, and it showed in her face. She leaned forward to inspect her eyes bags more closely when she heard a noise from outside in the bar.

She froze with the fag between her lips. No one was normally at Morton's at this time. The staff didn't get here until the late afternoon because Morton's only opened in the evening, and Martin never had meetings with his men in the mornings when Frieda might overhear them.

Frieda remembered she'd left the front door propped open. She shivered. If anyone nicked anything, she was bound to get the blame. She'd never had a problem leaving the door open before. It wasn't as if anyone would risk upsetting Martin Morton by entering his club without permission.

Still, Frieda felt nervous. She removed the cigarette from her mouth and stubbed it out in the sink before cautiously opening the door to the ladies' toilets and peering out into the club.

She couldn't see anything at first, so she took a couple of steps forward and suddenly there was a loud bang followed by a curse, and Frieda's bucket of water went flying.

Frieda let out a strangled shriek as she saw Frank the Face slipping and sliding through the spilled soapy liquid on the floor.

Bleeding hell. What the hell was he doing here?

Frieda just stared at him. The clothes he wore looked crumpled as if he'd slept in them.

Everyone around these parts knew that Frank the Face worked for Dave Carter, and was an arch enemy of Martin Morton. So the fact that he was here now made Frieda very nervous indeed.

"What are you doing here?" Frieda demanded.

Frank turned to face Frieda and seemed to notice her for the first time.

"Who the hell are you?" He snarled and then grimaced and put a hand against his forehead.

Frieda had seen that look many times before. It had clearly been a long night for Frank, and he'd had too much to drink. Frieda guessed he was now feeling the after-effects.

Frieda put her hands on her hips, pursed her lips together and then walked towards him. He must have had a ridiculous amount to drink last night to end up here. She couldn't imagine where he'd come from. Had he strolled in through the open door, or had he fallen asleep in the gents and spent the night there?

"You'd better not let Martin catch you here," Frieda warned, pointing a finger at Frank.

"What are you on about, you silly old bat?"

"Well, I never," Frieda said, outraged. She was ready to give Frank a stern telling off. The man might work for Dave Carter, but that didn't mean he could talk to her that way.

But before Frieda could put Frank back in his place, the back door behind the bar opened, and Big Tim walked out. His face creased in concern as he looked at Frank and then back at Frieda.

Tim nodded at her. "Can I have a quick word, love?"

Frieda hesitated. As much as she wanted the opportunity to put Frank in his place, she knew she couldn't afford to upset Big Tim. She needed this job.

"You had better get back upstairs, Frank," Tim said, looking at the dishevelled Frank angrily.

Tim pulled Frieda to one side and looked down at her. "I'm sure I don't need to remind you that Martin pays you very well to maintain his privacy. You mustn't mention who you saw here today, do you understand?"

Frieda bristled. Bloody cheek. What did he think she was? A grass? She'd worked for Martin Morton for years. Surely by now they knew they could trust her.

"I don't go round flapping my mouth," Frieda said. "You don't have to worry about me. I should think you've got your hands full with that one." Frieda said and nodded to Frank, who was just disappearing through the back door.

Frank was starting to regret his hasty actions last night. What had he been thinking? Dave Carter may have treated him like shit yesterday, but what he had done had been ten times worse. He had sold his boss out to his greatest enemy.

He felt like crap, too, and was suffering through the worst hangover of his life. He'd fallen asleep on the sofa upstairs in the flat and then wandered down here this morning to try and get away before anyone noticed him. Unfortunately, he hadn't spotted the cleaning lady's bucket on the floor.

Frank walked up the stairs taking each step slowly. Everything seemed to be an extra effort this morning. He had the shakes, and he wasn't sure whether that was his normal tremors or the after-effects of the Scotch he'd drunk last night. His rolling stomach and nausea were definitely down to the Scotch, though.

He reached the top of the stairs and walked into the open plan living area. Martin was sitting in an armchair sipping a cup of tea."

"Morning, Frank. You look like crap."

"I want to get home," Frank said, gesturing to the clothes he was wearing. "I need to get washed and changed."

Martin gave him a cold smile. "I don't think that would be wise, Frank. You should stay here today."

Frank was starting to feel stir-crazy already. How would he cope for the rest of the day stuck in here?

"You're treating me like some kind of prisoner," Frank protested.

Martin took another sip of his tea. "I prefer to think of you as a valued guest, Frank."

Frank looked down at the floor. What if he'd never let him go?

Sunlight streamed in through the windows. He knew it wouldn't be long before his former colleagues turned up for work at the warehouse. They always had a meeting first thing to discuss the plans for that day and any problems that might have arisen the night before.

Would they notice that something was wrong when he didn't show up at the warehouse this morning? Or would they just assume he was still upset at losing his position within the firm.

Frank felt the hope drain out of him and flopped down onto the sofa. He was now in bed with Martin Morton, and would regret it for the rest of his life.

15

CHARLIE WILLIAMS SAT IN THE front passenger seat of the van Brian had stolen earlier that day. It was ten-thirty pm, and it wouldn't be long until they started the raid. He buzzed with a nervous energy.

Dave had told them he didn't want any violence. Dave Carter never involved himself in petty squabbles like this, so it was just Charlie Williams, Brian Moore and Dave's brother Gary heading to The Three Grapes tonight.

Charlie was feeling uneasy and wished Frank was there. He didn't like how things had gone down yesterday and felt guilty that he had been the one to tell Dave that Frank was getting worse. Deep down, he knew that Frank was too ill to come out on a raid like this, but he missed Frank's steady common sense and reassuring presence.

A loud cackle of a laugh made Charlie look over his shoulder at Gary Carter in the back of the van. Dave's brother, Gary, could never be accused of having a calming presence. Charlie was worried about him. He sat in the back smiling to himself and looking far too eager to get things started. His eyes had an odd look, too, and his pupils were like pin pricks. Charlie hoped the stupid bastard hadn't taken anything.

Charlie swallowed back the guilt as he remembered how Frank had looked yesterday when he walked out of the warehouse. Perhaps eventually he would realise taking Dave up on his offer to oversee things on the car business was a good idea. It made sense, and it was a nice safe job for his retirement.

Charlie checked his watch again; it was almost time. He stared down at his gun, and out of habit, he checked the knife he kept in a holster around his ankle.

They weren't wearing masks tonight. The whole reason behind the raid was to make sure they were recognised so everyone would know that Dave Carter was striking back at the Mortons.

The seconds were slowly ticking by, and Charlie mumbled a prayer under his breath. He was a good Catholic boy when it suited him to be and still went to church every Sunday. He reached inside his shirt and touched his gold cross.

Meanwhile, Henry the Hand and Red-haired Freddie were upstairs in the flat over The Three Grapes. Red-haired Freddie was getting impatient, and he wandered over to the window, peeking behind the net curtains and looked out onto the street.

"What the hell are you doing? Get away from there. Do you want to give the game away, you daft apeth."

Red-haired Freddie gave a toss of his head, but he let go of the curtain and walked away from the window.

"Why are you so jumpy?" I bet nothing even happens tonight. I can't see anyone out there. I don't know where Martin got the tip off from anyway. Do you?"

They hadn't been allowed upstairs in Morton's today, which was unusual as they usually met up with Martin there in the afternoons, especially before a job like this.

Henry drummed the two fingers of his disfigured hand on the dining table. He was feeling impatient, and he didn't like being kept in the dark any more than Red-haired Freddie. The difference was Henry didn't make a song and dance about it. There wasn't any point.

"You don't think it's a setup, do you?" Red-haired Freddie asked. "I mean, we don't even know how many of Carter's men are going to turn up. We could be outnumbered."

Henry let Freddie mutter on and on and wished he could tune him out.

People reacted differently when they were nervous. You had people like Red-haired Freddie, who rabbited on and on, finding comfort in talking constantly. Henry was different. He liked silence.

The way he looked at it was, they had a job to do, and it was as simple as that.

Bernadette Shaw, known to everyone in the locality as Bernie, was having a terrible night. She'd only been at work for an hour or so when some idiot vomited all over the men's toilets. In Bernie's opinion, if a man couldn't hold his drink, he shouldn't be allowed so much as a sip.

Then there was the fact she was working with Clara tonight, the barmaid who was about as much use as a chocolate teapot. The dozy mare was pretty to look at, all tits and teeth, but it took her five minutes to serve just one customer.

Of course, the landlord loved her, the dirty old pervert.

Bernie was good at her job. She took pride in being quick and efficient. It might not take a genius to work behind a bar, but working next to someone like Clara reminded her just how much she was undervalued.

The landlord, being a typical man, thought the only qualification a barmaid needed was a pretty face and a large pair of breasts.

That was all well and good when they only had a few customers, but when the pub started to fill up and got busier, the customers weren't quite so happy to wait for their beer. Thanks to Clara's inability to do her job, Bernadette had been running around like a headless chicken all night and her feet were killing her.

She couldn't wait to get home, kick off her shoes and get back to her kids.

She had just handed Mick his change when there was a loud crash at the other end of the bar. She turned around to seek Clara had managed to drop a pint glass full of beer all over the floor.

As Bernie made her way over, Clara leant down and began to try to pick up the shards of the glass with her bare hands. She definitely wasn't the sharpest tool in the box. A split second later, Clara cursed and cradled her hand. She'd cut it on the glass. No surprise there, Bernie thought.

Bernie rolled her eyes and handed Clara a bar towel, and the girl wrapped it round her fingers to stop blood dripping on the floor. "Go and clean it up in the ladies," Bernie said.

As Clara walked out from the bar, Bernie turned her attention back to the customers. Old Bob waved at her from the other end of the bar and shouted out he was dying of thirst.

"I'll be with you in a minute," Bernie said.

Bernie was bending over behind the bar, mopping up the mess, when she heard the first gunshot.

16

CHARLIE WILLIAMS WAS SWEATING. HE was absolutely furious. He'd known deep down in his gut that Gary Carter couldn't be trusted.

Dave had specifically told them that they were not to use violence tonight. But Gary obviously thought he knew better. As soon as they had burst through the doors, Gary held his gun in the air, laughed like a madman and started firing at the ceiling.

The lights went out immediately, and the pub was full of shouting and screaming and people trying to run for safety.

It was chaos.

The Old Bill would be here in no time. It was a right royal cock-up.

Charlie looked around, desperately trying to make sense of what was going on. His ears were ringing from the gunshots, and it was so difficult to see in the dark. He tried to make his way towards the bar but tripped on an overturned table and went flying.

As he scrambled to his feet, the only person he could make out clearly was Gary Carter, who was standing a few feet away grinning like a madman. Charlie would have liked to smack the smirk off his face. Gary might be Dave Carter's brother, but the man was an idiot.

Charlie was so distracted by Gary and the punters running around that he didn't even see the other men burst into the bar until it was too late.

In a split second, Charlie noticed the smile dropped from Gary's face.

Gary held up his gun in front of him and tried to fire again, but nothing happened. The stupid bastard had used up all his bullets shooting out the lights.

Charlie raised his gun, but he couldn't fire. He couldn't see who was who and the last thing he wanted was to shoot some poor bugger who had nothing to do with the Morton and Carter feud.

All of a sudden, Charlie was tackled from behind, and he went tumbling over. He hit his head hard on a wooden chair leg. His gun went flying and came to a stop underneath a table a few feet away.

Charlie shuffled forward on his hands and knees and tried to dive for the gun. But he was too late.

He heard the crack of another gunshot and felt a searing pain shoot up his leg.

It was pandemonium in the bar now. People were screaming and jumping over him. One person actually trod on his back in their panic to get away.

Charlie turned his head and saw Gary. This time, he was by the door. Charlie reached out to him and shouted, "Help me. I've been shot."

Gary looked down at him. He blinked and hesitated for a moment and then he legged it out of the door, leaving Charlie sprawled out on the floor.

Charlie knew he was on his own now. He had no idea where Brian had gone, but he had likely followed Gary's example and done a runner. Charlie put a shaking hand on his thigh, and when he lifted it up, he moaned in terror. Even in the dark, he could see that his fingers were covered with blood.

His head swam, and he knew it wouldn't be long before he passed out. All of a sudden, he saw Red-haired Freddie looming over him, his face only inches from Charlie's.

A single thought worked its way through Charlie's jumbled mind – how had they known?

Charlie heard a voice above him. "Did you see Gary Carter? The big girl's blouse scarpered. Haha, the big brave Gary Carter, don't make me laugh."

When Charlie regained consciousness, it was still dark, and it took him a minute to realise he was outside. The night was cold, and he shivered convulsively. He was lying on something, but he couldn't quite work out what it is. It smelled terrible, though. Like rotting fish.

The bastards had dumped him and left him here to bleed out in a deserted alleyway.

It took all the effort he could muster to push himself up into a sitting position, and as the floor seemed to shift beneath him, he realised he was lying on a pile of rubbish. He looked around wildly, trying to gain some idea of where he was.

His leg was throbbing, and his trousers were soaked with blood. Each time he moved, the pain in his leg was close to unbearable.

He didn't know how long he'd been there, but it was still

dark, and against all odds, he was still alive. He reached into his shirt and held his gold crucifix between his thumb and forefinger. He thanked God he was still breathing.

But he wouldn't be for long if he stayed here. He needed to get help, and to do that, he needed to reach somewhere more populated than this stinking alleyway.

His arms and legs were shaking as he struggled to a standing position, and his leg screamed in pain as he put weight on it. He looked up and down the alley to try and work out which way to go. It looked like the alley ran along the back of a row of restaurants. In the distance, he could hear the murmur of people's voices and the muffled sound of some sort of music.

Charlie decided to head for the source of the noise. That would be his best chance of getting help. He staggered along the alley, which seem never-ending, and when he finally walked out onto the main road, he had to stop and lean against a brick wall to catch his breath.

He was so close now. He could see the illuminated front of an Italian restaurant. He could make out the candles and white and red chequered tablecloths. If he could just get closer…

He staggered on. He let out a shaky breath when he reached the large glass windows at the front of the restaurant and put his palm flat against the glass before banging on it loudly.

All the faces in the restaurant turned to look at him, but everything seemed to swim before his eyes. At that moment, Charlie's legs gave way under him, and he fell to the ground.

17

KATHLEEN DIAMOND KNOCKED ON LINDA'S front door, and Linda's mother answered.

"Hello, Mrs. Simpson. Is Linda at home, please?"

Linda's mother was the image of her daughter. She smiled at Kathleen, and her chubby cheeks dimpled.

Kathleen tried to smile back, but it wasn't easy. She felt like crying. Mrs. Simpson put a hand on Kathleen's arm. "We are just about to sit down for dinner, dear, are you all right? Why don't you come in and have a bit to eat, eh? You look practically dead on your feet. Have they been working you too hard at Bevels?"

Kathleen felt trapped. She couldn't imagine eating anything in her current state, but she didn't want to raise anyone's suspicions, least of all Linda's parents. So she followed Mrs. Simpson through into the hot kitchen and sat down beside Linda at the large kitchen table.

Linda's eyes widened as she saw her friend. She hadn't been expecting Kathleen's visit.

Mr. Simpson was a tall, thin, reserved man, who listened to his wife and children chatter on without adding to the conversation himself. Linda's younger brother Christopher took after his father in looks, but as he gabbled on like his mother and sister, Kathleen wished he took after his father in personality too.

It was torture sitting through dinner with Linda's family when all she really wanted to do was confide in her friend and talk things over in private. Instead, they had to talk about mundane things like the weather and the new girl who'd started at Bevels last week.

Linda's mother piled Kathleen's plate full of steak and kidney pudding, carrots and cabbage. Kathleen did her best to make some headway into the huge portion, but every mouthful seemed to get stuck in her throat.

When Linda accepted a second serving of the steak and kidney pudding, Kathleen shot her friend an angry look.

What was Linda playing at?

Finally, Linda sat back from the table and put her knife and fork together. "Is it okay if I do the dishes later, Mum? I want to go and show Kathleen the new record I bought last week."

Linda's mother pursed her lips, and for a moment, Kathleen thought she was going to say no, but after a moment, she nodded her head. "All right, Christopher can do the dishes tonight."

Christopher, Linda's twelve-year-old brother, did not like that idea much at all. "That's not fair. I did them last night."

"I'll do them tomorrow and the night after," Linda promised her brother and then stood up before her mother could change her mind.

Kathleen thanked the Simpsons for dinner and followed Linda upstairs.

As soon as they'd reached Linda's bedroom, Linda shut

the door and looked up at Kathleen.

"Well, did you get the result?" Linda asked.

Kathleen nodded sadly. "Yes, I'm pregnant. What am I going to do, Linda? My mum is going to kill me."

Now that she had actually told someone the news, it was like a dam had opened, and Kathleen began to sob.

Linda put an arm around her friend. "Don't cry, Kath. We'll sort something out. Things will work out in the end."

When Charlie Williams woke up in the hospital, he thought he had died and gone to heaven.

A gorgeous nurse, with strawberry blonde curls, who looked just like an angel, leaned over him, holding a thermometer.

He grinned up at her. "Hello, sweetheart."

A smile twitched on the nurses' mouth.

"Ah, I see you're finally awake," she said. "No, don't try and sit up. You'll feel very weak for a while. I'm just going to go and find the ward sister and tell her you're back with us."

As she walked away, Charlie admired the view. Perhaps things weren't so bad after all. He shifted in bed, and then wished he hadn't. A sharp pain shot up his leg and made it feel like it was on fire.

The sunlight streaming in through the large windows at the end of the ward told Charlie he'd made it through the night.

"So, what are you in for?" a voice asked.

Charlie turned and saw the man in the bed next to him had spoken and was looking at him curiously.

What should Charlie say? He needed to make up a good story and fast. Although, he could hardly pretend he hadn't been shot. No doubt, the doctors would have found the bullet embedded in his leg.

He decided to test a story on the patient next to him.

"I got shot," Charlie said. "Some nasty piece of work cornered me in an alley."

The old man's eyes widened. And then he nodded as if he'd expected as much. "It doesn't surprise me. The country is going to the dogs," he said. "I blame the immigrants. Was it an immigrant who shot you?"

Charlie shook his head. "It was dark. Couldn't see."

"You poor bastard. You were lucky they just got you in the leg."

Charlie nodded, but he didn't feel particularly lucky. Especially knowing that those bastards, Red-haired Freddie and Henry the Hand, had dumped him on a pile of rubbish and left him to die.

"I'm in for my prostate," the man said. "Been giving me gyp for years, it has."

Charlie nodded absent-mindedly. His mind was still on his own problems.

"Gave me the fright of my life when the doctor stuck a finger up me bum. I nearly had a heart attack. I thought he was a wooly woofter, but then he told me that's the way they have to check it these days. Have you ever heard of such a thing? I told him if it stops me needing a jimmy every five minutes, he could carry on."

Charlie let the man's voice drone on as he focused on what he would have to do next. He needed to get out of there as soon as possible. He bloody hated hospitals. They smelt funny.

Charlie smiled as he saw the pretty nurse walking back

towards him. He supposed there were some benefits to being in the hospital.

Maybe his luck was in, and he'd get a sponge bath later. Unfortunately for Charlie, the nurse didn't mention anything about a sponge bath. Instead, she delivered some bad news.

"The police are here. If you feel strong enough, they'd like to talk to you about what happened."

Charlie thought about pretending he wasn't strong enough, but then perhaps that might make him look guilty. Also, he would prefer just to get it over with. In his experience, it was best to get it all done and dusted as fast as possible. The Old Bill were probably just going through the motions anyway.

"Absolutely," Charlie said. "Anything to help catch the person who did this." Charlie almost smiled. He should have had a career on the stage. He'd almost convinced himself he was an indignant victim of a mugging.

After a moment, a policeman entered the ward and took a seat in the chair beside Charlie's bed. He had a long face and a tightly pinched mouth. His forehead was creased with lines from perpetual frowning.

"I'm Inspector Peel. I'd like to ask you a few questions, Mr. Williams. Perhaps we can begin with you telling me what you were doing last night?"

That got Charlie's back up straightaway. He was the innocent victim in all this. Why did it matter what he'd been doing last night?

"I was heading to a restaurant," Charlie said. "I thought I'd take a quick shortcut through the alley, but when I did, I saw a man with a gun and he shot me in the leg."

Charlie waited to see the reaction on the policeman's face. Would he fall for it? But Inspector Peel's face remained impassive.

"Did you have a reservation at the restaurant."

Charlie blinked. He hadn't thought of that. "Well, no, but I thought I might get lucky and score a table."

"So you're telling me this was a mugging?"

Charlie resisted the temptation to say something sarcastic. He was the bleeding copper. Did he always expect the victims to spell things out and do his job for him?

"Yes," Charlie said nodding. "That's right he was a mugger."

"It was very odd that he didn't take your wallet then, wasn't it, sir?"

Charlie paused. He would have to be more careful. This bloke wasn't as dumb as he looked.

"Well, I think it was an attempted mugging. I wouldn't hand over my wallet, that's when he shot me. I think he panicked after the gun went off. He disappeared."

"So, you were shot in the alley behind Giuseppe's restaurant?"

Charlie nodded. "Yeah, that's right." He couldn't remember what the restaurant had been called. Funnily enough, he'd had other things on his mind last night.

The policeman pulled a pencil from his pocket and wrote something in his notebook. Charlie couldn't quite make it out.

"It's strange then, isn't it?" Inspector Peel raised an eyebrow.

Charlie frowned. "What's strange?"

It was too hot in the hospital. The sweat was running off

him. Charlie pushed back the bedsheets.

"The fact that nobody heard a gunshot. There are numerous restaurants along that road, and nobody heard a thing. I find that very strange."

Charlie didn't like where this was heading. He was being treated like a suspect, not a victim.

"So," the policeman said. "Were you going to eat alone at the restaurant?"

Inspector Peel was trying to find holes in the story, and Charlie had to admit it did look a bit strange that he was going to a fancy Italian restaurant to eat on his own."

"Yeah," Charlie leaned forward and beckoned for the policeman to move closer. "I wanted to try my luck with one of the waitresses. She was a right looker." He winked. "Know what I mean?"

The policeman didn't respond.

"Have you ever been to The Three Grapes public house, Mr. Williams?"

Charlie licked his lips and tried his best to look innocent. It was getting hotter and hotter in the ward, and he was starting to feel sick. "Hmm, The Three Grapes," he repeated. "It does sound familiar. You'll have to remind me where it is."

The policeman looked at him through narrowed eyes. "Bethnal Green."

"Oh, yeah," Charlie said. "I know it. I've not been there for a while, though."

"So, you weren't there last night?"

Charlie shook his head. "No, definitely not."

Charlie leaned back against the cool cotton of his pillow and allowed his eyelids to close.

The nurse, who Charlie hadn't even realised was still hovering beside his bed, said, "I think that will have to be all for now, Inspector Peel. The patient needs his rest."

Charlie kept his eyes shut and pretended he was asleep.

He heard the inspector give a huff of impatience, and then he said, "I'll leave it there, for now, Mr. Williams. But I'll be back."

18

THE FOLLOWING MORNING, BRIAN MOORE turned up at the warehouse shaking in his boots. He knew Dave Carter was not going to be happy. He had kept a low profile last night in the hope that it would give Dave a chance to cool down.

He cringed every time he remembered what had happened last night at The Three Grapes. It all started to go wrong when Gary thought he should act like they were in the Wild West and decided to shoot a load of bullets into the ceiling. Bloody idiot. They couldn't see a thing after he'd shot out the lights.

To be honest, Brian had had a bad feeling about the raid from the get go.

He didn't like the way Dave was giving his brother more important roles in the company. As far as Brian was concerned, the man was a nutter and should have been certified.

As soon as Brian had got his first glimpse of Red-haired Freddie, he had scarpered. It was obvious the whole thing had been a setup. He hadn't even waited to see if Gary followed him. He heard footsteps and had assumed that both Gary and Charlie had made their way out. But then last night, he'd heard through the grapevine that Charlie had been shot and was now in hospital at death's door.

Brian ran a hand through his thinning hair. Dave Carter was definitely not going to be pleased.

As he walked inside the warehouse, he saw a couple of the day boys at the other end of the cavernous room, stacking boxes.

"Alright boys," Brian said and tried to sound cheerful even though he didn't feel it.

He got a few nods in the way of a greeting, but nobody replied. He glanced in the direction of Dave's office. The door was shut. That wasn't a good sign.

Brian ran his hand through his hair again, trying to smooth it down and knocked on the door.

There was a hesitation before Dave said, "Come in."

Brian couldn't hear anything different in Dave's voice. He was a softly spoken man normally, and he didn't sound particularly agitated. Brian tried to convince himself that this was a good sign as he opened the door.

Dave stood up behind his desk and nodded at Brian. He was dressed as he usually was — quite casually. He wore loose trousers, a shirt and tie but with a brown jumper over them. Dave Carter didn't look like a typical gangster. He didn't even look like a typical businessman. He seemed far more suited to working behind the counter of a hardware store or greengrocers.

His appearance had lulled many of his enemies into a false sense of security. But Brian had known him a long time and knew that in Dave Carter's case, appearances were deceptive.

His boss's face was bland and impassive. Brian searched it for clues to his mood, but it was no good. Dave kept his cards close to his chest. He always did.

"Hello, boss."

"I hear it didn't go well last night," Dave said, walking around his desk to come and stand in front of Brian.

Brian swallowed hard, then said, "It was a disaster, boss. They were already there. Lying in wait."

"The question is, Brian, how did they know we would be coming last night?"

"No idea," Brian stammered. His legs were feeling like jelly, and he wished Dave would invite him to sit down.

Dave jangled the keys in his pocket and paced the floor before looking back at Brian. "There were three of you. You, Charlie and Gary. There were only two of them, so how did they gain the upper hand?"

Dave's voice was soft, but Brian could hear the steel beneath.

"They had the element of surprise. And it didn't help matters when Gary shot the lights out. We couldn't see a bleeding thing." Brian licked his lips nervously. "Have you seen Gary yet?"

Dave turned away and continued to pace the floor. "I'm extremely disappointed along with you," he said. "Charlie is in the hospital. The Old Bill have already been around to talk to him. It's possible they might come and talk to you as well, Brian. I trust you know what to do."

"Of course." Brian nodded frantically. "I'll keep my mouth shut, boss. You can rely on me."

Personally, Brian thought it very unfair that he was getting the blame. If Gary hadn't been such a bloody fool, none of this would have happened. But he didn't feel brave enough to tell Dave Carter just what he thought of his brother.

Dave was quiet for so long, Brian began to sweat. They had screwed up big time, and Dave wasn't likely to let them get away with it scot-free.

"How is Charlie doing, boss? Is he going to be all right?"

"Looks like it. No thanks to you for running off and leaving him there."

Brian opened and shut his mouth like a goldfish. He wanted to protest his innocence, but he knew he couldn't. Dave was right he had run off and left for Charlie to face the music alone. He had wrongly assumed that Charlie had made his escape and followed him out.

Brian looked down at the floor. If it hadn't been for bloody Gary, none of this would have happened.

"All right, Brian, you can go now. I don't want to see your ugly mug right now. It just reminds me of the monumental cock-up you made last night. There will be trouble ahead, so keep your head down. Do you understand me?"

Brian nodded miserably and headed for the door.

After Brian had left, Dave sighed went back to sit behind his desk. Brian had merely confirmed his own suspicions. This whole mess could be laid firmly at his brother's door. Gary was becoming a liability.

Dave had always considered family important. He adored his wife Sandra and their children, Trevor and Lillian, and he'd always treated his brother well in the past. He'd given him handouts, a reliable wage, but Gary just accepted all that as if it was his birthright.

Dave shook his head. He was going to have to do

something about it.

Gary just couldn't be trusted any more.

He'd been going through the books and his accounts before Brian had arrived. Profits were up, and things were looking good with the business. The intelligent thing for Dave to do would be to ignore this feud with Martin Morton and keep his distance.

There was more than enough money making enterprises in the East End to keep them both happy. But unfortunately, the game wasn't played like that. If Dave let this thing with Martin Morton go on much longer, it would make him look weak.

He only had one option, and that was to end Martin Morton for good.

Dave closed the account book in front of him. He wouldn't be able to do it straight away. Morton would be expecting retribution. He'd be on his guard. But violence wasn't always the answer. Dave knew you could get a lot further in this world by using your head rather than using your fists. But Martin didn't know that. He wanted to play the big man and acted like he was ready for the big leagues, but he didn't have the staying power. Martin Morton was all about image.

He loved to wear sharp suits and had his hair slicked back and styled in the latest fashion. With the old scar that ran down his cheek, he really did fit the image of a gangster. But it was an illusion. He had a tough outward appearance, but inside Martin wasn't hard. He was made of jelly and scared to death of anyone finding that out.

In Dave's experience, the men who deep down were scared little boys were the most violent, always trying to cover up the terror they felt inside. But that wasn't Dave's problem. He didn't care about Martin Morton's insecurities. He just needed to wipe Morton's sticky fingerprints off the face of the East End.

But before he did that, he had more important things to be getting on with. Namely, making sure Charlie Williams didn't spill his guts, and then he had to deal with his brother, Gary. It had been a long time coming.

19

"OH, MY POOR BABY," DORIS Williams wailed as she trotted up to Charlie's bedside in the middle of the hospital ward. "I've been out of my mind with worry since I heard. I haven't been able to get a wink of sleep all night."

Charlie, who had been having a nice doze and dreaming about the pretty nurse he had developed quite a crush on, blinked his eyes opened. "Mum!"

"Yes, that's right. It's your poor old mother. Did you not think to try to telephone me and let me know what was going on? I've been worried sick."

Charlie rubbed his forehead. He was developing a headache that seemed to be directly related to the pitch of his mother's voice.

"I'm sorry, Mum. I lost a lot of blood. I wasn't in the position to phone anyone last night."

Doris Simpson gave her son a scathing look as though she believed getting shot was just an excuse and a pathetic one at that.

She slapped Charlie's arm. "You silly little bugger! What did you go and get shot for? Did I not bring you up right?"

Charlie stared at his mother. What on earth was the old

girl on about? He hadn't exactly been trying to get shot.

"It wasn't my fault, Mum. I was just in the wrong place at the wrong time. I was sitting there having a quiet drink, minding my own business when some crazy bastard came in waving a gun about."

"I wasn't born yesterday," Doris said, smacking Charlie over the head.

"Ow, Mum, pack it in!"

"So what should I do now? There's a copper waiting outside. I suppose that's for you, isn't it? What kind of trouble have you got yourself into now, Charlie? Honestly, your father will be turning in his grave."

Charlie didn't think so. His father had been a small-time crook who'd sold stolen goods out of a battered old leather suitcase. He thought his dad would be rather proud of how Charlie had progressed in the world. He'd be pleased to know Dave Carter had taken his son under his wing.

"I know you're worried, Mum, but I'll be fine."

"Really? And what am I supposed to do if you get banged up? Who's going to look after me when my rheumatism gets bad if you're inside, eh?"

Charlie shivered. "It won't come to that," he said and hoped that it wouldn't.

They both heard footsteps and turned to see Dave Carter himself strolling into the ward. He looked like a normal visitor as he walked in and smiled at the nurses by the desk.

"Oh, I'm afraid we can only permit one visitor at a time," the stern sister said.

Charlie scowled. She'd been giving him a hard time ever since he'd been admitted.

Dave smiled at her and murmured a few words. Charlie

couldn't hear what he said, but it seemed to work like a charm, and Dave left the ward sister blushing and giggling like a teenager.

As he approached the bed, Charlie struggled to sit up.

Dave held his hand out. "Hello, Charlie. I'm so sorry about what happened."

Charlie tried to gather his wits about him. He hadn't expected Dave Carter to come and see him in person. He shot a glance at his mother, who fortunately seemed to have been stunned into silence. Charlie thanked his lucky stars.

"I'm sorry we messed up, boss," Charlie said in a whisper. He didn't really want to talk about this in front of his mother.

"I brought you a bag of grapes." Dave put the brown paper bag on the bedside table.

"Mum, I don't suppose you could ask one of the nurses if I could have a glass of water, and I could do with an extra pillow? My back is killing me."

Doris Williams pursed her lips, but she nodded and reluctantly left the two men alone to talk.

"There was nothing I could do," Charlie said, twisting his fingers nervously in the bedsheets. "The lights went out, and then all of a sudden, Martin Morton's men were there."

"And they were definitely Morton's men?" Dave asked, his eyes fixed on Charlie's face.

"It was dark, but I saw Red-haired Freddie clear as anything. It was him, no doubt about it."

Charlie wanted to tell Dave about his coward of a brother running off and leaving him to face Morton's men alone, but he wasn't sure how Dave would react.

"And Brian and Gary, they both left you there? You were

there alone?" Dave asked as if he could read Charlie's mind.

Charlie didn't like where this was headed. Was Dave going to blame him for messing everything up?

Charlie nodded slowly.

Dave looked down at him. "They knew you'd been shot, and they ran away anyway?"

Sod them, Charlie thought. He wasn't about to accept the blame for this mess. "Gary saw me. I told him I'd been shot and asked him to help, but he ran away. I don't know about Brian. I didn't see him after we'd entered the room. Gary shot out the lights."

Dave nodded slowly. "I'm sure I don't have to remind you to handle this honourably, Charlie."

"Of course," Charlie said. "I've told the police I was shot by a mugger, in the alleyway where they found me." He leaned a little closer so that the man in the bed next door couldn't hear. Charlie could practically see the old bugger's ears waggling. "They've already asked me about The Three Grapes, though, Dave. I might be going down, but I won't sell you out. You can trust me."

Dave smiled and laid a hand on Charlie's shoulder. "Do you know, Charlie, I believe that I can. You are one of the few that I really do trust. I don't think you'll let me down."

Before Charlie could respond, his mother was marching up to the bed, escorted by a nurse, carrying an extra pillow. Doris yanked Charlie forward as the nurse placed the pillow behind his shoulders.

Charlie thanked the nurse and then turned back to Dave, but before he could continue the conversation, Doris piped up. "Of course, I don't know what I'll do if my poor boy gets locked away. I barely get by as it is. I need the money he gives me every week." She fumbled in her pocket for a handkerchief and pretended to dab her eyes.

Dave's mouth twitched with a smile. "Charlie's one of mine," he said. "And he won't go without. I'll make sure you're all right, Mrs. Williams."

Dave winked at her, and Charlie's mother sat down in the chair beside Charlie's bed, grinning like a cat who'd got the cream.

Charlie was glad someone was happy. His leg was bleeding killing him, and he knew he was due another visit from the coppers later that day. He certainly wasn't looking forward to that.

At least, he knew Dave Carter had his back, and that counted for a lot. He wondered what would happen to Gary, and a small part of him hoped that Dave would punish him severely. He wasn't sure he would ever forgive the fact that Gary had run away and left him to die, bleeding on the floor of The Three Grapes.

"I'll leave you to it then," Dave said. "It was lovely to see you again, Mrs. Williams."

Dave smiled, and Charlie's mother's grinned happily. "Always a pleasure, Mr. Carter," she said.

20

WHEN KATHLEEN HEARD THE KNOCK at the front door, she flew down the stairs. She knew it would be Linda, and she wanted to open the door before her mum got there. The last thing she wanted was for her mother to start talking to Linda in case her friend accidentally let something slip.

"I'll get it, Mum," Kathleen shouted as she opened the door.

Linda stood on the front step, beaming. Her skin was glowing, and she looked incredibly happy.

Why was she looking so pleased with herself? This was a serious situation, and Linda was smiling away like a dopey cow.

"Let's go up to my room," Kathleen said, waiting for Linda to enter and then shutting the front door behind her.

Mary appeared from the kitchen. "Oh, hello Linda, love. I hope your family are all right."

"They are, thank you, Mrs. Diamond."

Kathleen started to practically drag Linda up the stairs.

"Would you girls like a cup of tea?" Mary called after them. "I'm just about to make one."

Linda opened her mouth, but Kathleen, fearing Linda was

about to accept, spoke up first. "No thanks, Mum. We're just going up to my room. We're going to listen to some records."

Linda was a terrible liar, and Kathleen knew there was a good chance she would give the game away if they had to suffer through another conversation with Kathleen's mother.

Kathleen yanked Linda by the arm, leaving Mary staring after them with a bewildered expression.

"I can't wait to tell you about my day," Linda said as they reached Kathleen's room and the door was safely shut behind them. Kathleen frowned. What on earth was Linda on about? They'd spent all day together at Bevels.

"I was with you all day, Linda. What on earth would you have to tell me?"

Linda gave a smug smile. Kathleen narrowed her eyes and tapped her foot impatiently. "Well?"

Linda's eyes shone as she smiled. "I've met a man," she burst out.

Kathleen raised an eyebrow. Linda was a sweet girl, but she wasn't exactly a man magnet. Kathleen wouldn't have put it past her to make this up for a bit of attention.

"A man? And where exactly did you meet this man?" Kathleen asked sceptically.

"It was ever so romantic, Kath," Linda said, her cheeks glowing. "You remember I had to stay behind at work and finish off some extra hemming."

Kathleen nodded. Surely Linda wasn't talking about Mr. Bevel? There had been certain rumours flying about a little while ago when one young girl left the machines under a bit of a cloud.

"Well, I was leaving, and I was in a hurry, so I wasn't really looking where I was going. And just outside Bevels, I walked straight into him. You know how clumsy I am, Kath. I dropped my handbag and the contents went everywhere." Linda flushed a bright pink. "It was ever so embarrassing. I had my makeup and things in there, but he was ever such a gentleman. He helped me pick everything up and put it back in my bag." Linda's face took on a dreamy expression.

Kathleen nodded. This sounded more like it. She'd just bumped into some poor unsuspecting chap outside, and Linda had attached all sorts of romantic connotations to it.

Kathleen opened her mouth to tell Linda all about her problems, so they could discuss what Kathleen should do next, but Linda hadn't finished talking.

"After he helped me put everything back in my bag, he was ever so charming and said he thought it was fate that we'd met that way. Then he asked me to go out with him on Friday night. We're going to meet at the cinema." Linda said, looking ever so excited.

Kathleen was silent. She couldn't believe that Linda was thinking about going on a date when Kathleen had all these problems hanging over her head.

Linda suddenly noticed Kathleen was being very quiet, which was most unlike her. "What's wrong? Aren't you excited for me?"

"I never thought you were selfish, Linda, and I certainly hadn't pegged you as a mean girl," Kathleen said.

Linda's eyes widened. "Mean? I wasn't being mean. I was just telling you about the man I'd met. I thought you'd be pleased for me. You're always on at me to find a bloke, and now I've met someone."

"Right now, you meeting a man is the last thing on my mind, Linda. I do have bigger problems to deal with,"

Kathleen said irritably.

Linda looked repentant and patted Kathleen's hand. "You're right. I'm sorry. I thought my news might take your mind off everything."

"It can't take my mind off it. Nothing can. I'm in a lot of trouble here, Linda, and I could do with your support."

Linda bowed her head in shame. "Of course, let's talk about your problem and decide what you're going to do."

Kathleen nodded, feeling slightly mollified. She got up off of the bed and put one of her records on the record player just in case her mum was eavesdropping.

With the sound of Bing Crosby playing in the background, Kathleen sat back on the bed beside Linda. "I still don't know what I'm going to do," she said. "It's just so unfair. Why did it have to happen to me? We only did it a couple of times."

Linda pursed her lips together and then said, "Well, it only takes one time."

Kathleen narrowed her eyes. "Yes, thank you, Nurse Linda. You're clearly an expert on the matter."

Linda grimaced. She realised she was just irritating Kathleen even though she was trying to help.

Kathleen stared down at her hands on her lap. "A girl who used to work at Bevels called Claudine told me her cousin went to a place in Stepney. They can get rid of it."

Kathleen turned her eyes on her friend.

Linda looked pale. "I don't know if that's a good idea, Kath. You hear all sorts of stories about places like that. It could be dangerous." She tilted her head, so she was looking at Kathleen full in the face. "Why don't you tell your mum?"

Kathleen looked horrified. Had Linda lost her mind?

"There's no chance of that," Kathleen said, dismissing the idea immediately. "She would go mad. Then she'd never let me go out ever again."

The two girls sat silently for a moment.

"Look," Kathleen said, leaning back on the wall and biting down on her lower lip. "I need you to do me a favour."

Linda nodded her head, her shiny brown fringe falling forward over her eyes. "Of course. I'll do anything I can to help. You know that."

Kathleen nodded. That was exactly what she wanted to hear. "I need you to phone Claudine's cousin and find out exactly where this place is."

Linda's mouth dropped open in shock. "Why me? Why do I have to do it?"

"Well, I can't have anyone knowing it's me, can I?"

"But… But they'll think it's for me."

Kathleen laughed cruelly. "Of course, they won't. You can say you're calling about a friend. They will believe you. I mean," Kathleen looked her friend up and down. "It's not as if you're the type of girl that would drive a man wild, is it?"

The sparkle in Linda's eyes faded as Kathleen's words sunk in. Her shoulders slumped. "What do you need me to do?"

Kathleen reached over to the nightstand and took out the slip of paper that she'd kept hidden away from her mother. "I've got the number here. We need to go to the phone box now, and you can call Claudine's cousin and ask her where the clinic is. You can say you're asking for a friend."

"But won't they just assume it's for you if it's a friend of mine?" Linda asked. "After all, everybody knows you're my best friend."

Kathleen frowned. She hadn't thought of that. But it didn't matter. The important thing was that they got this address and got the matter sorted so that Kathleen could get back to her normal life.

Kathleen shrugged. "They might suspect that. But they can't prove it. Besides," she added grumpily. "It's not as if I have much choice, is it?"

21

ON FRIDAY LUNCHTIME, LINDA AND Kathleen left Bevels together. Linda had said she needed to go to the dentist, and Kathleen said she had a doctor's appointment.

Kathleen pushed back her hair from her pale face and felt sick with fear as she and Linda walked towards the address they'd been given in Stepney.

Linda linked arms with her friend and smiled up at her encouragingly.

"It will soon be over, Kath," she said.

But Kathleen knew that wasn't true. She'd already had to pay for the pregnancy test because the GP she'd visited wasn't her usual one. And now she knew this would cost money, too, and she hadn't got a clue how she was going to afford it. Kathleen wasn't one for saving her earnings. She paid a bit of money to her mother for her keep, and the rest of it went on records, clothes and makeup.

"Is this it?" Linda asked looking up at the red brick building. "It just looks like a normal house."

Kathleen looked at her friend with irritation. How was she supposed to know if it was the right address? She hadn't been here before either.

They knocked at the front door and waited until it was opened by a young girl, who couldn't have been much older than Kathleen and Linda. She looked them up and down but didn't say a word.

Kathleen flushed with embarrassment. What was she supposed to say? What if they'd got the wrong address?

"I've come for the clinic," Kathleen said in a shaky voice.

The young girl gave a nod and then jerked her thumb to indicate they should go inside. She still hadn't spoken a word. It was very odd.

As they walked inside, Kathleen whispered to her friend. "I'm not sure about this."

She felt Linda squeeze her hand reassuringly.

The young girl led them into the front room, but it didn't have any of the usual front room furniture. There was a set of hard plastic chairs lined up around the edges of the room, and Kathleen and Linda took a seat.

The young girl left them alone. "I hope we don't have to wait long," Linda said. "Otherwise, we're going to be back late at Bevels."

Getting back to work on time was the least of Kathleen's worries.

"Do you think they're going to do it today?" Linda asked, looking down at Kathleen's stomach. "How long does it take?"

Kathleen glared at her friend. Why was she asking such stupid questions? "I don't know. It's not as if I've done this before."

"Mrs. V will see you now," a voice said behind them. It was the young girl from earlier, who appeared out of nowhere, making Kathleen jump and clutch onto Linda's arm.

"Do you want me to come in with you, Kath?" Linda asked.

Kathleen hesitated, and then she shook her head. "No, I'll be okay. You'll wait for me, though, won't you?"

Linda nodded and patted her hand. "Of course, I will."

Kathleen took a deep breath and stood up. Then she followed the young girl out of the room. She was escorted down the hallway to another room, which Kathleen supposed under normal circumstances might be the dining room. Inside, there was a small woman with grey hair and rosy cheeks sitting behind a desk. If Kathleen had seen her under other circumstances, she'd have supposed she was somebody's grandmother. She really didn't look like the type of person who would perform an abortion.

After the young girl had shut the door behind her, leaving Kathleen and the elderly woman alone in the room, the grey-haired lady pointed at the chair in front of the desk. "Please sit down," she said.

Kathleen did as she was told, nervously licking her dry lips and feeling even sicker than before.

The woman pushed aside the papers in front of her on the desk. "I'm Mrs. V," she said. "I don't use my real name for obvious reasons, but please be assured I've performed the procedure many times in the past. Now, how far along are you?"

Kathleen looked at her blankly. "Um, I'm not really sure."

Kathleen's heart was pounding as Mrs. V frowned at her.

"Well, we can determine that upon examination. We won't be performing the abortion today. We will need payment up front. The total cost will be twenty-five pounds. Once you give us the money, we'll arrange a time for you to come back and have the abortion."

Kathleen felt the breath leave her lungs all in a rush. Twenty-five pounds! She could never afford that.

"Well, would you like me to schedule the appointment?" Miss V looked at Kathleen with piercing blue eyes.

Kathleen thought she didn't seem like such a friendly grandmother-type, after all. She didn't really care about Kathleen. She wasn't trying to help her. She probably dealt with girls like Kathleen all day long.

Kathleen shook her head and tried to fight back the tears that were gathering in her eyes. "I'll have to think about it and get back to you."

"Very well," Miss V said. "You know where we are."

Kathleen stood up, and her legs felt shaky as she walked to the door.

Her heart was pounding in her chest as she made her way down the corridor and back into the room where Linda sat waiting for her.

Linda stood up quickly.

"Let's go," Kathleen said.

Linda followed her out of the clinic and as they walked back to Bevels, Kathleen finally let the tears roll down her cheeks.

"What am I going to do, Linda? I can't afford to pay twenty-five pounds."

Linda thought for a moment and looked as though she were racking her brains. "I've got a bit of money saved," she said. "But it's nowhere near enough, I'm afraid. I think you're going to have to tell your mum."

"My mum will kill me," Kathleen sobbed.

Linda linked arms with her friend. More than anything she wanted to reassure Kathleen that things would work out all right in the end, but she knew Kathleen was right. Mary Diamond was going to go absolutely mental when she found out.

The following week, Mary Diamond was woken up early by the sound of the bathroom door closing.

Mary didn't sleep well these days, and she'd had a sleepless night.

When she heard the sound of retching coming from the bathroom, Mary quickly climbed out of bed and reached for her dressing gown. Her first thought was that Kathleen had some kind of bug, and she wanted to check on her, but when she opened her bedroom door, planning to go and comfort her daughter, she paused.

Kathleen had been acting very strangely lately, and now she was throwing up in the bathroom… A feeling of dread came over Mary. Surely not. Not her little girl.

But the more Mary thought it through, the more she realised her suspicions were right. It had been a couple of months since her daughter had been spending time with Martin Morton. Mary smothered a groan. It would be different if it had been a nice local lad, and Kathleen could settle down and get married. But Martin Morton!

Just then Kathleen opened the door to the bathroom and stepped out onto the landing. Her face was pale and had a greenish tint as she wiped her mouth with the back of her hand.

Her eyes widened in shock when she saw her mother standing there.

Mary folded her arms across her chest. "Have you got something to tell me, young lady?"

Kathleen's lower lip wobbled, just like it used to do when she was a toddler, and then she promptly burst into tears.

Mary sighed heavily. "Dry your eyes, my girl. Those tears aren't going to help anyone." Mary walked up to her daughter pointed to her stomach. "Is it Martin Morton's?"

Kathleen nodded and tried to swallow her sobs. "I'm sorry, Mum. But I loved him. I thought he was going to marry me."

Mary shook her head. Kathleen had been stupid, no doubt about that, but so had many other young girls before her.

Mary unfolded her arms and put her hand on her daughter's shoulder. She was still struggling to control her temper, but she knew that getting angry with Kathleen wasn't going to solve anything.

"Come on, love. Get your dressing gown on, and we'll go downstairs and make a nice brew. You'll feel better with a cup of tea inside you."

Kathleen looked relieved that Mary was taking the news so well. "I don't know what to do, Mum."

"We'll sort it out," Mary said, although she didn't really see much of a way forward. She wasn't about to let Kathleen give her grandchild up for adoption, and that didn't leave them with many choices.

The only thing Mary knew for certain was that Martin Morton must never know that the child was his.

22

THE FOLLOWING FRIDAY NIGHT, KATHLEEN sat on her bed, listening to records. She was incredibly bored. Although her mother had taken the news much better than she had hoped, Kathleen was starting to realise what life was going to be like from here on in.

She was young, and she should be out having fun. Instead, every day after work, she just had dinner with her mother and then stayed in her bedroom all night. It was so boring.

Even Linda was living a more exciting life than Kathleen now.

The man she was seeing, who Kathleen, at first, thought she had made up, was called Donovan Jenkins. He was tall and actually quite good looking. Kathleen had been very surprised when she'd seen him waiting for Linda outside Bevels a couple of days ago. She should have been pleased for her friend, but she couldn't help feeling jealous. It was normally Kathleen fighting off male attention, not Linda.

She'd asked Linda to come round to listen to records after work tonight, but Linda had informed her she was going out with Donovan again.

Just when Kathleen needed the support, Linda had gone

and landed herself a fellow. She was used to Linda doing everything she asked, so to be dumped for this new man Donovan was particularly annoying.

Kathleen sighed and got up and changed the record.

She remembered dancing to this one in Martin Morton's club. Those days were certainly over now. Once she had a screaming baby around, there wouldn't be any more nights out.

Kathleen flopped on the bed feeling very sorry for herself.

It would have been different if Martin hadn't been married. She could have been picking out her wedding dress right now, planning a whole exciting new life, but instead she was faced years of living with her mother and a demanding baby.

Kathleen turned on her side, bunching up the pillow beneath her head.

There could be a way out of this…

She knew that Martin was unavailable, but that didn't mean she had to be single for the rest of her life. Kathleen smiled to herself as a plan began to brew in her mind.

She hummed along to the record as she thought things through. Why should she waste her life stuck at home with the baby and her mother? If she acted quickly, she could still have an exciting life.

Kathleen smiled to herself. She wasn't the type to spend her life wondering what might have been. No, she was going to go out there and take what she needed. To hell with the consequences. But she had to act soon. Time was of the essence.

Martin Morton was at his mother's house. He hadn't been

able to get out of it, much to his displeasure. He should have been at work, making sure things were running smoothly. Friday night was their busiest night, and the bar would be packed. Plus, he still had Frank the Face hidden away in the flat over the club and that made him more reluctant than usual to be away from the club.

"Don't slouch, Martin," Violet Morton said.

Martin's mother was a formidable woman, and to avoid an argument, Martin did as he was told and sat up straight.

His brother, Tony, who was sitting beside him at the table, smirked.

Tony was slouching. He also had his elbows on the table and was eating with his mouth full, but of course, his mother never told Tony off.

Babs sat on Martin's right, looking fed up and bored. She'd never got on with Violet Morton, and Martin had to admit that his mother was very hard to please.

Little Ruby and Derek had been dressed up in their Sunday best to visit their grandmother, but Violet had taken one look at them and declared that Derek needed a haircut and Ruby's dress was too short.

"With all that money you're earning now, I would have thought you could afford to clothe them properly," his mother had said.

Martin had only just managed to swallow back the response he'd wanted to make.

They were having fish and chips tonight because Violet had thrown a fit at Babs and Martin for arriving ten minutes late. When they arrived, his mother had dramatically informed them she'd put the liver and bacon in the bin because it had been overcooked, so Martin had to walk round the corner to collect the fish suppers.

Of course, golden boy, Tony had been on time. He'd sat back with a grin on his face as Violet Morton laid into her eldest son.

Little Ruby dropped a chip on the floor, and Martin thought his mother was going to have a heart attack from the look on her face.

"Quick pick it up before the grease marks my new rug." She gave Ruby a sharp look. "You're a big girl now, Ruby. You shouldn't be dropping food on the floor. Have your mother and father not taught you how to use a knife and fork properly?"

"It's just a chip, Mum," Martin said and put his hand on Babs's knee as his wife looked as if she was about to explode.

"Well, it's a new rug, and it was expensive. She needs to be more careful."

Martin knew it was expensive. He was the one who'd paid for it! He'd paid for everything here. He'd moved his mother just round the corner from his own house and paid a small fortune to have it all redecorated and fitted with new furniture, but that wasn't enough to get any thanks from his mother.

Violet Morton stood up and began to clear the table.

Martin nudged Babs, encouraging her to get up and help, but she just shot him a nasty look in return and refused to budge. Instead, she leaned down and wiped Derek's greasy face with a bit of tissue.

"Sherry, Martin?" his mother asked, holding up the decanter, which was one of her most prized possessions.

Sherry was the last thing Martin wanted right now. He'd

much rather be having a Scotch back in his own bar, but if he refused, his mother would take it as a personal affront.

"Thanks, Mum."

She poured glasses for the four adults, and then sat down and lifted her glass to her mouth, sticking out her pinkie as she did so.

Martin eyed the brass clock on the mantelpiece. It had been given to his dad when he'd retired, after forty-five years of faithful service, working at the docks. He'd dropped dead six months later. Poor sucker, Martin thought. There was no way that Martin was following in his father's footsteps. Working his fingers to the bone was not part of his future plans. Although, he intended to make a success of himself and he was quite prepared to work hard to achieve that success.

"I'll just finish this, and then I better get off, Mum. I've got a bit of business to do tonight," Martin said.

His mother sucked in a scandalised breath. "Business? At this time of night?" She shook her head at him. "You want to be more like your brother," she said. "A good family man. He knows what's important.

Martin felt his tight control slipping. Tony didn't even have a bleeding family yet. He was out shagging a different bird every night.

"Someone has to pay for all this lot," Martin said, gesturing around the room at the new furniture that had recently been installed in his mother's dining room. "It's certainly not going to be Tony putting his hand in his pocket, is it, Mum?"

But his mother didn't answer the question. She set her sherry down on the table so she could fold her arms and directed a disgusted look at her eldest son. "Are you expecting your wife and children to walk home alone? Babs is six months along, Martin. You ought to be ashamed of yourself."

Martin gritted his teeth. It wasn't as if he was expecting them to trek home over the bloody Sahara Desert. The house was only around the corner.

"I'll walk them back, Mum," Tony said. He smiled at their mother, and then when he turned to Martin his eyes glinted as he enjoyed Martin's furious expression.

Martin knew he was so much better than Tony. He was cleverer than him, and he worked harder. He paid all his mother's bills, but for some reason, Tony was his mother's little darling boy, and Martin would never measure up.

He didn't know why he bothered even trying. He should go back to the club and spend the evening flirting with the curvy barmaid he'd recently employed. He'd had to give up Kathleen after Babs had found out.

Martin wasn't a stupid man. He didn't really care about hurting Babs's feelings, but he did prefer a quiet life at home, and if that meant he had to give up Kathleen and find a replacement, then so be it.

By dumping Kathleen, he had pacified Babs, which meant she wouldn't be scrutinising him quite so closely over the next few months.

Martin drained his drink and put the empty glass on the table.

He'd had enough of all this. "I'm off," he said, and without another word, he walked out of the dining room and left his mother's house.

No matter what his mother thought, Babs was quite

capable of getting home on her own. A lot of people underestimated Babs, but she was far more cunning than Martin could ever be.

He'd chosen wisely when he'd decided to marry her. It wasn't only that her father had given him some money to start up in business on his own. Of course, that had helped, but Babs knew the lay of the land.

She didn't make a fuss over most things. Granted, she got out of her tree over the thing with Kathleen Diamond, but that was because Kathleen was a stupid cow who had started flaunting her relationship with Martin. No woman, especially not Babs, liked to have their husband's infidelity rubbed in their face.

23

LESS THAN HALF A MILE away in Poplar, Dave Carter was spending Friday evening with his family, too. The difference was, he was enjoying it. The Carter's were having a birthday tea party for Dave's daughter, Lillian.

It was mayhem. Children of all ages were running everywhere. Lillian was wearing a brand-new pink dress, and her happy laughter made Dave smile. The girl was the apple of his eye. She had been since the day she'd been born. That first day, as he'd held her and looked down into her blue eyes, he'd fallen hook, line and sinker.

Dave was having a chinwag with two of Sandra's brothers when he caught his wife's eye and smiled. She was easing herself out of an armchair and looking a little tired. She was seven months pregnant, so it wouldn't be long before they had another little Carter running around, joining Lillian and Trevor.

Trevor trudged over to his father and held up his favourite toy. It was a little replica steam train. "The wheel has fallen off again, dad."

Dave leaned down and took the toy from Trevor. The wheel popped back on easily enough. He handed the train back to his son. "Are you having a nice time at the party, son?"

Trevor screwed up his face. "There's too many girls."

Dave laughed and nudged Sandra's brother in the ribs. "You wait until you get a bit older, son. You'll be glad to have lots of girls around then."

"No, I won't," Trevor insisted, looking at his father as if he'd gone mad.

He wandered off to play on his own. Sometimes Dave worried a little about Trevor. He did seem to prefer playing in his own little dream world rather than with other children his own age.

Lillian, on the other hand, loved being around people. There was something contagious about her happiness and her exuberance for life. He watched her now as she played chase around the living room, causing her mother to shout and tell her to slow down.

Dave crossed the room in two broad strides and scooped his daughter up in his arms. He chuckled as she squirmed in his arms as he tickled her.

"Are you having a nice birthday, Princess?"

"Yes, Daddy."

Unlike Trevor, who practically itemised every one of his toys, Lillian preferred to play and talk to other children. He and Sandra had bought Lillian a brand-new doll and some pretty outfits to go with it. Dave had also acquired a child-size pram for her to play with. However, since her friends had arrived and she'd shown them her presents, she barely looked at them again.

He set Lillian back down on her feet, and she ran off to join her friends playing outside.

The backyard was paved, and there wasn't much room out there. Dave swore to himself there and then that one day soon his kids would have a huge garden to play in.

It was starting to get dark, and even though the evening was mild, the kids would have to come in soon. Dave enjoyed watching them play for another five minutes.

Before he had the chance to call the children inside, he got a tap on the shoulder from Sandra. Her lips were pursed, and she looked annoyed, which was very unlike her. Sandra was generally very easy-going. This pregnancy had definitely taken it out of her, and Dave immediately assumed that something was wrong.

"What is it, love? Are you not feeling well?"

She shook her head. "No, nothing like that. I'm fine. You've got a visitor."

From the tone Sandra used, Dave knew she wasn't impressed. She looked over her shoulder and Dave followed her gaze. Bernie Goldstein stood there, shuffling from foot to foot, looking extremely nervous and clutching a small cap in his hands.

Sandra did not like him bringing business home, and to be fair, neither did Dave. He liked to keep his family life separate from his business dealings.

"I'll deal with it," Dave said, taking a step towards Bernie Goldstein.

"Make sure you do," Sandra said.

Bernie's eyes widened when he saw Dave, and he licked his lips nervously. "I'm ever so sorry to trouble you at home, Mr. Carter. And on your daughter's birthday…" He gestured around him and all the guests. "I had no idea. I'm truly sorry."

Dave stayed silent. Sometimes the threat of violence wasn't needed to scare someone. Sometimes the fear was all generated in their imagination, and all Dave had to do was say nothing. They'd scare themselves far more effectively than he ever could.

"I just wanted a quick word," Bernie stammered.

Still Dave said nothing.

Bernie's head drooped down. "I'm sorry. Shall I come back tomorrow?"

Dave found it hard to be angry with anyone on a day like today when he was in such a good mood. "I don't like people visiting me at home, Bernie."

Bernie now looked petrified as he realised the mistake he had made. "Oh, of course. How stupid of me. I'll come and speak to you at the warehouse."

Dave put one of his big meaty hands on Bernie's shoulder and felt the man shudder.

"No need for that, Bernie. You're here now. Just remember that in the future." Dave looked around at the crowded front room. "Let's go through to the yard and have a bit of privacy."

Bernie nodded, eager to please.

"Thank you ever so much for taking the time, Mr. Carter," he said as they walked through the front room and the kitchen and stepped out into the backyard.

Dave jerked his head at one of Sandra's brothers, indicating that he should go inside and leave him and Bernie alone to talk.

"Can I get you a drink Bernie?" Dave asked.

Bernie shook his head. "That's very kind of you, but no, thank you."

It seemed as if Bernie was having trouble saying what he wanted, so Dave prompted him. "What is it you need to speak to me about, Bernie?"

Bernie swallowed, and his Adam's apple bobbed up and down his neck. "I'm having a bit of trouble…" Bernie began looking frantically around him. His eyes flickered up to Dave's and then back down again to the floor.

"You see my son has been ill, and we have to pay the doctor's bills, and then my daughter's wedding is coming up. I'm struggling to make the payments this month."

Bernie Goldstein owned a cafe on Burdett Road. It was a popular little place, but it had been subject to racially targeted attacks, so Dave Carter had offered a bit of protection, which had worked well for both parties. Bernie could keep his cafe open without fearing any more attacks, and Dave earned a little extra money.

Bernie continued to babble on about how expensive the doctor's bills were.

He was so nervous. He couldn't stop talking.

Dave shook his head and studied Bernie's face. He considered himself a good judge of character, and he was sure that Bernie was telling him the truth. Even so, it wasn't good to look weak in this business.

If word got out that Dave had let Bernie off the hook, there would be more and more chancing their luck and trying to follow Bernie's example.

"I would very much like to help you, Bernie. As you know, I'm a family man myself."

For a moment, Bernie looked up hopefully, but his face fell when Dave continued, "Of course, I can't actually let you off the payments as that will make me look weak."

Bernie's shoulders slumped, and fresh beads of sweat appeared on his forehead.

"Look," Dave said putting a fatherly arm around Bernie Goldstein, even though the man was older than he was. "Like I said, I can't let people off payments but…"

Dave reached into his pocket and pulled out a roll of bills. He peeled off a few notes and handed them to Bernie, who took them, his eyes wide with surprise. "Let's call it a wedding present for your daughter," Dave said.

It had taken Kathleen four attempts to find something decent to wear. All of her clothes were now getting a little tight around her stomach. She settled on a pretty blue dress that normally she would have dismissed as too frumpy, but today she didn't have much choice.

She carefully applied her makeup and brushed her hair until it shone.

She quickly shoved her feet into her high-heeled shoes and rushed downstairs. She didn't have long if she was going to get there in time. And her plan all depended on getting there at exactly the right moment.

Kathleen caught the number twenty bus, which was ten minutes late, and she ended up running the short distance from the bus stop to the Odeon cinema. She was breathing heavily by the time she arrived, and at first, she couldn't see Linda. Her heart sunk in disappointment, but then, out of the corner of her eye, she saw them.

Linda was wearing her best knee-length dress with navy blue stripes. She'd worn her hair down, and she was gazing adoringly up at Donovan, her new bloke.

Kathleen pushed her shoulders back and swayed her hips

as she walked up to them. "Fancy seeing you two here!"

Donovan turned to her with a bemused expression on his face, but Kathleen noticed how his eyes slid up and down her body before returning to Linda.

Linda looked puzzled as she stared at her friend. "Kath, what are you doing here?"

Kathleen gave a tight little smile. "I was home on my own, and I was a bit bored. I thought I'd watch a film."

Linda frowned. "But you knew I was going to be…"

Kathleen cut her off. "Oh yes, you did mention something about it. I forgot. You don't mind me tagging along with you two, do you?"

Kathleen looked at Donovan and Linda, smiling brightly at them and ignoring the disappointed look on Linda's face.

"Of course, we don't mind if you join us," Donovan said. "Any friend of Linda, is a friend of mine."

That was exactly what Kathleen wanted to hear, and she linked arms with Donovan. "Oh, how lovely."

She quickly snuck a look at Linda, and then looked away again equally quickly when she saw the angry look on Linda's face.

When they went inside the cinema, Kathleen made sure she sat between Linda and Donovan. Donovan looked quite surprised, but he didn't make a fuss and sat down quietly.

As the lights in the theatre dimmed, Kathleen crossed her legs, making sure that her dress rode up over her thighs, giving Donovan an eyeful of her legs, which she knew was one of her best features.

Linda gave a little huff of annoyance and crossed her arms over her chest, staring stonily ahead at the screen. Kathleen ignored her and paid attention to Donovan.

She put her arm on the armrest, pretending to touch Donovan's hand accidentally.

He jumped as if he'd been electrocuted, and Kathleen frowned. This could be harder than she'd expected.

They watched the film in silence, and when the credits started to roll, Kathleen beamed at them both.

"Wasn't that a great film?" Kathleen said although she hadn't really been paying much attention. She'd been far too busy plotting.

As the lights in the cinema went up, Kathleen saw Linda's eyes were red. How strange, she thought. She hadn't noticed any sad scenes in the film.

24

WHEN MARTIN GOT BACK TO his club, things were just beginning to heat up for the evening. There was a line forming outside by the doormen, who stood aside to let Martin enter. He got a few respectful nods from some of the punters, but he ignored them. He was still in a foul mood, thanks to his mother.

The first thing Martin saw when he walked towards the bar was Frank the Face, looking pissed and cradling a glass of whisky. Martin gritted his teeth. What the hell was he doing downstairs?

A moment later, Big Tim was by his side. Martin jerked a thumb at the pathetic figure of Frank at the bar. "What's he doing down here? I thought I told you to keep him out of sight."

Big Tim frowned. "I don't think you said that, boss. You said to keep him at the club, not to keep him upstairs or out of sight."

Martin was feeling extremely irritable after spending the evening in his mother's company, so he turned on Big Tim and snarled. "Are you telling me I don't remember what I told you?"

Big Tim flinched. "No, boss. Sorry, I must have got it wrong."

Martin took a deep breath. He was filled with a burning fury, but it wasn't sensible to take it out on Big Tim. He was reliable and a good worker. Martin needed to keep him around.

But somebody was going to fall victim to his temper this evening. Martin's gaze fell back to Frank at the bar.

"Has he been any more forthcoming with details of Dave's future plans?"

"No, boss. He says it's all a mistake, and he never meant to betray Carter."

Martin's eyes narrowed. "Mistake, my arse. I'll show him just how big a mistake he's really made." Martin looked up at Tim. "Get him outside in the van."

Tim raised a questioning eyebrow, but wisely said nothing to contradict Martin. He'd seen his boss in this kind of mood before and didn't want to be on the receiving end of his anger.

Tim pushed his way through the crowds of punters gathering around the bar and slapped a hand on Frank's shoulder.

Frank whirled round. The alcohol had made him confident and given him an attitude to match. He looked at Tim with an angry glare.

"I've had enough of this," Frank said. "You can't keep me here any more against my will."

Big Tim smiled coldly. He'd once had a lot of respect for Frank the Face, but in the last couple of days that respect had gone out of the window.

He couldn't respect anyone who double-crossed people

like Frank had. Dave Carter might be Martin's enemy, and so he was Tim's enemy too, but you couldn't just skip from side to side like Frank had tried to do. It just wasn't done in this world.

"Don't worry," Tim said. "We're not keeping you here anymore."

Frank look shocked. "What?" He leaned forward cupping his hand behind his ear, so he could hear Tim more clearly over the loud music in the club. "What do you mean?"

"We're going for a little drive," Tim said.

Tim's words made the blood drain from Frank's face, and his eyes widened in shock. Tim had to hand it to him, though. He was a veteran at this. Frank didn't panic or try to scream down the club.

Frank's eyes shifted to the door, but he didn't try and make a run for it, and Tim was glad of that. It was better to take your punishment like a man, unlike Keith Parker who had pissed his pants in terror.

Frank slid off the barstool and followed Tim behind the bar. They moved through the small kitchen area and then finally walked out of the back door of the club.

When he saw Martin Morton waiting for him by the van, Frank's resolve nearly broke.

But he set his mouth in a firm line and met Martin's gaze without flinching.

"I hear you haven't been very talkative," Martin said. "That's very disappointing, Frank."

"I've got a lot of respect for you, Mr. Morton. I'm sorry I can't be more helpful, but I realise what I did was wrong, and I'll regret it till the day I die."

Martin rapped his knuckles on the bonnet of the van. "Get

in, Frank."

They hadn't tied Frank up. There was no point in that sort of thing. Frank the Face had earned enough respect over the years to forgo that particular humiliation.

But even Tim was wondering how far Martin was prepared to go on this one, though. Getting rid of a little runt like Keith Parker was nothing. It was about as simple as scraping some shit off their shoes. But Frank? Tim shook his head. Frank the Face was a huge player in Dave Carter's outfit, and if Martin killed Frank, Dave Carter would take that as a personal affront. He wouldn't take it lying down.

Tim indicated right, pulled off Jellows Lane and stopped the van in front of an old abandoned meatpacking factory.

To his credit, Frank had kept his counsel and hadn't yet started begging for his life.

They climbed out of the van, with Martin leading the way, Frank in the middle and Tim bringing up the rear, in case Frank tried to make a run for it.

They let themselves in through a side door and walked into a large open-plan space. Most of the cabinets and counters that had any value had been removed and flogged long ago, leaving a cavernous space behind.

"This will do," Martin said, his voice echoing around the large room.

He strolled around the room and then pulled out two wooden chairs. One had a broken leg. He held it above his head then threw it hard against the wall, smashing it.

Both Tim and Frank watched him uneasily.

Martin could be very unpredictable, and no one knew that better than Tim.

Martin carried over the one good chair and set it down in

the centre of the room. "Take a pew, Frank."

Reluctantly, Frank did as he was told and sat down on the rickety wooden chair.

It was cold tonight, and Frank's breath was forming circular, white puffs in the air.

Martin slapped his hands and then rubbed them together. "Have you changed your mind about talking yet, Frank?"

Frank closed his eyes briefly and muttered something; Tim thought it might be a prayer. That wasn't going to help him much now.

"I don't want to betray him anymore," Frank muttered, referring to Dave Carter.

"Well, you should have thought about that earlier. You've already betrayed him once. So what do a few extra titbits passed my way matter?"

Frank hung his head and then he looked up at Martin beseechingly. "Please, Mr. Morton. Be reasonable. Surely you can understand my predicament."

Martin smiled, and as he turned around, the moonlight streaming in the window lit up his face, highlighting that pale, silvery scar on his cheek. At that moment, Tim thought he looked truly evil.

"I'm not a reasonable man," Martin said. "If you wanted reasonable, you should have stuck with Dave Carter." Martin walked quickly up to Frank and clamped a hand around his neck, squeezing it so Frank's eyes bulged and his skin turned red.

Tim watched from a distance, giving Martin room but staying close by in case Frank retaliated.

Finally, just as Tim thought he was actually going to strangle Frank, Martin released his grip.

Frank panted for breath as Martin stood over him.

Martin gave him a moment to get his breath back and then grabbed a handful of Frank's hair, yanking his head back. "Ready to talk yet?"

Frank grimaced. The good side of his face tensed upwards, but the other side drooped down heavily, making his face look like one half was made of melted wax.

"I can't," Frank panted out.

Martin let go of Frank's hair, and his head dropped forward.

"Well, it looks like we have no choice, Tim." Martin nodded at Tim and gave him the signal.

Tim walked to the far side of the room and opened up the large, black holdall he'd stashed there earlier. He pulled out a huge, gleaming samurai sword and tested its weight between his hands.

Frank turned around, craning his neck, desperate to see what had put such a huge grin on Martin's face.

When he saw the sword in Tim's hands, his jaw dropped. "Jesus Christ," he said.

Martin cackled. "He ain't going to save you now."

25

CHARLIE WILLIAMS SHUFFLED ALONG THE prison corridor. The drawstring in the pair of trousers he'd been given was broken, so he was forced to walk along clutching them to his stomach, or have them falling down around his ankles.

He'd asked twice for a replacement pair, but all he'd received for his trouble was a shove in the back and a kick up the arse from the prison guards. Bastards.

He was on his way to the visiting room for another visit from his mother. He didn't much like seeing the disappointment in his mother's eyes when she came to see him, but that was better than having no visitors at all.

He'd been lucky enough to stay local so far. After the trial, he could be sent anywhere in England, and then his chances of getting any visitors would be very slim.

When he walked into the visitor's room, Charlie was so surprised to see Dave Carter sitting there that he released his grip on his trousers. Luckily he managed to grab them before they fell down completely.

He walked forward quickly, gripping his trousers with one hand and holding the other hand out to greet Dave.

"Mr. Carter, what a pleasant surprise."

Prison made most people act strangely, but Dave seemed relaxed and calm just as he always did. He'd stood up to shake Charlie's hand, but now he sat back down and gestured for Charlie to take the seat opposite him.

"How are you holding up, son?"

"It's not too bad in here," Charlie said, trying to be cheerful. "I reckon I'll be out soon. And I just want to say, you don't have to worry about me. I know where my loyalties lie."

Dave studied Charlie's face carefully making him feel nervous.

Dave leaned forward in his chair and put his hand on the table. "I'm afraid I've got a bit of bad news for you, son. The police have found a gun at The Three Grapes, and it had your fingerprints on it."

Charlie felt as if all the air had been sucked out of his lungs. He flopped back in the chair. That was it then. He would be in here forever.

"I don't want you to worry, Charlie. I've got you a brief, one of the best. I just need you to keep your wits about you, do you understand?"

Charlie nodded, glumly. He understood all right. He had to keep shtum. Otherwise, the consequences would be far worse than just going to prison. But Dave Carter didn't have to worry. Charlie would never rat him out. Dave Carter had given him a job and trusted him back when he was a seventeen-year-old kid with nothing, and there was no way that Charlie would repay him by squealing to the police.

"Are you really all right, son?" Dave asked, looking at Charlie with concern.

Charlie tried hard to smile, but his mouth just wouldn't turn up at the corners.

"I'm worried about my mum," Charlie said. "I'm all she's got, and she relies on me to put the food on the table. I don't know what she'll do while I'm inside."

"Now, Charlie. You know you don't have to worry about that. You're one of mine, and I take care of my own. I'm going to visit your mum personally and make sure she's all right. I promise you that. So I don't want you in here worrying, do you understand?"

Charlie nodded.

It was a weight off his mind not to have to fret about his mother. There were enough things to worry about in prison without worrying about her.

The following morning, Linda decided to confront Kathleen. She'd lain awake in bed last night thinking about it. She didn't really believe that Kathleen had done it on purpose. She obviously just didn't realise how important Donovan was to Linda. Kathleen had had a very difficult time of it over the past few days, and so it was quite understandable that she wanted some company on a Friday night.

Linda thought perhaps she'd been rather unfair to her friend. She didn't want Kathleen to think she was choosing a man over her. Kathleen would always be her best friend.

So after enjoying a Saturday morning lie-in, Linda had decided to talk things through with Kathleen and explain that although she wanted to spend time with Donovan, she still wanted to help her friend in any way she could.

As she passed Salmon Lane, she caught sight of Mary, Kathleen's mother, "Good morning, Mrs. Diamond," Linda said brightly.

Mary smiled. "Good morning, Linda. I'm off to the market. I promised Theresa I'd cover her stall for a couple of hours."

"I'm just going to see Kathleen."

"See if you can cheer her up," Mary said. "She's been a bit down in the dumps lately."

Linda wanted to tell Kathleen's mother that she knew all about the pregnancy and that she would do her best to support Kathleen, but she didn't know quite how to bring it up without sounding very rude and impertinent, so in the end, she decided to say nothing and waved Mary off and continued on to find Kathleen.

When she reached the Diamond's house, she knocked on the door, but there was no answer. Of course, she knew that Mary was out, but it was very unlike Kathleen to be out at this time on Saturday. She wouldn't be at the market spending money because she needed to save all her pennies now that she had a baby on the way.

Linda thought perhaps Kathleen hadn't heard her knock the first time, so she knocked again and waited.

Was that noise coming from inside? Linda wondered whether Kathleen was listening to the wireless and that was why she hadn't heard her knock.

She pushed on the door, and it opened. Mary had left it on the latch as she normally did.

Linda shut the door behind her and wandered through into the hallway.

She opened her mouth to call out to Kathleen, but a movement caught her eye as she walked past the doorway to the front room.

She turned in shock and blinked, unable to believe what she was seeing with her own eyes. Donovan and Kathleen were sitting on the sofa. Kathleen's blouse was draped over the back of the sofa, and she was just about to undo her brassiere.

Donovan paled when he noticed he and Kathleen were no longer alone. Kathleen gave a little squeak of shock and clutched a cushion to her chest.

Linda swallowed hard when she saw that Donavan's belt was unbuckled.

"Linda! Wait!" Donovan called out. "Let me explain."

But Linda didn't wait. She turned on her heel and rushed out of the house, feeling sick.

She ran nearly all the way home until she was panting and had a stitch in her side. She would never let either of them explain. What she had just seen didn't need an explanation. Even she wasn't that naive.

26

LATER THAT DAY, DAVE CARTER lived up to his word and went to visit Charlie's mum, Doris Williams. The Williams' lived in a two-up two-down on Bread Street. There was a large basement beneath the house that Doris let out to a lodger.

Doris had become very efficient and good at making money. As many East End women had before her, Doris has been forced to find a way to earn an extra bit of money to support her and Charlie after her husband passed. Not that he'd been much use to them when he'd been alive. Even when he'd managed to hold down a job for longer than five minutes, he'd been busy drinking his earnings away.

She had a reputation in the area for being a bit of a money grabber. But Dave Carter realised that this was only born out of necessity. He was determined that Charlie's mother would want for nothing while he was in prison. He still felt incredibly guilty that it was his own brother's fault that Charlie was in this predicament in the first place.

As if she'd been waiting behind the net curtains, Doris opened the door on Dave's first knock.

"Mr. Carter, what a pleasure to see you. Please do come

in," she said.

She led the way through a dark hallway, which smelled of beeswax polish, and into the small front room.

There were two armchairs set out by the fire and one hard backed chair.

"Please, take a seat," Doris said primly, pointing out one of the armchairs.

As Dave eased himself into the chair, Doris said. "I'll just put the kettle on and make us a pot of tea."

Dave had a lot to do today, and he wished he could refuse the offer of tea, but he knew ceremony was important to Doris, and she would feel most put out if he didn't stop for at least one cup.

As Doris bustled about in the kitchen, Dave leaned back in the seat and looked at a photograph on the mantelpiece. It was of Charlie, taken a couple of years ago. He stood proudly by the brick wall outside the house, smiling widely. He really was her pride and joy. Dave felt another pang of anger and regret over Gary's actions.

Doris bustled in, carrying a tray with two china cups and a matching teapot.

"Milk?"

"Thank you."

Dave noticed that one of the dainty cups had a chip on the rim. Doris was careful to make sure he got the one without the chip.

Dave smiled at her as he took his cup of tea and vowed to himself that he would make sure that Doris was all right.

"I wanted to pay a visit, Doris, because I want you to know that your Charlie is a good boy. He's been caught up in this mess through no fault of his own. The police are trying to wrongly pin a charge on him."

Doris leaned forward eagerly in her seat, her face glowing. "You mean he is innocent? Oh, Mr. Carter." She pressed a hand to her chest. "I'm ever so relieved. I was worried he'd got himself into so much trouble."

Dave gave her a small smile and then sipped his tea. Charlie Williams could never be described as innocent, but he wasn't a bad kid, and Dave was telling the truth when he said it wasn't his fault that he'd been caught.

Carefully avoiding the issue of innocence, he said, "I've hired him a brief, and it won't be long until he's out. I'm confident of that. I'm going to do whatever I can to help him, and that includes helping you, Mrs. Williams. I hope you don't take this the wrong way, but I would like to contribute a little something every week to make up for Charlie's absence. I know it can't be easy with him inside."

Doris's eyes teared up. "Oh, Mr. Carter, you are a good man. I told Charlie you wouldn't see us go without."

After he had left the Williams' house, Dave was feeling very pleased with himself. It had gone smoothly. He was glad Doris was a sensible woman and had agreed to accept the money. Sometimes people could be proud and refuse. But Doris Williams knew what it was to be poor. She wasn't silly enough to let her pride get in the way and complicate something as straightforward as money.

He'd only walked to the end of Bread Street when he came face-to-face with a very angry looking woman.

She stormed right up to him and poked him firmly in the chest. At first, Dave was so shocked he couldn't do anything. It had been many years since anyone had dared to confront him in such a fashion.

He studied the woman's face, and then the pieces fell into place. It was Frank's wife, Maisie.

"I want to know what you've done," she demanded shrilly.

"Maisie, isn't it? Frank's wife?"

"Yes, that's right. And I'm not about to let you get away with this!"

Dave frowned. He had no idea what the stupid cow was going on about. "Sorry, Maisie, you'll have to explain."

Maisie's face was red and shiny, and she had clearly been crying recently.

"You know exactly what I mean! Don't try and pretend you don't. You tell me what you've done to my Frank, or I'm going to the police."

Dave grabbed Maisie by the elbow, escorting her along the street.

"What are you doing?" Maisie cried out.

"We need to talk," Dave said. "There's a cafe just at the end of Salmon Lane. We'll talk there."

Once they were safely in the cafe, sipping cups of tea, Dave said, "Now, tell me what all this is about."

Maisie set her cup of tea down on the table with trembling hands. "Frank's missing," she said quietly. "Have you done something to him?" The look she gave him was so raw and pleading that Dave's heart went out to her.

He leaned forward and put a hand over Maisie's, but she snatched it away. Dave realised she suspected that he had done something to Frank.

"I need you to listen to me, Maisie, love," Dave said. "Frank hasn't turned up for work. I wasn't worried because I thought it was due to the disagreement we'd had."

Maisie glared him. "What disagreement?"

Dave leaned back in his chair and sighed. This was going to be difficult.

"I've been noticing that Frank has been getting a little worse recently. His trembling has increased, and I was worried about him at work. I offered him a job, overseeing the expansion of my workshops. As you know, motorcars are getting popular around here, and I want to expand. I told him I needed someone like Frank, who I could trust to be in charge of the operation. Unfortunately, Frank didn't see it that way. He'd thought I was trying to get rid of him."

Maisie looked down at the table as though she were processing what Dave had said.

"I thought he was just spending some time at home thinking things through. I hoped he was going to come back to work."

Maisie shook her head. "He didn't tell me about any of that. He came home, acting very strangely, and he went straight out again. I haven't seen him since."

Dave frowned. That wasn't good. He had a very bad feeling about this.

"And nobody else has seen him?"

Maisie shook her head and looked miserably down at the table. "No, I've asked people at our local. I even went to see his brother in Mile End, but no one's seen hide nor hair of him."

Dave leaned forward and patted Maisie's hand. This time, she didn't snatch her hand away. "Try to keep calm, Maisie, love. I'll see what I can find out for you."

27

LINDA CHECKED HERSELF QUICKLY IN the hall mirror on the way out to work. She tucked a stray strand of hair back into her ponytail. Her eyes were still red, but that couldn't be helped. She'd cried herself to sleep last night.

She took a deep breath and reached for the handle on the front door. She was shaking at the thought of seeing Kathleen at Bevels. But she didn't have a choice. She had to go to work.

"Bye, Mum," she said, shutting the door firmly behind her and marching down the steps.

When she turned the corner, she stopped dead.

Donovan was standing there with a bunch of carnations in his hand. He shoved them at her.

"These are for you," he said, his eyes scanning her face, looking for some sign of forgiveness.

Linda clamped her mouth in a firm line and shoved the flowers back at Donovan. He had a bloody cheek, thinking flowers would work after everything she'd seen.

"Get out of my way. I'm late for work," Linda ordered.

When he didn't move, she simply walked around him, striding along as fast as she could.

Donovan followed at her heels, chasing after her, "I'm sorry, Linda. You have to forgive me."

"I do not!" Linda said. "I will never forgive you."

Donovan reached out and put a hand on her arm, but Linda shook him off.

She was walking fast, but Donovan had much longer legs, and he could quite easily keep up.

"I couldn't resist it, Linda. I'm only a man, and she offered herself up on a plate. But I don't like her, not really. It's you I like."

Linda ignored him and kept walking. She wouldn't turn her head and carried on pretending he wasn't there.

"I'm not stupid, Linda. I know you're ten times the girl she ever will be."

That was the last straw. Linda whirled around and used her handbag to whack him on the arm. "You are stupid, Donovan. You really have no idea, do you?"

Donovan gaped at her in shock. He'd never seen Linda angry before.

Linda continued, "Kathleen is pregnant, you fool. She just wants an idiot like you to pass off as the baby's father!"

Linda was gratified to see that those words had finally got Donovan to shut up. He was opening and closing his mouth like a goldfish, so Linda turned around and marched on to Bevels, leaving Donovan staring after her.

She felt a slight twinge of guilt for sharing Kathleen's secret but quickly extinguished it. Why should she care about Kathleen? Kathleen quite clearly had no regard for Linda at all.

Frank the Face woke up, his body stung all over, and the

scent of blood was thick in his nostrils. He wasn't sure how long he'd been lying there alone. He'd been drifting in and out of consciousness, willing himself to die. But it hadn't happened. The pain told him that much.

He winced as he tried to sit up. He blinked his bleary eyes and looked down at his arms. They were covered with thin slivers of cuts. He shuddered as the memories came back to him.

Martin Morton had enjoyed using the large sword to slice thin layers of Frank's skin. He was careful not to make the cuts too deep, so Frank didn't bleed out. The sadistic bastard had wanted to keep him alive.

It felt like Martin had carefully worked away on him for hours. They'd tied him to the chair before Martin set to work. Even Big Tim had turned pale as Frank's entire body had turned scarlet with blood.

It had mostly dried now, crusting on his skin, and it cracked as he moved.

He couldn't remember them leaving, or even remember them untying him from the chair. Frank thought he must have passed out.

Frank struggled to get to his knees. The floor was freezing cold.

He had to get out of there. London was not safe for Frank the Face anymore. It wouldn't be long until Dave Carter found out what he'd done. His reaction would probably be worse than Martin's.

Dave didn't have the same sadistic streak as Martin, but Frank knew he'd have his throat slit within the week once Dave found out he'd betrayed him.

Feeling thoroughly sorry for himself, Frank heaved

himself to his feet, clenching his teeth against the stinging pain of the thousands of cuts all over his body.

He made his way outside, blinking in the bright morning sunlight. He took a deep breath, breathing in the fumes and familiar scent of London, trying to get rid of that horrible lingering smell of blood.

He knew what he had to do now. He was going to have to leave London for good and leave his family behind. He hoped that Dave would feel compelled to look after Maisie and bung her a few quid. He couldn't take her and the kids with him. It simply wasn't practical.

Once Frank had settled on his plan, he set off for the corner of Jellows Road. He stepped inside the phone box and dialled the police.

"I want to report a murder," Frank said. "Frank Briggs has been murdered at the old meat factory on Jellows Lane."

Before the police officer on the other end of the phone could ask any questions, Frank had hung up.

This was it now. There was no going back. He bit down hard on the inside of his mouth. He was going to miss Maisie and the kids like mad, but they would be far better off without him.

With any luck, the police would find the blood on the floor of the old factory and assume he'd been murdered there, and his body dumped somewhere else.

Frank stepped out of the phone box and staggered down the lane; he still had his wallet in his trousers, and there was enough money in there to get him to Victoria where he could get on a coach. He didn't know where he was heading yet. He would just take the first coach he saw, as long as it got him far away from London.

A little old lady, who'd been walking towards him, suddenly saw the state of his skin and scuttled over to the other side of the road, giving him a terrified look.

Frank pulled a handkerchief out of his pocket and tried to tidy himself up the best he could. But it was no good. The blood was dried on. He would have to wait until he got to Victoria and then use the bathrooms there.

He looked up at the watery sun in the sky and realised that this was the first day of the rest of his life.

28

WHEN LINDA GOT TO BEVELS, she was scolded by Mrs. McClair for being late. She could feel Kathleen's eyes on her from across the room, but she studiously ignored her.

She apologised to Mrs. McClair and then quickly slid into her seat behind her sewing machine.

Kathleen leaned forward and tried to get her attention. "Psst," she said. "I'm sorry, Linda. Truly I am."

It took all of Linda's willpower to ignore her and focus on setting up her machine.

She was on waistbands today, so she quickly threaded her machine with the blue cotton and began to sew. Luckily, Linda was an excellent seamstress, and she could have done this particular job with her eyes closed because right now her eyes were filled with tears and everything was very hazy.

The morning passed agonisingly slowly, and Linda developed a headache. She hadn't gotten enough sleep last night because she'd been so upset.

Despite the fact she was so distracted, Linda's ears pricked up as she heard Kathleen's name mentioned by a couple of girls on the other side of the room.

"She should have kept her legs together."

"My mother says no good will come of her. She's ruined for life now. Stuck at home with a screaming baby and no husband. Can you imagine the shame?"

Linda drew in a sharp breath. How had they found out so quickly? Despite her intentions to ignore Kathleen, she turned around in her seat to see whether Kathleen had also heard the whispered gossip.

Kathleen's face was pale as she turned her head and looked at Linda with a baleful gaze.

Linda tried to harden her heart. It served her right. Kathleen Diamond had betrayed her in the worst possible way.

But despite her anger at Kathleen, Linda couldn't help feeling sorry for her old friend. This little bit of gossip was only the start. Things would get a lot rougher for Kathleen from here on in.

She would need all of her friends about her for support, but Linda wasn't ready to forgive her. Not yet.

Kathleen angrily rearranged the fabric on her sewing station. Linda was completely overreacting. It wasn't as if she'd been engaged. Linda had only just met Donovan. As far as Kathleen was concerned, Linda was being ridiculous.

Every time Kathleen tried to catch her eye, Linda looked away. It wasn't like her at all. Linda had always been the one person she could rely on, and Kathleen didn't like feeling that she was now on her own.

At lunchtime, Kathleen decided to approach Linda. She picked up her handbag and stopped in front of Linda's workstation.

"It's nice and sunny outside," she said. "Shall we take our sandwiches over to the park. It might be the last chance we get before winter."

Linda slowly raised her eyes to meet Kathleen's.

Kathleen was quite taken aback by the fierce glare Linda gave her. She pursed her lips together as if she was afraid she was going to say something she'd regret.

"Come on, Linda. You know I didn't mean to hurt you, and if you think about it, I'm sure you'll see you're overreacting."

Linda looked around the room and saw that all the other girls were looking at them.

"Not here," she said, grabbed her handbag and stormed out of the machine room.

Kathleen quickly followed her past Mrs. McClair's desk and headed for the stairs.

Once they got outside, Kathleen shivered. She'd been in such a rush to chase after Linda she'd forgotten her coat.

She wrapped her arms around herself, trying to keep warm.

She was regretting suggesting the park now; she was far too cold.

Linda's warm, woollen coat made her look twice the size she really was, Kathleen thought.

When Linda turned back and saw Kathleen following her, she huffed out a breath in frustration. Then she slowed her walking pace and gave Kathleen a sideways look. "For goodness sake, Kath, where is your coat? You'll freeze. You shouldn't be so silly, not in your condition."

Kathleen scowled. She didn't appreciate being reminded of her condition as Linda put it.

"I'll go back and get my coat," she said. "But will you wait for me here. We need to talk."

Linda shook her head. "No, we don't need to talk, and I'm not going to wait for you. I'm sorry, Kath, but you really hurt me, and I'm not going to forgive you."

After Linda turned and walked off towards the park, hurrying after another couple of machinists from Bevels, Kathleen stood on the pavement shivering and watching her friend.

She couldn't believe it. Linda had never spoken to her like that before. She'd always been there, good old, reliable Linda.

Kathleen felt her lower lip wobble, and she felt very sorry for herself as she turned around, heading back into Bevels to go and get her coat.

It didn't occur to her that she was the one in the wrong; she truly believed that Linda was overreacting. She didn't understand how the girl could be so cruel, especially considering everything that Kathleen had been through recently.

Kathleen walked back inside the large room, weaving between the sewing workstations, and grabbed her coat.

Before she could put it on, she realised she wasn't alone in the room.

All of the girls had gone to lunch, but there, standing in the doorway blocking Kathleen's path, was Mr. Bevel himself.

Mr. Bevel rarely addressed the girls. He preferred to keep himself holed up in his office, and left Mrs. McClair in charge of the day-to-day supervision of the girls.

Kathleen swallowed uneasily and gripped her coat in front

of her. "Mr. Bevel?"

Mr. Bevel was a short man. Kathleen guessed he was only around forty, but he was almost completely bald. He had a nervous disposition, and his eyes were darting about, looking at everything in the room apart from Kathleen.

"Ah, Miss Diamond. Kathleen, isn't it?"

"Yes, that's right, Mr. Bevel."

"Ah, I see. Well, this is rather awkward. I don't like to have conversations like this, but I'm afraid, in this case, it's necessary."

Kathleen frowned and wished the man would get to the point. What was necessary?

"I'm afraid I've heard the most scandalous rumours about you. I thought the best thing to do would be to ask you if they were true."

Kathleen's eyes widened. How on earth could Mr. Bevel know she was pregnant? Or was he talking about something else? She didn't want to reveal the truth if she didn't have to. But she was unsure how much Mr. Bevel really knew.

Kathleen's heart was thundering in her chest.

"Of course, if these rumours are completely unfounded, I apologise unreservedly, but I'm sure you understand that I have to ask."

"Ask what?" Kathleen's voice was very shaky.

Her fingers were white as she gripped her coat.

"I've been informed that you're pregnant, and according to our records, you're not married, are you?"

Kathleen's cheeks burned as her gaze fell to the floor. This was so humiliating.

This was not how she imagined her life turning out.

"So it's true?" Mr. Bevel queried.

Kathleen didn't trust her voice to speak, so she simply nodded.

Mr. Bevel was silent for a moment and then he said, "Ah, well, I see. I'm terribly sorry, but I'm afraid I'm going to have to let you go. People talk, you see, and I can't have a girl with loose morals around setting a bad example for the other girls. I'm sure you understand, don't you, Kathleen?"

Kathleen looked up then and glared at the horrible little man. Loose morals? Bad example to the other girls? She wasn't half as bad as some of them. She was just one of the ones that got caught! Bloody men. It was all their fault, Kathleen thought, scowling at Mr. Bevel.

"Perhaps it's better if you pack up now, to avoid a scene when the other girls come back from lunch," Mr. Bevel said.

"Better for who? It's certainly not better for me, is it? Just when I need reliable money coming in, you're turfing me out."

Mr. Bevel looked horrified that Kathleen could retaliate. He'd expected her to go quietly. He began to bluster and turned bright red.

"Well, you can stick your job. I don't need you. I don't need anyone," Kathleen said, rushing to her workstation and making sure she'd taken every single personal belonging out of the drawer under her desk.

"You're going to regret this. Mark my words," Kathleen spat at Mr. Bevel, pointing at him.

She grabbed her belongings and stormed past him, leaving Mr. Bevel open-mouthed in horror.

As she clattered down the stairs, tears stinging her eyes, cheeks burning with humiliation, she burst out onto the street and ran straight into Linda.

"Kath?"

Kathleen turned on her. "I've been fired. Are you happy now? Is that enough punishment to satisfy you?"

Linda's big, brown eyes grew wide with pity.

Kathleen dropped her handbag on the floor and shrugged on her coat before picking up the bag again. She walked off, pushing past Linda and a couple of the other girls from Bevels.

Kathleen didn't need anyone's pity. She was Kathleen Diamond, and she would show all of them. No one treated Kathleen like that and got away with it.

One way or another, she was going to make sure they'd all be sorry.

29

KATHLEEN DIDN'T GO STRAIGHT HOME. She knew her mother would be there, and she was not up to answering any questions. She decided to walk home via the Whitechapel Road passing some of the stalls and the shops displaying pretty dresses and costume jewellery.

One particular navy blue dress with a sweetheart neckline made Kathleen pause and stare into the shop window. It was gorgeous, and it would have suited Kathleen to a tee. She deserved it after such an awful day. The kind of life she'd always wanted included being able to walk in and buy a dress like that without worrying about the money, or thinking that it wasn't suitable for work. Why shouldn't she get what she wanted?

But she didn't have the money, and with a baby on the way, she wouldn't have any money for some time to come. She walked on, clutching her coat to her chest, trying to keep warm.

She stepped to the side of the pavement to allow a woman with a pram to pass.

The woman was everything Kathleen wanted to be. She had her hair carefully done up in the latest style. She had a beautiful shade of lipstick on and wore an expensive coat with a mink collar. Kathleen couldn't help noticing the gold ring on her finger, too.

The woman obviously had a husband with a good job, who enjoyed treating his wife.

Why couldn't Kathleen have that? It wasn't fair that she was going to have to live on the breadline with a baby stuck at her mother's. After all, it wasn't entirely her fault.

Kathleen's hand slid down to her stomach as she considered her options.

She'd been looking about this all wrong. She was absolutely determined not to be a victim any longer. This baby didn't have to be a burden. It could be her ticket out of here.

Kathleen smiled. This baby just might be the best thing that had ever happened to her.

She whirled around, changing direction, and walked quickly towards Martin Morton's club.

When Kathleen reached Martin Morton's club, the door was open. Inside Frieda Longbottom was swirling her mob in a bucket of hot, soapy water.

Kathleen strolled in as if she owned the place.

"Is Martin here?" she asked Frieda, putting her hands on her hips and looking over Frieda's shoulder.

Frieda looked her up and down in a disapproving fashion.

Kathleen felt her temper rise. Who on earth did old Frieda think she was? She couldn't judge Kathleen. She certainly wasn't any better than her.

"Well, is he?" Kathleen demanded.

Frieda narrowed her eyes and leaned her mop against the

wall. "Yes," she said slowly. "He's upstairs, but he's busy."

Kathleen ignored the warning and stepped around the old woman and the bucket, walking over the floor that Frieda had just mopped.

"Oi, where do you think you're going, missy? He's busy; I told you. He's doing paperwork, and he doesn't like people going up there during the day."

Kathleen ignored her and strode on, walking towards the door behind the bar.

Despite her outward display of confidence, Kathleen was starting to feel very nervous.

She took a deep breath. There was no turning back now.

She walked through the doorway behind the bar and started to climb the stairs to Martin's flat.

Before she reached the top of the stairs, the door to Martin's flat flew open. He stood at the top of the stairs, glaring angrily down the stairwell. "Who's there?"

He growled the question, and Kathleen flushed in mortification. It hadn't been that long ago. Surely he couldn't have forgotten about her already. She swallowed nervously. The light was dim in the stairwell, so perhaps he just couldn't see her properly.

Kathleen had paused, but now she continued up the stairs on shaky legs. "It's me, Martin. It's Kathleen, Kathleen Diamond."

Martin stayed silent, his eyes watchful, as Kathleen climbed the rest of the stairs. When she finally reached the top, his eyes narrowed, and he said, "What are you doing here? Couldn't stay away from me, eh?"

"I need to talk to you, Martin."

"I'm quite busy at the moment."

"It won't take long," Kathleen persisted. "It's important."

"I suppose you'd better come in then." Martin stood aside and let Kathleen pass and into his flat.

Kathleen looked around. It looked exactly the same. All modern furnishings. It must have cost a fortune. Surely he wouldn't begrudge passing a few quid to a woman who was pregnant with his baby.

"I thought you knew the score," Martin said. "You're a smart girl. It was nice while it lasted. But it was just a bit of fun, wasn't it?"

Kathleen swallowed hard and gritted her teeth. This was so humiliating, but she had to see it through. She really didn't have a choice.

"You see, Martin –"

"I hope you're not going to make a fuss, Kathleen. I can't stand women who make a fuss."

Kathleen was starting to wonder why she'd ever found Martin Morton an exciting prospect. He was very handsome in a sleek, dangerous kind of way. His dark hair and tanned skin had set her heart fluttering the first time she'd met him, but standing here in the cold light of day, looking at the scowl on his face, she realised just how a person's personality could change their looks. Deep down, despite the suave suits, and carefully styled hair, Martin Morton was ugly.

"I'm pregnant, Martin."

There. She'd said it. That was the worst bit out of the way.

The expression on Martin's face cleared. It was eerily blank. Kathleen tried to reassure herself that she didn't care how he reacted. She hadn't really expected him to be happy about it. But she did expect him to take care of her and the baby. It was his responsibility, and she wasn't about to let him off the hook.

Despite the warmth of the small fire in Martin's front room, Kathleen shivered.

"All right," Martin said. "It's not a disaster. There are things we can do, people who can make this go away."

"It's too late for that," Kathleen snapped, finally coming to the end of her tether and finding her backbone. "I need to know you're prepared to take responsibility. The baby will need a father to provide for it."

Kathleen's tone was brisk and businesslike. As far as she was concerned that was just what it was now. A business transaction.

A flash of dislike passed over Martin's face, but it was only there for an instant before it disappeared. He smiled. "Yeah, of course, darling. I'm not going to let a kid of mine go without. Don't you worry your pretty little head about it. I'll take care of everything."

Kathleen was taken aback. She hadn't expected it to be so easy. She thought Martin would take a little bit of convincing to cough up.

She looked at him sceptically. "And what about Babs?"

That same look of dislike passed over Martin's face, but again it cleared before Kathleen could really know for sure whether she'd imagined it or not.

"Don't you worry about Babs. I said I'd deal with it, and I will."

Kathleen nodded. "Okay. Well, that's good. I'm glad you're taking your responsibility seriously."

A moment of awkward silence passed between them as Martin's eyes bored into her.

"I'll be off then," Kathleen said, thinking that was quite enough for one day. She was sure they could sort out the details at a later date after the news had sunk in.

Martin called out to her just before she left. "Just one thing, Kathleen."

Kathleen turned around with a hand on the door handle. "What's that?"

"Keep it quiet. I don't want everybody knowing about this. Understand?"

Kathleen thought for a moment. It didn't really seem an unreasonable request. Kathleen didn't particularly want everybody to know her situation either, but Martin was kidding himself if he thought no one would ever find out.

Still, they wouldn't hear it from her.

"Whatever you think's best, Martin."

As soon as Kathleen had made her way downstairs, Martin Morton threw a punch at the wall, followed up with a couple of kicks for good measure. The little tramp!

When she'd stood in front of him, his hands had been itching to wrap around her scrawny little neck and get rid of her once and for all. But that would have been rash, and Martin had learned over the years that rashness was quickly followed by repercussions.

He clenched his fists, aimed for another hit on the wall, but then paused and studied his bloodied knuckles.

He needed to think things through before acting. And as much as he hated the thought of it, he needed to keep the bitch sweet for now until he decided what to do.

How she'd got up the nerve to come around here and confront him, he would never know. Did she really think he would just hand over a blank cheque? He wouldn't have put it past the conniving slut to have planned this all along.

And when Babs found out, which of course she would, she would scream bloody blue murder. Not that Martin was one of those men who gave a toss about what their wives thought, but Babs had it in her power to make his life bloody difficult, and Martin just didn't need that hassle.

And God forbid what would happen if his mother found out. If Violet Morton got wind of this little scandal, she would never let him hear the end of it. She'd have his guts for garters.

Martin shook his head. Kathleen Diamond was going to pay for this. No one got one over on Martin Morton, especially not some little tart.

Downstairs, Frieda had finished her mopping. She watched Kathleen walk past her, keeping her snooty little nose in the air. She could look down her nose at Frieda all she liked. Frieda had overheard every single word of that conversation, and she knew one thing for sure, Kathleen Diamond had no right to look down her nose at anybody. The silly little cow should have kept her drawers on.

Frieda flinched as she heard Martin knocking something over upstairs. Clearly he hadn't taken the news well.

Frieda definitely wasn't one for gossip, particularly about Martin Morton. For one thing, he was a dangerous bastard, and for another, Frieda was loyal, and she knew where her bread was buttered.

The trouble was this had put her in quite a dilemma because Babs Morton was the one who had gotten her the job here in the first place. Frieda had been ever so close to

Babs's mother Eileen. They'd gone back a long way. Frieda had seen Babs grow up, and she'd been very pleased to see her do so well for herself. She hated the thought of all this going on behind Babs's back. But she knew at the same time that she could get into a great deal of trouble by telling Babs.

Frieda leaned down to pick up the bucket of water. She had almost finished. She just needed to do the small section by the door.

She winced again as a big bang sounded upstairs. Frieda gave a little huff. He was just like a little boy, throwing his toys around because he hadn't gotten his own way. She raised her eyes to the ceiling. Yes, Martin paid her wages, but it was to Babs she owed her loyalty. As soon as she'd finished here, Frieda decided she'd pop round and break the news.

30

AS GOOD AS HER WORD, Frieda went to see Babs Morton as soon as she'd finished cleaning Martin's club.

Babs opened the door with a broad smile. "Frieda, what a lovely surprise."

Babs welcomed her inside with a kiss on the cheek. There was a screech as Derek ran out of the front room being chased by Ruby, who was giggling incessantly.

Babs put a hand to her forehead. "They are driving me to distraction today."

Frieda beamed at the little ones. "They are growing up ever so fast. Just you make the most of this time, Babs. After they grow up, they're even more trouble." Frieda chuckled.

Babs smiled fondly down at the children, who were now throwing pieces of a jigsaw puzzle at each other. "They are naughty little tykes sometimes, but I wouldn't be without them for the world."

"Come in and have a cup of tea, Frieda. You look like you could do with one. Have you finished at the club?"

Frieda nodded. "Yes. I have to admit it seems to get harder day by day. Mopping that bleeding floor takes it out of me. I swear it gets bigger every time I do it."

Babs filled the kettle and turned to look over her shoulder at Frieda. "You work too hard, Frieda. Do you want me to have a word with Martin about getting someone to help you out a bit?"

Frieda shook her head. To be honest, she liked the job, and she liked working on her own. It meant she could sneak off for a crafty fag whenever she wanted. Besides, she had always worked better alone.

"Don't worry yourself. I'm just grumbling. I'm still quite capable of handling the cleaning."

As Babs prepared the tea, Frieda sat down at the kitchen table and started to worry about how to bring up the subject of Martin's little floozy.

When Babs set the teapot on the table and sat down opposite Frieda, she studied her closely. "I can tell you want to tell me something, Frieda. You look ever so worried. What is it? If I can help in any way, you know I will, don't you?"

Frieda swallowed the lump in her throat. Babs clearly thought it was Frieda who had the problem, and the fact that she offered to help touched Frieda deeply.

"You're a good girl, Babs. Your mum would be ever so proud of how you turned out."

Babs smiled and put a hand on Frieda's.

"The thing is," Frieda said, gathering courage. "There's no way easy way to say this, sweetheart. It's about Martin."

The pleasant smile left Babs' face in an instant. "Go on."

"I was working this morning when Martin had a visitor. It was that trollop, Kathleen Diamond."

Babs inhaled sharply. "He promised me that was over. Are you telling me they've been carrying on again behind my back?"

Worse than that, Frieda thought, and hated the fact that she had to be the one to break the news to Babs.

"I'm afraid he's got her in the family way, love. I overheard them talking about it this morning."

The colour drained out of Babs' face, but other than that she made no reaction, apart from gripping her teacup a little tighter.

"He's a fool," Frieda said. "Why on earth he would mess around with a little tart like that when he's got a lovely girl like you at home is beyond me. He needs his head testing."

Babs gave Frieda a strained smile. "I appreciate you telling me, Frieda. God knows, I miss my mum, but I'm so lucky to have you in my corner."

"Oh, sweetheart," Frieda said, deeply touched. "You deserve so much better. He's an idiot."

"As most men are," Babs said pointedly.

"You got that right, sweetheart," Frieda said and cackled. Glad that Babs had taken the news reasonably well so far.

She'd expected to have to mop up some tears and produce lots of tea and sympathy. But Babs was now clearly a woman of the world. She had the full measure of her husband, and Frieda was willing to bet she was a formidable force to be reckoned with when it came to dealing with Martin Morton.

As Babs waved Frieda off, the bracelet on her wrist jingled. Babs glared at it. Sometimes the jewellery Martin bought her felt like shackles rather than the fancy gold it really was.

Frieda was a good friend, and Babs did not appreciate the fact Martin had put the woman in such a difficult position.

She was well aware that Frieda had been surprised she'd taken it so well. But in Babs' opinion, there was no point getting hysterical over the matter. She wasn't stupid. She had known Martin was a ladies' man when she married him, but there was a difference. He used to be discrete. Now he just liked to rub her nose in it, showing a complete lack of respect, which wasn't acceptable.

Martin thought he could do whatever he wanted these days. Well, he could think again. Babs had loved him once, but now she had grown to despise him.

But the cool resentment she felt towards her husband actually played in her favour. There was no passion there, no fury. She was able to think calmly, and that was important. It meant she could take her time and hit Martin where it hurt, and she had a plan to do just that.

Frieda turned just before she reached the turning to Burdett Road, intending to turn around and give Babs one last wave, but Babs was no longer at the door. Someone else was.

Frieda did a double take. Her eyes weren't what they used to be, but she could have sworn that that was Dave Carter going into the Morton house.

Frieda shook her head and chuckled to herself. Her eyes were playing tricks on her. There was no way Dave Carter would be going to Martin Morton's house.

Frieda hitched up the handbag on her shoulder and carried on walking home, dismissing the idea completely from her mind.

31

GARY CARTER APPROACHED THE WAREHOUSE on Blocksy Road nervously. He hadn't seen his brother since the day of The Three Grapes fiasco, and he wasn't sure what kind of reception he would get. He'd heard that Dave was still furious, so he'd decided to give him some time to cool off. He'd gone and stayed with a mate out in Essex, waiting for the heat to die down. But now Gary's money had run out, so he needed to talk to Dave and clear the air.

Gary licked his lips as he approached the big, metal, rolling door. He tried to force himself to relax. He'd screwed up plenty of times in the past, and Dave always forgave him in the end. Family was important to him, and Gary was his brother after all.

For a second or two, Gary looked about in confusion, expecting Charlie Williams to be in his normal spot, guarding the door, but there was no sign of him. Gary grimaced when he remembered that Charlie was still inside. Dave had a lot of influence with the police, and he paid a couple of inspectors to smooth his business dealings, so Gary was surprised that Charlie hadn't yet managed to get out.

"Oh, it's you," A voice said behind Gary, deep, gruff and scornful.

Gary turned and saw the squat, broad figure of Brian Moore.

Brian was giving him a look that Gary found disagreeable.

"You finally decided to show your face around here then, have you?" Brian asked with a smirk.

The cheeky little bastard. Gary glared at the short man. He was a fine one to talk. Gary had heard all the gossip afterwards, and he knew for a fact that Brian had been hot on Gary's heels and ran away leaving Charlie behind. So he was just as much at fault as Gary was.

Gary shot a look down at Brian's crotch. "I hope you've got some new trousers on, Brian. I heard you pissed yourself when you saw Red-haired Freddie."

"You what?" Brian said, his big, chubby face turning bright red.

"Nothing to be ashamed of, Brian. We can't all be brave in the heat of the moment now, can we?"

"It was you that shot the bloody lights out!" Brian growled. "If you hadn't done that none of this would have happened."

Gary narrowed his eyes and took a menacing step towards Brian. Dave had plenty of men working for him, but over the last few years, there were only three he'd let close to him: Gary, Charlie Williams and Brian Moore. What Brian had failed to remember was that out of the three of them only Gary was family, and, therefore, would not suffer this kind of lack of respect.

"I think you're forgetting who you're talking to, Brian," Gary said coldly.

Brian opened his mouth to respond but then thought better of it.

Gary smiled. "That's more like it. Now, is my brother around?"

Brian nodded. "Inside."

Gary followed Brian inside, their footsteps echoing in the cavernous warehouse. He headed over to the small office on the right-hand side, where Dave conducted most of his business. The blinds were only half lowered, and the door was open, so Gary strolled right in.

Dave was alone in the office, sitting behind the desk making some notes. He looked up as his brother entered.

"Well, look what the cat dragged in."

Gary heard Brian chuckle behind him and turned, angrily slamming the door shut in Brian's face. He might have to suffer his brother's taunts, but he didn't have to allow Brian the pleasure of listening to it.

Gary turned back around and then sat down in the seat in front of Dave's desk without waiting for an invitation.

Dave put down his pen and leaned back in the seat, interlinking his fingers and resting them on the desk.

"So what's your excuse this time?"

Gary scowled. He hated Dave lording it over him. It wasn't Gary's fault that Dave had all the opportunities. If he'd had half the luck Dave had had, their situations would be reversed, and he would never talk to Dave in such a fashion.

"I went out to Essex for a while until things cooled down a bit."

Dave sighed. "I mean what was your excuse for the absolute mayhem at The Three Grapes. What the hell happened, Gary? There were three of you and only two of them. How did they manage to get the better of you, eh?"

Gary shrugged and stared moodily at the floor. Dave was clearly putting the blame squarely at his door, but in Gary's opinion, he hadn't really done anything wrong.

When had Dave last put himself at risk by going out on a job? It had been years since he'd done anything like that. He stayed safely holed-up at home, or here in his little office, counting his money. It was old-silly-bollocks, Gary, who did all the grunt work and never got any thanks for it.

"Just for once, Dave, I'd like a little bit of appreciation. Does it really make you feel that good to put me down all the time?"

Dave shook his head in disbelief. "What are you going on about? I pay you handsomely for what you do. Nobody else would put up with all your rubbish. You let me down that night, Gary. And worse than that, you left a man lying on the floor, bleeding. One of our own."

"See! This is exactly what I'm talking about. You're blaming me again. I didn't bleeding well know he got shot, did I? I couldn't see anything. It was a nightmare, absolute chaos. The coppers were going to arrive at any second, so I did the only sensible thing I could. I left."

"Funny," Dave said, narrowing his eyes, "Charlie told me he called out to you. He told you he'd been shot, and you looked at him and then ran away."

Gary sprung to his feet. "He's lying!"

Dave said nothing but raised one eyebrow as he stared at Gary.

Gary slammed his hand on the desk. "Don't tell me you believe that little bastard over your own brother?"

Still Dave didn't say anything, and now Gary was getting really wound up.

He did see Charlie on the floor, but he wasn't about to admit it. Besides, it wasn't his fault the stupid bastard went and got himself shot. But that wasn't the important thing here. The outrageous thing was the fact that Dave believed Charlie's word over his. He trusted someone else over his own brother.

"Dad would be turning in his grave if he could see you treating me this way," Gary said spitefully.

Dave shook his head. "These screwups of yours keep happening, Gary. I want to trust you. I'd love to have a brother to share all this with, but when you keep going off the deep end, I can't rely on you. When you look me straight in the eye and lie to me, how am I supposed to trust you?"

Gary slumped back down in his chair. This was going far worse than he'd expected. He'd love to slam his fist into his brother's face and run out of there, but he couldn't. Dave controlled the purse strings, and he was bloody tight with his money. Gary needed cash, so he was going to have to listen to this little lecture yet again.

Dave leaned forward, propping his elbows on the desk. "Tell me the truth, Gary. Are you using? Did you take something that night?"

Gary licked his lips, trying to work out whether or not he should tell Dave the truth. He had had a touch of cocaine that night just to see him through. He'd had a long session the night before, and he was tired and hungover. He'd just needed a little bit of coke to perk himself up. It wasn't as if it was dangerous.

"I just had a little sniff. It was nothing. It keeps me alert."

Dave shook his head in disgust. "When are you going to learn that stuff makes you paranoid? You can't operate properly when you're on it. And if you've come back here thinking I'm going to give you money just so you can snort it up your nostrils, you've got another think coming, son."

Gary felt a cold rush of panic flood over him. No. Dave couldn't cut him off. He wouldn't. How the hell did Dave expect him to survive?

"You are joking aren't you?"

Dave shook his head. "I'm sorry, Gary, but this is the last straw. There is no place for cowards here."

Gary got to his feet, placed his hands on the desk and pushed his face into Dave's. "You're going to regret this!" he spat.

With a snarl of frustration, Gary stormed out of the office, slamming the door behind him so hard the windows rattled.

32

AFTER HIS BROTHER HAD LEFT, Dave leaned back in his chair and sighed. Gary would never know how much it hurt Dave to cut him off, but it had been brewing for years. No matter how much Dave encouraged him to take the business seriously, Gary just wanted to spend money on booze, girls and drugs. He didn't want to make anything of his life.

He seemed to be missing the drive and motivation to want to be someone in the East End. He liked the respect that came with being Dave Carter's brother, of course, but he didn't want to put in the work to become a man of influence in his own right.

Dave wondered if it was his fault. As the elder brother, he'd always looked out for Gary, making sure he wasn't bullied and even doling out his pocket money.

Gary had been much younger when their father had died, so Dave had taken on the paternal role, trying to guide Gary as he grew up. He'd obviously made a monumental mistake somewhere along the way because Gary had turned into a nasty, selfish piece of work who Dave was ashamed to call his brother.

Dave ran a weary hand over his face. Hopefully, this shock

to the system would be just what Gary needed to get his life back on track. Dave had been telling the truth when he told Gary he wanted nothing more than a brother he could share this with. He would have loved to have had a brotherly relationship like the Krays, to have someone there he could rely on, no matter what. It must be a comforting thought to know there was someone who always had your back, Dave thought. But he would never trust Gary enough for that. He trusted Charlie Williams far more than he'd ever trusted Gary.

Dave leaned forward and tried to concentrate on the notes he'd been making. He needed to push Gary out of his mind and focus as he had a very important decision to make. Martin Morton was getting far too big for his boots.

Two big gangs trying to operate in overlapping areas in the East End was a recipe for disaster.

And Dave was determined to emerge the winner in this particular fight. He knew he needed to hit Martin Morton where it hurt. The key to that was money. He needed to target his suppliers.

Dave looked down at his notes. He'd written down everything he knew about Morton's suppliers. He intended to target them one by one, so slowly that Morton wouldn't even realise what was happening until it was too late.

Dave nodded and looked down at the list again. It felt good to work like this. With a clear head and a definite plan. It had never failed him in the past, and he was sure he would be successful this time, too.

He'd seen off many wannabe gangsters over the last few years. He had to give Martin Morton credit; he was the most serious threat he'd come across so far, but Dave would still win out. He always did.

He called Brian into the office along with a couple of younger men he'd decided to promote. With Gary out of the picture and Charlie inside, he needed to let a couple more men into the inner circle.

The two new boys entered the room looking extremely nervous.

Brian followed them in, his bulk and broad shoulders forcing him to turn sideways to pass through the doorway.

"There's no need to look worried, boys." Dave began addressing the two new recruits. "I've been pleased with your work, and I've decided you've earned the chance to prove yourselves."

The two new boys exchanged excited glances, and Dave hoped he was right in trusting them. It was a risk, but all business involved calculated risks.

Not for the first time, he regretted how things had turned out with Frank the Face. He hadn't found out the whole story yet, but it was looking more and more likely that Frank was dead.

"I've got some news," Dave said. "It isn't public knowledge yet, so I'm going to need you to keep this under your hats, but you will have probably noticed that Frank's been missing for the past couple of days."

Everyone in the room stared at Dave.

He thought they probably realised what was coming next. He hated to be the one to break the news. Frank had been a very good worker, and he'd worked for Dave for a number of years.

"Martin Morton killed Frank."

The two new boys were so shocked they couldn't say

anything. They just stood there with their mouths open, but Brian took a step forward shaking his head. "How do you know? Are you sure?"

Dave nodded. "I got the news from one of the inspectors on our payroll. And let's just say I have another informant, someone very close to Martin Morton." Dave allowed himself a little smile.

Brian was quiet for a moment, looking up at the ceiling and Dave could almost hear the cogs turning in the man's brain as he tried to work out who Dave's informant was.

"Have you turned someone in Morton's gang?" Brian finally asked.

Dave kept his face blank. He kept the identity of his informants on a need-to-know basis, and Brian and the other lads definitely did not need to know the identity of this particular informant.

"That's not important," Dave said impatiently. "What is important is that we are going to hit Martin where it hurts."

"We should bloody kill him," Brian said passionately. He'd liked Frank, and the two men had been close.

Dave stood up from behind his desk and walked around it before placing a hand on the squat man's shoulder. "I know how you're feeling, Brian. And I promise you we will get Martin Morton for this. He won't get away with it."

33

KATHLEEN HADN'T SEEN HER FRIEND Linda for
months. Now that she no longer worked at Bevels, Kathleen
spent her days looking in the shops up the West End and
stopping in fancy places for lunch. A week ago, she'd taken
tea in Selfridges. She decided she needed a treat and ordered
tea and a scone. But sitting there in the cafe, she felt
strangely out of place, which wasn't helped by the snooty
waitress.

Kathleen had left her half-eaten scone on her plate, and on
the way home, she had popped to Maureen's for pie and
mash.

She felt much more comfortable in the little cafe, but she
wouldn't have admitted that to anyone. Kathleen knew it
would take a little bit of adjustment, but soon her life would
change for good. She couldn't wait to get rid of the grunge of
the East End, but at the moment, she didn't quite fit in up
West End either. Not yet anyway.

Martin had been bunging her a few quid each week, and it
was lovely not to have to worry about money. However,
without having to turn up to work every day, she felt a bit at
a loss for things to do. Especially as she wasn't friends with

Linda anymore.

The novelty of being a kept woman was wearing thin. There was no one to share it with. She remembered the last time she'd gone up the West End with Linda. They'd had a right laugh, making fun of the snobby sales assistants in the shops. With Linda, she hadn't given a rat's arse whether some silly old sales assistant was looking down her nose at them. It didn't seem to matter when she had Linda.

She missed Linda more than she'd ever imagined. She missed the kind, faithful, loyalty Linda's friendship had provided. And she was very surprised that Linda had kept her distance for so long. After that thing with Donavan, Kathleen was convinced it would all blow over in a few weeks, and Linda would be round apologising for overreacting.

Kathleen tightened her coat around her as she walked up the road.

She walked up the path towards the house and let herself in. The door was on the latch as it always was. Mary Diamond never locked the door during the day.

"It's only me, Mum," Kathleen called out.

Kathleen put the bag full of clothes she'd bought on the floor and started to take off her coat. Mary appeared in the doorway. Strands of her greying hair had escaped her bun. She wore an apron and held a large ladle in her hand.

Mary glanced disapprovingly at the carrier bag on the floor. "I don't suppose you got anything for the baby, did you?"

Kathleen sighed. Not this again. "There's plenty of time for all that," she said dismissively.

Kathleen really didn't see the point in buying all sorts of

fancy clothes for the baby. It would grow out of anything she bought within a couple of weeks anyway. She didn't see the irony in buying dresses that didn't even fit her at the moment. She was confident she would regain her figure as soon as the baby was born.

"I've made shepherd's pie," Mary said. "Why don't we sit in the kitchen and I'll serve up?"

Kathleen left the bag where it was, hung her coat on the peg and followed Mary into the kitchen.

She sat down at the table as her mother waited on her, dishing up a large portion of shepherd's pie along with some boiled carrots.

"I thought we should sort out a few things in preparation," Mary said after Kathleen had taken her first bite of the shepherds' pie. "It won't be long now, and we'll have to think about what we're going to do when you go back to work."

Kathleen's fork clattered against her plate. "What do you mean?" she demanded.

"Well, you can hardly take the baby with you when you go out to work, can you? So that means I'll have to stay home and look after it. That's going to take a bit of rearranging because you know I cover the stall for Theresa two days a week. I suppose I can take the baby with me eventually, but not when it's very young."

Kathleen pushed her plate away. She couldn't believe her mother had the gall to try and run her life for her. Kathleen had absolutely no intention of going back to work. She had planned for Martin to provide for her and the baby.

"You've got it wrong, Mum. I'm not going back to work. I'm looking after the baby after it's born."

"And just how are we supposed to get by with no money?" Mary asked cuttingly.

"Martin will pay. It's his kid, and he'll provide for it."

Mary huffed. "I'll believe that when I see it. I know his type. He's paying you a bit of money now to keep it quiet, but he will soon get bored of that and then where will we be?"

Her mother could be so spiteful. Kathleen shoved the chair back from the table, scraping it along the floor and stood up. "I'm going out."

"Where on earth are you going at this time? And you haven't even finished dinner."

"I need a bit of peace and quiet," Kathleen said and stormed out of the kitchen.

She'd only taken a couple of steps along the road when she ran straight into Linda.

Kathleen blinked rapidly, hoping Linda wouldn't see the tears in her eyes.

For a moment, she thought that Linda might cross the road and deliberately ignore her, but she didn't.

Her hair was gleaming, and she wore a smart dark brown coat that suited her creamy complexion and matched her dark brown shiny hair.

"You look nice, Linda. Are you off out?" Kathleen asked hoping that Linda would stop and chat for a while.

Linda looked tense. "Yes," she said shortly, obviously not wanting to get into a long conversation with Kathleen.

"With Donovan?"

Linda gave her a scathing look. "No!"

She glared angrily at Kathleen for a moment before she continued, "I'm going to the pictures with some girls from work."

Kathleen nodded sadly. It seemed Linda was finding it far easier to make friends without Kathleen around. Kathleen had always found it hard to make friends. Linda was really the only friend she'd had since she'd been at school.

Linda's expression softened. "Are you feeling okay?" She looked down at Kathleen's bump beneath her coat.

Kathleen smiled. "Not too bad, although I'm fed up with being the size of a house." Kathleen's voice took on a dreamy tone as she continued, "Martin can't wait until I get my figure back of course."

Linda's mouth set in a firm line as she stared at her friend and then she said, "Martin? He's still on the scene then?"

Kathleen bristled. "Of course, he is. He is the baby's father, isn't he?"

Kathleen tried to relax a little. Linda did still care about her. Maybe she was ready to put everything behind them, and they could be friends again just like before. "He's ever so good, Linda. He gives me money each week, and it's only a matter of time, of course, before he leaves Babs."

Linda's eyes widened, and she shook her head. "You're delusional. He's not going to leave his wife. You can't really believe that."

"What would you know?" Kathleen asked. "For your information, he's trying to get us a place. Obviously, we can't live over the club with the baby. That's entirely unsuitable, but as soon as he finds a place, we'll be moving in together," Kathleen insisted, although Martin had said nothing of the sort.

Kathleen wasn't sure why she was lying. She just couldn't stand Linda feeling sorry for her.

"So you're still living at your mum's now then?" Linda asked.

"Not for long," Kathleen said crisply. "And a good thing, too. She's driving me round the bend at the moment."

Linda sighed. "She cares about you, Kath. More than Martin ever will. You're lucky to have her."

Kathleen didn't appreciate being told she should appreciate her mother more. "What's come over you? Why are you suddenly my mother's appreciation society?"

Linda looked at her sadly. "I just think you should live in the real world. It's not so bad. You've got people who care about you." Linda reached out and put her hand on Kathleen's arm. "I worry about you, Kath."

Kathleen narrowed her eyes. Linda worried about her? The very idea was ridiculous. She must be jealous. That was the only explanation. Linda was jealous that Kathleen was making a life for herself.

"I'm perfectly fine, thank you, Linda. And I certainly don't need you to worry about me."

"Fine. Goodbye then." Linda squared her shoulders and walked off.

Kathleen turned around and watched her friend walk away. She had so much to look forward to now with the baby and Martin, so she really couldn't understand why she felt a sharp pang of regret as Linda walked away.

34

WHEN DAVE CARTER CAME HOME for lunch, his wife Sandra put a cheese and pickle sandwich on the table in front of him and then massaged her back.

"Are you all right, love?"

Sandra shook her head. "I'm run off my feet. Lillian's come down with measles now, so they're both supposed to be in bed, but the pair of them are running me ragged."

Dave tucked into his cheese and pickle sandwich.

"Why don't you take the weight off, love?" he said, nodding to the empty chair beside him at the kitchen table.

Sandra looked around at the mountain of washing she was supposed to be doing, but then she sighed and sat down next to Dave.

"How's work?" Sandra asked, rubbing a tired hand through her hair.

"It's going well. We're opening the new car workshop tomorrow. It's been a lot of work, but I think it'll be worth it." He took another bite of sandwich and then looked up. "It's the way of the future. Everyone will have a car soon... Hey, Sandra, love, what's wrong?"

A tear trickled down Sandra's cheek. "I don't care about

the bleeding future, Dave. I care about the here and now. The kids are ill, and I've got so much to do here. I can't manage. Can't you stay here this afternoon and look after the kids. You're so good with them."

Dave reached out and took his wife's hand in his.

"Of course, I will. I'll pop back after lunch and tell Brian he's in charge. I can trust him to hold the fort for a few hours. I'll tuck the kids up in bed and tell them to stay there before I go, and then I'll get some chips for tea, so you just put your feet up this afternoon.

"Thanks, love," Sandra said tearfully.

Dave polished off his sandwich then leaned over and kissed her on the cheek before standing up and making his way to Trevor's room.

The little boy's eyes were half closed as he looked up at his father. "Dad, I don't feel very well."

"I know you don't, son. You just need to get some sleep, and you'll be right as rain in a couple of days."

Dave reached out and touched Trevor's forehead. He was warm, but not hot enough to make Dave worry he had a fever. "You get some rest, and we'll have some chips for tea does that sound good?"

Trevor gave a weak little smile, and Dave pulled up the covers, making sure the little boy's body was fully wrapped up.

Before Dave even left the room, Trevor had fallen asleep.

In complete contrast to her little brother, Lillian was full of beans, sitting upright in bed, playing with a doll.

"Daddy!" she said excitedly when Dave came in the room.

Dave put a finger to his lips. "Now what are you doing up playing? You're supposed to be going to sleep. You're not well."

Lillian flopped back against the pillows and pouted. "It's so boring."

Dave sat beside her on the bed.

"Come on, young lady. Get under those covers and close your eyes. The doctor said sleep is the best thing for you."

"I think I could probably fall asleep if you told me a story," Lillian said, and Dave had to smile at her persistence.

"All right then, one story and then you go to sleep, promise?"

Lillian nodded happily and snuggled under the covers.

"Well," Dave began. "Once upon a time, there was a girl called Cinderella. She was a princess."

Lillian's face puckered in a frown, but she stayed quiet to let her father continue.

"But there was a nasty old queen who didn't believe that Cinderella was really a princess so she decided to put a pea under her mattress because if Cinderella really was a princess she'd be able to feel it."

Lillian sat bolt upright in bed. "No! That's not right, Daddy! You're mixing up the stories. *Cinderella* is a different story to the *Princess and the Pea*. Cinderella had the ugly sisters!"

"Is that right?" Dave said chucking her under the chin.

"Yes," Lillian giggled.

"Well, I don't think there's much wrong with you, is there? You're still a clever little thing."

Sandra's voice suddenly boomed out from the kitchen. "Lillian! I hope you're not giving your father the runaround! I expect you to be asleep in five minutes flat."

Dave pulled the funny face at Lillian. "That's blown it," he said. "I'd better tuck you in. Now get some sleep, sweetheart." He kissed her cheek and pulled the blankets up to her chin.

When he returned to the kitchen, Sandra looked up at him. She was trying to keep her face stern, but she couldn't quite quash the smile that spread over her face. "You spoil the girl."

"Never," Dave said, grinning. "How about I spoil you a bit now, eh? Come here."

Dave opened up his arms and pulled Sandra in for a cuddle. She rested her head against his chest as he stroked her hair.

He planted a kiss on her forehead and said, "I don't tell you this enough, love, but you and the kids are my world."

Kathleen Diamond gave birth to a healthy baby boy after being in labour for twenty-four hours. She was now lying in a hospital bed, thoroughly worn out. She'd thought the pain would never end, and the whole ordeal had left her exhausted.

It was visiting hours, and her mother was perched on a chair by her bedside. They'd taken Kathleen's little boy off to the baby ward, and her mother had just been along to see him.

"Honestly, love, he is ever so handsome. He'll break some hearts when he's older," Mary Diamond said.

Kathleen smiled weakly. When she'd looked down at the little baby's bright red face, she'd noticed that he had a mop of dark hair, very like Martin Morton. She hadn't seen any of her own features in the baby, but it was early days.

"Yes, he does look like Martin, doesn't he?"

The smile slid from Mary Diamond's face. "Actually, I was thinking he looked quite like your Great Uncle Fred. He had very dark hair, too."

"Well, I hope he does look like Martin," Kathleen said.

Martin Morton was much more likely to fork out money if the baby looked like him. In Kathleen's dreams, the kid grew up to be amazingly talented and gorgeous, and Martin grew to adore him.

She leaned back against the pillows. "He hasn't been around asking after me, has he?"

Kathleen hadn't heard anything from Martin, and as she knew her mother didn't like him, she wouldn't put it past her to make sure he stayed away.

Mary frowned. "No, I haven't seen hide nor hair of him. I wouldn't be surprised if we never see him again."

"Don't be ridiculous. It's his son," Kathleen snapped, but truthfully she was a little worried. She didn't know what she would do if Martin decided he didn't want to support the baby.

She'd hoped he'd come with a bunch of flowers, like one of the other fathers had done. The sister on the ward had forbidden him from bringing them in, but Kathleen thought it was ever so romantic that he'd tried. It was the thought that counted, and she wasn't sure if Martin had thought of her and the baby once.

She'd heard through the grapevine that Babs had given birth to a little girl just days earlier. They'd named her Emily.

All of the other women on the ward were married, and they'd had their husbands to visit. Kathleen felt quite out of place with only her mum coming to see her. She felt as if all the other women on the ward were judging her.

"So what are you going to call him?" Mary asked, breaking into Kathleen's thoughts.

Kathleen chewed on her lip. She'd been hoping to talk the matter over with Martin and get his input on the baby's name, but it didn't look like he was interested.

"I quite like the name Jimmy. James Diamond, and I'll call him Jimmy."

Mary smiled. Her own father had been named James, and everyone had called him Jimmy. Touched, she reached over and patted her daughter's hand. "It suits him. Jimmy Diamond. Perfect."

"Did the nurse tell you how long they expect me to be in here?" Kathleen asked.

She couldn't wait to get out and get things sorted. When she was back home, she'd be able to talk to Martin properly and make sure he understood his responsibilities. Stuck inside the hospital, she didn't have a hope in hell of doing that.

"You'll be here at least another week yet," Mary said. "To make sure you know how to feed the little mite and change him, that sort of thing."

Kathleen's shoulders slumped, and she sighed. A whole week stuck in the hospital! How would she cope?

"Are you feeling all right, sweetheart?"

Kathleen nodded. "Just a bit tired."

She leaned back on the pillows and shut her eyes. They'd be bringing the baby back round for his feed soon, and she intended to catch up on her beauty sleep. After she left, she was planning to go straight to see Martin Morton, and she needed to look her best for that.

35

THE FOLLOWING DAY, DAVE CARTER was back at his new workshop for the grand opening. Both the kids had been feeling a little better that morning after a good night's sleep, and no doubt within a few days, they would be back at school.

Dave gazed proudly around the workshop. It had been kitted out with all the latest machinery, and no expense had been spared.

Carter's Cars. Dave looked up at the simple sign over the door. His old man would be proud if he could see him now. Dave was planning to keep this business legit. Mostly, anyway. Obviously, he'd have to spend a few quid here and there for bribes, but there would be no stolen motors or any of that sort of stuff going on in his new business.

He'd bunged some money to a friend of his to assure a contract with a group of black cabs, and he's also secured a contract from a small bus firm, who arranged things like day trips to Southend. That would be his bread-and-butter work.

Dave grinned. The sky was the limit, and he intended to expand soon. He would have places all over the East End and then maybe even other places in the country.

Brian stood by his side, and Dave slapped him on the back. "Thanks for yesterday, Brian. You did a great job holding things together for me."

"Not a problem, Dave," Brian said, grinning broadly. "It really does look good, doesn't it?"

The mechanics had arrived for work, dressed in their brand-new navy blue overalls with Carter's Cars stitched above the breast pockets.

Dave gave them a little guided tour around the workshop, then turned to them and asked, "So what do you men think?"

The man he'd employed as the supervisor was first to speak up. "I can say without a doubt it's the best equipped workshop I've ever worked in. Thank you for the opportunity, Mr. Carter."

"Just do me proud boys, okay?"

He turned to Brian. "What do you say to going for a drink to celebrate?"

"Sounds like a smashing idea."

But before Dave and Brian had even turned around there was a voice shouting for Dave. A little boy ran into the workshop, panting for breath.

"What are you doing here?" Brian boomed. "This isn't a bleeding playground. Go on, skedaddle."

The little boy ignored Brian and ran up to Dave. "Mr. Carter...Mr. Carter, come quick! Something bad has happened, and you've got to go home."

Dave stared down at the little boy's dirty face. He'd recognised him from somewhere. He was one of the neighbours' boys.

"What's happened?"

The little boy shrugged. "I was playing outside your house, and Mrs. Carter told me to come and get you. She said it was very important. Something bad has happened."

Dave didn't bother to ask any more questions and strode quickly outside the workshop, breaking into a jog. Luckily the workshop was only a few minutes' walk from home.

Brian tried to jog after him, but he was a big bloke and didn't find it easy to keep up. "Anything I can do Dave?" he wheezed as he tried to catch Dave.

"Just keep an eye on the workshop, Brian," Dave called over his shoulder and then picked up speed until he was running flat-out.

When Dave burst through his front door, he immediately knew something was wrong. There were people in the house he didn't recognise.

From the hallway, he saw a woman with dyed red hair sat at his kitchen table with her arm around Sandra. As he got closer, he realised it was Rita from next door.

A tall, skinny man in a brown suit, stood by the sink. He definitely didn't recognise him.

"What the hell is going on?" Dave demanded.

The tall man stepped forward and looked like he was about to say something, but Sandra got there first.

She let out a wail. "Dave it's Lillian. I went into her bedroom, and she was all limp. She wouldn't wake up."

Dave didn't wait for the rest of the story. He quickly turned around and rushed up the stairs to Lillian's bedroom.

His little girl lay back on the bed as if she was sleeping peacefully. Other than a few spots scattered over her face and arms, she looked exactly the same as she always did. Dave rushed to her bedside and shook her arm gently.

"Lillian! Lillian, wake up. It's daddy."

But Lillian didn't wake up.

When Dave realised Sandra, Rita and the tall, thin man were standing behind him in the doorway, he turned around to face them.

"Why how long has she been like this?" He couldn't understand why they were just standing around doing nothing.

"I found her an hour ago," Sandra said in a trembling voice.

She shook her head, and then Rita spoke up, "She called me, and I went to get the doctor straight away." She turned to the tall, lanky man beside her in the brown suit.

Dave's blood turned to ice in his veins.

"I'm terribly sorry, Mr. Carter," the tall man said. "It was too late when I got here."

Dave's mind wouldn't process the doctor's words. He just wouldn't let them sink in. He pushed back the blankets and scooped up his daughter in his arms. "Why are you all standing there like a bunch of lemons? She needs the hospital, doesn't she? Quick, out of my way."

Before Dave could pass through the door, the doctor put his hands firmly on his shoulders. "Listen to me, Mr. Carter. It's too late. I'm very sorry, but Lillian has passed on."

Dave shook his head. What was the stupid pillock on about?

He looked down at Lillian in his arms and then held her up so the doctor could see her. "She's just asleep. Does she really look dead to you? She's still warm for God's sake."

Sandra was openly sobbing now, and Rita put her arm around her and led her away.

The doctor said nothing for a moment. He looked at Dave with sad, grey eyes and then carefully guided Dave back towards Lillian's bed.

"It's time to put her down now, Mr. Carter."

With shaking hands, for once in his life, Dave did as he was told. He carefully laid his little girl back in her bed, pulling up the covers one last time.

36

KATHLEEN WAS FINALLY GOING HOME. She'd been in hospital for over a week. The sister on the ward had wanted her to remain for another day or so, to make sure that she'd properly bonded with the baby. But there was no chance of that. Kathleen wasn't staying there a second longer than she had to.

After she had gotten back home, she decided maybe she'd been a little hasty. She was back in her old bedroom, with a little crib set up against the wall for young Jimmy. It was cramped and miserable.

Kathleen glanced through the rain-splattered window out onto the line of dreary houses opposite and looked at the grey street beyond.

She was sick of this place. She was going to get out of there the first chance she got.

She needed to see Martin Morton. The selfish bastard hadn't even bothered to come and see his son once.

He obviously believed he could treat Kathleen like dirt and she wouldn't put up a fight. Well, she wasn't about to take it lying down, not now that she had Jimmy to think about.

She looked down at the baby in the crib, his flushed cheeks and his dark hair. He hadn't been an easy baby so far. He was up most of the night screaming the place down.

Even the nurses had found him a difficult baby. All Jimmy did was eat, sleep or scream.

At least he was quite a good looking baby. She'd seen some at the hospital who were downright ugly. She wanted to play on Martin's ego, and so she wanted Jimmy to look his best when he first saw his father.

Jimmy stirred in his sleep again, and Kathleen held her breath. Too late. The baby began to scream the place down. Kathleen sighed. It was never ending.

She got up and walked over to the crib, scooping Jimmy out.

"Mum," Kathleen called as she carried the baby down the stairs carefully. "Can you look after Jimmy? I've already fed him. I've absolutely no idea why he's decided to cry again. I just want to pop out for a little while."

Mary Diamond took her grandson from Kathleen's arms. "There now, what's all this fuss, Jimmy," she said, cradling the little boy and rocking him in her arms.

"Where are you off to?"

Kathleen deliberately ignored her mother's question. "I won't be long."

In the hallway, she paused and looked at her reflection in the mirror hanging on the wall. She carefully applied some pink lipstick. She was well aware she wasn't looking her best. She had bags under eyes, and she hadn't slept properly since Jimmy was born.

But that couldn't be helped. She left the house and headed in the direction of Martin's club. It didn't matter how much

Martin wanted to ignore Jimmy. The fact was the baby existed, and Martin had to pay for it. This time, Kathleen wasn't going to take no for an answer.

It was mid-afternoon, and the club wasn't open yet. Kathleen hammered on the door, and after a minute or so Big Tim opened up.

He looked down at her, his big face solemn.

"Is Martin about? I just need a quick word." Kathleen said, trying to peer around Tim and look into the club.

Tim didn't budge, and he didn't invite her in, even though the rain was falling steadily now, and Kathleen was getting absolutely drenched.

Kathleen tried to smile at him as if she wasn't at all bothered by this slight, and this was all perfectly normal. "I'm getting a bit wet out here. Is it all right if I come in for five minutes?"

Big Tim shook his head. "Sorry, love. I'm under orders not to let anyone in during the afternoons. Martin's not here anyway."

Kathleen clenched her teeth. She wouldn't put it past Big Tim to be feeding her a lie.

Martin was probably upstairs right now.

"I really won't take long. I just need a quick word." She lifted her foot and tried to step inside, but Big Tim blocked her path. "I said he isn't here."

Kathleen cursed under her breath.

Finally, as if he'd taken pity on her, Big Tim said, "He's taken Babs and the kids out to the country for a couple of days. They're looking at the new house."

Kathleen felt like the wind had been knocked out of her as Big Tim shut the door in her face. Was Martin moving to the country?

She turned away and walked back home, barely noticing the rain seeping through her clothes.

She'd just turned the corner and was only a few yards from her front door when a thought occurred to her.

This house in the country wasn't just for Martin. He probably wanted Babs and her little brats out of the way. She smiled. With Babs and the kids out in the country, and Martin still in London, things would be a lot easier for Kathleen.

By the time she stepped back inside, she was dripping wet. But she didn't care. Things were looking up.

The day of Lillian's funeral would haunt Dave Carter for the rest of his life. The day had dawned bleak and grey, and as they lowered Lillian's tiny coffin into the ground, the heavens opened, soaking everyone attending the service.

Beside him, Sandra gave a raw, strangled sob. He wrapped his arm around her and felt his heart break in two. They hadn't brought Trevor to the funeral. Rita, from next door, was minding him, but the poor kid didn't know what was going on.

Dave had caught him poking his head into his sister's bedroom, not quite understanding or believing that Lillian had really gone. It was a hard thing for a kid to get his head around. Dave was finding it hard enough himself.

The horror he'd felt at that dreadful moment when he'd realised there was nothing he could do to save his daughter wouldn't leave him. He'd had nightmares every night since.

He'd wanted to hate that doctor. He'd wanted to punch him into next week, but he couldn't because deep down he knew the doctor had done his best. Lillian was dead before he'd even arrived.

The doctor had sat beside Dave for an hour afterwards, patiently answering all his questions and demands.

He demanded to know how on earth it was possible that Lillian had died when just yesterday she was full of beans. She hadn't even been that ill. Trevor's initial symptoms had been much worse.

The doctor had explained that sometimes these things happen, and there was no predicting them. He believed that Lillian had suffered from encephalitis, a fancy word for swelling on the brain. It wasn't common, but it happened.

The doctor tried to reassure Dave that he was sure Lillian hadn't felt any pain and had simply gone to sleep. Dave hoped to God that was true.

As they turned away from the graveside, he tried to support Sandra's weight. She was beside herself with grief and could hardly walk.

When they were halfway back to the church, she gave out a sharp cry, different to her previous sobbing, and Dave looked down at his wife.

Sandra was clutching her stomach. "The baby!"

The next few minutes passed in a blur as everyone helped to bundle Sandra and Dave into the back of one of the workshop's motors and sent them off to the hospital.

Although he murmured reassuring words and held his wife's hand in the back of the car, Dave didn't feel like he was really there. Somehow, he was detached from all of it.

"Nothing is ready," Sandra muttered. "I haven't laundered all the clothes, and we haven't even given a thought what to call him or her," she said, looking down at her bump. Then she doubled over as another wave of pain hit her.

Dave felt a shiver of impatience. What did it matter? It shocked him to the core when he realised he didn't want this child, not now. It would forever be tied to the loss of Lillian. It felt like his whole body had been filled with despair, infecting every good thought and turning it around into something bad.

He rubbed Sandra's shoulders. "It'll be all right. You'll see," he said, but even as he said the words, he could feel the cold venom in his heart. He didn't want this child. No baby could ever take Lillian's place.

37

KATHLEEN WAS ABSOLUTELY FURIOUS. SHE knew Martin must be back from the country by now, but he still hadn't shown his face. She gazed down at little Jimmy, who after his last little screaming session, had finally gone to sleep.

She knew now that Martin was not taking her seriously. If he thought she would go away quietly, then he had another think coming. It was early evening, and she knew the club would just be opening. The club was no place for a baby, but Martin really hadn't left her much choice.

Kathleen reached for a blanket and started to wrap Jimmy up and then transferred him to his pram.

Mary looked up from her knitting. "What are you doing?"

"I need some fresh air," Kathleen said. "I won't be long."

"Do you want me to look after Jimmy?"

Kathleen shook her head. "No, I'm taking him with me."

Mary looked out of the window and then back to Jimmy's pram. "Well, keep him wrapped up. There's a chill in the air this evening."

Kathleen walked briskly along the road, not wanting to give herself a chance to change her mind. The club would be busy and full of people. People who would love to gossip about her situation. This wasn't exactly the way she planned everything to go, but it was all Martin's fault. He could have come to see them quietly, and nobody would have had to know. He was forcing her to do this.

There was only a short line outside the club, and Kathleen wheeled the pram right up to the doormen. She couldn't see Big Tim, and she didn't recognise the two men on the door.

She cleared her throat, feeling embarrassed because the line of people were gawping at her. "I'm Kathleen Diamond," she said. "I'm here to see Martin."

She leaned on the pram, to tip the wheels up, so she could get inside the door, but the two men stood in front of her blocking her way.

"No kids in here."

Kathleen was close to tears now. "I need to see him," she hissed. "So you get him out here now to talk to me, or I'm going in there." She jabbed a finger in the direction of the club.

"No, you're not," one of the doormen said, standing beside the other man blocking her path. "We are under orders not to let you in."

Kathleen's cheeks flamed with embarrassment. How could Martin treat her like this? The bastard. And what about poor Jimmy? He'd never done anything to deserve this.

"This," Kathleen began in a high-pitched shriek, pointing at the baby. "Is Martin Morton's son. I'm here so we can see him."

Everyone in the line outside the club was now looking in Kathleen's direction, and quite a few people inside the club were now peering through the windows and gathering by the door to see what all the fuss was about.

Kathleen felt her lower lip wobble.

One of the doormen took pity on her and patted her on the shoulder. "Look, it's not the time or the place. Why don't you see him tomorrow, eh?"

It slowly sunk in. Kathleen was never going to get past these two on the door, and all she was doing was making a spectacle of herself.

She took a step back, pulling the pram with her, and she just happened to look upstairs. A curtain twitched and then closed, but not quickly enough.

Martin bloody Morton had been up there, looking down at her, enjoying every moment of her humiliation.

Kathleen was fuming as she tightly gripped the pram, wheeled it around and stalked off up the road.

But she wasn't going home. She was going to get her own back on Martin Morton, and she was going to do it now.

Kathleen walked along Bread Street looking for number thirty-six. She'd never visited Martin's house before, but she knew the address. The door had been painted in thick, green, glossy paint. It was a large three-storey townhouse, much larger than the house Kathleen shared with her mother, Mary.

Kathleen began to feel a little less confident. The last time she'd seen Babs, the woman had scared the life out of her. But she glanced down at little Jimmy lying quietly in his pram and decided she had to act now. She had a responsibility to him.

She raised a hand and rapped twice on the door.

She could hear the laughing and joking of children from

inside and then held her breath as the door opened.

The house was warm and well lit, and Kathleen felt a pang of resentment.

When Babs saw her standing on the doorstep, her eyes widened, but otherwise, she showed no sign outward sign of her emotions at all.

Babs crossed her arms over her chest. "What are you doing here?" she asked in a low, dangerous voice.

Kathleen's knees were practically knocking together, but she gathered up her courage and stuck her chin in the air. "We have a matter to discuss," she said. "May I come in?"

Babs pursed her red lips in a tight line then looked across the street and saw the curtains twitching. The lady opposite was having a right old nosy, so Babs nodded, and stood back to let Kathleen enter.

Kathleen gathered Jimmy in her arms and left the empty pram against the wall outside.

The house was lovely and warm and had been freshly decorated. This was the kind of place she and Jimmy should be living in. Martin could clearly afford it.

"Hello," said a little voice, and Kathleen looked down to see Martin's daughter staring up at her. "Can I see your baby?" she asked.

Kathleen didn't know where to look or what to say. Babs stood rigidly by her side.

Finally, Kathleen kneeled down, so that Ruby could get a look at little Jimmy.

She reached out and stroked his cheek with her chubby hand and then grinned up at Kathleen.

"Go in the front room, Ruby, and play with your brother. Keep an eye on baby Emily. I'm going to talk to this lady in the kitchen."

Ruby did as she was told, and Kathleen followed Babs into the kitchen.

Babs closed the door behind them so that the children couldn't overhear.

"You've got some bloody nerve coming here, lady," Babs snarled as soon as the door was shut.

Kathleen clutched Jimmy to her chest. "I didn't have a choice."

Babs crossed her arms and leaned back against the kitchen worktop. "Explain yourself."

Kathleen licked her lips and then held up Jimmy. "Martin got me pregnant," she said. "This is Jimmy."

Babs sneered at her. "And what do you expect me to do about it?"

This wasn't going the way Kathleen had planned. She'd expected a little bit of anger from Babs, but she'd hoped Babs would be a little more sympathetic. After all, Martin had treated them both badly.

"I was naive," Kathleen said. "And he took advantage of me. I'm sorry. I never meant to hurt you. I had no idea you were pregnant."

Babs's expression was still hard.

Kathleen thought frantically. She didn't know what else to say. She could only hope that this surprise visit had been enough, to shock Martin into action. Once Babs told Martin about Kathleen's visit, surely that would be enough to force Martin to come and talk to her.

"It's hard to look after a baby on my own. You know what it's like. It's worse for me as I don't have a job, and I'm living at my mother's," Kathleen said, pleading for Babs to understand and offer a little bit of sympathy.

But she was out of luck. Babs shook her head. "I can't believe your nerve. You've actually come around here to ask me to help you, haven't you?"

Kathleen swallowed hard. "I thought you could just have a word with him. You know, tell him that Jimmy is his responsibility."

"Get out of here before I throw you out, you stupid cow," Babs roared.

Kathleen didn't need to be told twice. She ran as fast as she could out of the kitchen and along the hallway, practically throwing poor Jimmy back in his pram before hightailing it up the road.

38

THEY HAD ALL LEFT HIM. His mum, his dad and even his sister. And to make it worse, they'd left him with Rita from next door. He didn't like Rita. She smelled funny. Mummy had said that was because she wore too much scent, but Trevor just didn't like her.

Rita was calling his name now, but she'd never find him. He was hiding in his secret place. The same place he'd hidden during hide and seek games with Lillian, and she'd never managed to find him.

He shifted his position to get more comfortable beneath a pile of blankets at the bottom of the wardrobe.

Everything had gone crazy recently. Just after they'd been ill with measles. Mummy said Lillian had gone to heaven, but Trevor didn't know whether to believe her or not. All of Lillian's things were still in her bedroom as if she might come back. Trevor thought perhaps she'd gone to heaven for a visit. He liked the idea of that. When she came home, Trevor had lots of questions he'd like to ask.

"Trevor! Trevor!" Rita's voice came bouncing through the walls.

Trevor rearranged his blankets to get more comfortable.

Mummy had said she'd only be an hour, but they'd been gone nearly all day. Trevor had eaten breakfast and lunch, and he knew it was almost dinnertime now because it was getting dark.

He hoped they hadn't gone after Lillian. They'd always preferred Lillian to him, especially his dad.

Trevor felt very sorry for himself and rubbed his eyes with the blanket. He wasn't crying. He didn't cry anymore because he was a big boy.

"Trevor! Where are you, you little bastard?"

Rita was only calling him that because there was nobody else here. She was always nice to him when his mum or dad were around. She wouldn't dare call him a little bastard then. But what if they never came back, and he was stuck with Rita for good?

The hinges on the front door squeaked as they opened, and Trevor's heart soared as he heard the familiar booming voice of his father.

They were back!

Trevor pushed back the blankets and quickly sprung up from his hiding place, carefully climbing out of the wardrobe and shutting the door behind him. He didn't want anything to give away his secret.

As he ran towards the kitchen, he could hear Rita talking, "He's disappeared. I know he's still in the house somewhere because I kept the door locked after last time."

Last time Rita had been asked to look after Trevor, he'd taken himself off to his friend's house down the road, and the whole street had been out looking for him. He'd gotten a slap on the backside from his mother for that one.

Trevor burst into the kitchen, saw his dad standing there

and broke into a broad smile. They hadn't left him. But then he peered behind his father and saw that his mother wasn't there. And he promptly burst into tears.

Dave had a banging headache, and Trevor's screeching went right through him.

He got down on his knees and wrapped his arms around his son. "Calm down, Daddy is here."

He wanted to tell Trevor everything would be all right, but he couldn't because nothing would be all right again.

He scooped the boy up in his arms and stood up.

"Thanks for everything, Rita. I can take it from here."

Rita looked at him dubiously. "Are you sure? I could stick around and prepare something for dinner? I know Sandra probably—"

Dave cut her off. "I can manage. Thanks again." He walked her to the door.

She reached up to ruffle Trevor's hair before she left, but the boy flinched away from her, burrowing his head into Dave's chest.

After Rita had left and Dave had shut the door behind her. He carried his son into the kitchen.

"Now, tell me what's the matter," Dave said although he knew exactly what the matter was. The little boy had just lost his sister.

"Where's Mummy? Has she gone too?"

Dave sat down at the kitchen table and balanced Trevor on his knee. "She'll be back in a week. She's just had your baby brother. We'll go and visit them tomorrow."

Trevor looked up at Dave and blinked. "Is Lillian coming back, too?"

"No, come on, Trevor, we talked about this already. Lillian can't come back. She's gone to heaven with the angels."

Little Trevor's face screwed up as if he was concentrating hard and then he shrugged and nodded as if he accepted what Dave said was true.

Dave wrapped his arms around his son and kissed the top of his head. He needed to be strong for Trevor, Sandra and the new baby. He needed somehow to get back to a normal life, but he didn't know how. He knew he would never feel right again. A part of him would always be missing.

39

AS SOON AS KATHLEEN LEFT, Babs Morton gathered up the children, took them next door and asked old Mrs. Morrison to keep an eye on them.

She then marched straight to Martin's club. It was still drizzling, so she pulled up the collar on her coat. With each step, she imagined stomping Martin's face. It was quite therapeutic.

It only took her a couple of minutes to get to the club. She didn't often make an appearance these days, but everybody knew who she was. She marched up to the doormen, and they stood aside to let her enter.

She didn't even bother to look at their faces as she passed. She was just concerned about getting her hands on Martin. He was going to pay for humiliating her.

She scanned the club, but she couldn't see him, and then she felt a large, meaty hand on her shoulder. She turned around and saw Big Tim standing there. Babs gave him a stiff nod. "Evening, Tim. I need a word with Martin."

Tim nodded. "He's still upstairs. He hasn't come down yet this evening. Would you like to go up?"

The fact that Tim was asking that question told Babs that

Martin didn't have some floozy upstairs with him right now. Now that he'd gotten Kathleen in the family way, Martin had probably dumped her and moved onto some other tart.

"Who else is up there?"

"Tony. They are discussing business, but I'm sure Martin won't mind you interrupting."

Babs didn't give a flying fig whether Martin minded or not.

She pushed up her sleeves. "I'll have a drink. Tell Martin to come down here."

Tim looked taken aback, but after a moment, he nodded and headed off behind the bar. He whispered Babs' drink order to one of the barmaids and then slipped through the door to go and get Martin.

Although the bar was already busy, people made room for Babs. They were all younger than her, Babs noted, sourly. It wasn't like the old days where she could go into Martin's clubs and know everyone by name. These days it was all youngsters and blaring, modern music. All that rock 'n' roll stuff. It made Babs feel old.

The barmaid pushed a port and lemon across the bar, and Babs thanked her and then swallowed half of it down in one gulp.

She didn't want to go upstairs and have this out with Martin. She wanted him to come home tonight. For once, she wanted her husband to be under the same roof as her, so the gossips would be able to see that they were still together and stronger than ever.

It might not be true, but Babs cared about appearances. Fair or not, the woman always got sneered at if her husband strayed away from home.

Martin appeared in the doorway behind the bar and regarded Babs warily.

Babs gave him a tight smile, and Martin sauntered up to her. "Hello, sweetheart. What's wrong?"

There was a time in the early days of their marriage when Martin would have been glad to see her, although that was a long time ago now. Now, when she came to visit him in the evening, he assumed something was wrong. That said it all.

"I'd like you to come home tonight, Martin," Babs said.

She was well aware her voice sounded brittle, but she was doing her best to sound pleasant, even though she really wanted to throw the rest of her port and lemon in his face.

Martin frowned. "I was planning on staying at the club. I'll be working late tonight, and you know I don't like to disturb you."

That was Martin's way of pretending he stayed at the club every night out of consideration for Babs and the children. Even though his bloody club was just around the corner from where they lived.

"I don't care what time you get back, Martin," Babs said. "Just make sure you do."

Martin frowned at the venom in Babs's tone. "What's the matter, babe? Tell me now, and we'll sort it out."

Babs shook her head. There was no way she was airing their dirty linen in public. Martin could wait until he got home. Only then would she really let him have it. She'd tear strips off the bloody bastard once they were in the privacy of their own home.

After Babs had left, Big Tim strolled up to Martin. "Is everything all right boss?"

Martin nodded. "Yeah, I think so. Babs has just got a bee in her bonnet about something."

"About Kathleen Diamond? You know she's been sniffing around recently."

"Nah, Babs knows all about her. As far as she's concerned that's all over."

"Anyway, I'd better get back to Tony." Martin lowered his voice and leaned into Tim. "We're discussing our options. Dave Carter is not on top of his game at the moment, so that means it's the best time to exploit any weaknesses, if you know what I mean?" Martin winked at him.

Tim nodded. "Do you need me upstairs?"

"No, we are just bouncing around some ideas at the moment. You keep an eye on things down here, and I'll fill you in later, all right?" Martin slapped him on the back.

When Babs got home, she collected the children from the neighbour and then put them straight to bed. She made a pot of tea and sat down at the kitchen table.

She poured herself a cup. She liked it strong and dark, with just a splash of milk, no sugar. She glanced at the clock and knew she was in for a long wait, but she was determined she wouldn't go to bed before Martin came home. They were going to get this situation sorted out once and for all.

She took a sip of tea and then lit a cigarette, rehearsing what she was going to say over and over in her mind.

40

MARTIN CAME HOME AT TWO in the morning. Babs
ground out her cigarette in the glass ashtray and pushed the
stewed cup of tea away from her.

Her eyes felt gritty and red, but she suddenly felt awake,
ready for this confrontation.

Martin was creeping around, trying to be quiet. He
obviously hoped Babs was asleep already. But he slowly
eased open the door to the kitchen and then did a double
take when he saw Babs at the kitchen table.

"Hello, Babs. Sorry, I'm so late. You didn't have to wait
up."

"Sit down, Martin."

She saw Martin's body tense. He didn't like being told
what to do, especially not by his wife.

But he pulled out a chair and sat down at the kitchen table
opposite her, pulling out his own packet of cigarettes and
lighting one up. He offered the packet to Babs, but she shook
her head. She'd been chain-smoking all evening and the last
thing she needed was another cigarette.

"What's all this about then?" Martin asked.

"Kathleen Diamond," Babs said.

"What? All that's all over, Babs. We've talked about this. She didn't mean anything to me. You know that."

Babs waited for a moment to see whether or not Martin would confess that he was the father of Kathleen's baby, and admit there was a little half-brother to Ruby, Derek and Emily living only a few streets away.

When Martin didn't say anything, Babs shook her head.

"And when exactly were you intending to tell me that you'd fathered a child by another woman, Martin? It's disgusting! There's only a few days separating Emily and that little brat."

Martin's face looked like it had been set in stone. "Who the hell told you that?" he growled. "You know better than to listen to gossip, Babs."

"I don't need to listen to gossip, Martin. Not when the trollop comes around to show me her bloody kid! How do you think I felt when she kneeled down to show Ruby her half-brother?"

Martin shot up, knocking the chair back onto the floor with a clatter. "She did what?" he roared.

"Quiet!" Babs ordered. "You'll wake the children, and they've had quite enough disruption for one day."

Martin's eyes were wild as he clenched his fists by his side. He'd obviously expected to be able to sweep this one under the carpet, and he didn't much like Kathleen showing any backbone.

"I don't believe it," he muttered to himself.

"Well, you'd better believe it. She came to visit me early this evening. All the neighbours saw her. She is after money Martin. She says the baby is yours, and she wants you to support it. What I want to know is, what are you going to do about it?"

Martin, who had been angrily staring out of the kitchen window, turned slowly to face Babs. "What do you want me to do about it?"

"I want you to get rid of her! Send her and that baby off somewhere. I don't want Ruby, Derek and Emily growing up with a little half-brother not five minutes' walk away."

Martin curled his lip in disgust. "I'll sort it."

"You'd better, Martin. I'm warning you. I've had enough. I've had it up to here with your antics."

"Give it a rest. You're lucky to have me, and you know it. All you do all day is sit on your backside, or go out shopping. You'd be nothing without me. You've got it easy Babs, and you know it!"

Babs folded her arms across her chest and stared at Martin with hatred. How could she ever have fallen for this man? Where had the charming, good-looking man she'd married disappeared to?

Martin always tried to win arguments this way. When he was at fault, he would just try and turn the argument around to something he could win.

Well, Babs wasn't about to let him get away with it that easily. "I want to know what you're going to do about it, Martin."

"I said I would sort it, didn't I? And I will." Martin turned around. "I'm going back to the club. I can't stay here tonight."

He began to walk down the hallway towards the front door.

"Just you make sure you sort this out like you promised, Martin. Otherwise, I'm going to make you pay."

Martin chuckled cruelly as he picked up his coat from the coat stand. "You'll make me pay? Don't make me laugh, Babs. You can't do a bleeding thing about it. Just you remember that before you start mouthing off next time."

After Martin stormed out and slammed the door behind him, Babs leaned against the wall. "Oh, you'd be surprised, Martin," she muttered to herself. "You'd be surprised just how much I could make you suffer."

41

FURIOUS, MARTIN STORMED BACK TO the club. He was damned if he was going to stand around and listen to Babs go on at him about something he'd finished ages ago.

It wasn't his fault if that daft cow, Kathleen, wasn't sensible enough to avoid getting herself in the family way. Babs was being completely unreasonable.

The club was closed when Martin let himself in the front door. All the punters had long gone, even his bar staff had cleaned up and finished for the night. All the glasses had been collected and washed, ready for the next day, but the floor was still sticky under his feet.

Martin made his way behind the bar and reached for a bottle of whisky. He poured himself a generous measure and downed it.

He was going to make sure that little bitch never crossed him again. He poured himself another whisky, tucked the bottle under his arm, made his way to the doorway at the back of the bar and started climbing the stairs to his flat.

He was a couple of steps from the top when he heard a noise.

There was some bastard in there!

This was Martin's flat. It was his domain. Who the hell would have had the nerve not only to break into Martin Morton's club, but to actually get into his private living space, too?

Martin was in no mood to be crossed tonight. He was going to show the cheeky bastard what for.

He flung open the door, holding the bottle of whisky by the neck, ready to smash it down on whoever had the nerve to break into his property.

He stalked down the corridor, but the main living space was empty. Then a noise caught his attention, and the door to the spare bedroom door opened. Martin whirled around and held up the bottle of Scotch.

"All right bruv," Tony said, grinning at him. He didn't have a shirt on, and his trousers were slung low on his hips, showing off the body he was so proud of.

Martin gritted his teeth, but he lowered the bottle of whisky. "What the bloody hell are you doing here?" he asked his brother.

Tony gave a shrug and another grin. "Entertaining."

Martin looked over Tony's shoulder and could just make out a woman hiding in the shadows in the bedroom.

Martin turned his back on Tony and walked back towards the open plan living area and sat down on the sofa.

Tony followed him.

"And what is wrong with your gaffe?" Martin said pointedly.

"That's where Melinda is. She's moved in. I could hardly take this one back there, could I?" Tony whispered.

Martin shook his head at the sheer nerve of his brother.

Tony had a flat above the bookies on Titan Street because

Martin paid the rent. Up until a year ago, Tony was still living at home with his mother, and Violet Morton still hadn't forgiven her eldest son for helping her youngest boy move out.

"What are you doing back here anyway? I thought you were back at the house with Babs tonight?" Tony asked reaching for the bottle of whisky and then rummaging around in the kitchenette for a glass.

"Above the sink," Martin said, pointing to where he kept glasses. "And don't talk to me about that bloody pain in the arse."

"Babs?"

"The woman's got a screw loose. She got me to go home just so she could have a go at me about getting Kathleen Diamond up the duff."

Tony spluttered a laugh and then covered his mouth with his hand. "Sorry, bruv. Did you really get her pregnant? Blimey. No wonder Babs is giving you a hard time."

Martin shot Tony a dark look, snatched the bottle from his brother and poured himself another whisky. "Babs thinks she can tell me what to do. It's a joke. All this time I've spent building up my reputation in the East End, and two women think they can take me on and make a fool of me? They've got another think coming."

Tony frowned. He liked Babs. She was a good woman, and in Tony's opinion, she put up with a lot from Martin.

"I don't think Babs is trying to play you, Martin. I imagine she's just a bit hurt."

Martin looked at his brother as if he'd grown two heads.

"Well, I can't do much about Babs because I'm married to the silly mare. But Kathleen Diamond is going to regret she ever met me."

"And what about the kid?"

Martin sneered. "What about it? How do I know it's even mine? She probably dropped her knickers for every Tom, Dick and Harry. I'm not being conned. I bunged her a few quid while she was pregnant to keep her quiet, but she's gone back on her word. She went to Babs and told her all about it."

Tony gave a low whistle. "The girl has got some nerve."

Martin shook his head. "Cheeky bitch. She's going to regret it. I promise you that."

"So what are you going to do about it?"

Martin stared down into his glass of whisky, swirling the glass and watching the amber liquid glitter in the light. "I'm going to make sure she never bothers me again, bruv."

Martin gave a cruel smile, distorting his handsome features, and then he raised his glass of whisky to his brother in a toast.

"Here's to getting rid of meddlesome bitches."

Tony raised his own glass and clinked it against his brother's. "Right you are. Now, do you mind if I get back to my lady?" he asked, nodding at the spare bedroom.

Martin shook his head. "Go right ahead. I suppose I should at least be thankful you had the decency to not use my own bed."

Tony got up with a grin and headed back to the woman he'd left in the bedroom, while Martin nursed his drink.

He didn't mind being left alone. It gave him more time to plot his revenge. Kathleen bloody Diamond was going to pay for this.

42

AT ELEVEN O'CLOCK THE FOLLOWING morning, Martin was nursing a hangover. He'd polished off the bottle of whisky last night, and his head was pounding. Tony and his bit of fluff hadn't left yet, and Big Tim was due to arrive at any minute. Martin took his extra strong cup of tea downstairs with him.

Tim used the little office behind the bar, which was barely more than a cupboard under the stairs. Every day, he looked at the takings, made sure the staffing levels were adequate and placed any orders the club needed, but before he made a start on that today, Martin needed to have a word.

Unfortunately, Frieda hadn't yet finished cleaning. She clattered the metal bucket against the floor as she moved it a few inches and then continued to mop.

The noise set Martin's teeth on edge.

"Morning. Heavy night, was it?" Frieda asked as she eyed him warily.

Martin didn't dislike Frieda particularly. He really had no feelings towards her at all one way or the other. He'd given her the job years ago because she'd been a friend of Babs's mother. He'd never had any complaints. She did the job she was paid to do and kept her mouth shut. As far as Martin was concerned, that was good enough

"Something like that." Martin took a sip of his tea.

A shadow fell across the doorway as Big Tim entered the club. He walked inside, shrugging his big shoulders and taking off his coat. "Morning, Frieda."

Tim had removed his coat by the time he noticed Martin sitting at the bar. "Morning, boss. Is everything all right?"

Martin didn't normally talk to Tim at this time of day. He didn't usually talk to anyone until the afternoon. But today was different.

"I need a word about something," Martin said

Frieda looked up, her tired, old eyes now bright and alert.

Although she'd worked for him for years, and Martin thought he could probably trust her, there was no way he was going to chance her overhearing this.

"Let's go upstairs," Martin said, shooting a pointed look Frieda.

He'd just have to turf Tony and his fancy woman out of bed. He didn't want anyone overhearing what he was about to say to Tim, not even his brother.

As they walked upstairs, Martin said, "We have a problem, Tim, and I need someone I trust to sort it."

Big Tim nodded his large head. "You know me, Martin. I'll do whatever needs to be done."

Martin nodded with satisfaction. He was pleased with Tim. He'd killed Keith Parker without even questioning Martin's reasons. He was a good and loyal worker.

As Martin pushed open the door to the flat, he turned to Tim and looked up at him. "I rely on you, Tim. You know I appreciate loyalty, and your work hasn't gone unnoticed.

You've earned a pay rise. An extra fiver a week, plus I want you to be my number two."

Tim's face opened up in surprise. "Number two? But I thought Tony…"

Speak of the devil. Tony chose that moment to appear.

At least he had a shirt on this time.

"I need you and your bird out of here," Martin barked.

Tony scratched his head and looked at Martin through bleary eyes. "Can't we at least have a cup of tea first? I've only just woken up."

"I don't care, and no you can't."

Tony stared at Martin for a second as if he was considering arguing with his brother, but then thought better of it. Mumbling under his breath, he went back to the bedroom, and Tim and Martin heard him cajoling the woman to get out of bed.

Martin moved over to the small kitchenette and began to fill the kettle.

He was going to make another cup of tea, but only for him and Tim. He'd had enough of Tony. It said a lot when he didn't trust his own brother with the most important aspects of the business. But deep down, Martin knew that Tony wasn't trustworthy. Tim was.

After Tony and his bimbo had shuffled out of the flat, Martin turned back to Tim and put a mug of tea in front of him.

"It's a personal matter," Martin began, leaning on the counter, staring at his strong cup of tea. "Kathleen Diamond."

Big Tim frowned. "What about her?"

"She's been causing me a lot of grief. You know me, Tim.

I'm a reasonable man. I've given her money, supported her, ignored her little tantrums, but now she's gone and brought my family into it. I can't be having that. She went round there with her baby, showing it to my kids. Can you believe it? And what proof do I have that the baby is even mine?"

Tim stayed silent. He really wasn't sure what the best approach was in the circumstances, so he thought it was better to keep shtum.

"I have certain rules, Tim. My number one rule is to come down like a ton of bricks on anyone who messes with my family. And that's what Kathleen has done."

Tim nodded his head in agreement. He'd met Kathleen on numerous occasions, and she'd always come across to him as a little too big for her boots. He agreed with Martin. She could do with taking down a peg or two.

"Do you want me to have a word?" Big Tim asked. "I could go round there and put the fear of God into the girl. She wouldn't bother you again."

Martin gave a slow smile that set Tim's teeth on edge. "For any normal girl, I think you might be right. Trouble is, this Kathleen is a vindictive bitch. She thinks I owe her, and she's not just going to take this lying down. I was planning to bung her a bit of money and set her up somewhere out in Essex. I figured keeping her and Babs apart would be the best thing to do under the circumstances."

Tim nodded as if that made a lot of sense to him.

"But I'm afraid that's just not going to work now. We need a more permanent solution." Martin looked at Tim meaningfully.

"Permanent?" Big Tim's eyes widened in shock. He couldn't believe it. "Do you mean…?"

Martin nodded and drew a finger across his neck in a cutthroat gesture. He watched Tim carefully for his response. This was a true test of his loyalty.

Tim's face grew pale, but other than that, he displayed no reaction.

That was good. It reassured Martin that he'd made the right choice. He could trust Big Tim.

Big Tim felt his stomach churn as he stared at Martin's cold, impassive face.

Big Tim was no angel. He'd done plenty of things in the past he wasn't particularly proud of, but somehow he'd always managed to explain it away and tell himself that there was a reason behind it.

But in all his days on earth, Big Tim had never so much as raised a hand against a woman, let alone killed one.

His career path was decided at an early age. The sheer size of him meant he was a valuable commodity even in the playground. He'd taken money from the other kids to act as their protector.

In those days, his sheer size was enough to deter people. As he got older, though, it seemed as though older lads wanted to make the name for themselves by challenging Big Tim to fight.

He'd been a gentle boy until he was ten or eleven, and then he'd realised people were not going to let him be. To stop the constant challenges, he had to prove his point.

The next boy who picked a fight with him, went down hard. Tim left him with a broken collar bone. He'd had to do it so word would get out that Big Tim was not someone to be messed with.

It was a hard lesson but one he'd remembered for the rest

of his life. Go in hard. Go in brutal.

As time went on, people didn't just want him as a protector. They employed him as an enforcer. He'd started working for Martin over five years ago, and in that time, he had personally been responsible for the deaths of three men. Most of the time it was an easy job. He usually just had to rough someone up and put the fear of God into them, so they paid Martin whatever they owed.

But on occasion, he'd stepped across that line and committed murder. Somehow Tim managed to justify it.

The three men he'd killed were nasty pieces of work. One of them was a wife beater, the other a grass and finally, the most recent, Keith Parker, had been a double-crossing little bastard.

In Tim's opinion, they'd all gotten what was coming to them. But a woman... Actually killing a women...Doing something as horrendous as that had never crossed Tim's mind before.

His mouth felt dry as he stared at Martin. His boss's mouth was moving as he issued Tim instructions and told him about his plan. But Tim couldn't take it all in. His mind was whirring.

He'd never let Martin down, not once. He'd taken on every job assigned to him and done it well.

The trouble was, he'd done it so well that Martin wouldn't let him get away without seeing this through.

Now Martin had confided in him, they were locked together by this secret, and he knew that if he didn't do it, somebody else would. Would Martin really let him live, knowing the dreadful secret?

He didn't have a choice. Like it or not, he was going to

have to do it.

43

THAT AFTERNOON, MARTIN MORTON TOOK himself off to the Diamond household. When Kathleen's mother, Mary, opened the door, he could hear a baby screaming from inside.

Mary narrowed her eyes when she saw it was him. "Oh, it's you. I wondered when you might show your face."

Martin wanted to tell her where to go, but instead he smiled and said, "Lovely to see you, Mrs. Diamond. Is Kathleen home?"

Mary sighed and moved to one side so Martin could enter. "She's in the kitchen.

Martin walked through the entrance hall towards the back of the house. All the houses in this area were practically identical, with the same layout, so he didn't need to wait for Mary to show him the way.

Kathleen was in the kitchen, balancing the baby on her hip while trying to fill the kettle at the sink.

"Please stop crying, Jimmy. You're doing my head in," Kathleen muttered as she jiggled the baby in her arms, trying to get it to shut it up.

"Kathleen."

Kathleen whirled around, spilling water onto the kitchen floor, and looked up at Martin in shock.

She stared at him open-mouthed.

"I thought I should come around and see the baby. Sorry I haven't been round before. I've been busy recently."

Mary bustled into the kitchen behind him. She obviously wasn't going to give them any privacy, the nosy old bat.

"Well, it's about time you did the decent thing," Mary said scornfully.

"If you wouldn't mind, Mrs. Diamond, I'd like to have a few moments alone with Kathleen."

Mary looked indignant as if she was going to argue with him, but Kathleen said, "Please Mum. Give us a minute."

Reluctantly, Mary left the kitchen, closing the door behind her.

Stepping around the puddle of water on the floor, Kathleen walked up to Martin and held out the baby.

Martin stared down dispassionately at the chubby little thing. He had dark hair and dark blue eyes. Martin supposed it could be his. But then he saw something that changed his mind. The baby had a little dimple in the centre of his chin.

He didn't know anyone in his family who had a dimple like that. He was pretty sure something like that got passed down through the family.

Martin bit down on his tongue so hard he tasted blood. The baby wasn't his. She was cheating him. If Kathleen thought she was on easy street now, she could think again.

"Don't you want to hold him?" Kathleen asked, looking up hopefully at Martin.

"Babies aren't really my thing, love."

"Oh," Kathleen pulled the baby against her chest and gazed down at him. "He looks a lot like you, though, doesn't he?"

Martin forced himself to smile through gritted teeth. "Yeah, I suppose he does. Look, Kathleen, I don't want things to be bad between us, but Babs told me you went round to the house."

Kathleen paled. "I'm sorry. It was a stupid thing to do, but I was desperate. I tried to see you at the club, but they wouldn't let me in."

"That's because I was busy," Martin said impatiently. "Look you can't see Babs again, do you understand me?"

Kathleen nodded. "Of course, whatever you say."

"I will provide for my own," Martin said. "So you have no worries on that score. But I don't want you going around telling everybody that the baby is mine."

Kathleen's face crumpled in confusion. "But he is yours."

"But it's not very nice for Babs to have all these people gossiping behind her back, is it? If you keep quiet, then I'll provide for you and the baby. You'll want for nothing. Okay?"

Kathleen nodded, but Martin could see the rebellious spark in her eye. The stupid cow didn't know what was good for her. It confirmed to him that the decision he'd made was the right one.

"Right, I'd better be off," Martin said, taking a roll of bills from his pocket, peeling off a couple and leaving them on the kitchen table for Kathleen.

"Don't you want to at least stay for a cup of tea?" Kathleen pleaded. "Look, Jimmy has stopped crying now. He must know you're his dad. He must sense it."

Martin stared at her as if she was the most stupid woman on the planet. The baby was only a couple weeks old. "No. I can't stay. I've got things to do. But maybe I'll see you tomorrow, if you're free?"

"Yes, of course. That would be great," Kathleen said, beaming at him.

Martin nodded and then swaggered out of the kitchen, heading down the hallway and then out onto the street.

The silly cow had fallen for it. Hook line and sinker.

As soon as Martin left, Kathleen quickly wrapped little Jimmy in a blanket and put him in his pram.

Ignoring her mother's questions and insistent warnings about Martin Morton, Kathleen headed outside. She needed to talk to somebody — someone who would understand. So she headed to Linda's house.

Although they were by no means back to their normal friendly terms, Linda had at least stopped ignoring her, and Kathleen was determined to make her come around to her way of thinking. She was the only real friend Kathleen had, and it got lonely sitting at home all day with a baby.

She was so excited after Martin's visit. She was fit to burst and wanted to share her happy news with someone, but when Mrs. Simpson opened the door, Kathleen couldn't help but notice the pinched features of the woman's face. She clearly disapproved of Jimmy.

Kathleen swallowed nervously. "I'm sorry to disturb you, Mrs. Simpson. I hoped Linda would be home?"

Linda's mother hesitated on the doorstep as though she couldn't decide whether to slam the door in Kathleen's face or drag her inside quickly before the neighbours saw. In the end, she decided for the latter, although her welcome was none too warm.

"Linda, you have a visitor," Mrs. Simpson called up the stairs.

Linda barrelled down the stairs, two at a time. Her shiny, brown hair bounced about her shoulders.

When she saw Kathleen standing there, she paused and exchanged a look with her mother.

All three of them stood there in awkward silence for a few moments before Linda's mother finally said, "It's none of my business what you do with your life, Kathleen. But Linda's life is my business, and I don't want her to be led astray by your wicked ways. I think it's best if you don't call around here anymore."

Kathleen's cheeks flamed red.

"Mum!" Linda said as she jumped down the last two stairs. "Kathleen got herself in trouble, but she's not a bad person. I can't just drop my friend because she made a mistake."

Mrs. Simpson gave Linda a look that said that was exactly what she expected her daughter to do.

"I'm not having a daughter of mine following such an example."

Kathleen stood there in abject misery, feeling completely humiliated. All her excitement and desire to share her news about Martin with Linda had dissipated. She had never felt so embarrassed in all of her life. She'd always liked the Simpsons. She enjoyed the fact that they were a traditional family. Linda's mum and dad were still together, and Linda and her brother were very much loved by their parents.

Kathleen knew that her upbringing had been very

different. Although her mother had brought her up on her own, she at least had the respectability of being married when she'd given birth to Kathleen.

Kathleen tilted her chin in the air. "That's a very old-fashioned point of view," she said scornfully. "I am still the same person, you know. And I know a lot of people are looking down their noses at me because I've had little Jimmy out of wedlock. But I'm glad I had him. He's a lovely little baby."

To Kathleen's horror, she felt her eyes fill with tears. She bit down hard on her lip. There was no way she was going to burst out crying in front of Mrs. Simpson.

Mrs. Simpson looked at Kathleen as though she were a bit of dog dirt on the street.

"Come on," Linda said, easing her body between her mother and Kathleen. "Let's go outside and take Jimmy for a walk."

Kathleen stepped outside and put Jimmy back in his pram. The little mite hadn't even woken up. He was completely oblivious to all the trouble he'd caused his mother, Kathleen thought ruefully.

"Don't be late," Linda's mother ordered as Linda stepped out of the front door.

"I'm sorry about that," Linda said as they walked along the street together. "Mum can be very prim and proper about things, and there has been ever so much gossip."

Kathleen nodded miserably. When it was just her and Jimmy, it was easier to ignore the gossip. Obviously, she'd noticed the pointed looks in the street, and the fact that people even crossed to the other side of the road to avoid her, but she'd never had a great number of friends, and because Kathleen's ego was so great, she put it down to the fact that people were jealous. In her mind, most of the silly women responsible for spreading the gossip would give their eye teeth to have a relationship with Martin Morton.

But for the first time, Kathleen realised perhaps it wasn't jealousy. Perhaps they really were disappointed in her.

She didn't like that idea at all.

"Your mum is just very old-fashioned. I understand. It's not your fault."

Linda looked at her doubtfully. "Most people around here are quite set in their ways."

Kathleen sighed and looked down at Jimmy, who was now sleeping peacefully. Linda peered over the pram and pulled the blanket out of the way so she could see the baby's face. "He is ever so sweet, and look at that dimple in his chin. I think that gives him character. My grandma always said a dimple in the chin was lucky. It meant you were going to be lucky in money and love... or something like that." Linda shrugged and smiled. "It's a good thing anyway."

Kathleen beamed down at Jimmy proudly. No matter what anyone said about him, he was definitely a handsome little baby.

She would bring him up to make sure he wasn't ashamed of his roots. She wanted him to be proud of his father. One day, she would get Martin to come around to her way of thinking, and he would treat Jimmy as well as his other children. Kathleen had visions of Jimmy, Derek and Ruby all playing happily together in the future. Kathleen was so carried away with her daydream, she hadn't realised Linda was still talking to her.

"Hello? Are you even listening to me?"

"Sorry, Linda. I was just thinking about Jimmy and his future if he stays around here."

"Why? You're not going anywhere, are you?"

"I get the feeling Martin would prefer it if we weren't quite so close to Babs." She shrugged. "He's agreed to pay me some money every week and find us somewhere to live."

"Are you sure that's a good idea? I mean, I know everyone around here can be quite judgemental, but at least you know people. If you needed help, you've got your mum nearby and you've got me."

Kathleen smiled at her friend. "Thanks, Linda. That means a lot. But I'm going to do what's best for Jimmy, and I think that means having a relationship with his father. If Martin wants us to move out of the area, then that's what we'll do."

As Kathleen continued to walk companionably along the street with Linda, her head was full of plans for the future. She had no idea what Martin really had planned for her and Jimmy.

As good as his word, the following day, Martin called for Kathleen. This time, there was no sign of Kathleen's mother, as she was helping out on the stall at Chrisp Street Market.

Martin gave Kathleen his most dazzling smile, and Kathleen felt her stomach fill with butterflies in response.

"Come in," she said, smiling. "I've just put Jimmy down for his nap."

Martin followed her inside, and she led him into the cramped front room, which was stuffed with lots of mismatched furniture polished to a gleaming shine.

"Can I get you a drink?" Kathleen offered.

"No, thanks. You all right?"

Kathleen blinked in surprise. "Yes, I'm fine. Why?"

"You're looking tired, girl. You've got bags the size of suitcases under your eyes."

Kathleen turned away and pouted as she put her hands against her face. She was very tired because Jimmy had been up quite a few times in the night, but she hadn't thought she looked that bad. She'd even put on lipstick this morning because she'd expected Martin might pop in today.

"Sorry, I didn't mean to hurt your feelings," Martin said. "I'm just concerned. Are you sure you're getting enough rest?"

Kathleen shrugged. "Well, it's not easy with a new baby, Martin."

Martin nodded soberly. "That's what I thought. You know what you need to do, don't you? Get out and treat yourself. I tell you what…" Martin pulled a roll of bills from his pocket and peeled off twenty-five quid. He held it out to Kathleen. "Why don't you take yourself up West and buy a new dress or something, eh?"

Kathleen's face lit up, but then she bit her lip and shook her head. "I can't. Getting the pram on the bus is a bleeding nightmare. Plus, I need to take all Jimmy things with me."

"Surely he won't need that much. It will only be for an hour or two, and it will do you good to get out of the house. You can't stay at home all day just because you've had a baby. Other women do it. I see prams on the buses all the time."

Kathleen looked at him doubtfully.

"If I'm not too busy later, I'll take you out to dinner."

"All right," Kathleen said, smiling at him. "It's really good of you. I could do with a break from washing dirty nappies.

Martin gave a dazzling smile. "That's my girl," he said.

44

KATHLEEN SHOULD HAVE BEEN FEELING happy. She had money in her pocket, and she was making her way to the West End, her favourite haunt.

She'd decided against the hassle of trying to get the pram on the bus and left little Jimmy with his grandmother. But for some reason, she just couldn't get up the enthusiasm for shopping.

Linda was at work today, which meant she had no one to go with and no one to boast to about the fact that Martin was taking her to dinner. She hadn't even been able to mention it to her mother because Martin had expressly forbidden her from telling anyone.

She tried to think positively. It was a step in the right direction. This time next year, anything could have happened. Martin could have turfed Babs out on her ear, and it could be Kathleen and Jimmy moving into the fancy house down in the country.

She'd enjoy showing her mother around the big house. Showing her that, despite all her fears, Kathleen had done all right in the end.

Kathleen got on the double-decker bus and paid the

conductor.

She stared out of the rain-splattered window and wondered what the future might hold.

She wished she'd worn something a bit more comfortable. She'd convinced herself that her body had sprung back to its original form shortly after giving birth, but the dark red dress that had previously been one of her favourites was feeling very tight around her waist.

She shuffled around in the seat and tugged at the dress, trying to get comfortable, which earned her an annoyed look from the old lady on the seat next to her.

Kathleen was relieved to be finally free of the steamy confines of the bus when she stepped out onto Oxford Street. It had stopped raining, and the sun was coming out. Kathleen took that as an omen things were going to get better.

She did a bit of window shopping first, enjoying the confidence of knowing that she had money in her pocket. If she wanted to buy something she could.

She saw one small boutique called Lydia's that had a gorgeous bright yellow dress in the centre. The waist was narrow, but the skirt flared out and looked terribly elegant.

Kathleen glowed with excitement. If she could wear that dress tonight for dinner with Martin, he'd be so impressed.

She stepped inside the boutique and the bell above the door rang. The shop was far more spacious inside than she'd expected, and there were a number of customers perusing the rails.

Kathleen looked around the shop searching out the yellow dress, but she couldn't find it, so in the end, she walked up to the sales assistant standing beside the counter.

"I'd like to try on that dress," Kathleen said in her poshest voice, pointing at the dress in the window.

The sales assistant looked her up and down, rather cheekily in Kathleen's opinion, but then gave her a tight smile.

"We've only got two left. I'll get them for you. Wait there," the sales assistant ordered, pointing to a spot by the ladies fitting rooms.

Kathleen did as she was told, and when the sales assistant returned, she had the beautiful bright yellow dress in her arms.

"I was mistaken," she said. "We only have one left." Her gaze raked over Kathleen's figure. "I'm not sure it's in your size."

"Thank you," Kathleen said politely, although she thought the sales assistant was a cheeky mare.

She took the dress inside the changing room, even though the sales assistant seemed very reluctant to hand it over.

She quickly stripped off her own dark red dress and examined the label inside the yellow dress, looking for the size. She frowned. What was that silly sales assistant on about? The dress was the perfect size for Kathleen. She'd never needed a bigger size than that in her life.

She stripped off. Standing there in her petticoat, she shivered as she ran her fingers over the luxurious fabric of the yellow dress. She grinned and slipped the beautiful flared dress over her head.

It was a struggle. She tugged and tugged and finally pulled it down, but there was no way she was going to be able to do up the buttons on the back.

She stared at her image in the wall-mounted mirror in

shock. She looked horrendous. The dress pinched the skin around her arms making them bulge outwards, and the yellow fabric rippled around her body leaving no lump or bump unseen.

Distressed, Kathleen tried to pull the dress over her head, but it got stuck halfway. She gave a cry of dismay and yanked on the dress again.

It wouldn't budge.

Close to tears, Kathleen called out for some assistance.

Very sheepishly, she asked, "Could you help me? The dress has gotten stuck."

The sales assistant stepped inside the dressing room and gave a snort of disapproval.

What happened next was the most humiliating five minutes of Kathleen's life. The sales assistant made Kathleen bend over at the waist and used her foot on Kathleen's leg to give extra purchase as she pulled.

When the dress was finally yanked off, Kathleen tumbled backwards, landing on her arse on the floor.

The sales assistant began to frantically check the yellow dress for damage, while Kathleen grabbed her red dress and pulled it on quickly.

She reached for her coat, and the sales assistant said, "Not so fast. If there's any damage to this dress, you're going to be paying for it."

She spoke in such a large booming voice Kathleen knew everyone in the shop must have heard her.

Her cheeks flamed with embarrassment, and she wanted to curl up into a little ball, but instead, she thrust out her chin and screamed, abandoning any pretence of her posh accent, "Like hell I will. It's a bloody horrible dress anyway!"

And with that, Kathleen stormed out of the shop with the sales assistant protesting behind her.

Outside the shop, Kathleen quickly buttoned up her coat and kept her head down, feeling stupid.

That was it. There was no way she was going to have lunch today. She was going to get her figure back if it killed her.

The next shop Kathleen went in was one she knew. She wanted something familiar after that disaster. So she turned off the main street and headed to a cheaper, less exclusive store, one she had been to many times before.

There was a pretty black dress printed with pink flowers on display in the window. The skirt was flared, although nowhere near as flared as the yellow dress had been. But Kathleen thought the material might be more flattering, so she headed inside.

"Kathleen Diamond! Is that really you?"

Kathleen looked up to see Carrie Horrocks, a girl she'd been at school with. Standing next to her was Brenda Wightly. The two girls had been inseparable at school. Kathleen had never really liked them, and they'd never been friends as such, but Carrie looked friendly enough as she walked over with a beaming smile on her face.

"Oh, hello, girls," Kathleen said. "I haven't seen you for a while. How have you been?"

Carrie wiggled her fingers in Kathleen's face, showing off a plain wedding band and an engagement ring with a minuscule stone in it. Kathleen doubted it was a diamond.

"I'm married now," Carrie said. "I'm Mrs. O'Brien."

Kathleen smirked. She was pretty sure Carrie had married

Patrick O'Brien, the same lad she'd been with during their time at school. Patrick worked down at the docks and was a coarse man. Not exactly what Kathleen would consider a catch.

She gave Carrie a fake smile. "Oh, how lovely for you," she said.

She knew the next part of the conversation would include Carrie asking about her life, and Kathleen considered making something up. Not that she was ashamed of Jimmy, of course, but Carrie wouldn't understand. She didn't want to tell either of the girls about Jimmy or Martin. She wasn't going to give them a chance to lord it over her.

So rather than continue the conversation, Kathleen quickly ducked behind a rail. "Lovely to see you, but I must pick out my dress. I'm in a terrible rush today."

Carrie exchanged a look with her friend Brenda, and they both smirked.

Kathleen felt her cheeks grow hot. She kept her head down, determined to ignore them and find the dress that she'd seen in the window.

She found it hanging on the second rail. As her fingers closed around it, she felt the material of the dress. It was much thinner than the yellow dress, but it felt soft, and Kathleen smiled. This one would look nice on her.

She carried the dress over to the counter, and the sales assistant, who had a South London accent and was definitely not as snobby as the assistant in Lydia's, escorted her to the fitting room.

"Just let me know if I can get you another size," the sales assistant said as she swished the curtain across on the changing cubicle.

Kathleen pulled on the dress and gave a sigh of relief. This time, the dress fit perfectly. Okay, so it was one size bigger than she normally wore, but that didn't matter. It looked nice, and it didn't cling to her stomach like her old dresses did.

Smiling to herself, Kathleen took the dress off and carefully hung it back on the hanger. After getting dressed, she carried it back to the sales counter and handed over the money.

The sales assistant rang the transaction up on the till, gave Kathleen her change and then pushed the dress, wrapped up in tissue paper, back to Kathleen.

Kathleen tucked her bag over her arm and prepared to head back to Oxford Street, but as she did so, she had to walk past Carrie and Brenda.

"Oh, goodness," Carrie said. "Would you look at this awful dress, Brenda?" Carrie held aloft the same dress that Kathleen had just purchased.

Kathleen paused. What was wrong with the dress? She thought it looked very pretty.

Brenda shook her head disapprovingly. "It is ever so low-cut. You wouldn't catch a nice girl wearing a dress like that."

"No," Carrie said in agreement, pretending to be studying the dress very seriously, but Kathleen could see the beginnings of a smirk on the girl's mouth. "But it would be perfect for a girl who has lost her knicker elastic, wouldn't it?"

Brenda cackled. "Oh, yes," she said. "It would be perfect for a girl with loose morals."

Both girls collapsed into giggles as they turned around and saw Kathleen was still watching their little show.

Kathleen took a deep breath. She would rather have her life with little Jimmy, ten times over, than put up with a boring life married to somebody like Patrick O'Brien.

But Kathleen had never been particularly articulate when she was angry, so instead of saying that, she just screamed, "Get stuffed, the bleeding lot of you!"

Every other customer in the shop and the sales assistant turned to look at Kathleen.

An older lady in the far corner put a hand to her chest and muttered, "Well, I never."

Kathleen turned on her heels and ran from the shop.

45

KATHLEEN GOT OFF THE BUS on Burdett Road feeling even more depressed than she had been when she set off. She knew this was how her life would be from now on, full of people laughing and gossiping behind her back.

She looked down at the bag that held the new dress and her lip wobbled. She felt so sorry for herself. She'd really liked the dress and had been looking forward to wearing it, but thanks to those nasty cows, Carrie and Brenda, she wouldn't be able to wear it without thinking of their spiteful words.

She pulled uncomfortably at her, too tight, red dress. It would be a relief to get home and change into something more comfortable. Although goodness knows what she was going to wear tonight for dinner with Martin. None of her nice clothes fitted anymore. Maybe she would have to wear this new dress, after all. She shouldn't really let Carrie and Brenda spoil it for her. They were two boring girls, with boring lives, who would never amount to anything.

Compared to Kathleen, their lives were pathetic. They were just jealous because she was going places and they weren't.

As she turned the corner, she saw a large, dark car parked up at the end of her road.

Kathleen looked at it curiously. No one in the street owned a car. So it had to be a visitor. As she drew closer, she saw there was somebody behind the wheel. The driver wound down the window, and Kathleen was expecting to be asked for directions. Probably some old toff had gotten himself lost.

To her surprise, when she peered in the window, she saw that it was Big Tim, one of Martin Morton's men.

"All right, Kathleen."

Kathleen blinked at him in surprise. "What are you doing around here?"

"Martin told me to give you a lift."

"A lift? But I'm supposed to be meeting him for dinner, and it's only five thirty."

Big Tim shrugged, and Kathleen noticed his fingers tightened on the steering wheel.

"I just do what I'm told. He asked me to pick you up. Maybe his plans have changed. Do you want a lift or not?"

Kathleen nodded, but she looked down the street. She could just make out her front door. "Can I just tell my mum I'm going out?"

"No, there's no time. You don't want to keep Martin waiting, Kathleen. He's not the sort of man to wait around for a woman."

Reluctantly, Kathleen walked around the car and opened the door to the passenger side. She would have preferred it if Tim had acted like a gentleman and opened it for her, but she got the feeling that Big Tim didn't like her very much.

"No kid?" Tim asked her gruffly.

"I left him with my mum today."

Tim nodded and then with his jaw clenched and his eyes fixed on the road, he drove away from the curb.

Linda was walking home from Bevels and saw Kathleen step into the large, black car. She frowned. It was quite unusual to see such a fancy car around these streets. She assumed it was Martin Morton's. He was the type of man to have a car like that. Linda shivered when she thought about Martin Morton. She hoped Kathleen knew what she was doing, because despite the fact her friend could be a selfish cow at times, Linda really did worry about her.

As the car disappeared from view, Linda buttoned up her coat against the cold winter chill and quickened her steps. Her mum was cooking cottage pie this evening, and she didn't want to be late for that.

46

KATHLEEN SAT IN THE FRONT passenger seat, feeling very annoyed. She'd planned to take her time getting ready tonight and had wanted to dress up and fix her face before going out. But Tim hadn't given her time for any of that.

She hadn't even had a chance to change her outfit, so she was still wearing the uncomfortable red dress. It was so tight it felt like it was cutting her stomach in half right now.

Kathleen reached into her handbag and pulled out her powder compact. At least, she could fix her face before she got there.

As she applied the powder, she took a sideways glance at Tim, but he was staring straight ahead.

Kathleen powdered her nose and said, "So which restaurant are we going to?"

Tim shot her a look and then hesitated. "An Italian one," he said. "I've forgotten what it's called."

Kathleen smiled to herself. Italian! That was very romantic. It seemed as if Martin was finally coming around to her way of thinking. She fished out a red lipstick from her bag and tried to apply it carefully, cursing the bumps in the road.

After Kathleen had snapped the lid back on the lipstick and closed her powder compact, she noticed that the roads they were travelling on were very quiet. Residential roads. "Where is this restaurant anyway?"

"Bethnal Green," Tim said.

Kathleen had lived in the area all her life, and she knew all the little side roads like the back of her hand. She knew for sure that this little road was not the most direct route to Bethnal Green.

"You're not going the right way," Kathleen said. "You need to turn around and get back on St Paul's Way."

"A few roads have been closed. It's due to a burst pipe or something, so I'm taking another route."

Kathleen sunk back into the seat and licked her lips. She was suddenly feeling nervous.

She stared out at the dark road. As they drove on, the houses got fewer and fewer and gave way to old warehouses as they headed closer to the docks.

She suddenly wished more than anything she could be at home with little Jimmy in her arms.

She shot another anxious look at Tim. "We're not going to the restaurant, are we?"

Tim refused to look at her, and that told her everything.

She reached out her hand for the door lever, wondering how badly hurt she would be if she jumped from a moving vehicle.

"Don't even try it," Tim snapped as he glanced down at her hand.

She put both hands back in her lap, and realised even if she did manage to get out of the car, there was nobody around here who would help her, and Tim would soon catch up with her. Her best chance was to try and talk her way out of it.

"Please, I want to go home," she said, her eyes filling with tears.

When Tim wouldn't turn around or look at her, she put her hand on his arm. "Please,"

When Tim finally did turn around and looked her in the eye, she could see that he was struggling with the situation. He didn't really want to do it.

What had Martin told him to do? Threaten to beat her up?

"Look, Tim. I understand how all this works. I know you've got a job to do. Martin's told you to warn me off. But you don't have to hurt me. I'll leave. I'll take little Jimmy and leave tonight. You'll never see me again. How's that?" Kathleen's words left her mouth all in a rush. She could feel her heart thundering in her chest.

Her lower lip wobbled as she waited for Tim to respond.

He turned the car into a small side street and then parked up by the canal.

"It's nothing personal," he said.

Kathleen felt her throat tighten. "No, please. Please don't hurt me."

Big Tim's huge frame was shaking as he got out of the car and walked around to Kathleen side.

She struggled for a moment, pulling the door closed, but her strength was no match for Tim's, and he wrenched it open, grabbing her by the arm and pulling her out.

She stumbled on her heels and fell to her knees on the cobbles. From that position, she looked up at him beseechingly.

"Please, please, please."

She was so scared. She couldn't form a coherent sentence now. All she had was that single, solitary word. She pinned all her hopes onto it and repeated it over and over.

Tim took a deep breath and looked up at the sky. It was a clear night, and his breath came out in streaming puffs of white.

Kathleen's mind was whirring. She was sure he didn't really want to do it… She had a chance.

But she couldn't wait for him to change his mind. She quickly scrambled to her feet and lurched off, trying to get away from the docks and the canal. She kicked off her shoes and ran as fast as she'd ever run in her life.

But it was no good.

With a couple of huge strides, Tim was by her side, and then his hands closed around her throat.

Kathleen's eyes bulged, and her legs kicked out as she desperately fought for life.

The last thing she saw were the tears pouring down Big Tim's face as his hands tightened around her throat and he squeezed the life out of her.

Afterwards, when it was done, Big Tim fell on his hands and knees and retched. He didn't stop for five long minutes. His whole body was desperate to rid itself of the evil act he just committed.

But it was no good. When he turned back, he could still see Kathleen's lifeless figure splayed out on the edge of the canal.

His hands were trembling, as he reached out and stumbled towards her.

For a moment, he looked down at her large, empty eyes

staring up at him.

"I'm sorry," he muttered, and then he leaned down and pushed Kathleen's body into the canal.

There was a splash, and for a few seconds, she floated on the surface, her eyes still open, staring accusingly at him before she drifted away.

47

AT THE VERY MOMENT KATHLEEN'S life drained away, Martin and Babs were hosting a party at their new house in Essex.

Martin had purchased a four-bedroom house in a cul-de-sac. It was tastefully decorated. The kitchen was the latest model, with gleaming, shiny surfaces, and it was fitted with all the latest equipment. The beautifully manicured garden was the icing on the cake. Despite the fact the whole place was a knock-out, Babs was moaning. She hated it out there.

"All the neighbours turn their noses up at me," Babs said.

"That's why we're having the party, ain't it? To get to know the neighbours, let them see we are decent people."

Martin shuffled his pack of cigarettes and plucked one out. He handed one to Babs. Martin had hired a little firm to lay on a few fancy nibbles and staff to serve the cocktails. Babs hadn't had to lift a finger, but there was no pleasing the woman.

Martin took a whisky sour from a tray carried by one of the waitresses he'd hired. He smiled at her. She was a tasty little number. He might follow up later if Babs ever let him out of her sight.

"This is supposed to be a party," he hissed at Babs. "So for God's sake, look like you're enjoying yourself."

Babs scowled as Martin turned away from her. It was no good. Martin might have his heart set on a place in the country, but it wasn't him that had to bleeding live there!

It was Babs who had to suffer, and the kids who had to go to a swanky new school they hated.

Babs knew nobody in Essex, apart from her snobby neighbours who hadn't been friendly or welcoming at all. The only reason they'd come tonight was to get an eyeful of the nouveau riche element that moved into their exclusive little cul-de-sac.

The bespectacled man from next door approached her. "You have a lovely home, Mrs. Morton."

Babs knew from talking to him once before that he had some kind of job in advertising, in the city. The boring bastard hadn't stopped going on about his job when he'd cornered Babs one day as she came back from the shops. Ten tedious minutes had passed before she thought up an excuse to run back to the house.

"Thanks," Babs said. He had exactly the same layout in his gaffe. All the houses were the same on this estate.

"I hope you don't mind me bringing this up, but I have noticed that the leaves hadn't been swept up from under your sycamore tree. I wouldn't have mentioned it, but we do like to keep the neighbourhood looking smart."

Babs blinked at him. Was this really what she had to look forward to? Conversations about bloody leaves falling in the garden!

She couldn't remember the man's name — Morrissey...

Morrison, or something like that.

Babs glared at him. "Well, that's what trees do, isn't it? They lose their leaves in the winter. It's nature."

The man chuckled as if Babs had made a particularly funny joke. "Yes, very good. But you still need to rake them up, dear. Or at least, employ someone to do it. I know your husband isn't home much."

Babs did not like this man's tone one bit. If he wasn't careful, he was going to have a face full of her bloody cocktail in a minute.

"I can give you a number of a very good gardener if you'd like." The man persisted.

Babs sneered. "Why don't you give it to my husband? He deals with things like that, even though he is not here that much."

Babs walked away from the man. She needed a break from these people. Martin had some stupid, social ambitions. When would the silly sod realise that these were not his people?

She escaped into the kitchen and leaned back against the wall, taking a sip of her drink. She only wished she could hide in the kitchen all night.

They'd had the telephone installed just after they moved in, but as no one else Babs knew had a phone, she didn't see the point.

The kids were being teased at school about the way they pronounced certain words, and Babs felt guilty. It was all her fault. If she had stood up to Martin, then they would be back in the East End where they belonged.

Babs suddenly realised she wasn't as alone as she'd thought. There were voices coming from the garden. It was a cold, frosty night. Why anyone would want to be out there, freezing their bits off, was beyond Babs.

She quietly lifted the latch on the kitchen window and opened it an inch so she could hear better.

She instantly recognised the voices. It was Martin and his brother, Tony.

"Carter is beside himself. You are missing out on a prime opportunity, bruv," Tony said. "Carter is off his game. If you don't do something now—"

When he replied, Martin's voice was scornful. "I don't give a monkey's if he is off his game. Even when he's on his game, I can beat him fair and square. I'm ten times the man Carter will ever be. Besides, I've got something else on my mind at the moment. I need to give that my full attention."

"Oh yeah, what's that?"

"None of your beeswax," Martin said.

The shrill ring of the telephone made Babs jump, and she quickly stepped back from the window, afraid Martin would catch her eavesdropping. She put her drink down on the kitchen counter and hurried out to answer the telephone.

She picked up the receiver. "Hello?"

At first, no one answered, but Babs could definitely hear the sound of someone breathing on the other end of the line. "Hello, I'm sorry…I can't hear you. Is anyone there?"

Finally, the person on the other end of the line spoke, "Babs, it's Tim. I… I need to speak to Martin, please."

Tim didn't sound right. If he hadn't identified himself, Babs would never have recognised his voice. It was barely a whisper.

"All right, love. I'll just go and get him for you."

She headed back over to the sink and rapped on the

kitchen window.

Martin's face appeared at the window, and Babs moved to the kitchen door to let him in.

He stepped inside and looked at Babs suspiciously. She knew he suspected her of eavesdropping.

"Big Tim's on the phone for you," Babs said. "And what are you two doing out there on a freezing night like this? Up to no good, I bet."

Martin moved past Babs quickly, eager to get to the phone. "Don't talk daft, Babs."

Tony stepped into the kitchen behind Martin and gave Babs a dazzling smile. "Hello, Babs, you're looking gorgeous as usual."

Babs smiled and preened under Tony's attention. It was hard not to like Tony. He certainly knew how to lay on the charm. Babs wished Martin could be a little more like him, but the brothers were like chalk and cheese.

Babs knew that her hiding was over for the evening. She needed to go and play hostess, so with a sigh, she picked up her drink and headed back to the front room, where the guests were milling about, gossiping over the furniture choices, no doubt.

She walked past the telephone table and saw Martin with the phone clamped to his ear. His face was pale, but his eyes glittered with excitement, and Babs couldn't help wondering what news Big Tim had been delivering.

As she walked past, Martin said, "Take it easy. You've not done anything wrong. We didn't have any choice. Now get yourself home and get a couple of drinks inside you."

They were clearly talking about another one of Martin's shady exploits. He'd probably got his hands on some more of those knocked-off cigarettes, Babs thought as she headed into the living room and put it out of her mind.

48

MARY DIAMOND BOUNCED LITTLE JIMMY on her knee. He'd been tetchy all evening, and now he was getting hungry, the poor little mite.

"It's all right, sweetheart. Mummy will be home soon," she said and carried the baby into the kitchen.

She'd bought a nice bit of fish for supper tonight, which would make a change from the cheap potato stew she'd been serving up the past few nights.

Mary had to admit, although she didn't like the man, the money Martin had given Kathleen this week had certainly helped. The small amount Mary earned from the stall didn't touch the sides, and with Kathleen out of work and a new baby to take care of, they needed every penny they could get.

Mary had already chopped up all the vegetables, and she now transferred them to a saucepan, holding baby Jimmy tightly in her other arm.

Holding him was the only way to get him to stop crying. He was a very demanding baby, and he needed to be held and occupied at all times.

Mary returned to the front room and glanced at the clock

on the mantelpiece. Kathleen should have been home ages ago. Jimmy was hungry, and Mary's stomach was starting to think her throat had been cut. She was really looking forward to this bit of fish. She planned to pan fry it, and it wasn't something you could cook in advance and keep warm or reheat without spoiling. So she'd have to wait for Kathleen to get back.

As the minutes ticked past and turned into another hour, Mary started to get really angry. Surely Kathleen wouldn't just have gone off. She knew Jimmy would need feeding. She'd promised her mother she'd only be two hours at the shops, at the most.

Mary carried Jimmy over to the window and peered out at the dark street.

Mary had lived in the same house for years, and despite the comings and goings of different gangsters and petty criminals, she'd always felt safe there, so she couldn't explain the reason why she suddenly felt a cold shiver of dread pass through her body.

Mary didn't believe in mother's intuition or any of that other mumbo-jumbo. All she knew was that she was scared out of her wits.

Why hadn't Kathleen come home?

Kathleen was now a full two hours late. Something must have happened. Mary wrapped little Jimmy up in a blanket. She didn't bother putting him in his pram as she was only going to walk up the road. As she stepped out onto the street and shivered, she hugged little Jimmy tightly to her. His dark blue eyes were bright and watchful as they looked up into her face.

Mary quickly walked along the street and then turned left.

Maybe she was just being silly, but it was driving her mad, sitting at home waiting. When she reached the Simpsons' front door, she hesitated then knocked three times.

The door was opened by Mrs. Simpson, Linda's mother. Mary had never really got along with the Simpsons. The whole family, apart from Linda, acted as if they considered themselves a class above the likes of the Diamonds.

But desperate times called for desperate measures, and Mary needed help.

"I'm sorry to interrupt," Mary said. "Kathleen hasn't come home, and I'm a bit worried. I wondered whether Linda had seen her."

Mrs. Simpson cast her disapproving eyes onto baby Jimmy in Mary's arms, but then she stood aside. "You'd better come in."

To Mary's embarrassment, when Mrs. Simpson showed her inside, she saw that the family were all sitting down to dinner.

Mortified, she turned again to apologise to Mrs. Simpson and then quickly asked Linda whether she'd seen Kathleen. "She hasn't come home, and I'm worried. She's a good girl usually and gets home on time."

Linda's brother snorted at that. "A good girl?" He spluttered with laughter.

Mary's temper flared. "I'm well aware that Kathleen is not perfect, but she would not let little Jimmy go hungry." She shifted the baby in her arms, and even as she said the words, she wondered if she was making a fool of herself.

As much as she loved her daughter, she knew that Kathleen was inherently selfish. She'd never left Jimmy like this before, but that didn't mean there couldn't be a first time. If Kathleen came with her tail between her legs later, Mary would personally throttle the girl.

She felt Mrs. Simpson's hand on her arm. "I understand," she said. "It's a mother's instinct to worry."

Linda piped up, "She wouldn't have left Jimmy, Mum."

Mary felt the hope that she'd held onto evaporate. "So you haven't seen her, Linda?"

"I saw her earlier after I left work. I was walking home. She didn't see me, but I saw her get into a big black car at the end of the street."

Mary thought she might be sick. Who on earth did Kathleen know who owned a car? But as she asked herself the question, she realised the answer: Martin Morton.

He better not have harmed her. Mary didn't trust the man as far she could throw him.

"Was it Martin's car?" she asked Linda urgently.

Linda shook her head. "I'm sorry it was dark, and I couldn't see who was driving. I didn't recognise the car either."

Mary nodded and to her horror, she felt tears prickle in her eyes.

She turned away, burying her head in little Jimmy's blankets. She would not cry in front of the Simpsons.

How had this all gone so wrong? She hadn't had it easy bringing up Kathleen alone, but she thought she'd done a good job in the circumstances. Deep down, she knew Kathleen wasn't a bad girl.

Mrs. Simpson's voice was cool and calm as she took charge of the situation. "I don't like the sound of this, at all. I think we should notify the police."

"Oh, no!" Mary Diamond didn't have the same abhorrence

of the police as some of the people in the area did, but she didn't want to get the police involved and then be humiliated when Kathleen turned up a few hours later.

She couldn't help hoping that the girl was going to come home of her own accord, and laugh it off. Knowing Kathleen, it was possible she'd been caught up having a good time and completely forgotten about the baby.

Mrs. Simpson shook her head. "I'm sorry, Mrs. Diamond. But I really must insist. If Kathleen got into a car with a man we don't know, and we delay in calling the police..." She shook her head, leaving the rest of her words unsaid.

Mary nodded her head sadly. She was right. They would have to call the police. Mary couldn't take the chance.

"Right," Mrs. Simpson said, turning to her daughter. "Linda, you go back to Mrs. Diamond's house and make sure she's okay. Somebody needs to be there in case Kathleen comes home. Christopher and Alfred will go out looking for Kathleen in the local area, and I will go around to Mrs. Wright's. I think she's been feeding her baby formula, and that will tide little Jimmy over until we find Kathleen."

Mary was ever so thankful that Mrs. Simpson seemed so confident. "I'm sure I'm making a fuss over nothing, but I do appreciate your help."

Mrs. Simpson smiled kindly and patted her on the arm, but she stopped short of telling Mary everything would be all right.

Linda escorted a tearful Mary and little Jimmy back to their house.

Mary sat at the kitchen table, and Linda had just started heating a saucepan full of milk ready to make some cocoa when there was a knock at the front door.

Linda turned to Mrs. Diamond with a smile. "That will be my dad. I bet they've found Kathleen already."

She wiped her hands and headed out for the front door. "I'll get it."

Mary stayed sitting at the table. She'd fed Jimmy the formula, and afterwards, he'd fallen fast asleep as if all the excitement this evening had been too much for him.

When Linda opened the door, she was surprised to see it wasn't her father. She was confronted by a very tall policeman who removed his hat. "Mrs. Mary Diamond?"

Linda was too shocked to say anything, so she simply nodded and gestured for the policeman to come inside.

From her seat at the kitchen table, Mary turned around and craned her neck, so she could see who was at the door.

"Send him through, Linda," she said. "I'm sure they just want to take some details about Kathleen's disappearance."

Linda ushered the policeman through to the kitchen.

"May I sit down?" the policeman asked.

Mary nodded, and the policeman pulled out a chair and sat down opposite her. Linda hovered beside them, wringing her hands nervously.

"I know you want more information, officer. But the truth is, I don't know anything other than what Mrs. Simpson would have told you already. Kathleen went out, but she should have been back to feed the baby over three hours ago. I've no idea where she is. Linda saw her getting in a black car at the end of the street at about half past five. There's not much else I can tell you."

The policeman was starting to look extremely uncomfortable. He couldn't get a word in edgeways with all

Mary's chatter.

Linda took a step forward and put a hand on Mary's shoulder. "Maybe the policeman can tell us something, Mrs. Diamond."

Mary nodded and smiled. "Sorry, I'm babbling on. I'm just ever so worried about her, you know? Would you like a drink? We were just about to have some cocoa?"

The policeman shook his head and then cleared his throat nervously. "I'm ever so sorry to tell you this, Mrs. Diamond..."

Mary let out a little gasp, and Linda's shaking arms wrapped around her shoulders as they braced themselves for what the policeman was about to say next.

"We have found a body of a girl who has been strangled and dumped into the canal. We believe it's your daughter, Mrs. Diamond."

49

BIG TIM WAS STRUGGLING. HE'D taken himself off to the Blind Beggar in Whitechapel. He usually drank at Martin's club because he liked to be around faces he knew, but today he didn't want to talk to anyone.

The regular crowd at the Blind Beggar looked up, surprised to see him as he walked in, but Tim kept his eyes straight ahead, not wanting to attract conversation. Molly, one of the regular barmaids, was soon in front of him.

"We don't often see you in here these days," she said, giving him a flirtatious wink.

Tim didn't engage. Usually, he liked the attention he got from being part of Martin's gang, but today he just wanted to be left alone, to dwell on the awful act he had committed.

Tim ordered a pint of beer and a whisky chaser. He was planning to get blind drunk, and hoped to God when he woke up tomorrow morning, he was feeling a little better. Or at least, he hoped he'd find a way to live with this awful guilt.

Tim was on his third pint when he overheard some geezer at the bar talking loudly about Dave Carter.

Tim had made it his business over the years to know

everybody related to the Carter gang, at least, the ones who were openly affiliated with him.

The man talking was Terry Pulchetti, the son of Italian immigrants who'd moved to the East End twenty years ago.

He was a flamboyant character and very passionate. As he talked, he was gesturing with his hands. Clearly, he was quite a fan of Dave Carter and hadn't noticed that Tim, one of Martin Morton's henchmen, was sitting quietly at a table in the corner.

The people Terry was talking to had noticed Tim's presence, though. They were exchanging nervous glances and looking over at Tim. But the Italian was having far too much fun being the centre of attention to pay heed to any of their warnings.

"He has a nobility," the Italian said. "How anyone can get through the loss of a daughter like that and then come back the way he has." He shook his head and then took a deep breath as if he was getting emotional. "It's not like it was in the old days. Dave Carter is the only one left. He is a man you can trust, a man with principles." The man raised his drink in the air and said in a booming voice, "To Dave Carter, may he find strength in this difficult time."

A few people raise their drinks, but most of them had their eyes fixed on Tim, looking terrified. They needn't have worried. Tim was in no mood to defend Martin Morton tonight.

If he were honest, Tim had always had a sneaking admiration for Dave Carter. He knew lots of people laughed at his background, coming from a family of greengrocers like he did. But Tim couldn't see anything wrong in that. Dave Carter was a hard-working, fair man. Like any man with that amount of power, he had a ruthless streak, but Tim doubted Dave Carter would have given the order to kill the mother of one of his children.

As far as Tim knew, Dave Carter didn't even play around on the side.

If Martin Morton had been an intelligent man, he would have begun organising his operation to take advantage of Dave Carter right now when he was most vulnerable. That, in Tim's opinion, wouldn't have been despicable. It was purely business.

It was difficult to know where to draw the line. All Tim knew was that he had crossed his own particular moral line tonight, and he wasn't sure he would ever get over that. He looked up and sighed when he saw the swaggering Italian walking over to him.

"My apologies, Tim. I didn't see you there. I meant no disrespect."

The Italian wasn't talking so loudly now. He wasn't broadcasting his apology to the rest of the pub. He was talking fast and nervously licking his lips between each word.

What was the point in any of this? Tim just couldn't be bothered with it.

He stood up and picked up his coat. "Get out of my way," he growled and pushed through the crowd of people in the pub to get to the exit.

The following morning in Pentonville Prison, Charlie Williams carried his tray away from the serving counter and stared down at his breakfast. Weak tea and lumpy porridge. Prison food was bloody awful. He could kill for one of his mum's full English breakfasts right now.

He walked forward, weaving between the rows of men sitting at the benches. Most of them were already full. There were a few spare seats scattered about, but he had to be ever so careful about who he picked to sit next to. It was all political. You chose your mates from the start and stuck with them.

Charlie had fallen in with a couple of young men around his age. They weren't bad lads, and it always helped to have someone to watch your back in prison. As he searched the room for his mates, his gaze fell on a nasty weasel-faced man, called Alfie Harris.

Alfie didn't really hold much sway in prison. He was a South Londoner, and a good ten years older than Charlie, but he had a vindictive streak a mile long. He was the kind of man who enjoyed suffering. And he would play horrible practical jokes on other inmates just to get a sick kick out of it.

Charlie had determined from day one to avoid him. That was the best way to handle prison, keep your head down and not upset anybody.

But from the way Alfie Harris's eyes were fixed on him, it looked like Charlie Williams's luck had just run out.

Charlie carried on walking and pretended not to notice. Maybe if he didn't give the sadistic sod any attention, he'd grow bored. But as he went to pass Alfie, he tripped and went flying.

His tray clattered to the floor, porridge splattering up, covering his face and hair, and his tea burned his hands. For a moment, he lay there, dazed, as a great roar went up from his fellow prisoners, who were laughing and pointing.

Charlie rolled onto his side and then pushed himself up to his feet. It was then that he saw Alfie Harris's leg pushed out and crossing his path.

He had tripped Charlie deliberately.

Charlie felt his blood boiling in his veins and clenched his fists at his sides. He would have absolutely loved to wipe the smirk off that bastard's face. But Alfie was surrounded with a crowd of his cronies, and Charlie was wise enough to know he couldn't take them all on.

"Oh, dear," Alfie said, his voice dripping with sarcasm. "Charlie Williams, ain't it? Don't you work for the great Dave Carter?"

Charlie didn't reply. He just stared back stonily at him.

"Well, you really should be more careful." Alfie got to his feet, pushed his finished breakfast tray away from him and shoved his face close to Charlie's. "Prison can be a very dangerous place."

"Is that a threat?" Charlie asked, making sure he kept a broad grin on his face so Alfie knew exactly what he thought of his threats.

"No, son," Alfie Harris chuckled. "It's just a friendly warning. Watch your back. And stay out of my way."

That was exactly what Charlie had been trying to do, but obviously, he hadn't quite managed it.

Charlie bent down to pick up his spilled breakfast tray, and a prison guard wandered over. He took his bleeding time, Charlie thought.

"Clean up this mess, Williams," the prison guard ordered, hooking his thumbs through the belt loops of his trousers."

That was what he was trying to do. Charlie shook his head, but he knew better than to complain about his treatment. He picked up pieces of the broken bowl and lumps of soggy porridge with his fingers.

"Do you think I could have a cloth or something?"

The prison guard stared down at Charlie with indignation. "What do you think I am? Your bleeding maid? You can get yourself down to the kitchen and ask for one. Get a mop and bucket while you're at it. Perhaps after mopping the cafeteria floor you'll be a little more careful in future."

To catcalls and cries from the other prisoners, Charlie stomped off towards the kitchen. It was just another day in the wonderful world of prison.

By the time Charlie finished mopping the floor, everyone else had gone.

He put the mop and bucket away in the cupboard in the kitchen and then headed out. He was missing exercise time in the yard over this, and he was desperate for a ciggie. He intended to make a quick detour and go back to his cell to pick up his baccy before going outside. Unfortunately, Alfie Harris and his cronies had predicted Charlie's route.

Charlie sighed when he saw them.

"Really? You haven't had enough for one day?" Charlie said, shaking his head.

Alfie Harris put his ugly, red face right up to Charlie's.

"I'll tell you when I've had enough, Williams. We've heard you're the big man. So why don't you prove it, eh? Come on, I'll give you first punch," Alfie said.

Charlie laughed. "You've got to be joking. Do I look stupid? As soon as I land a punch, you and all your mates will pile on. It's hardly going to be a fair fight, is it?"

For his cheek, Charlie got a shove from behind. Although he was itching to land one right on Alfie Harris's nose, he managed to keep both his arms at his sides.

"Come on, I just wanted a cigarette. I don't want any trouble, Alfie."

But Alfie Harris clearly wasn't in the mood to be reasonable. He delivered an open-handed smack to the side of Charlie's face.

That was the trigger. It was a fight that Charlie couldn't hope to win, but he couldn't take disrespect like that. He launched himself at Alfie, delivering an uppercut to the jaw and one hard punch to Alfie's soft belly before the other men pulled him off.

As Charlie predicted, they all piled on. He was punched and kicked until his whole body felt bruised. Alfie screamed insults at him the whole time.

When they'd finally decided he'd had enough, Charlie was sprawled out on the floor with blood pouring out of a cut on his head and another at the side of his mouth.

He spat the blood on the floor. "Is that all you've got?" Charlie murmured weakly before he passed out.

50

AFTER TAKING A THOROUGH BEATING from Alfie Harris and his friends, Charlie William's woke up on the medical ward. His ribs had been bandaged and all his cuts cleaned, but he still ached all over.

He'd only been awake for five minutes when he was ordered out of bed and escorted back to his cell.

He slept until dinnertime. The bell rang out, and Charlie could hear the shouts and clanging footsteps of the other inmates making their way to the cafeteria. But he couldn't bring himself to go with them.

At least, the other bed in his cell was empty. He'd had to put up with a kid from Bermondsey crying his eyes out every night for the last month, but they'd moved him on two days ago. No doubt, another inmate would fill the empty bed soon.

Later that evening, the prison guard on night duty, took pity on him and passed him a hunk of bread and some cheese. But Charlie couldn't even stomach that. The doctor had been by to administer some more painkillers, which at least helped him sleep. Charlie dozed on and off, wincing every time he tried to turn over.

Something woke him in the early hours and made him open his eyes. A little squeak sounded near to his ear. He jumped off the bed and then held his ribs in pain.

There, beside the bed, was a dirty, great rat, munching on his cheese.

"Gerroff!" Charlie yelled, flapping his hands to scare the horrible thing away.

He peered at the plate where his cheese sat, half-eaten by the giant rat. The rat left some dirty, black droppings next to the plate as well.

As if life couldn't get any more depressing, Charlie thought. He didn't know how much more of it he could take. At least, the pain in his ribs took his mind off the pain in his leg. It still ached when it rained, although the bullet wound had healed quite nicely in the end.

Charlie stared grouchily at the cheese, prepared to kill the bloody rat if it came back. He'd really hoped to have gotten out of prison by now. The police investigation made no sense at all. He was the victim, but as well as getting shot that night, he'd also been stitched up somehow and blamed for the shooting. It was ridiculous. He hadn't shot himself in the leg!

As Charlie sat back down on the bed, he reached inside his bedside cabinet, which was bolted to the floor and only had one little drawer, for his tobacco. Then an idea occurred to him. For the first time in a long while, Charlie Williams smiled. That rat had done him a favour.

Pushing himself back on the bed, Charlie cradled his ribs. The bastards really had given him a thorough beating. He opened up his pouch of tobacco and then looked at the rat droppings. He grinned. Perfect.

* * *

On Monday afternoon, Martin was back in his flat after a weekend in Essex. He left Babs and the kids at the new house, much to Babs' disappointment. She'd told him in no uncertain terms that she wasn't happy there. He wished she wouldn't moan so much. Sometimes it seemed like that was all she ever did.

He'd given her a blinding house with a gorgeous garden and all she did was moan about the neighbours.

Martin would never understand it. He couldn't give a damn about a bunch of snobby neighbours. He didn't mind people thinking he was working class; that suited him down to the ground. All he wanted was for people to respect him, and he got that respect through fear.

Martin looked at Tim, who was sitting on one of Martin's leather armchairs and staring out of the window with a blank expression on his face.

Martin frowned. "Are you even listening to me?"

Tim blinked a couple of times as if he was just coming to after a trance. "Of course."

"I was asking you what happened to the kid? Kathleen didn't have it with her?"

Tim's face grew pale, and his eyes widened. "The kid? You don't want me to..."

"What's the matter with you?" Martin asked sharply. "Are you coming down with something?"

Tim shook his head. "Kathleen had left the baby with her mother."

Martin shrugged as if the news didn't bother him one way or another, and then he looked up and scowled as his brother walked into the dining room.

Tony had the confidence of an angel. He grinned at them both and then dropped down into a chair, sprawling over it.

"Sit up. You're making the place look untidy," Martin ordered.

Martin's sharp words didn't dent Tony's confidence. His smile grew wider, but he did sit up. He was wearing an expensive tailored suit, and Martin knew he thought he was a good-looking bastard.

"I've got some news," Tony said. "But you're not going to like it."

Martin shook his head. He'd been off his game over the last few days, too caught up in sorting out issues of a personal nature. Never before had his personal life encroached on his business, and he was determined to keep them separate in the future.

"What is it? Spit it out."

"It's Dave Carter. He's taken over Ronnie Baxter."

Martin bit down on his tongue. Of all the nerve! He clenched his fists and banged them down on the arms of the chair he was sitting in.

Ronnie Baxter was a supplier of knockoff booze, one of the biggest suppliers in the East End. He supplied Martin's club directly, as well as a number of the pubs under Martin's protection.

For a moment, Martin was so furious he couldn't speak. He stood up and paced the room, shaking his head.

Tim and Tony watched him. Tony still had that infuriating smile on his face, but Tim's face was expressionless.

"I can't believe that bastard hasn't yet learned his lesson."

"Maybe he needs another one," Tony suggested, looking down at the gold watch on his wrist.

Martin paused. He paid Tony handsomely, but he didn't pay him enough to buy a bloody gold watch. "Where did you get that?"

"What this old thing?" Tony held up his wrist, chuckling. "It was payment for a debt. A private payment."

Tony's eyes met Martin in a challenging fashion. Martin was about to dig further, but then he stopped himself. He couldn't let himself get sidetracked. Dave Carter was the important issue here.

"I have shown him how serious I am," Martin ranted. "We eliminated Keith Parker when he was playing both sides, and after everything that went down at The Three Grapes, Dave Carter should know enough to give me a wide berth. I've outclassed him in every way. One of his lads is still in prison."

Martin ran his hands through his hair, exasperated. "That bloody greengrocer should go back to selling bleeding apples and get his nose out my business."

Martin spun round to face Tony and Tim, his eyes glinting evilly. "This is war, boys. And it's not over until we have annihilated Carter."

51

MARY WALKED ALONG HOLLINS ROAD. The rain was steadily coming down and splashing into puddles as she walked. Her shoes were soaked through, and her grey hair was plastered to her head, but she barely noticed.

The past couple of days had passed in a blur with concerned neighbours delivering food. The East End pulled together when someone suffered a tragedy like this, and Mary had been touched by her neighbours' consideration. Especially Mrs. Simpson, Linda's mother. She'd taken control that night, and Mary would be forever grateful.

She hadn't known what to do with herself after the policeman had left. What was someone supposed to do when they'd been told their only child had been murdered?

Mrs. Simpson had made sure Jimmy was fed and changed, and then she told Linda to spend the night.

Linda was a good, sweet, kind girl and had been a comfort to Mary. The only trouble was that the little house only had two bedrooms, so Linda stayed in Kathleen's room and kept an eye on Jimmy overnight.

The following morning when Mary woke up and the memory of last night came crashing around her, she could hear the sound of steady breathing coming from Kathleen's room, and she'd almost convinced herself the whole thing had been a dream.

Even though she knew deep down it wasn't true, she couldn't help the hope that grew in her chest. She pushed open Kathleen's bedroom door, hoping to see her daughter asleep in the bed. Instead, her gaze fell on Linda's plump figure half-hidden under the covers.

Quietly, Mary had taken little Jimmy from his crib and carried him downstairs, leaving Linda to sleep.

Jimmy was determined to be difficult and didn't want to take the formula milk.

Mary was almost beside herself. "I'm sorry, little lamb," she muttered. "But you don't have a choice. It's this or nothing, so you'd better get used to it."

Jimmy squirmed in Mary's arms, refusing to suck at the bottle, leaving his grandmother in tears by the time Linda came downstairs.

Linda stepped up and took the baby from her. "Don't you worry, Mrs. Diamond. I'll look after him. Why don't you go and get yourself dressed?"

Later that day, Linda took the baby to visit her mother, to give Mary a chance to catch up on some sleep. But Mary couldn't sleep. Sleep was the last thing she wanted. As soon as she closed her eyes, she had horrible visions of Kathleen floating in the canal.

So she'd decided to go out for a walk, and that was how she found herself, soaking wet, looking up at the outside of Martin Morton's club.

It was busy already, and the music was pumping. How

could he? How could he just go on as if nothing had happened?

Her poor little girl would never see another day. She spotted Martin Morton through the window, chatting with some men, propped up against the bar, and he was smiling.

That smarmy smile tipped Mary over the edge.

She slipped past the doormen, who didn't know what to do. They'd never had to manhandle a woman of Mary's age before.

The two big men in suits tried to guide her back outside, but they weren't quick enough, and she made a beeline for Martin.

"You bastard! You killed her. I know you did," Mary screamed at him, and despite the loud music in the bar, everybody turned around to see who was daring to talk to Martin Morton in that way.

Martin's whole body was tense as he turned. He was like a loaded spring, only just in control. He shot an irritated look at the two huge men behind Mary.

The tallest of the men shrugged. "Sorry, boss. She just slipped past us."

Martin shook his head in disgust, but then he turned back to Mary. "I've answered all the questions the police had for me, and they are satisfied, so if you don't mind, I'd like you to leave."

Tears were freely falling down Mary's cheeks as she shook her head and pointed a finger in Martin's direction. "I will have you for this, Martin Morton. I swear to God, I will make you sorry you ever met my Kathleen."

The men around Martin were looking shocked at Mary's daring. But she didn't care. She'd already lost everything.

There was nothing Martin could do to her now that would make her feel any worse.

Martin took a menacing step towards Mary. "I am already sorry, you old bat. I wish I had never laid eyes on your tart of a daughter."

There was a collective intake of breath all around the bar. Martin Morton might rule the area with an iron fist, but the people of the East End had respect for the dead, and no one liked to hear that kind of language. Although no one would say anything, they all thought that Martin had gone too far.

But Martin was oblivious to their reaction. "I have an alibi. I was in bleeding Essex all weekend." Martin gave Mary a smug smile. "So you tell me, how am I supposed to have done her in?"

Mary's chest was rising and falling rapidly as she struggled for breath. "You got one of your lackeys to do it," Mary screamed.

She walked right up to Martin and poked a finger in his chest. She opened her mouth, about to shout another insult, when out of the corner of her eye, she spotted Big Tim. One look at his slack face and his haunted eyes, and she knew that he had done it.

She pointed at Big Tim. "You got him to do it, didn't you?"

"Get the stupid bitch out of here," Martin said, waving his hand in dismissal as he turned his back on Mary.

The doormen had to drag Mary out, kicking and screaming. And although the music in the bar continued, the conversations all around the club ended as everybody watched how Martin Morton was treating Mary Diamond.

As Mary was shoved back out in the rain, she took a large gasping breath. Her chest felt so tight she could hardly breathe.

She stared up at the outside of Martin's club and vowed to herself that one day she would get revenge for this. One day Martin Morton would get what was coming to him.

52

MEALTIMES WERE THE WORST. THAT and bedtimes. Those were the times he missed Lillian the most. When they sat together as a family around the dinner table, Dave felt Lillian's absence keenly.

Trevor sat opposite him pushing the peas around his plate and not eating.

Sandra was watching her son intently.

For the last couple of days, Trevor had been refusing to talk. In two whole days, he hadn't uttered a word.

Dave had told Sandra it was just a phase, a reaction to the death of his sister. He thought if they ignored it for a while, Trevor would go back to normal, but Sandra was convinced he was acting up.

Trevor put down his knife and fork and pushed his plate away. He turned in his seat and went to climb down, but Sandra reached down and gripped his arm. "Oh, no, you don't. You do not leave this table without asking to be excused."

Trevor sat back at the table, but still he said nothing. He leaned back in his chair and looked up at his father. Trevor's big eyes regarded Dave reproachfully. It seemed to Dave,

Trevor was silently asking how could he trust a father who would let his sister die.

"As if we haven't had enough to deal with," Sandra muttered under her breath. "Trevor, I'm not in the mood to deal with your naughtiness. I know perfectly well you can talk."

Trevor stared down at his plate.

"How would you feel if I refused to talk to you?" Sandra demanded of her little boy.

Dave sighed and started to stack the plates. "Come on love. Just let it go for now."

But Sandra shook her head. "No, I won't. If we don't nip this in the bud now, he'll think he can get away with anything."

Sandra turned back to Trevor. "Well, are you going to ask to be excused?"

Trevor silently shook his head.

And then, unexpectedly, Sandra's fierce anger disappeared, and she began to sob.

Grief had ripped their family apart. Everyone was reacting to Lillian's death in a different way. Dave was trying to hold it all together, but truthfully, he didn't know where to start. Sandra now had a new baby to look after on top of everything else, and it was all too much for her.

As the tears rolled down Sandra's cheeks, Trevor reached out and put his little hand on top of his mother's, to try and comfort her, but still he didn't speak.

Dave stood up and kissed his wife on the forehead. "Come on, love. Why don't you get yourself up to bed, eh? I'll clear up the dinner things."

He scooped the little boy out of his chair and carried him

up to his bedroom. "Do you want me to read you a story, Trevor?"

Trevor looked up at his father and hesitated, but then he nodded.

"Right, well, get your pyjamas on and clean your teeth, and I'll be back in a minute."

While Trevor was getting ready for bed, Dave washed up the plates from dinner. Before he could go to Trevor's bedroom, and begin telling the story, there was a knock at the front door.

When Dave answered the door, he felt the tension in his body ratchet up several levels.

It was Gary.

Gary looked up at him sheepishly. "I'm so sorry, bruv. I'm sorry I didn't make the funeral. I didn't hear about it until afterwards."

Dave didn't invite his brother in, but Gary stepped through the door anyway and enveloped his brother in a hug. "Let's not argue anymore, eh? Family is just too important."

Dave didn't return the hug. His body was stiff and unresponsive before he pulled away, but he let Gary follow him inside the house.

"How's Sandra?" Gary asked.

Dave shook his head. He didn't know where to start. "Not good. In fact, you could do me a favour."

Gary nodded eagerly. "Of course. Anything. What do you need me to do?"

"Go and get Dr. Spencer."

Dave gave him Dr. Spencer's address and moved towards the stairs, intending to read Trevor his story.

Gary turned just before he left the house. "I really am sorry, bruv. I promise I'm never going to let you down again."

Dave said nothing. He just trudged up the stairs towards Trevor's bedroom.

Dave had just finished reading Trevor his story when the doctor arrived with Gary.

Dave shook the doctor's hand. "Dr. Spencer, thank you for coming."

"What seems to be the trouble?" the doctor asked as he followed Dave into the kitchen.

"I need you to give Sandra something. She is beside herself, crying all the time, getting upset with Trevor. She can't cope."

The doctor sighed and looked uncomfortable as he regarded Dave steadily for a moment. Then he said, "I can give Mrs. Carter a sedative to help her sleep. There are some tablets I can prescribe that may improve her mood, but I'm sorry Mr, Carter, I don't have a magic pill for grief. The only cure for that is time. And it never really goes away. It just hurts a little less as time goes by."

Dave nodded sadly. "While you're here, maybe you could take a look at Trevor, too. He is refusing to talk."

The doctor frowned and then nodded. "Of course."

"I'll put the kettle on," Gary said, leaving Dave and the doctor to climb the stairs together.

The little boy was tucked under the covers, but he wasn't asleep.

"This is Dr Spencer," Dave said. "He's going have a look at you and make sure you're all right."

The doctor took his time examining Trevor. He asked him lots of questions that went unanswered. Trevor just regarded him silently with his big grey eyes. But the doctor didn't make a fuss over Trevor's silence.

Finally, when he'd finished his examination, the doctor said, "Now, Trevor. Your father tells me you haven't been talking much over the past couple of days. I've examined you and determined there's no physical reason for that. I understand that you're feeling very sad and confused because your sister has gone. Sometimes these things make us feel so sad we can't express them."

The little boy's eyes filled with tears, but he didn't speak.

The doctor smiled kindly and pulled up the bed covers to tuck him in. "Things will get better, Trevor."

Dave followed the doctor out of Trevor's bedroom. "So there's no reason he's not talking? There's nothing wrong with him?"

"The only reason is his grief. It's hard for a child to understand the loss of a sibling at the best of times. Maybe he blames himself. No doubt he's heard people talking about how he was the sickest out of the pair of them, yet he was the one who survived."

As they entered the kitchen, Gary turned to look at them. He held up a bottle of Dave's brandy. "I decided against tea. I thought we'd better have something stronger."

He poured Dave and the doctor a glass of brandy, too.

The doctor took his glass with a nod. "Thank you. You're lucky to have such a supportive family, Mr. Carter."

Dave ignored his brother and his glass of brandy. "So, Doctor, are you telling me this is only temporary? Trevor will get over this at some point, won't he?"

The doctor nodded. "Yes, I think he'll grow out of it. It could last a couple of days, maybe a few weeks, but eventually he'll start talking again."

Dave felt a rush of relief wash over him as he reached for his brandy.

After the doctor had left them with a prescription for Sandra, Dave sat down at the kitchen table opposite Gary. "Where have you been?"

"Here and there," Gary said. "I went up to Manchester for a few days and did a bit of business."

"Are you still taking that stuff?" Dave asked, examining Gary's face and eyes for any telltale signs that he was still hooked on drugs.

Gary shook his head emphatically. "No, I'm hundred percent clean. I mean it, Dave. I've turned over a new leaf. I've come to realise how important family is."

Dave searched his brother's face, looking for any signs to indicate he was lying. But it was no good. Dave was seriously off his game. The senses that he normally relied on had deserted him, and all he could think about was that his brother was family, and family was precious.

53

MARTIN MORTON LOOKED AROUND THE room, surveying the men he'd summoned to the meeting. They were gathered in the flat above the club. Red-haired Freddie sat on one of the armchairs. Henry the Hand, Tony and Big Tim were squeezed together on the sofa, and Martin stood in front of them.

He'd only invited his core men here. Men he could trust. He planned to take his business to the next level, and he didn't want to take the unnecessary risks that came with revealing his scheme to his less trustworthy underlings.

He believed he could trust all of the men in this room.

"Good news, boys. We are expanding. It's time we really made our mark. We need a few more places under our protection, and the first one I've picked out for us is The Lamb."

There were a few confused looks from the men before Red-haired Freddie spoke up.

"The Lamb? Are you talking about the pub in Poplar?"

Martin nodded. "Yes, that's the one."

"But isn't that on Dave Carter's patch, boss."

"Not anymore, Freddie. As far as I'm concerned, Dave

Carter doesn't have a patch. I'm going to take every single one of his properties and chase him out of the East End for good."

A heavy silence fell over the room, and Martin studied each one of his men in turn.

If any of them had any doubts, it was better that they spoke up now. He didn't want anyone working for him who wasn't one hundred percent committed.

He knew he was better than Dave Carter, and he intended to prove it. But a leader was only as good as the men he had working for him, and if any of these men were yellow, he needed to know now.

Henry the Hand was the next man to speak up. "Sounds good to me, boss. Dave Carter has been asking for a smack for a long time. It's time we put him in his place once and for all."

There were murmurs of agreement from around the room.

Notably, Big Tim stayed silent. He'd been acting very strangely recently. Martin narrowed his eyes as he looked at him. Big Tim had always been his most trusted man. Martin didn't want to believe that that had changed.

"What do you think, Tim?"

Big Tim turned his head to look at Martin. He gave a single nod. "Absolutely. The time is right."

Red-haired Freddie still held back. Out of all of the men, Martin considered him the smartest. He could be a coarse bastard, and definitely enjoyed his drink a bit too much for Martin's liking, but there was no denying that Red-haired Freddie had a way of looking at problems with an analytical mind.

"The Lamb is a big move, boss. It's a statement. Don't you

think it might be better to start off with one of the smaller properties and take him by surprise? We could edge our way in. Take control slowly before he even knows what's happening."

Red-haired Freddie might be smart, but Martin thought he was wrong on this occasion. He'd underestimated how good Martin was.

Martin Morton was worth ten of Dave Carter, and he wasn't afraid of anything that pathetic waste of space could throw at him.

"I don't think we need to be too worried about Dave Carter, Freddie. The man comes from a long line of greengrocers for goodness sake. He's just playing at this. Once we take away the central piece of his little empire, it will collapse. Trust me. It will fall down like a line of dominoes."

Red-haired Freddie narrowed his eyes, but he nodded. "Okay, boss. The Lamb it is."

At that same moment, just over a mile away, Dave Carter was also holding a meeting. He was pleased with how his two new recruits had turned out. Patrick Cunnings, in particular, seemed to have a knack for the roles Dave had assigned to him so far. Dave was currently employing him as a heavy, but he could see the kid had a natural ability for the work and had decided to promote him soon.

He'd asked his brother, Gary, Brian Moore and Patrick Cunnings to come and see him at the warehouse.

Getting back to work wasn't easy. Lillian's death had knocked him for six, and he'd taken quite a bit of time off to spend with his family. The new baby was sickly and was struggling to feed. Trevor was still in his silent phase, and Sandra still cried herself to sleep at night.

Dave knew grief took time to heal, and he wasn't sure he'd ever get over the loss of Lillian, but he couldn't afford to let the business slide.

Luckily for him, the shops and pubs under his protection carried on much the same as usual, thankfully earning money. The new car workshop he'd set up was also ticking over nicely, thanks to Brian's careful supervision. But in this business, Dave couldn't afford to take his eye off the game.

There were plenty of wannabes, waiting in the wings, looking for a piece of the action and the chance to take over his patch. The most dangerous of these men was Martin Morton, and Dave had known that for a long time.

Dave leaned back in his chair, hands resting on his desk, and listened to his men's condolences.

"I appreciate that," Dave said to Patrick, who'd just murmured how sorry he was about Lillian's passing.

"I'm not going to lie to you, lads. It's been a very hard few weeks, but I need to get back to work for my own sanity and to keep this business running."

Dave exhaled and leaned forward. "Charlie Williams is still behind bars, and it's looking like Martin Morton killed Frank. He thinks he's gotten away with it."

Dave clenched his fists and shook his head. "But he hasn't."

Dave looked at his men in turn. "I've got it on good authority Martin Morton is planning a major hit on us, soon."

Gary piped up, "Who told you that?"

Dave was known for playing the long game. He had

always been a firm believer in informants. Information was critical in this business. It wasn't all threats and violence. Most of the time, you could play on people's emotions. If someone felt they had been slighted or hurt in the past by one of his rivals, Dave made it his business to reach out to them. It was surprising how long grudges could last, and Dave liked to exploit that. There was no extortion or violence. It was simply talking and extracting knowledge.

"I have an informant close to Martin Morton."

"How close is this person to Martin?" Brian asked.

"Close enough. I'm not going to be sharing their identity, so there's no point asking," Dave said and gave a pointed look to his brother.

Gary shrugged.

"I want you all to be on your guard. We might need to react quickly, and when we do, we need to be ruthless. The way I see it, all of our properties are at risk. Although, I doubt he's going to bother with the chain of greengrocers," Dave said, and everyone chuckled.

All the men in the room were aware of Dave's nickname among his enemies — the greengrocer, and while Dave himself could make a joke about it, none of them would have dared.

"The warehouse could also be a target," Dave continued. "It's prime real estate and perfect for selling and distributing booze and fags, so Martin will want a piece of the action."

"So it could be one of the pubs or the warehouse. The informant doesn't know where he is planning to hit us?" Brian asked.

Dave shook his head. "Not yet."

Despite the unease of everyone else in the room, Dave

smiled. It felt good to be back in the game and take his mind off the problems at home.

He needed to focus his full energy on beating Martin Morton, and that was exactly what he intended to do.

54

GARY CARTER TUGGED ON THE sleeves of his shirt. He had just taken a little pick me up. Not too much, as he didn't want Dave to catch wind of it, but he needed a little to get going today. Things were about to get serious between the Morton gang and the Carters, and he needed to be on top of his game.

He hadn't been lying exactly when he'd told Dave he'd given the stuff up. He'd tried. He really had, and he was determined to kick the habit again just as soon as they got past all these troubles with Martin Morton.

Gary knew Dave considered him a live wire, and it hurt that his own brother couldn't trust him. Although he wouldn't admit it to anyone else, he was well aware of the fact that he had screwed up the raid on The Three Grapes.

He'd let Martin Morton get the better of them on that occasion, and for that, he owed Dave big time.

To see his brother devastated after the death of his niece, poor little Lillian, cut Gary's heart in two. Dave and Sandra had been such a happy little family. Life just wasn't fair.

Gary was determined to help Dave out, whether he wanted his help or not. To do that, he needed to make sure his brother wasn't hiding anything from him. Like this informant, for example. He was concerned it could be a trap laid by Martin Morton.

Ever since they were kids, Dave had always been a fan of talking things through, of using his brain over his fists. Which was all well and good, but Martin Morton was a sneaky bastard, and he didn't want to risk his brother getting caught out.

Gary sniffed and wiped his nose on the back of his hand as Dave walked past.

Dave looked at him with narrowed eyes. "Are you all right, Gary?"

Gary nodded. "Never better. Where are you off to?" Gary asked as Dave put on his coat.

"Bit of business," Dave said and then, without another word, headed out the warehouse.

Gary chewed on his thumbnail and wondered what to do. He only hesitated for a moment before he followed Dave out of the warehouse.

He paused beside the door, waiting for Dave to get a safe enough distance away. Gary didn't want to be seen following him.

He licked his lips, nervously and raked a hand through his hair. Dave would not be happy if he knew he was being trailed.

He kept a safe distance from Dave all the way up Blocksy Road. Despite the fact Dave owned a huge car workshop now, he still didn't use the motors. He preferred to walk and always had done. He liked to know the lay of the land and to see the locals running their businesses in the area.

Dave had always said knowledge was power, and if he

drove everywhere, he'd miss all those little things that added up to a wealth of knowledge. But it was bloody freezing today, and Gary wished he could have followed Dave in a car.

His hand shook as he lit a cigarette. He held it to his lips and breathed in deeply.

When Dave stopped to talk to an old geezer outside The Lamb, Gary made sure he stayed a safe distance away and hid in a shop doorway. He couldn't hear what they were discussing, but he imagined it wasn't anything important. The old geezer was very unlikely to be the informant. Whoever was spilling Martin Morton's secrets to Dave, had to be close enough to Martin to get quality information.

Bleeding well get a move on.

Gary gave an impatient huff. He was freezing his knackers off, and Dave had just stopped to exchange a few pleasantries. Did his brother not feel the cold?

Gary wished his brother would hurry up. His hiding place was not ideal. He was blocking the entrance to the butcher's shop, and two women had already passed by, looking at him curiously.

The shopkeeper tried to nudge open the door behind him, and Gary turned on him furiously.

Gary hissed, "Get back inside, you nosy bastard!"

The shopkeeper quickly did as he was told, turning the sign hanging on the window around to say closed and locking the door.

Gary peered round the corner and saw Dave had started walking again, so he slid out of his hiding place and continued to follow him.

They walked for some time, and Gary was on his third

cigarette by the time they arrived at East India Dock Road.

Gary was starting to think this had been a wasted exercise. What was the point? Dave was probably just on one of his normal walkabouts. Gary hadn't seen anyone that could possibly be Dave's informant.

There was a cafe just up the road, on the right, and Gary thought about calling it a day and getting a nice hot cup of tea inside him. It was brass monkeys outside today.

Just when he was about to give up, he saw Dave turn off the pavement and head inside the Poplar Baths.

Gary frowned. What on earth was Dave doing going in there?

Keeping a safe distance from Dave, Gary also entered the baths. As soon as he went through the main entrance, he smelled the distinctive pong of chlorine, and he wrinkled his nose. Inside the little lobby, Gary turned in a circle, but there was no sign of Dave.

Flaming hell, he'd missed him. He'd frozen his balls off for the last half an hour, and it was all for nothing.

Gary was just about to give up when a movement caught the corner of his eye. When he turned, he saw a woman with dark hair, wearing a fitted red dress. She looked a little overdressed for the Poplar Baths and that intrigued Gary. He walked a little closer and saw Dave standing just around the corner, staring at the woman in red.

Now that was interesting. Dave was very proud of the fact he was a family man. Gary couldn't understand it himself, but Dave was dedicated to Sandra and never so much as looked at another bird. So this was definitely a turn-up for the books. Gary smirked. So his dear old brother wasn't perfect after all.

East End Trouble

He could only see the woman from behind and wished he was a little closer. He'd like to see the woman who'd managed to turn Dave's head.

Gary leaned back against the wall where he was half hidden by a noticeboard and watched as Dave approached the woman and started to talk.

Gary cursed under his breath. He wasn't close enough to hear what they were saying, but he was worried about getting too close in case Dave saw him.

He hung back in the shadows as a gaggle of children passed by, heading towards the swimming baths.

Rather them than me, Gary thought. He didn't fancy going outside today with wet hair.

Just when Gary was thinking he'd never find out the identity of this mystery woman, she turned around, and Gary Carter got the shock of his life. It was Babs Morton.

Dave was standing there, bold as brass, talking to Babs Morton. It all clicked into place for Gary. Babs would have overheard a lot about Martin's business. She was the perfect informant.

Gary grinned in admiration. Take that, Martin Morton. People might mockingly call him the greengrocer gangster, but Dave was a clever bastard.

All his life, people had underestimated Dave, but standing there watching his brother in action, Gary was astounded.

He'd always been a little jealous of his brother, and he tried to suppress that envy. Right now, that bitterness had disappeared out the window. Gary felt nothing but admiration.

He couldn't deny the fact his brother had outclassed Martin Morton by a bleeding mile.

* * *

Babs Morton gave a tight smile as she said goodbye to Dave Carter.

She still had twenty minutes to wait before the children came back from the baths.

She'd been meeting Dave Carter there for a little while, but she was going to suggest they met somewhere else next time. She couldn't explain it, but she'd had the feeling someone was watching them.

But when she'd turned and looked around, there hadn't been anyone there, so it was probably just her imagination. The whole affair made her a little nervous. She didn't feel guilty at all because Martin deserved it. But it didn't mean she wanted him to find out.

Babs sighed and looked down at her wedding ring. That was the problem with having men in charge. If women were in charge, no one would have these issues. They wouldn't endanger their livelihood, or risk going to prison over some silly little tart.

Women dealt with things logically.

Pushing the pram up and down the corridor as she waited for Ruby and Derek, she reached in to comfort baby Emily as she started to grizzle.

She'd told Dave everything she knew about Martin, every scrap she thought he might be able to use against her husband. Of course, there had been plenty of gossip over Kathleen Diamond going missing after her relationship with Martin.

Dave had asked her if she thought Martin had done it. She was convinced he had. If he hadn't put his own hands around the poor girl's neck, then he'd definitely gotten one of his men to do it.

Babs shivered. Life with Martin had taught her to be ruthless, but thinking about that girl being strangled and then dumped in a canal like a piece of rubbish turned her stomach.

Kathleen had been a stupid little bitch; there was no doubt about that. She'd annoyed Babs no end by showing up like that in front of the children, but no one deserved to end up like that. No one.

She heard a commotion to her left, and when she turned, she saw Ruby and Derek coming out of the baths, arguing and pushing each other. Behind them, was the older child who Babs had paid to look after them.

"Stop your fighting. Or I'll tan both of your backsides when we get home," Babs ordered and leaned down to forcibly separate her squabbling children.

She opened her purse, ready to pay the girl for babysitting, and when she did so, her purse opened to reveal a photograph of her Martin, taken just after they'd married.

Babs smiled coldly at the picture. She felt nothing anymore. Absolutely nothing.

Martin would regret the day he'd humiliated her for the rest of his life.

55

THE DAY OF KATHLEEN'S FUNERAL was bright and cold. Linda dressed in her best black, woollen skirt and blinked away the tears as she remembered how Kathleen had nagged her to buy one that was flared and more fashionable.

She swallowed hard as she remembered Kathleen would never try to impart her fashion advice on her again.

It was hard to believe Kathleen had really gone. After they'd argued over Kathleen's behaviour with Donovan, Linda had been so furious she was determined never to speak to her again, but that seemed so petty now.

If only she'd known what was around the corner. Linda shook her head sadly. She should have forgiven Kathleen sooner.

Linda brushed away a tear as they walked from the church after the service to the graveyard.

Kathleen's mother was walking with her neighbour, Alice Pringle, who had looped her arm through Mary's and was supporting her.

Mary Diamond's face was grey, and she looked like she'd aged twenty years overnight. Linda had done her best over the past week to pop in regularly and make sure Mary and little Jimmy were okay.

All of the neighbours had pitched in. Gossipy, old Alice Pringle had been a surprise. She'd been an absolute angel. She'd cooked Mary dinner every night and listened to her talk about Kathleen for hours.

Linda's mother was looking after Jimmy today. A funeral was no place for a baby. Linda was determined to do everything she could to help the poor little mite. When he was older, Linda wanted to be able to tell him what his mother had been like. Obviously, she wouldn't tell him everything. She certainly wouldn't mention Donovan, but she hoped to let him know how beautiful his mother had been and how much fun and zest for life she'd had.

The poor little lad was going to have to grow up without his mother. It just wasn't fair.

Linda's teeth chattered together as she watched them slowly lower Kathleen's coffin into the hole. The priest was droning on, but Linda couldn't hear what he was saying over the blood rushing in her ears.

She suddenly had a horrendous image of Kathleen's body being eaten by maggots and earthworms, and she put a hand to her mouth to smother a sob.

Standing a couple of feet away, Mary let out a pain-filled wail, and Linda moved quickly to take her arm and try to comfort her.

Linda and Alice Pringle supported Mary between them. Mary's whole body was racked with sobs and Linda heard a woman mutter behind her, "It's just not right. A mother should never have to bury her child."

Across London, while Kathleen's funeral was still in

progress, Martin Morton was being questioned by police. This was the second time he'd been brought in, but each time, he made sure his highly-paid solicitor was present.

After each question the Inspector asked, Martin's brief gave a tight smile and said, "You don't have to answer that, Mr Morton."

It seemed forking out a fortune for a top level brief was worth it. Martin really didn't have to answer many questions at all, which suited him down to the ground.

The police may have suspected him of having a hand in Kathleen's murder, but they could not dispute the fact he had a perfect alibi.

Martin wasn't worried. All that linked him to Kathleen was idle gossip. The police would soon realise they didn't have enough evidence for a case and would be forced to drop the matter completely, at least, that's what his brief had advised.

He should have known it was too easy. Just when he thought the questioning was all over, the Inspector dropped a bombshell.

"Have you heard Keith Parker's body has been found?"

Martin tried to keep his face blank, but he could feel the confident grin slipping from his mouth. "Keith Parker? Well, that's a blast from the past. I thought he'd gone to Manchester."

The Inspector nodded. "Yes, that's what you told the police when he went missing. We wasted a lot of police hours searching for him in the Manchester area, and all this time, he was rotting under a pile of leaves in Epping Forest."

The Inspector watched Martin for a reaction, but if he was expecting to see guilt or remorse, he was out of luck. Martin didn't give a toss about a small-timer like Keith Parker. He'd double-crossed him, and so he'd paid. That's the way it worked.

Keith had been well aware of the risk when he decided to start working with Dave Carter at the same time as Martin.

"Do you have any further information regarding Keith Parker's murder?"

Martin rolled his eyes. That was the trouble with coppers these days. They expected everyone to confess so they didn't have to do any real work.

"Like I said, I thought he was up in Manchester. Maybe he died of natural causes," Martin added cheekily.

"A bullet through the brain is hardly natural causes."

Martin shrugged. "True enough. Well, as lovely as this chat has been, I do have work to do. So if we're done today, I'd like to leave."

Inspector Peel stood aside to let him pass, and Martin could feel the intensity of the man's gaze.

Martin walked out of the interview room and paused beside the custody desk to deliver his most dazzling smile to the Inspector in charge of the case.

Inspector Peel turned his large, hooded eyes on Martin. "You haven't gotten away with this yet, Morton. You'd better watch your step."

Martin grinned, delighted to have riled the Inspector. "Was that a threat, officer? Maybe my solicitor would be interested in hearing what you just said?"

The Inspector's face screwed up in distaste as he studied Martin Morton.

Martin felt his hackles rise. Inspector Peel had no right to look down at him.

Some of the fools working at this station thought they were something special, but Martin had a couple of high-ranking officers on the payroll, and he was sure most of the rest of them were bent, too. The more bent coppers, the better as far as Martin was concerned. As Big Tim was fond of saying, there was nothing so dangerous as a clean copper.

Martin would very much have liked to teach Inspector Peel a lesson, but common sense told him he would be better letting the whole thing go.

Having a girl murdered and dumping her body in the canal was nothing compared to the bother of having a squeaky clean copper on his tail. And right now, Martin didn't need any more enemies.

He needed all these distractions out of the way so he could concentrate on wiping out Dave Carter.

Once he got rid of Dave Carter, Martin would have more money coming in, which meant more coppers on the payroll. That meant that he would be practically untouchable. Maybe when he got to that stage, Martin would come back and teach Inspector Peel a lesson he wouldn't forget.

56

THAT EVENING, AFTER THE LAST of the guests had left, Mary Diamond walked into the kitchen. Alice, Linda and a couple of Mary's other neighbours had worked tirelessly to clean up after the wake, and there was hardly a sign in the kitchen that anything out of the ordinary had happened that day.

Jimmy was asleep upstairs in his crib, and the house was quiet. Too quiet. Mary missed Kathleen's voice. She even missed the sound of her records.

Linda had offered to stay the night again, but Mary told her to go home. She was a good girl but, she had her own life to be getting on with. She had to work at Bevels every day, and the last thing a girl of her age should be doing was worrying about Mary. Linda had her own grief to deal with.

Mary sat down at the table and poured herself a cup of tea. She stared down at the steam and tried to think things through.

She wasn't getting any younger, and now she had little Jimmy to worry about. Of course, she was glad she had him. Every time she looked at him, she thought he looked more and more like her lost daughter.

The colour of his eyes was changing now, going from that lovely blue that all babies seemed to have, to a deeper shade — almost violet— just like Kathleen's.

She didn't know what she would do if she didn't have Jimmy's welfare to focus on. She'd probably have fallen apart.

The situation was utterly hopeless. Sometimes she felt she'd never be able to get back at Martin Morton for what he'd done. She still suffered from flashes of uncontrollable rage, but that red-hot fury had dissipated and had been replaced with a cold, intense hatred of the man.

Mary might not be able to get her revenge yet, but she would one day.

She'd heard talk about men for hire who would kill or maim your enemy, but Mary couldn't afford anything like that, especially not with the baby to look after.

Mary sipped her tea. She hadn't been able to stomach any food, despite the fact that her neighbours had been pushing sandwiches and sausage rolls at her all day. She'd taken the plates of food politely and then dumped them in the kitchen.

But she was going to have to start looking after herself. She had to live long enough to see Jimmy grow into a man.

One step at a time, that's all she could do. Life would never go back to normal, but somehow she would have to get through it.

Mary heaved herself to her feet. Even her bones felt tired. She intended to put a drop of whisky in her tea to help her sleep. No doubt Jimmy would be up at the crack of dawn. There would be no time to mope in bed feeling sorry for herself.

When she heard the front door creak open, Mary assumed

it was Linda popping in to check on her again.

Mary sighed. "Really, love, I told you I'd be fine, and I will. You don't need to keep checking up on me."

But when she heard footsteps in the hallway, Mary knew something wasn't quite right.

The footsteps were heavy...far too heavy to be Linda's.

As Mary looked up, her heart skipped a beat and then began to thunder in her chest.

There, looming in the doorway of her kitchen, was Big Tim, one of Martin Morton's most feared henchmen, and the man Mary strongly suspected of killing her precious Kathleen.

"Where's the baby?" Tim's gravelly voice was almost a whisper.

Adrenaline flooded Mary system. This man had killed her daughter, but there was no way he was going to get his hands on her grandson. Over her dead body.

Mary lunged towards the sink. A sharp carving knife glinted on the draining board. She grabbed hold of the handle and turned around, brandishing it at Tim.

"Don't you come near us, you murdering bastard."

She slashed the knife in front of her, the blade just inches away from Tim's chest.

"I'll slit your bloody throat," Mary snarled at him.

Big Tim's blank face remained impassive, and in one quick movement, he grabbed Mary by the wrist and twisted her arm painfully until she dropped the knife.

He kicked the blade across the floor.

Mary struggled fiercely. He might be ten times stronger than she was, but she wasn't going to make it easy for the bastard. As he wrapped his huge arms around her, stifling her movements, a fleeting, happy thought flashed through Mary's mind: she would soon see Kathleen again.

"Sit down," Tim demanded, shoving Mary into one of the kitchen chairs.

He held her in place for a few seconds while Mary got her breath back.

"There's no point struggling," he said. "I'm here to warn you off, not to kill you."

"Like you killed my Kathleen, you mean," Mary spat at him. Her whole body was trembling with absolute fury.

Big Tim didn't deny it, but he let go of Mary's shoulders and walked around the table to take the seat opposite her.

Mary eyed him warily, not trusting him for a moment.

"The baby is not here, anyway. A friend is looking after him while I get myself together," Mary lied.

She hoped Big Tim didn't check upstairs after he'd finished her off and prayed Jimmy stayed silent in his crib.

Tim bowed his head. "Officially, I'm here to warn you off."

When he looked up at Mary, she was surprised to see tears were glistening in the corner of his eyes.

Mary glared back at him but said nothing.

"You need to get out of here, Mary," Big Tim said. "Martin is not going to forget the things you said in his club. You can't say those sorts of things and expect him not to retaliate."

"Retaliate? The bastard had my daughter killed. You'd better believe I'm going to retaliate."

Tim sighed. Then he shook his huge head and looked into Mary's eyes.

"I'm sorry," he said simply. "You can't win with someone like Martin Morton. He's ruthless. He sent me around here today. Please, think about moving away with the boy, somewhere you'll be out of harm's way."

"What?"

Mary shook her head. Where on earth could she go? She'd lived in the area all her life. She only just managed to support herself by working on the market stalls as and when she was needed. So how could she move away with no money and no job? At least here she had a roof over her head.

Besides, Mary wanted to be around to see Martin's downfall and make sure he suffered.

"He wouldn't really do anything to hurt his own son, would he?" Mary asked even though she knew the answer to her question already.

Tim took a deep breath. "I wouldn't put anything past him. If I were you, I would get that child as far away from him as I could."

Tim stood up and made his way towards the door.

"What? Is that it?" Mary scraped her chair along the floor as she stood up quickly.

When Tim put his large hand on the front door, he turned back to face Mary. "I really hope this is it, Mary. I don't want to see you again. If you care anything for that baby, you'll get him somewhere safe. Next time, the warning won't be so gentle."

Big Tim walked out the front door and shut it behind him.

Mary stood in the hallway waiting for her speeding pulse to slowly come back down to normal.

He was right. Jimmy wasn't safe here. But how on earth was she going to get him out of the East End and support him without a job. Mary wandered back into the kitchen, picked up her cold cup of tea and carried the cup and saucer to the sink.

As she washed up, she considered her options. She couldn't leave Poplar, but that didn't mean Jimmy couldn't. She had a friend who lived out in Romford. He would be safe there.

It would kill Mary not to be able to see him every day, but if that was what was best for the child, and if that kept him safe, she would have to bear it.

Her friend, Bev, had lived just two streets away before she'd moved out to Romford with her husband five years ago. Her husband had passed away a couple of years ago, and Mary knew Bev had been lonely. Would she take Jimmy? It was one hell of an ask, and Mary wouldn't be able to pay her a fortune toward the boy's keep. There was only one way to find out. Mary would have to go to Romford and ask for Bev's help.

As Mary dried her hands, she looked up at the ceiling. "I'll do everything I can to take care of him, darling. I promise you that much."

With a heavy heart, Mary trudged upstairs to bed.

57

CHARLIE HAD SPENT THE LAST week collecting rat droppings from the rat he'd named Roland.

He selected the driest droppings and then opened his pouch of tobacco and crumbled the droppings on top. When he'd used up most of the droppings, he mixed the contents up carefully and inspected the package.

He would never notice the difference, Charlie thought with a grin.

He hobbled up from the bed. The bruises around his ribs had almost gone, but they still felt tender, a timely reminder of just how much he hated Alfie Harris. He stuffed the package of tobacco in the pocket of his trousers and then wandered off to the washroom where he washed his hands thoroughly with soap and water. The soap was a little better there, not much, but at least, it created a few suds.

He then headed off towards the recreation room, which was really just a wide corridor between the two wings of the men's prison.

Alfie was sitting at a table playing cards with some of his cronies when Charlie approached.

One of the men sitting next to Alfie laughed. "Well, look

who it is. He's come back for more."

Alfie Harris turned his weasel-like face towards Charlie. "What do you want?"

"Look, I don't want any trouble. I just wanted to clear the air."

Alfie sneered at him, but Charlie pressed on. He set the packet of tobacco on the table in front of Alfie. "A peace offering."

Alfie smiled up at him and gave him an evil-looking smirk. He obviously thought he had Charlie Williams just where he wanted him. Running scared. He had pegged Charlie as another prisoner he could bully and extort.

Despite his intense dislike of the man, Charlie managed to smile pleasantly. "No strings," he said. "I just thought it was a nice gesture."

Alfie smirked and put his thin, veiny hand over the packet of tobacco. He hesitated a moment and then snatched it up and stuffed it in the breast pocket of his prison uniform. "It will take more than that to buy my goodwill, son."

Charlie wanted to laugh. It had worked.

"I realise that, Mr. Harris," he said with mock sincerity. "But it's a step in the right direction, isn't it?"

Charlie could hardly suppress his laughter as he walked away from Alfie Harris.

The stupid fool had fallen for it hook, line and sinker. He walked over to another table and took a seat beside two young lads who were starting a game of rummy.

"Want to join?" one of them asked Charlie.

Charlie nodded as he sat down. "Go on then, deal me in for the next hand."

But Charlie didn't look up as the cards were dealt. His

eyes were still fixed on Alfie Harris.

Alfie had opened up the pouch and was peering inside. He took a large pinch of the tobacco mixed with rat droppings and sprinkled it on a cigarette paper. He rolled it up expertly and then raised it to his lips.

Charlie held his breath.

They weren't allowed matches or lighters in the prison, so a prison guard had to come over and light it with a match for him.

The prison guard lit the cigarette, and Alfie took a deep breath in.

Charlie put a hand over his mouth to suppress his sniggers as Alfie breathed out the white smoke and then coughed a couple of times.

Alfie stared at the cigarette. "It's strong stuff. I reckon it must be foreign," he said to the prison guard before shrugging and raising the roll-up to his lips and inhaling again.

Charlie laughed until tears ran down his cheeks, and the two blokes he was sitting next to looked at him as if he had lost his mind.

That was prison for you, Charlie thought. A man had to make his own entertainment.

58

THE FOLLOWING AFTERNOON, GARY CARTER burst into his brother's office at the warehouse. Dave had been going over some figures from the workshop with Brian and looked up surprised at the interruption.

Gary was breathless, and his eyes shone with excitement. "I need a word, Bruv."

Brian Moore, who was sitting on the other side of Dave's desk, turned his squat neck, looked at Gary and raised an eyebrow.

"In private," Gary added, scowling at Brian.

Brian Moore considered himself a vital part of Dave Carter's business, and he didn't like the fact that Gary didn't trust him enough to talk in front of him.

Gary's eyes glittered with excitement, and his skin was itching. He couldn't wait to share this news with Dave, but it wasn't something he wanted to do in front of anyone else, even Brian.

Finally, Dave nodded at Brian. "We'll continue this later."

Looking, majorly disgruntled, Brian stood up and shrugged his broad shoulders.

He gave Gary an obstinate look as he passed, but Gary

barely noticed. He quickly sat down in Brian's vacated chair.

"You're going to love this, bruv."

Dave regarded him steadily as he leaned back in his chair, interlinked his fingers and placed his hands on the desk in front of him.

Gary knew he seemed volatile. He'd just taken a bit of coke, and the last thing he wanted was for his behaviour to tip Dave off. He tried to get his enthusiasm under control, but it was impossible.

"It's Big Tim," Gary burst out unable to hold it back any longer. "He's been in the Blind Beggar since lunchtime, and he's absolutely wasted. He has been muttering all sorts about Martin Morton. I reckon we've got a chance to turn him."

Dave stared at Gary but said nothing.

Gary's legs were jittery, and his knees were jumping beneath the desk. He was so eager to get started. He had no idea why Dave was wasting so much time.

"We have to act now, bruv. We won't have much time. I'll go now," Gary said, starting to stand up again.

"No," Dave said firmly.

Gary looked at him puzzled. His brother wasn't one for turning down an intelligent opportunity, and this was a prime chance to screw over Martin Morton.

"What do you mean, no? We won't get another chance like this again."

"You can't go; he knows you're my brother."

"Yeah," Gary said, waving Dave's words away dismissively. "But if he's ready to turn on Martin Morton then, he is not going to care, is he? He'll be pleased to speak to me because I'm your brother."

"No," Dave said again. "You're missing the point. Tim will know you're my brother, and so will everyone else in the pub. If he is seen talking to you, it will get straight back to Martin Morton within minutes."

Gary slumped back down in the chair. He hadn't thought about that. "Well, who else can you trust to send. Everyone knows Brian is working for you. Most of the people in our outfit are well-known faces around here."

Dave nodded slowly. "We'll send Patrick."

Gary's eyebrows shot up into his hair. "The new boy?"

"Yes. Tell Patrick to approach Tim and tell him we'd like to talk to him in private."

Gary swallowed and nodded slowly. It made sense. Although it would put a big onus on Patrick to show he had what it took. He nodded again. He wished he'd thought of that.

Gary grinned at Dave. "I'll get right on it."

Gary walked swiftly out of Dave's office, closing the door behind him and heading down to the other end of the warehouse where the other boys were sitting around playing cards.

"Patrick, I need a word."

All the boys were gathered around an upturned wooden crate and looked up as Gary spoke.

"I've got a job for you."

Patrick smiled broadly as he walked beside Gary, and Gary shook his head. The boy was so young. He had a cocky walk and a level of overconfidence that made Gary nervous. He hoped Dave wasn't making a mistake by trusting him with this.

"This job is important, right? You don't screw it up."

Patrick nodded eagerly. "Of course, boss. You can rely on me."

As Gary filled Patrick in on the plans, he couldn't help thinking they were taking one hell of a risk using this young lad to approach Big Tim.

Patrick Cunnings was on top of the world as he swaggered down the Whitechapel Road toward the Blind Beggar. He'd had a pint or two in there on numerous occasions but never for work.

He couldn't help grinning to himself. This was the start of a new life. He was going to do this job well and get Dave Carter to trust him. Then the sky was the limit. Patrick Cunnings had plans, plenty of them.

Cunning by name, cunning by nature that's what one of his teachers at school had said, and it was true enough. Patrick knew he was bright, although he'd been awful at school. His patchy attendance hadn't helped, and neither had the fact that both his parents believed teaching their son silly things like maths was a daft idea when he could be working and bringing home some money.

His dad had been most eager to get him out earning, mainly because he spent most of his own wages down the pub every night.

Patrick beamed as he imagined his mother's face lighting up when he passed her a few extra quid this week. She would be made up.

Patrick pushed open the door and entered the pub. It was lovely and warm inside and already quite busy. He took a quick butchers at the other punters inside the pub. Most of the old-timers were propped up at the bar, and he couldn't see Big Tim among them. He scanned the tables and caught sight of Big Tim, sitting at a table in the corner on his own.

Big Tim was a well-known character in these parts, and Patrick had seen him on numerous occasions. He'd known how big the man was, but today for some reason, he seemed even larger than usual. Everything about the man was massive. His suit jacket strained at the seams as he lifted his drinking arm, bringing his pint to his mouth.

For the first time, Patrick felt a twinge of nerves. It wouldn't be clever to get on the bad side of a man like Tim. Still, he had been given a job to do, and he was determined to do it.

He squared his shoulders and then smiling at everyone around him, he walked up to the bar with a swagger.

Molly walked over to him quickly. "What can I get you, love?"

Patrick ordered a pint of beer but kept his eyes on Big Tim.

When Molly handed him his pint, he took a long drink and then wiped his mouth with the back of his hand.

He took a deep breath and started to walk over to Tim's table.

He felt a bit like a condemned man, but he tried to reassure himself that all he was doing was talking. That was easy enough. And if he managed to pull this off, Dave Carter would be sure to show his appreciation.

"Er, you mind if I sit down?" Patrick said to Big Tim.

The big man's head moved up slowly, and Patrick could see for the first time just how pissed he was. His eyes struggled to focus on Patrick.

"Do I know you?" Big Tim asked suspiciously.

Patrick slid down into the chair opposite Tim, put his pint

on the table and leaned in close.

"I've got a message for you," he said in a quiet voice. "Gary Carter would very much like to have a word with you...if you have the time, sir."

Patrick had added the sir on the end for good measure because he thought it sounded respectful. He licked his lips nervously as Big Tim leaned forward, staring at him with bleary eyes.

Patrick swallowed hard. "Gary said he can meet you at The Three Grapes in half an hour if you're willing to talk."

For the longest time, Tim said nothing and Patrick started to think that perhaps he was too drunk to understand English. This was going to be harder than he'd expected.

He leaned further forward, intending to try to get through to him again, when all of a sudden Tim moved like lightning.

Patrick was quick on his feet, which he was very thankful for because as Big Tim's huge fist came crashing towards his face, he dodged it just in time. It missed his jaw by less than an inch.

For a moment, Patrick just stood there, blinking in shock, and then suddenly his wits came back to him. He turned around and legged it out of the bar.

Clearly Big Tim wasn't in the mood to talk.

Patrick didn't stop running until he'd turned off Whitechapel Road. He leaned back against the rough brick wall and panted. That had been a close call, and far too close for comfort for his liking. He'd been lulled into a false sense of security because Tim had appeared so drunk. He was still a dangerous bastard, though. If that punch had connected, Patrick would have been knocked out cold on the floor.

He was disappointed that Tim hadn't decided to take Gary up on his offer, but he hoped Dave wouldn't be displeased with his work today. He had done exactly what he was told, and in this game, that was important.

59

MARY CARRIED LITTLE JIMMY UP the path to the front door of the small bungalow in Romford. She hadn't visited Bev since Bev and her husband had left the East End, and she was really surprised at how lovely the bungalow was.

It was in a little cul-de-sac, surrounded by other identical bungalows. The front garden was lovely and filled with flowers. Everything about the little bungalow seemed fresh and new. They'd been newly built when Bev and her husband had moved in five years ago.

Mary felt a pang of envy. Life would have been very different if she'd moved out here with Kathleen.

But there was no point regretting the past. Things couldn't be changed. All she could do now was make sure that Jimmy was safe.

She raised a hand and knocked on the door.

The door opened, and Bev's jaw dropped open. "Flaming Nora, Mary. Is that really you?"

Bev broke out into a broad grin as she opened the door wider. "Come in, love. It's wonderful to see you again. It's been far too long."

Bev looked great. Her skin was fresh and glowing, and she

looked younger than her fifty years. Her hair was free of grey, and Mary wondered if she had it tinted. She touched her own hair self-consciously.

Mary stepped inside the bungalow, and her breath caught in her throat as she saw how tastefully it had been decorated. Pretty wallpaper printed with rosebuds covered the walls, and the carpet was thick beneath her feet. Mary would have killed for a place like this.

Bev's husband, Fred, had worked like a demon over the years and done very well for himself, but at forty-five, he'd had a heart attack and decided to retire early. They'd moved to this bungalow in Romford, but unfortunately, Fred didn't get a chance to enjoy his retirement. Less than a year later he died after another heart attack.

Mary followed Bev into the front room, which was lovely and bright as there were great big windows looking out onto the back garden.

"Are you all right, girl?" Bev asked, noticing Mary looked quite overwhelmed. "Sit yourself down, and I'll make a cup of tea."

Bev leaned over and chucked little Jimmy under the chin. "Who is this good-looking little chap then?"

"This is Jimmy," Mary said and smiled proudly. "My grandson."

"Oh, how lovely! You lucky thing. I didn't even know Kathleen had married. Did my invitation get lost in the post?" Bev teased, but then the smile fell from her face as she saw the expression on Mary's face.

Mary shook her head sadly. "She didn't get married."

Bev pursed her lips then she patted Mary's arm. "Let me make that tea, and then you can tell me all about it."

When Bev left the room to make the tea, Mary took the opportunity to have a good nosy around. Jimmy squirmed in her arms as she admired Bev's furnishings. There was a nice picture of Bev and Fred on the mantelpiece. It must have been one of the last ones they'd had taken before her old man had died.

The last time she'd seen Bev had been at Fred's funeral, and she regretted not visiting sooner to see how a friend was coping with widowhood.

They'd been ever so close once. They'd attended the same school and once Mary had envied Bev's good fortune in landing a man like Fred. Kathleen's father had been the polar opposite of Fred in every way. The man had been a complete scallywag. Bev and Mary had their daughters just a few months apart, and they'd bonded over cups of tea and chats about motherhood. Then tragedy struck when the girls were just five years old: Kathleen and Bev's daughter, Claire, contracted diphtheria.

It had been one of the worst times in Mary's life. Eventually, Kathleen had pulled through, but poor little Claire hadn't been so lucky. Bev had had a complete breakdown at the funeral, and for a year afterwards, she couldn't cope with everyday things. She didn't clean the house or cook, but with Fred and Mary's help, she'd managed to pull through those dark days.

Mary knew she was about to ask Bev a huge favour, and she would have understood if Bev turned her down, but this was the one chance she had to make sure Jimmy was safe, and so Mary was determined to be as persuasive as possible.

Bev brought out the tea and then listened in silence as Mary told her what had happened. She didn't spare any details. Bev had grown up in the East End and was well aware of what life could be like. When she'd moved out to Romford, Martin Morton had just been a little upstart with no power to speak of, but she listened with horror as Mary told her what sort of man he had become and how Kathleen had been trapped in his web.

By the time Mary had finished, both women were in tears.

"So, the thing is, they've warned me to get Jimmy out of the area. I don't have anyone else I can turn to, Bev… I was hoping you'd look after him for me, just for a little while until things settle down. Of course, I can pay you some money for his keep…" Mary's voice trailed away as she looked beseechingly at her friend.

Beverley got up from her armchair and came and sat beside Mary on the sofa. She put her arm around her old friend's shoulders.

"I'm so sorry, Mary. I can't imagine how awful this has been for you. Of course, I'll look after him for you. I'll do my best to help; you know that."

Bev stroked little Jimmy's cheek.

Mary broke into fresh tears at her friend's generosity. "I'm sorry, Bev. I know it's a huge ask. And you're happy here in your lovely home. The last thing you want is a screaming infant around."

Bev shook her head. "It will make a nice change. It's too quiet around here. To tell you the truth, I've been ever so lonely after Fred died. I even considered moving back to the East End."

Mary looked at her friend in shock.

Beverley chuckled. "I only thought about it for a little while then came to my senses. It's lovely out here, Mary.

Neighbours are nice, and it helps that I got a little bit of money from the insurance when Fred passed. I remember how good to me you were after I lost my Claire. I told you then I'd never forget your kindness, and I meant it. I'll help you through this, Mary. Together, we'll make sure little Jimmy is all right."

60

BIG TIM STOOD OUTSIDE THE Three Grapes, swaying. It was still only mid-afternoon, but he was absolutely plastered. He hesitated at the doorway and then decided to make his way around the back, as he didn't want anyone to see him enter the main bar.

Martin Morton's fierce face loomed before him in his imagination, and it almost made him turn around and leave, but then that image was immediately followed by one of Kathleen's pleading eyes, staring up at him as his hands wrapped around her neck.

Tim squeezed his eyes shut and shuddered.

He stepped through the doorway and into the little passage at the back of the pub. The landlord was just walking in to get a container full of pork scratchings, and when he looked up and saw Big Tim, he flinched.

Big Tim put a hand out against the wall to steady himself. "Where are they?" he asked, his voice slurred.

The landlord raised his eyes and pointed upstairs.

So Tim started to ascend the stairs steadily, taking them one at a time with his thudding steps.

When he reached the top, a door opened, and cigarette

smoke swirled out. There in front of him stood Gary Carter.

"Hello, Tim. Nice of you to pop by. Come in here and take the weight off."

Tim had heard rumours about Gary Carter. Namely that he was partial to certain drugs. The other thing he'd heard was that he wasn't trustworthy. But Tim told himself that didn't matter. He was only here to see what Gary had to say, that was all.

He followed Gary inside the room. He was surprised to see they were not alone.

Sitting at a large, laminate-topped dining table was Dave Carter.

Tim stopped and blinked. Dave Carter was the absolute opposite of Martin Morton. He looked fresh-faced, trustworthy and honourable. Tim wasn't green enough to think you could tell that by a person's appearance, but although Dave Carter might be ruthless, Tim was sure he didn't have the vindictive downright nasty nature Martin did.

"Mr. Carter," Tim said with a nod, suddenly feeling far more sober.

Dave smiled at him. "Take a seat, son."

Tim did as he was told, and the wooden chair squeaked beneath his weight as he sat on it.

"What's all this about then?" Tim asked. "I ain't no grass, and I'm not talking about the girl."

He said the words all in a rush as he raised a shaking hand to rub his short, spiky hair.

"This isn't about the girl."

Tim was intrigued. He couldn't figure out Dave Carter's angle. Did he want to know what happened to Frank the

Face? Tim would never tell him that.

Finally after a long silence as he tried to work out why the Carter brothers had asked him to meet them, he said, "What do you want to know then?"

Dave smiled again. It wasn't a dazzling, handsome smile like Martin's, but it was friendly. It gave his face a warm and genuine expression.

"It was something that happened a while ago now," Dave said. "It's not really a big deal. I wanted to ask you about Keith Parker."

Tim frowned. Keith Parker, that little worm! Why did Dave care about him? Keith had been was playing the two men against each other, so Martin had really done Dave Carter a favour.

Big Tim shrugged. He was very ashamed of what he'd done to Kathleen, and he wasn't particularly proud of watching Martin Morton torture Frank the Face, but he felt no remorse at all for what he'd done to Keith Parker. In his opinion, Keith Parker had deserved everything that he got.

"He was cheating. Playing both sides. Martin ordered a hit. But he got one of his men to pull the trigger."

It had been Henry the Hand who'd shot Keith straight between the eyes, but Tim wasn't about to grass him up.

Gary turned to stare at his brother, looking almost as confused as Tim.

Dave nodded encouragingly. "And have you still got that gun?"

"Or did you dump it?" Gary asked.

Tim shook his head. "I don't know where all this is going. I don't even know why you're talking to me. If Martin was to find out—"

"He won't find out," Dave said. "You've been working with Martin for a while. You're loyal, and I admire that quality. But you have to put yourself first for once. An honourable man like you, Tim, must find it hard to talk to us like this."

Tim swallowed and looked at the carpet. "You have no idea."

"I'm not going to ask a lot of you, Tim; I'm giving you a friendly warning. Martin Morton is going down. I'm going to make sure of that. I know he was involved in Frank the Face's disappearance."

Dave held up as Tim went to speak. "No, I'm not asking you to grass him up on that. I'm not asking you to grass, at all. All I want is that gun. Now, you can choose your side carefully. You're no coward. I know that for a fact. All I need from you is the gun. If you get it for me, when Martin is finished, there will be a place for you with us."

As Tim frowned, Gary turned to face his brother, the shock plastered all over his face. He hadn't been expecting him to say that.

"You don't want any information?" Tim smothered a hiccup, and Dave shook his head.

"The only thing I need from you is the gun.

Tim thought about it for a moment. Despite everything that Martin had put him through, and the fact he knew for certain the man was evil through and through, he hesitated. Once his loyalty to Martin would have been impenetrable, but now…

Martin had ordered Tim to get rid of Kathleen. If her mother hadn't taken the baby to Essex, Tim was sure the little boy would have met the same fate as his mother.

Martin was evil. He deserved to lose everything.

Tim shrugged. "All right."

"You've still got it?" Gary asked, looking mistrustful.

Tim nodded. He kept it along with other weapons in an abandoned house that had been bombed in the war.

That particular row of houses on Victoria Road hadn't been demolished and replaced yet, and it was as good a hiding place as any.

Martin had told him to get rid of the gun, meaning to dump it in the canal or something similar, but guns cost a lot of money, and they weren't easy to come by. So Tim had taken to stashing his weapons in the abandoned house on Victoria Road.

Sometimes kids played around there, but he wasn't worried about them stumbling over anything they shouldn't because he kept all the weapons in a locked metal case.

Tim rummaged in his pockets and pulled out a ring of keys. With fumbling fingers, he selected the smallest.

He smiled at Dave and Gary. "Yes, I've still got it."

61

GARY CARTER FOLLOWED BIG TIM along Victoria Road. The abandoned, bombed-out houses loomed over them and gave the street an eerie feel. Gary was as jumpy as hell and very agitated. He shouldn't have taken quite so much coke. There was such a thin line between feeling bright and alert and a nervous wreck.

It was a freezing cold night, but Gary wiped sweat from his forehead. Jobs like this made him nervous.

He watched Tim's huge frame lumbering up the road ahead of him and eyed him warily. Who was to say this wasn't all an act to get Gary alone?

He'd never had Big Tim down as much of a mastermind or that great an actor, but he couldn't be too careful.

Gary looked over his shoulder to make sure they were alone. The street was deserted and dark.

"It's this one," Tim said.

Gary noticed he had stopped slurring his words. That made him nervous, too. Was he just slowly sobering up? Or had it all been an act?

Tim nodded again and gestured for Gary to go in the derelict house first.

"Not on your Nelly," Gary said.

Tim studied him carefully, and Gary realised that his nerves were showing. It wasn't a good idea to show fear in front of your enemy.

"Age before beauty and all that," Gary said, forcing a chuckle.

Big Tim had to stoop to get through the doorway, and Gary followed him in.

He fumbled in his pockets for some matches, lit one and then almost wished he hadn't as he caught sight of the shiny eyes of a rat, staring right at him from a broken cabinet.

"Jesus."

"It's just a rat," Tim said. "Or are you worried I'm going to double-cross you?"

"Just hurry up. We haven't got all night."

"It's upstairs," Tim said.

Gary looked up at the rickety staircase. It was wooden, and half the banisters had fallen down. It didn't look like it could hold Gary's weight let alone Big Tim's.

"That doesn't look safe."

"If you're scared, I'll go up and get it and bring it down." Big Tim grinned. "You can wait here."

Gary considered that for a moment and then shook his head. "No way. Go on, you first. I'll follow."

As Big Tim ascended the stairs, they creaked noisily under his bulk. Gary's match flickered out, and he quickly lit another one, so he could see and avoid the gaping holes in the staircase.

Luckily the main part of the stairs seemed pretty solid, and they made it up to the top in one piece.

"It's through here," Tim said, lumbering into a bedroom.

Gary followed him and watched as Tim levered up one of the floorboards. He pulled out a black metal case and used the tiny key on his key ring to open it.

Gary took a step closer, looked at the contents of the case and gave a low whistle. "Bleeding hell. You've got a lot of stuff there."

From his position on the floor, Tim looked up at Gary and gave him a gruesome smile.

"True enough. I'll have to find somewhere else to stash it now. I can't have you knowing where I keep my secrets, can I?"

Gary suppressed a shiver. He did not want to know Tim's secrets. He had a feeling they would give him nightmares.

"Is that the gun?" he said, looking down at a small, black hand piece.

Tim nodded, pulled a handkerchief from his pocket, wrapping around the gun before handing it to Gary. "It ain't loaded, and I wiped it off for fingerprints."

Gary nodded. "Fine. Thanks. Now, let's get out of here."

Tim locked his case, but instead of putting it back under the floorboards, he stood up and held it under one arm.

"You're bringing that with you?" Gary asked, looking suspiciously at the metal box.

Tim nodded. "I'm not leaving it here now that you know about it. I've got somewhere else it can go."

Gary shook his head. Big Tim was mental. He was going to carry that down the road as if it were a bag of groceries. He had knives and all sorts in there.

As they walked down the stairs and out onto the street, Tim said, "So, tell me, what does Dave want this gun for?"

Gary grinned and tapped the side of his nose. "You'll find

out soon enough."

Truthfully, Gary had absolutely no idea what Dave had in mind. It irked him that his brother hadn't trusted him enough to confide his plans, but he wasn't about to admit that to Big Tim.

He wanted Tim to believe he was his brother's second-in-command because admitting he didn't know anything about Dave's plans would make him look like a complete foot soldier.

To Gary, appearances were important, especially in front of people like Big Tim.

Outside the abandoned house, both men turned to each other.

"So what now? Big Tim asked.

"Now, we wait," Gary said.

He looked up and down the deserted Victoria Road and then gave Big Tim a nod. "A pleasure doing business with you."

"Is that it?" Big Tim asked. "Do I just get on with life as normal now?"

Gary nodded. "Yes, that's exactly what you do."

"And Martin won't find out about this?"

"That's the plan."

Maybe it was Gary's imagination, but he thought Big Tim looked a bit anxious. He'd never imagined Tim to be the type of man to get nervous or to even have feelings.

After a moment's hesitation, Gary reached out and slapped the big man on the shoulder. "He won't find out from us, Tim. He'll never know it was you that gave us the gun. But he's going down. Once Dave has made a decision, nothing stands in his way. I know people think of Martin

Morton as the dangerous, ruthless one, but once my brother forms a plan, there is no stopping him. Martin Morton doesn't stand a chance."

62

THE FOLLOWING DAY, THE LANDLORD of The Lamb, Barney Newell, was flushing through the lines of the new barrel when there was hammering at the front door.

"All right, I'm coming. Don't break the door down."

He wasn't supposed to open for another five minutes. Barney expected it to be one of his regulars, one of the old blokes who were here every lunchtime as soon as he opened.

But when he unbolted the door and opened it, he was horrified to see that he was staring into the face of Martin Morton. Behind him, loomed the huge figure of Big Tim.

Barney felt his bowels loosen as Martin Morton gave him a dazzling, evil smile.

"Hello, Barney. Is it all right if we come in?"

Without waiting for an answer, Martin pushed past Barney and Big Tim followed.

Barney staggered backwards. His mind was reeling with all the possibilities that could have brought Martin Morton to his pub.

It was widely known that Barney was under the protection of Dave Carter, and he had been for years. He paid Dave a little bit of money every month and knew that his interests were safely looked after.

So he didn't understand what the hell Martin Morton was doing here. But whatever the reason for Martin Morton's presence, Barney knew it couldn't be good.

His wife was out back, preparing sandwiches for a quick lunch before they opened. Barney didn't want her involved in all this.

"What brings you to this neck of the woods?" Barney said, trying to smile at the two men, but his mouth wouldn't quite turn up at the corners, and he ended up giving them a grimace rather than a smile.

"We are expanding. And luckily for you, you're slap bang in the middle of our expansion. We've come to offer you a little bit of protection."

Barney shook his head, opened and shut his mouth a couple of times, and then he said. "But I pay Dave Carter. You know that, Mr Morton."

The charming smile left Martin's face, and he took a step closer to Barney. "Not anymore you don't, Barney. From this day on, your pub is mine. I'm taking over all of Carter's premises."

Barney frowned, frantically trying to wrack his brains for a way out of this mess. He kept his ear to the ground, and as landlord to a pub, he was privy to plenty of gossip. If there really had been a takeover coming, he would have heard something about it.

Was Martin Morton simply chancing his luck?

Barney decided to tough it out. He'd get them to leave, and then he'd go straight round to Dave Carter and explain the situation. Dave could sort it out.

Dave was a far more reasonable man, and although

dangerous in his own way, Barney felt he could trust him and that he was a fair man. Barney wouldn't have trusted Martin Morton as far as he could throw him.

"Sandwiches ready, darling," Barney's wife's voice carried out into the bar.

Barney paled as he saw Martin's smile widen.

"Your wife is here. How lovely. How is she?"

Barney's eyes opened wide in panic, and then he quickly leaned over the bar and called out to his wife. "Go and get some milk from the corner shop. I've got some visitors."

Barney's wife wandered into the bar. A blowsy blonde, she was the apple of Barney's eye, and he would have done anything to protect her.

"What are you talking about, you daft sod? We've got plenty of milk…"

She suddenly stopped in her tracks when she saw Martin Morton and Big Tim in the bar. She exchanged an anxious glance with her husband and then gave a little nod. "Gentlemen, I'm just off to get some milk."

Barney nodded, and when his wife had left the bar, he turned back to face Martin Morton.

"Look, I don't know where this confusion has come from, but I'm under Dave Carter's protection, and I am loyal to Dave." Barney's voice faltered as he saw the glare he got from Martin Morton.

With his lips trembling slightly, he continued, "You've got to sort this out with Dave. I can't give you any more money. I can't afford to pay the two of you."

Martin was silent. His intense eyes bored into Barney.

Barney started to babble. "I'm sure you can see my point of view. Now, if you don't mind, I got a pub to run, and I'm going to have to ask you both to leave," Barney finished up, trying to keep his nerve.

"You what?" Martin looked at Big Tim. "Did you hear that? He's asking us to leave."

Big Tim shook his huge head. "That's not very polite, Barney. Martin doesn't like to be asked to leave."

Barney put both his hands in the air in a placatory gesture. "I'm sorry. I didn't mean any disrespect. You know that. It's just that my hands are tied. I can't do anything."

"You can open up your till and pay me the money you owe me," Martin said.

Barney shook his head rapidly. "No, I can't."

Martin gave an evil chuckle. "Did he just say no to me, Tim?"

"I think he did, boss."

"He obviously needs a little bit of persuasion."

Big Tim made a move for Barney, who yelped and jumped out of the way. He fled up the stairs, running as fast as his little legs could carry him, but he was no match for Big Tim. Despite Tim's size, he could move bloody quickly for a big lad. He grabbed hold of Barney by the scruff of the neck and half-pulled and half-carried him into the front room above the pub.

Barney was now a blubbering wreck. He was so glad his wife wasn't here to see this.

"Be reasonable, please," Barney begged.

He knew he was about to get a hiding, but there wasn't much he could do about it. If he paid Martin Morton, he wouldn't be able to afford to pay Dave Carter, so he was in for a beating either way.

It wasn't fair. He'd paid Dave Carter good money to make

sure that things like this didn't happen.

He could hear Martin's footsteps as he slowly climbed the stairs. Barney's stomach churned in response. He'd heard that Martin Morton could be a sadistic bastard.

When Martin entered the room, his eyes fixed on the sash window, and he grinned.

He turned to Tim. "It's a bit stuffy in here. What do you think, Tim? Shall we open the window?"

Understanding his boss, Tim carried a squealing Barney over to the window. Opening up the window as wide as it would go, he then shoved Barney's head outside.

Martin joined them by the window. "Breathe in that nice, fresh, East End air, Barney. Isn't that nice?"

Tim was holding Barney so he couldn't get his feet on the floor and the top part of his body hung out of the window. His arms waved manically.

"I think he needs a bit more fresh air, Tim. Fresh air can be ever so persuasive."

With a grunt, Big Tim scooped up Barney's legs and stuffed him out of the window. Hanging onto his ankles, he dangled Barney over the street.

Barney screamed like a girl. He could see the paving slabs beneath him and knew his skull would crack like a coconut if he were to fall.

Then to his horror, he saw his wife returning from the shop. She dropped the bottle of milk on the pavement, and her hands went up to cover her mouth. "Oh, my God. Let him go!"

Martin stuck his head out of the window. "Do you really want us to let go? That's not very nice." He chuckled, clearly enjoying every moment of the entertainment.

Thoroughly humiliated and scared out of his wits, Barney conceded. "All right, all right. I'll pay you whatever you want. Please, just get me back inside."

Martin nodded, and Tim heaved Barney back inside, scraping his ribs all along the frame.

Barney collapsed into a heap on the floor. He was a quivering wreck.

"Get up," Martin said with disgust. "Get your arse downstairs and get my money. This better not be a sign of things to come, Barney. The next time I visit, I don't want all this fuss, do you understand me?"

Barney had been rendered speechless with fright, but he managed to nod and scrambled to his feet and then hobbled down the stairs.

After he had paid Martin Morton, they left, and Barney poured himself an extra-large brandy and flopped onto one of the chairs. This was not fair. He was a pub landlord, not a bloody gangster. He paid Dave Carter for protection, and he hadn't bloody got it.

Now he was going to be broke.

His wife ran into the pub, her heels clacking on the wooden floor as she rushed up to him.

"Oh, Barney. Thank God you're all right."

But Barney was far from all right. He was slap bang in the middle of a gang war, through no fault of his own.

63

CHARLIE WILLIAMS WALKED ALONG TO the prison visiting room with none of his usual swagger. Prison had sucked all the life out of him and all his hope for the future. His brief had told him that he was looking at least another five years inside.

All the days seemed to blend into one in prison. It was one, long, monotonous grind. The only breaks in the tedious days were fights in the prison yard, or Alfie Harris trying to make Charlie's life more of a misery than it already was.

Since he'd been incarcerated, he'd had a couple of visits from a copper, promising him a reduced sentence if he ratted out his boss. But that wasn't going to happen. Charlie would never grass on Dave Carter.

As he walked further up the corridor, he saw a group of men loitering, clustered tightly around Alfie Harris. For some reason, Alfie had had it in for him from the start. He just didn't like the look of Charlie's mug.

Charlie had managed to get his revenge in subtle ways, but he could do without any stupid fights now.

He kept his eyes straight ahead, trying not to antagonise Alfie. If a fight broke out now, he would be banned from visiting hours, and he knew Dave was coming in today. So he couldn't risk a punch-up.

Luckily, Alfie seemed to be preoccupied, arguing with a bald bloke, so Charlie made his way past without any problems.

He was patted down at the entrance of the visiting room by a guard, and then when he walked inside, he saw Dave sitting at one of the centre tables.

He did his best to smile, but he couldn't help noticing Dave's shocked reaction. Charlie knew he was looking gaunt. Prison food wasn't exactly appetising. His old dear cried every time she'd visited him. He had dark circles under his eyes through lack of sleep. There was always someone shouting and making a fuss even in the early hours.

"It's good to see you, Dave," Charlie said trying to muster up his old grin.

Dave stood up, his face a mask of concern as he held out his hand to shake Charlie's.

"How's life treating you in here, son?"

"Well, it ain't a Sunday picnic that's for sure. But I'm taking it day by day. You don't need to worry about me."

Dave nodded slowly, and they both sat down. "Are you having any trouble with anyone in here? Anything I can help with?"

Charlie thought for a moment. It was only Alfie Harris on his back, and really he was only a minor irritation. It could have been a lot worse. So Charlie shook his head.

"No, I'm fine. So how's life on the outside?"

Dave took a deep breath and then said, "Gary has come back."

Charlie tried to minimise his reaction, but he couldn't help clenching his teeth as he thought about Dave's brother. It was all his bleeding fault Charlie was in here.

"I know he let you down," Dave said. "You've been a good worker, Charlie. And I'm not going to forget this in a hurry. I've been looking after your mother as I promised."

Charlie nodded. His mother had been very keen to sing Dave's praises on her last visit. She'd been wearing a lovely new winter coat and had even been to get her hair done. She was better off money-wise now than she had been before Charlie got locked up.

"I know," Charlie said. "I appreciate it."

"I look after my own, Charlie, which brings me to my reason for visiting you."

Charlie leaned forward in his chair, eager to hear whatever bit of news Dave had brought with him.

"I've got a plan to get you out of here."

Charlie felt his heart leap in his chest but then quickly pushed down the bubble of hope that rose up inside him.

When he first got sent down, he had been expecting to get out within a few days, and it was soul destroying to slowly come to terms with the fact he was here for the duration. It was better if he didn't get his hopes up because then he didn't have to deal with the crushing disappointment at a later date.

"Now, I'm well aware from my contacts that you've had a visit from a copper, asking you to provide information on your boss in exchange for your freedom."

Charlie's gaze flew up to meet Dave's. "I would never rat you out, boss. Never. I can't believe you'd even think it."

Dave shook his head. "I know that, son. But I have a plan."

Dave talked Charlie through his thought process. He explained all the aspects of his plan and how he expected it all to work. When he had finished, Charlie looked up and frowned.

"But I'm no grass, boss."

"I know that, son, but this is different. I'm giving you permission. Do you trust me?"

Charlie bit down on his lower lip and then nodded his head. "Yes, of course, I do."

"Then believe me when I tell you I will get you out of here soon."

Later that day, Barney Newell trudged up Blocksy Road towards the warehouse where he knew Dave Carter had an office. He never usually dealt directly with Dave. Barney usually handed over the money to one of his underlings every week. Dave hadn't collected the money himself for years.

He'd never had a problem before, and never needed to talk to Dave about an issue like this. He was still trembling from his ordeal earlier, and he'd left his wife in charge of the pub to go and try and get this matter sorted as soon as possible.

As he approached the entrance to the doorway, the short, stocky figure of Brian Moore stepped out of the shadows.

"Barney? What are you doing here?"

Barney ran a hand nervously through his thinning hair. "I need to speak to Dave. It's urgent."

Brian frowned for a moment then pressed the button on the side of the wall, which made the big metal door roll upwards. "What's it about?" Brian asked over the noise of the rattling door.

"I had a visit from Martin Morton earlier. He reckons the pub is under his protection now, and he made me pay. I don't understand what's going on. I've always paid Dave before."

Brian snarled. "Martin Morton, that piece of trash. What on earth did you give him money for?"

Barney was getting close to the end of his tether. "I didn't really have much choice, did I? He hung me out the window by my blooming ankles. It was either pay up or get splattered on the pavement."

"Come in," Brian said. "I'll check if Dave's got a moment to see you now."

Barney followed Brian into the huge warehouse, and as they wound their way through the piles of boxes, he grew more and more nervous. He really hoped Dave Carter had a solution because the last thing he wanted was to be caught up in a war of territory between Martin Morton and Dave Carter.

It was just his bleeding luck to be piggy-in-the-middle.

Brian disappeared into the side office for a moment then he came out and gestured for Barney to follow him.

When Barney walked inside the office, he saw Dave sitting behind a large, wooden desk.

"I hear you've had a visit from Martin Morton this morning, Barney?"

As he looked at Dave's kind face and friendly expression, Barney suddenly felt guilty. Somehow he felt this was all his fault, and he'd betrayed Dave by giving Martin the money. "He demanded protection money, and I had to pay up," Barney said. "The trouble is, Dave, I don't have any money to pay you now. Otherwise I'll have nothing left to give the brewery for me rent."

Dave nodded slowly. "I certainly wouldn't expect you to pay this week, Barney. We've let you down. You're paying me money to make sure you don't get hassled like this. Now, Martin Morton is a nasty piece of work, and he needs to be put in his place. I'm very sorry that you've been caught up in this, but I need to ask you a favour."

The relief that Barney had felt when Dave told him he didn't need to pay this week's protection money faded instantly when Dave asked for a favour. That didn't sound good. Barney was just a landlord. He wasn't cut out for all this gangster stuff. He should have moved out of London while he still had the chance and gotten away from all this.

But there was no way he could refuse Dave Carter a favour, so Barney reluctantly nodded. "What do you need?"

"I know you don't want to get caught in the middle," Dave said as if he was reading Barney's mind. "All I need from you is the use of your pub for an hour tomorrow morning, at eleven o'clock."

Barney nodded eagerly, glad Dave hadn't asked more of him. "Of course, no problem."

Dave got up from his seat and walked around the desk, holding out his hand to shake Barney's. "In a couple weeks' time, I promise you'll never have to worry about Martin Morton again."

After Barney had thanked Dave profusely and left them, Brian shut the office door.

"What's the plan, boss?"

Dave smiled. Brian was a good worker but one thing Dave

had learned over the years was not to reveal his full hand to anyone.

Instead of disclosing his plan, he said, "We need to get word to Martin Morton. Tell him to meet me in The Lamb tomorrow, at eleven AM."

Brian's face creased up in a frown as he looked at Dave in shock. "You're going to meet him yourself?"

Dave nodded.

"But shouldn't we get Gary in on this and have some backup? What if Martin Morton brings the rest of his crew?"

"We ask him to come alone, and hope that he is honourable."

"Pah," Brian snorted. "I think we both know that Martin Morton is not honourable."

Dave tilted his head to the side and gave a little shrug.

"So you really want to do this on your own, boss? You're going to meet up with him on your tod?"

Dave nodded and smiled at Brian before saying, "Yes, it's time we sorted this once and for all."

64

THE FOLLOWING MORNING, MARTIN MORTON made his way to The Lamb. He'd been shocked at first when Red-haired Freddie had passed on the message that Dave Carter wanted to meet, but then he'd thought it actually might be a good sign. His visit to Barney Newell at The Lamb yesterday had certainly shaken things up, and that was his intention. He wanted to make Dave Carter aware that he was a force to be reckoned with and that Martin was going to be top dog in the area.

He thought the message from Dave was a sign of desperation on his part. Dave was bound to try to persuade him to be reasonable. Dave Carter was an old-fashioned sort of man. He believed that there was honour between gangsters. But as far as Martin was concerned, honour was just another sign of weakness.

Although the message had requested that Martin come alone, he wasn't stupid and had brought Red-haired Freddie with him.

When they reached the outside of The Lamb pub, Martin turned to him and said, "You stay here."

Red-haired Freddie tried to peer in the pub windows. "Are

you sure, boss? It could be a trap."

"No, I don't think so. Dave Carter hasn't got the balls. You keep watch out here, and if you hear me shout, come running. Shoot first, ask questions later, all right?"

Red-haired Freddie nodded nervously.

Martin plastered a confident smile on his face and pushed open the doors, striding into The Lamb. To his surprise, the pub was completely empty. He hadn't been expecting that.

It was all mind games. Dave Carter was trying to mess with his head. He thought he was very intelligent, but at the end of the day, Martin was the better man, and he wasn't going to fall for any of Dave's cheap tricks.

As if he wasn't bothered at all, Martin strolled around the bar. He noticed on one table there was a half-drunk cup of tea and a pile of papers. He did a double-take as his eyes focused on an object on top of the newspapers. It was a gun.

Martin frowned. What kind of a joke was this? Had Dave just left the gun lying around?

Martin looked around the bar, but it was still empty. He reached out and touched the cold metal of the gun before picking it up and testing its weight in his hands. At that moment, there was noise from behind him and Martin, still holding the gun, turned around quickly.

Dave Carter stepped out from behind the bar. He was alone as far as Martin could see, and despite the fact that Martin was holding a gun in his hand, Dave looked remarkably relaxed as he walked over.

"Morton. It's been a long time," Dave said.

Martin said nothing but raised the gun.

"It's not loaded. I was just cleaning it. It relaxes me. Now, let's have our talk and clear the air, shall we?"

Martin put the gun down, not paying attention to the fact there were no cleaning materials anywhere near the gun. He pushed it to one side and squared off against Dave. He didn't like the way Dave was taking charge of this meeting.

"What do you want?" Martin said.

Dave reached down for his half-drunk cup of tea. "Can I get you anything to drink?"

Martin scowled. He hadn't come here for a bloody tea party.

He was getting really irritated now. He shook his head.

Dave took a sip of his tea and then said, "I was hoping we could come to an agreement. I respect how you've made a name for yourself, and I'm not out to take anything away from you. I think maybe we should think about boundaries. You could stick to your patch, and I'd stick to mine, and never the twain shall meet, and all that."

Martin gave a tight smile. "Of course," he lied smoothly. "The last thing I want is any more trouble."

"That's right. There's no point in us getting caught up in a petty squabble when it's just losing us both money. We're businessmen, and as such we need to focus on business."

Martin nodded casually and stuffed his hands in his trouser pockets. "I want The Lamb, though."

Martin knew that this would be a sticking point for Dave Carter. There was no way Dave could back down from The Lamb without looking weak.

Martin grinned as he saw Dave flinch.

"That's quite some request," Dave said. "But I'm prepared to compromise for the sake of an agreement."

Martin's eyebrows shot up. He was so surprised. He most definitely hadn't expected that. Dave Carter must be more worried than he'd thought. He would be able to annihilate him. Martin couldn't wait.

Once he had The Lamb, all of Dave's other properties would start to fall like dominoes and land in Martin's lap.

"We could come to an arrangement," Dave said. "I'll give you The Lamb if you give me access to all the warehouses you control on Victoria Docks.

Martin shrugged. He didn't give a shit about Victoria Docks. Those places were all abandoned. Dave Carter really had lost his touch. "Yes, you can have those."

Dave nodded slowly. "Well, I'm glad we had this little talk and got things straightened out. There was one question I had for you, though."

Martin narrowed his eyes. "Go on?"

"Do you know what happened to Frank the Face?"

Martin shrugged. "Frank the Face? One of your lads, wasn't he?"

Dave nodded.

"No idea."

Dave Carter's eyes never left Martin's face, and for the first time, Martin felt a slight sense of unease as if Dave knew far more than he was letting on.

"So you didn't kill him?"

Martin shook his head. "No."

"And you swear that on your mother's life?" Dave asked, his tone cold.

Martin exploded. "What the hell is this? I didn't bloody kill him. I swear it on my mother's life, good enough for you, Carter?"

Martin was seething, and Dave looked as cool and collected as could be.

Dave nodded. "Thank you for being so honest."

Martin clenched his teeth, annoyed that he'd let Dave rattle him. "Are we done here?

Dave drained his cup of tea and then smiled at Martin Morton.

"Oh, Yes. We are done," Dave said.

Outside The Lamb, Martin met up with Red-haired Freddie.

"How did it go boss?" Red-haired Freddie asked, rushing over to Martin's side.

"I've got him stitched up like a kipper." Martin grinned, feeling very satisfied with the morning's work. "He's handing over The Lamb in exchange for a couple of warehouses on Victoria Docks. Bloody idiot. They're derelict. We've got him on the back foot now, Freddie. It won't be long until all this is ours."

"So what exactly did he say?"

Martin gave Freddie an irritated look. He didn't like the fact that Freddie obviously thought Carter wouldn't roll over that easily because it reminded Martin of that niggling worry at the back of his mind. It had been almost too easy.

"I agreed to a truce, and we agreed to maintain boundaries."

Freddie's jaw dropped open. "But you didn't really mean it, did you?"

"Of course, I bleeding didn't, you idiot. This is just the first step. We lull Dave into a false sense of security, and then we take his premises over one by one."

65

CHARLIE WILLIAMS HESITATED OUTSIDE THE large steel door.

It creaked open, but still Charlie stood there frozen to the spot until a shove behind him sent him staggering into the room.

The room contained a table that was bolted to the floor and two chairs. Sitting in one and facing Charlie, was Inspector Peel.

His large hooded eyes stared up at Charlie for a moment before he said, "Sit down, Charlie. I hear you had a change of heart."

Charlie swallowed hard and sat down on the chair opposite Inspector Peel.

He ran a hand through his hair. "How does this work then?" he asked suspiciously.

Inspector Peel's eyes flickered up behind Charlie and nodded at the prison guard behind his back. "We'll be all right now. You can shut the door."

The prison guard scratched his forehead. "I don't know. I was told there should be a prison guard with him all the time."

"Get out!" Inspector Peel ordered.

Charlie didn't turn around, but he heard the heavy metal door clanging shut behind him.

Inspector Peel gave him a very tentative smile. "It's really very simple, Charlie. You give me information, and if the information is deemed sufficient by my boss, I either reduce your sentence or possibly even let you out in the next couple of weeks. Wouldn't that be nice?"

Nice wasn't the word. Charlie ached to have the freedom to walk down the road again, to pop into the pub for a pint and to have a bath on his own, without a hundred other men crowded into the large bathroom at the same time.

But Charlie was nervous. This was a big deal, and it went against everything he'd been told growing up. You don't grass on your own.

Charlie nervously raked a hand through his hair. "All right."

The Inspector's eyes narrowed. "You're really going through with it then? Can I ask what changed your mind this time? You've been visited on numerous occasions and every time you told them you weren't interested in helping our investigations."

Charlie shook his head and shrugged. "I've had enough of being inside. I don't see why I should take the fall while the people that were responsible go scot-free."

Inspector Peel studied him silently for a few moments as if he was weighing up whether Charlie was telling the truth.

Charlie needed to keep his nerve. He linked his hands together in his lap so that Inspector Peel wouldn't see they were shaking, and he stared straight ahead.

Inspector Peel nodded. "Very well. What have you got for

me?" he asked as he held his pen above the notepad on the table in front of him.

Charlie took a deep breath and then began to talk. "It's about the murder of Keith Parker."

The Inspector smiled feeling very pleased with himself. His boss would be over the moon with a result like this. The Keith Parker case had gone cold on them. He hated open cases as they reflected badly on the whole Police Department. Charlie Williams was small potatoes, but his boss on the other hand…He was the big time. They'd been trying to get Dave Carter for years.

"Go on, Charlie. If this is good stuff, you could be out there breathing in the fresh air in no time.

Charlie felt nervous. He wished he had his brief with him. Although he didn't really bond with the stuffy, grey-haired suit, at least, the man knew his stuff. Charlie was worried about incriminating himself or the wrong person.

But he'd promised Dave, so he sniffed and then continued, "I was there when Keith Parker was murdered. I saw who pulled the trigger."

Inspector Peel leaned over the desk eager for Charlie's next words, "So, was it Dave Carter who pulled the trigger?"

Charlie shook his head. "I wasn't working for Dave back then. It was Martin Morton who pulled the trigger. I saw him kill Keith."

For a moment, Inspector Peel was rendered speechless, and then his eyes glowed with excitement. If he could trust Charlie Williams's testimony and land Martin Morton, he would be in for a promotion. He couldn't just rely on Charlie's story alone, though. They'd need some concrete evidence.

"Wait here, Charlie. I need to have a word with my boss."

Charlie looked up, panicked. "Why? Don't you believe me?"

Inspector Peel's eyes narrowed. "Don't panic Charlie. It's good stuff. As long as you answer the questions we put to you, I think this information will guarantee your release."

They questioned Charlie for the rest of the day, trying to get the story straight. Charlie kept everything very simple. Dave had told him that was the best way. He didn't mention any other names, not even any of Morton's gang. The aim behind this was to neutralise Martin Morton, nothing more.

Charlie felt sick at the thought Martin Morton might find out he had stitched him up, but the choice was between that and jail, and he refused to feel guilty over it because Martin was the one who had ordered Keith to be killed anyway. All right, so it wasn't Martin Morton who actually pulled the trigger, but Martin was the one who had ordered Keith to be killed, which was the same thing in Charlie's book as actually killing him.

The police had been offering him a reduced sentence if he rolled on his boss, but not one of them ever specified that his boss had to be Dave Carter.

Charlie couldn't help smiling to himself. It was one hell of a plan and pretty audacious really. He was glad he was on Dave Carter's side that was for sure. He wouldn't want to get on the wrong side of him.

Charlie was a little worried about getting caught out in a lie, but as he saw it, he was already in prison for the foreseeable future, so could things really get any worse? Besides, Dave had said the police would find evidence. They just needed Charlie to point the finger at Martin Morton and nudge them in the right direction

He walked down the prison corridor with his hands stuffed in his pockets. Inspector Peel hadn't exactly been forthcoming on when he would be released, but they had said it should be within the next week.

He tried to imagine what it would feel like to have his freedom back. He reckoned the first thing he'd do was visit the Blind Beggar for a few beers. Then he'd have a roast dinner at his mum's and then pie and mash the following day. The prison food had been absolutely atrocious, and Charlie would enjoy putting the weight back on.

As he strolled past the recreation area, he saw Alfie Harris out of the corner of his eye and smirked. Soon he would be out of Harris's reach for good.

66

BEV BALANCED JIMMY ON HER hip and stood by the large living room window. They were waiting for Mary, who was supposed to be arriving any minute. Bev knew it had been a wrench for Mary to leave her little grandson here in Romford.

Jimmy had been an angel. He had settled into a well-contented baby and was oblivious to all the turmoil that been going on around him.

When she caught sight of Mary walking up the road, Bev turned to Jimmy and said, "Look, who's that? It's your grandma."

Jimmy gave her a toothless smile, and his chubby cheeks dimpled.

She opened up the door just as Mary reached the garden path. Mary's voice cracked as she said, "Oh, hello, my darling boy."

The smile on Mary's face grew huge as she saw Jimmy looking healthy and happy in Bev's arms. She walked quickly down the path and opened up her arms to give Jimmy a cuddle.

"How has he been, Bev?"

"He has been an absolute angel. I suppose we're lucky he's so young and doesn't have a clue what's going on," she said as she stepped aside to let Mary enter and then closed the front door behind them.

"Why don't you take Jimmy in the front room, and I'll make a cup of tea?

As Bev prepared tea in the kitchen, she could hear Mary cooing over Jimmy.

She couldn't even imagine the horrors that Mary had been through. Bev remembered Kathleen as a little girl. She'd been bonny in those days and a cheeky little thing but, deep down, she'd been a sweet kid.

It broke her heart to know Mary was going through the same pain she had suffered when she'd lost Claire. At least, Mary had little Jimmy, though, and Bev was prepared to do anything she could to keep them together.

Mary had been an absolute love after Bev had lost her daughter, Claire, to diphtheria. She'd never really gotten over it, but as time passed the horrible torment eased slightly. Hopefully, it would for Mary, too, and she had Jimmy to help her through it.

Bev carried the teapot and cups on a tray back into the living room.

"Thanks ever so much for looking after him, Bev," Mary said. "I know it's not easy looking after an infant at our age."

"Nonsense. It keeps me feeling young."

Truthfully, Bev had been in her absolute element with Jimmy. She enjoyed taking him out in his pram every day and liked talking to the grandmothers and mothers in the park. She'd been desperately lonely since old Fred had died, and she would never have grandchildren of her own, so she was grateful for this opportunity.

"How have you been, Mary?" Bev asked.

"Not too bad, love. The house feels really strange. Every time the clock chimes five-thirty, I expect Kathleen to walk through the front door... And then I remember." Mary's face creased in pain. "I suppose I'll get used to it in time."

"Well, I'm quite happy to look after young Jimmy here for as long as you want. I'll be honest; I've loved having him. Jimmy is a good baby, and he sleeps through the night already. You know me, I've never been one for sleeping in, so him getting up early doesn't bother me."

Mary nodded and then lifted Jimmy onto her hip before coming to sit beside Bev on the sofa. "I hoped you could look after him for a little while longer. Just until I get something sorted. I don't trust that Martin Morton, Bev."

Bev stared down at Jimmy's chubby face. She couldn't believe anyone would consider hurting such an innocent little soul. "Don't you worry. I can look after him just as long as you need me to."

Mary smiled as she looked down at Jimmy. "He does look ever so much like his mum, doesn't he? When he was born, I was worried he was going to look like Martin Morton, but I swear Jimmy's eyes are the exact same shade that Kathleen's were."

Bev reached over, picked up her tea and took a sip. "He's certainly going to be a very good looking lad."

Mary's gaze didn't lift from Jimmy's face as she said, "Yes. He's special. I know it. He is going to grow up to be a very important man. He'll be bigger than Martin Morton, and mark my words, Bev, he'll get revenge for his mother's death."

Mary looked up at Bev with tears in her eyes. "I just hope I'm alive to see it."

Bev felt a tremor of unease. It wasn't right to bring a child into the world with all that on his shoulders. The poor kid would grow up bitter and twisted.

Jimmy needed a safe environment with people who loved him, not someone who was set on revenge. But then, Bev told herself, Mary was still in shock. She'd only just lost Kathleen so it was understandable she'd react this way. No doubt in time, Mary would mellow, and Jimmy would get the happy childhood he deserved.

67

THE FOLLOWING DAY, MARY WAS wandering through Chrisp Street Market. It had almost killed her to leave Jimmy behind yesterday. He was all she had left of Kathleen, but she knew Bev would take very good care of him, and right now that had to be enough.

She'd lost weight over the past few weeks as she never seemed to have an appetite for anything. She knew she needed to keep her strength up if she wanted to be around to see Jimmy grow up, so she decided to pop into Maureen's and get pie and mash for supper.

No doubt her neighbour, Alice Pringle, would be horrified that she wasn't eating a home-cooked meal, but Mary had more important things to worry about.

The pie and mash shop was quiet when she entered, and Mary got served quickly. Carrying the parcel of hot pie and mash under her arm, she headed back home. She passed the half-empty stalls as the traders began to pack up.

Old Bob was folding up the tea towels on his stall. She paused and inspected a display of white net curtains but then felt guilty. Every spare penny she had, she needed for Jimmy's upkeep. She should really make do with her old net curtains for now.

But the lacey-style of the curtains was very attractive, and she'd love a new pair to replace her greying old ones. She paused to have a look at the lace, and as she did so, she heard something that made her stomach turn.

Martin Morton's voice.

Blood rushed in Mary's ears, and her mouth grew dry.

He was swaggering along with that brother of his, looking like butter wouldn't melt. He grinned and laughed at something his brother had said then slapped him on the back. He looked like he didn't have a care in the world. Bastard.

Before she could think better of it, Mary stuffed her hand in her food parcel and pulled out the hot liquor that was supposed to accompany the pie and mash.

She strode up to Martin, brandishing the liquor in front of her. "Oi, you murdering bastard! Don't you think you're going to get away with it. I'll see you pay for this, Morton."

And with those words, Mary chucked the liquor all over his expensive suit.

Martin's face grew red, and a crowd gathered around them. Everyone had horrified looks on their faces, but Mary cackled with uncontrollable laughter. She only wished the liquor had been hotter.

Martin Morton lunged for her, but his brother put an arm out and held him back.

"You stupid bitch," Martin Morton growled.

"Calm down, bruv," Tony said, desperately trying to hold his brother back.

"You'll regret that," Martin snarled at her, but Mary just couldn't stop laughing. She knew she was getting hysterical.

Martin slipped through his brother's arms and grabbed Mary by the neck.

Still, she couldn't stop laughing. Tears were running down her face as he shook her viciously, trying to throttle the life out of her.

She heard somebody screaming and wondered for a moment whether the noise was coming from her own throat, but then she saw Linda bashing Martin over the head with a handbag. "You get off her. Get off her right now, or I'm going straight to the police!"

Finally, Martin relaxed his grip. The crowd of people that had gathered round were talking in hushed whispers. This would be all over the East End before the day was over.

Martin turned his furious attention onto Linda. "Keep your nose out of it, you interfering little bitch."

Linda was trembling, but she didn't back down. "You should be ashamed of yourself for attacking a woman like that."

Martin scowled, but he didn't say anything else and allowed his brother to pull him away.

Once they were out of sight, Linda turned to Mary, "Oh my goodness, are you all right? I thought he was going to strangle you."

Mary slumped against Linda as the girl put her arm around her shoulders. It all seemed so pathetic. All she'd managed to do was get a little bit of liquor on his suit, and he'd gotten away with murdering her daughter. It was hardly tit for tat.

"I'm going to get him for this, Linda," Mary said. "If it's the last thing I do, I'm going to make him pay."

* * *

Martin Morton stormed back to his club and went straight upstairs to the kitchen in his flat. He grabbed a cloth and tried to clean off the liquor splattered all over his expensive suit.

The silly bitch! How dare she talk to him like that. Did she really think she would get away with it? He might not be able to act right now; he'd attracted enough attention from the police, but given time, he would exact revenge on Mary Diamond for her disrespect.

She'd started off as a pain in the arse and had gotten worse and worse.

He'd have to talk to Tim again about putting the fear of God into the bitch, and after that, in a couple of years when everything had died down, he'd slit her throat himself.

"You all right, bruv?" Tony called out from downstairs.

Martin ignored him and continued rubbing the dirty marks on his suit. It was bloody ruined. He should make her pay for it. The stupid cow.

He heard a disturbance downstairs and wondered what his brother was doing down there.

He walked into the landing, stood by the edge of the stairs and peered down. "Tony? What's going on down there?"

A few seconds passed before Tony appeared at the bottom of the stairs. His tanned skin was paler than Martin had ever seen it, and his eyes were wide as he looked up at his brother.

"You'd better come downstairs, Martin."

"What for? Can you deal with it?" Martin wasn't in the mood for any more pathetic little complications today.

"No." Tony shook his head slowly and then looked over his shoulder. "Martin, the police are here. They want to talk to you about the murder of Keith Parker."

Martin's hand froze. He strode into the kitchen and threw the cloth back in the sink. He'd been expecting this. It wasn't a big deal. He just would have preferred it happened on another day. He was already fuming due to that stupid bitch, Mary Diamond, and he didn't want to deal with a flat-footed copper asking questions on top of all that.

Martin shrugged, and shouted out, "Fine. Give me brief a ring then."

Keith's body may have been found, but by Martin's reckoning, it had to be pretty decomposed by now, and Tim had gotten rid of the gun, so there was nothing to point back to him. Martin even had a perfect alibi. He had nothing to worry about. Even so, he could do without this headache.

Martin had a lot of pride in his appearance. It was all part of the package and helped him feel confident. "I'll be right down. I'm just getting changed."

"There's no time for that," a deep voice that sounded vaguely familiar said.

Martin turned back to look and saw Inspector Peel climbing the stairs in front of Tony.

"Hello, Mr. Morton," he said, walking into the living area. "I've found the evidence. You're going down, my son."

Martin sneered. He wasn't worried about Inspector Peel. He was just a jobsworth copper, just like an irritating little fly that wouldn't go away.

"In your dreams, mate," Martin said, but then he was stunned as two uniformed officers appeared behind Inspector Peel.

Martin took a step back as Inspector Peel began to read his rights.

"What the bleeding hell are you lot doing? I wasn't there. I had an alibi, remember?"

"An alibi from your long-suffering wife," Inspector Peel said. "I didn't believe it at the time. And now I've got the proof you were lying."

Martin shook his head. His alibi had not been a lie. He had been at home with Babs. He twisted and turned, trying to wrench himself free as the uniformed officers held him, pulling his arms behind his back.

"Get your hands off me," Martin roared.

"Calm down, bruv. I'll get your brief. You'll be out of there in no time," Tony said. "Just take it easy."

Inspector Peel smirked and looked at Tony. "Oh, I'm afraid your brother won't be out so quickly this time. Not when we've got the gun that killed Keith Parker with your brother's fingerprints all over it."

Tony's jaw fell open, and he stared at Martin open-mouthed.

Martin shook his head. That wasn't possible. He hadn't shot Keith. He'd ordered his men to do it, but he'd never touched the gun himself…

Then the memory came back to him. Meeting with Dave… The gun on the table…

"The bastard. It's Dave Carter. He's fitted me up for this. He got me to hold the gun, but it wasn't me. I never killed him."

Inspector Peel chuckled, and Martin turned on him. "You're going to regret this. I'm innocent."

"That's what they all say, Mr. Morton," Inspector Peel said as he walked beside the struggling Martin Morton and escorted him out of the club.

* * *

Dave was in his office at the warehouse on Blocksy Road when Gary burst in with a grin on his face. "He's been nicked!"

Dave looked up from his paperwork. "About time, too."

It had taken the police longer than he'd hoped to build their case.

"I just saw the Old Bill leading Martin Morton out of his club. Rumour has it, he's going down for a long time," Gary said gleefully.

Just as Gary finished speaking, Brian Moore also burst into the office. "Have you heard about Morton?"

Dave smiled. He may have had to wait longer than he wanted for the police to build their case, but it was worth it. Charlie would be free within days.

Dave leaned back in his chair and looked with satisfaction at Brian and Gary. They'd waited for this day for a very long time.

"It's been a long time coming, but we've done it, boys. We got revenge on that piece of scum for taking out Frank the Face and for leaving poor old Charlie to bleed to death on a pile of rubbish. But our hard work has only just started."

Gary and Brian exchanged puzzled looks.

"The real work starts now," Dave said. "We expand, and we annihilate anyone who might want to step into Martin Morton's shoes."

Gary grinned. "Right you are, bruv. We'll be behind you one hundred percent."

Dave chucked his pen down on the desk. Things had worked out perfectly. With Martin Morton out of the picture, nothing could stop him from taking over the whole of the

East End, and that was exactly what he intended to do.

Epilogue

JIMMY DIAMOND was dressed in his new school uniform for his first day of school. He looked so grown up, Bev thought with a sigh. She wished Mary could have seen him today. Bev walked Jimmy to school, and when he turned to wave at her at the school gates, she felt a lump in her throat.

When she got home, she sat down to write a letter to Mary, telling her all about it. She'd been taking care of Jimmy for five years now, and she loved him as if he was her own grandchild. She felt sad that Mary had to miss out on all these milestones.

She tried to write down every little bit of description in the letter so Mary would feel like she'd been a part of it.

Bev spent the rest of the day anxiously worrying about Jimmy, hoping he'd be all right at school. He was a good lad, and there was no reason to think he wouldn't get on well, but Bev couldn't help fretting.

When three o'clock finally rolled around, and she was able to go and pick him up, she couldn't race around to the school fast enough.

Although she'd made sure to get to the school by three fifteen, there was absolutely no sign of Jimmy. She waited by the school gates for a little while until all the mothers had left with their children. Then the panic really set in.

She rushed into the school and asked the first teacher she saw where she could find Jimmy Diamond.

"Oh, he left a little while ago. Someone came to pick him up."

Bev felt as if a bucket of cold water had just been thrown over her. "Who? Who picked him up?"

Her heart was thundering in her chest as the teacher frowned. "A woman picked him up. Jimmy seemed perfectly happy to go with her. Is something wrong?"

Bev was practically in tears, and her heart was beating nineteen to the dozen as she raced back home. As she approached her bungalow, she caught sight of Jimmy sitting on the wall, waiting for her.

The rush of relief she felt was quickly replaced by anger when she saw Mary sitting on the wall beside him.

"What the bleeding hell are you playing at? I nearly had kittens when I turned up at the school and found Jimmy wasn't there."

Bev's voice trailed away as she looked at Mary.

Her face was gaunt and heavily lined. She'd aged quickly after Kathleen had passed, and she now looked at least ten years older than she really was.

Bev's heart softened. She understood that Mary missed her grandson desperately.

"Oh, well, no real harm was done, I suppose. Why don't we go indoors and have a nice cup of tea?

Mary shook her head. "There's no time for that, Bev. I just

called in so we could say goodbye."

"Goodbye? What do you mean?"

"I'm taking him back home, Bev. Back to where he belongs. Jimmy is coming back with me to the East End."

"You can't do that! It's not safe, and he's happy here with me."

Mary shook her head and set her mouth in a firm line as she regarded Bev steadily. "I appreciate everything you've done for Jimmy and me. But it's safe enough now. Martin Morton has been locked up a long time, and all his old henchmen are working for other people or keeping their heads down."

Bev felt sick. Surely, Mary couldn't be serious?

"So," Mary said, looking down at Jimmy with a smile. "I'm taking him home, Bev. It's time he learned the truth about his mother."

If you enjoyed this book, don't forget to sign up to the mailing list : http://www.danioakleybooks.com/newsletter/ so you are first to know when the next book is out.

It would really help me if you left a review, telling me what characters you would enjoy to read about in the next book. Reviews help the book's visibility and help me see what my readers would like to read next. So if you have the time to leave a review that would be fantastic!

I really do appreciate each and every review. Thank you so much for reading.

I also write under the name D.S Butler and you can find a list of those books on the next page.

Dani x

Dani Oakley also writes police procedurals under the name D. S. Butler. You can find all the books on Amazon.

Here is the series reading order:
> Deadly Obsession
> Deadly Motive
> Deadly Revenge
> Deadly Justice
> Deadly Ritual
> Deadly Payback

If you would like to be informed when the new Dani Oakley book is released, sign up for the newsletter:
http://www.danioakleybooks.com/newsletter/

Printed in Great Britain
by Amazon